DEATH SQUEEZE

Dear John,

Sent this on the chance that you might not have read it yet.

Have a happy, healthy, safe and prosperous holiday Season & New Year.

Love you.

Mary & Ross

More Latin American Literature
from Avon Books

by Marcio Souza
MAD MARIA

by Jorge Amado
CAPTAINS OF THE SANDS
DONA FLOR AND HER TWO HUSBANDS
GABRIELA, CLOVE AND CINNAMON
THE GOLDEN HARVEST
HOME IS THE SAILOR
JUBIABA
PEN, SWORD, CAMISOLE
SEA OF DEATH
SHEPHERDS OF THE NIGHT
TENT OF MIRACLES
TEREZA BATISTA
TIETA
THE TWO DEATHS OF QUINCAS WATERYELL
THE VIOLENT LAND

by Mario Vargas Llosa
AUNT JULIA AND THE SCRIPTWRITER
THE WAR OF THE END OF THE WORLD

by Gabriel Garcia Marquez
ONE HUNDRED YEARS OF SOLITUDE

edited by Barbara Howes
THE EYE OF THE HEART

DEATH SQUEEZE

Marcio Souza

Translated by Ellen Watson

AVON BOOKS ◆ NEW YORK

Originally published as *A Condolência* by Marcio Souza, Rio de Janeiro.

This work is a novel. Any similarity to actual persons or events is purely coincidental.

AVON BOOKS
A division of
The Hearst Corporation
1350 Avenue of the Americas
New York, New York 10019

First Avon Books Trade Printing: December 1992

AVON TRADEMARK REG. U.S. PAT. OFF. AND IN OTHER COUNTRIES, MARCA REGISTRADA, HECHO EN U.S.A.

Printed in the U.S.A.

OPM   10   9   8   7   6   5   4   3   2   1

For Eduarda and Floriza,
from the heart

1978.

That was the year the Rio de Janeiro Museum of Modern Art caught fire; General Figueiredo, the military candidate for president of Brazil, declared that he preferred the smell of horses to the smell of the people; and Jimmy Carter visited Brazil.

Part 1

The Hand of King Wu

S he had waited to call until just before the close of business hours and of course the Rebouças Tunnel was completely bottled up. Plus it was raining—a steady drizzle that promised to continue through the night. Miguel followed the metronome of the windshield wipers in front of him. Raindrops struck the glass and were swept away by the tireless routine of the curved blades, arcing concentrically like a mandala. Horns honked in irritating unison as the interminable line of cars inched forward down rua Humaitá, one lane branching off for the clogged tunnel.

Miguel concentrated on the shiny wet streaks the rain left on the windshield. Nothing going on outside the car interested him; there were more truths and mutations in the design of water on glass in front of him than in the tense faces of the people locked in the traffic jam. Miguel himself was determined not to succumb to impatience; some time ago he had simply stopped believing in it. He liked to think of this revelation as the first real discovery in an ongoing search. With humility and courage, others would follow. Miguel felt protected somehow from the people furiously honking or cursing the traffic, racing their motors like maniacs.

Caught in the rain at the height of rush hour, he confined himself to emptying his thoughts, because that was the most he could do at the moment. Admitting he was tired of what he was doing would be dangerously close to expressing what he felt. Which wasn't tiredness exactly, but something larger, a kind of discontent, a thirst that reduced everything to insignificant proportions. And the answers, he knew, were not simple. Meanwhile, in just a few minutes he would have to feign professional interest and enthusiasm, both of which he had lost a long time ago.

Miguel was beginning to feel hungry and knew a headache was not far behind. He had to eat on schedule or else, a sign of just how sedentary he had become. The line of cars was creeping along rua Jardim Botânico now, squeezing past trucks and crew at work on the power lines, which made that block even more chaotic and obliged pedestrians to dash through the rain outside the wooden barricades and compete with the crazed cars for room. A pretty girl carrying an armload of books caught his attention. She had bright red lips and a nice tan. She was weaving her way across the street, almost at a trot, nimbly avoiding cars and puddles of water. Miguel noticed, surprised, that he recognized one of the books she held clasped to her chest, a memoir by a dissident general. All kinds of generals had been writing their memoirs lately—they were becoming best-sellers, even reading matter for young girls. Just the sight of one of these books made Miguel sick to his stomach.

He turned onto rua Lopes Quintas and headed up the hill toward a house partially hidden from view behind vine-covered walls. It was a truly magnificent edifice, and its owner had clearly done remarkably well navigating the troubled economic waters of Brazil. Finding the gates wide open, Miguel pulled up the flawless driveway lined with haughty palms to the awning in front of the main entrance. Floodlights lit the door; potted plants and vines could be seen hanging from a kind of balcony overhead. A young woman in uniform stood waiting.

"Dona Haidèe isn't here," she said.

Nonplussed, Miguel opened his mouth to protest, but the girl went on, indifferent to his reaction.

"But her secretary is waiting for you. Please, come in."

She stepped aside and Miguel walked in. Irritation overcame him thoroughly now. The secretary was a mere formality, because the woman of the house was not in the habit of delegating business authority. In the hallways of Multimedia, the advertising agency where Miguel worked, the secretary was known as "the Gorilla," an appropriate enough nickname for a muscle-bound character whose true baptismal name was Hercules. The guy looked more like a bodyguard than an executive secretary.

The maid shepherded Miguel to the office, a spacious room looking out onto a garden. There were several drawing boards and a conference table surrounded by eight chairs. One wall was taken over by a floor-to-ceiling bookcase filled with hardback books.

Hercules stood gazing out the window, his back to the door. He seemed distant, worried, apparently so lost in thought that he was unaware of Miguel's arrival. Indirect lighting set the mood; the room was free of ostentation, free of even the scent of dubious taste. The place reeked of refinement.

Miguel knew this house well, its discreet perfume, its serenity, its air of casual luxury. He imagined he knew the woman who lived here quite well too.

Hercules turned to find Miguel standing motionless in the doorway. Outside, the garden remained dark, wet. Hercules seemed not at all himself. His forehead was beaded with sweat, and he looked nervous and a bit forlorn.

"I'm sorry, I didn't hear you come in," he said, pointing Miguel to one of the chairs at the conference table.

"Did I get the time wrong or something?"

Hercules was too tense to attempt a smile.

"Haidèe called this afternoon," said Miguel, "just as I was leaving the office. She asked me to stop by. She said she needed to talk to me about the preview of the winter line."

Hercules sat down at the table and mopped his brow with a rumpled, damp handkerchief. He was breathing heavily and avoiding Miguel's eyes.

"Is there a problem?" Miguel was on the verge of leaving. It was unsettling, the way he was being received. The place seemed as familiar as always, with the same calm and silence that had always impressed him. He had been visiting this house since he was a boy, though not as frequently now as he used to, when his parents would come spend Sunday around the pool and have lunch in the garden, while he explored every nook and cranny of the yard, trees covered with lichens and enormous ferns big enough to hide behind. Haidèe's husband, now deceased, had been a college buddy of Miguel's father; they had graduated together in law and were great, intimate friends, though radically different in personality. The house was the same as ever, but something had changed beneath the surface so familiar to him.

"This morning, the minute she woke up, Haidèe noticed the canvases were dusty."

Miguel looked at the secretary without understanding what he was implying, if in fact he was implying anything.

"The paintings," Hercules explained.

Haidèe had a considerable collection of paintings scattered throughout the house. The fruit of one of her passions, gathered during her wandering life as the wife of a diplomat, it was an extremely valuable collection.

"And sure enough, dona Haidèe ran her fingers over them and they were covered with a film of dust."

"A film of dust?"

"They're so slipshod."

"Who?"

"The servants . . ."

Miguel nodded, as if in agreement. Could it be that Haidèe had summoned him here to listen to Hercules complain about the servants? Where had she gone, anyway? Why wasn't she here to meet him as they'd arranged? Miguel tried to block the return of his impatience, but it was no use. He should be at home by now, reading one of his books on meditation.

"Do you know what she did? She asked me if I didn't think it sad for the paintings to be so dusty."

Miguel said nothing. He was trying his hardest to understand what was going on and to not give in to irritation.

"She had me call the maid and stood there watching until the job was done," continued Hercules. "You know how she is. She said all kinds of things, how such and such was not being cared for properly and how the house looked abandoned. Of course she was exaggerating."

"Where is she?"

The secretary went on as if he hadn't heard Miguel's question.

"Dona Haidèe was so depressed this morning. I think she had some kind of premonition. She's always like that, she seems to know about things before they happen. Remember when her car was stolen? Well, she warned me beforehand, I know it sounds incredible, but she knew, she had a dream or something."

He paused and returned to mopping his brow.

"Haven't you noticed how she just knows things?"

"No," said Miguel.

"That's because you're not around her as much as I am. I've been with Haidèe for fifteen years—practically a lifetime. And she's always astounding me."

Miguel nodded and braced to leave. As if sensing his intent, Hercules' voice changed, emphasizing each word.

"This morning I knew right away it was going to be one of those days. She had breakfast in the kitchen and spent the day in here working." He pointed to the drawing boards littered with dress designs. "New styles for next year's line. I think that's what she wanted to talk to you about, Miguel."

"She called me at around five o'clock and asked me to stop by . . ."

"Dona Haidèe's been putting in a lot of time on these designs. She hadn't been out of the house the last two days. Anything that needed taking care of, she did by phone."

A thought crossed Miguel's mind: what if the secretary was just trying to throw him off the track? The old bag had gone off on some last-minute tryst and now he didn't know what to say. No, that didn't make sense, the secretary was a straightforward sort of guy. If Haidèe really had taken off with some lover, he would have announced that very fact with a sense of pride, because he was proud to work for that woman. In any case, there was no reason for Miguel to just sit there, waiting for the secretary to dismiss him.

"Look, Hercules, I'm going to head home. Haidèe had to go out, no problem, I can talk to her tomorrow."

The secretary seemed to be fighting the urge to leap from his seat, and his puzzled look suggested that Miguel had made a wrong move in some game he didn't even know he was playing. Miguel attributed Hercules' reaction to the fact that he himself was no longer properly hiding his impatience.

Hercules mopped his brow once more and stuffed the handkerchief back into his jacket pocket. As he did, Miguel got a glimpse of the gun in the holster under his left arm.

Miguel stood up stiffly.

"I'm sorry," he said, "but I really must go."

Hercules shook his head, dispirited.

"I'm the one who should apologize," he said, no longer trying to conceal his nervousness.

"Never mind, I'll talk to her tomorrow," said Miguel. "No problem."

Miguel replaced his chair in the exact spot he'd found it and started for the door, very businesslike, without another look at the nervous secretary.

"No, don't go," the other man begged. It was very strange to hear a man like him beg.

Miguel stopped in his tracks. He had a sudden urge to rip the tie off his sweaty neck. His palms were clammy too, and a few drops of perspiration ran down his body inside his clothes, making him itchy and even more irritable. But he'd run out of reasons to be upset; Hercules was neither changing the subject nor trying to cover for the rudeness of his boss. The man was just plain scared.

The very idea that Hercules was scared gave Miguel a start; maybe his timing was bad, trying to slip away during an uncomfortable moment that had nothing to do with him. Suddenly he felt like a stray cat on the roof, about to get a pan of scalding hot water flung at him.

"Something terrible is going on," said Hercules.

Miguel loosened his tie and went back to the table. The secretary was positively oozing, sweat running down his face, his hair shiny with grease.

"What did you say?" Miguel's heart began to race.

"She's being threatened. They call her on the phone all the time."

"What do they say?"

"Threats. Four times today."

"What kind of threats?"

"They say they're going to kill her."

It couldn't be true, things like this didn't happen. Miguel was trying desperately not to believe what he was hearing.

"It must be a joke. Are you sure it's not some kind of prank or something?"

"It's no joke, it's for real."

"It could be some kind of sick joke . . . or just some loony making phone calls. This town is full of crazy people."

Hercules shook his head sadly.

"No, she's sure it's the real thing."

An icy finger ran down Miguel's spine.

"She's sure? But what's the motive?" Miguel knew, even as he asked, that it wouldn't be such an awfully difficult question to answer. Haidèe wasn't exactly one of the most popular women in Rio, and there were probably lots of people who had their reasons.

"Where is she?"

"She's safe."

"What's being done? Have you called the police?"

"Haidèe doesn't want the police involved."

"It's blackmail, then. They're trying to scare her, right?" Miguel tried to fix the logic of this idea, something that would inspire less fear and more reassurance. "Has she ever been blackmailed before?"

"Not that I know of. She's really terrified, Miguel."

"Why isn't she here? Are they watching the house?"

"I don't think so. I have a little experience with this, and I spent the day checking out the area. If they're watching the house they're real professionals. I didn't notice anything unusual."

Miguel walked to the office door and stared out into the living room. Shadows and silence.

"I took one of the calls myself," said Hercules.

"What did they say? What did the voice sound like?"

"It was a man. Disguising his voice, I think. But he seemed to sense that it was someone else on the phone. All he said was that they were going to kill her. Froze my blood, Miguel. And I've been around the block a few times."

But Miguel refused to believe it; he didn't want to. He had no desire to get mixed up in any violence again, even vicariously.

"Even so, I still think it's some lunatic," said Miguel, hoping the secretary would admit that was the most rational explanation. But Hercules looked doubtful. "Haidèe should have her number changed. The phone company will do it on the spot."

"Her number's been unlisted for a long time."

"But everyone has it. The manager of every textile company around has her number on his Rolodex."

The maid came in with a tray of coffee. Her arrival at least served to break the impasse of Miguel's resistance to accept what was happening. The maid set the tray on the table and poured coffee. She handed a cup first to Miguel and then, with visible disdain, to Hercules. She left the room, swaying inside her thin knit dress, secure in her beauty and exempt from the facts, which in Miguel's eyes placed her in an enviable category.

"So this afternoon, when she called me, Haidèe had already received several of these phone calls. Why did she want to see me?"

"Because she trusts you, Miguel."

"Me? What can I do?" Miguel did not conceal his surprise.

"The truth is I have no idea what you can do, and neither does she. So of course you don't, either. But by the second call she was so terrified she needed someone. And you're the only one she trusts."

"I have to talk to her. That's the only way to find out what she wants."

"You *will* talk to her, Miguel."

"When? Now?"

"Soon."

"What do you mean, soon? I want the whole story, from Haidèe herself. I'm sorry, Hercules, but this is all very peculiar. First she calls me here to meet with her. She says she wants to talk about the opening of her new collection. She insists on setting the meeting for tonight after hours. Then when I get here, she's gone. Instead I find you, acting rather strange, and you tell me some disturbing things. No, it doesn't figure. I guess I'm going to have to be the one to call the police. Right now. And you're going to have a little explaining to do."

"I wouldn't do that if I were you."

"Why not?"

"Because dona Haidèe wouldn't like it. She doesn't want the police involved. And she knows what she's doing."

Hercules got up and stood beside the table, one hand disappearing beneath his jacket.

"What's going on here?"

"Nothing, Miguel. Stay calm, I just don't want you to do anything stupid."

Miguel realized Hercules was not going to let him leave, afraid he'd call the police. Sizing up his adversary, Miguel knew he didn't stand much of a chance of winning a direct confrontation. The man was almost a foot taller and much stronger. He was also in good shape, no doubt, whereas Miguel's only exercise was pickup soccer with friends on weekends. Plus, Hercules was armed.

"I'm not going to hurt you, Miguel. Why are you looking at me like that?"

"Stay away from me, you hear? I'm warning you! I'm going to walk out of here just like I walked in. You're hiding something, Hercules, and I'm going to find out what it is."

"I'm not hiding anything, Miguel. Come on, sit down and finish your coffee."

"Fuck the coffee," shouted Miguel. "I want to know what the hell is going on here!"

"I already told you, Miguel. Dona Haidèe does want to talk to you. It's just that she had to leave."

"If she's getting threatening phone calls, why did she go out alone? No, there's a lot that doesn't figure here."

"She knows how to defend herself, Miguel. At least I hope so. But you've got to help her. She trusts you. For some reason you're her only hope. She asked me to make that clear to you, but I got nervous, I guess, and blew it."

Keeping one eye on the gun under Hercules' jacket, Miguel resolved to change tactics.

"Okay," he said. "Let's work on this coffee."

"Thank God you understand. We can't tell anyone else about this. It would be too dangerous, that's what she told me. Only the three of us."

"I agree."

"Not even your wife," warned Hercules. "It's for her own safety. At least that's what dona Haidèe said."

"Okay, I won't tell her a thing. But she must be getting worried by now. I don't usually get home late."

"This shouldn't take very long."

Miguel sat down again. He needed to get his thoughts in order. Haidèe wasn't home, though she'd asked him to come see her. The secretary was here in her place, with a gun and a confused story. Miguel strained to review the recent events, but nothing made sense.

"Hercules, you said you took one of the calls. I want you to tell me, word for word, what was said."

"Dona Haidèe answered the phone and then passed it to me. I think they must have realized she wasn't on the line anymore because they didn't say much. Just that if she didn't do what they told her, she could consider herself dead."

"You say *they*, as if there was more than one."

Hercules looked blank, as if he'd fallen into a contradiction.

"I think there's a group of them. The voice on the phone didn't sound like he was acting alone."

"You mean the voice spoke in the plural?"

"What?"

"Did he say 'we'?"

"Yes, he said, If you don't do what we say, we'll make good on our threats. There was more than one, for sure."

"That changes things. I can't imagine a whole group of mad-men playing practical jokes. Unless the voice was just bluffing."

"I don't know, Miguel. But she believed him. When I hung up,

she was white as a sheet. And then she asked me if I thought she
was getting old."

"What?"

"She said, 'Hercules, do you think I'm getting old?' "

Hercules dabbed at his forehead for a moment.

"I know what she meant," he continued. "She's a tough lady,
she's never been afraid of anything before. And she's not the type
to go down without a fight. But she was really scared."

"She's not that old," said Miguel.

"She's getting there. You probably don't know what it means
to be old. The head can still feel young but the damn body refuses
to cooperate, it's getting weak, your legs shake after any kind of
exertion."

"I don't recognize the person you're describing."

"Maybe not, but she is afraid of giving in to age."

Miguel pushed aside the cup of cold coffee in front of him and
decided to test the waters.

"So, what now? Are we going to sit here all night?"

"She wants your help."

"You said that already."

"Well!" he said, consulting his watch. "Now we'll find out if
you really are her friend."

"Of course I want to help," said Miguel without conviction. "If
you could tell me where to start."

"Before she left, Haidèe said some strange things."

"What kinds of things?"

"That there was a big shake-up going on. The metalworkers'
strikes, the amnesty movement, the denunciations, complete with
photos, of military and police involved in torture splashed all
over the papers. She said it was like an earthquake, shaking the
ground we walk on, and throwing up layers that had been buried
underneath."

"She said that?"

"More or less. She said the phone calls were voices from
the past, from people who had become invisible, or something
like that."

"You should have told me all this from the start," complained
Miguel. "Haidèe must really be in danger. It scares the hell out
of me just thinking about it."

"Me, too."

When the metalworkers had gone on strike, Miguel had known

that some kind of eruption was beginning. He remembered standing in front of a newsstand with his mouth hanging open one morning—he never thought he'd live to see the day that a leftist newspaper would print photographs of various army officers, accusing them of torture. Miguel listened silently when his colleagues at the ad agency talked about the workers' courage and when they speculated about the end of the military regime. He kept his peace because he knew it wasn't going to be easy. The military was not about to be scared off by a handful of strikes and was no doubt already preparing an appropriate response to the brash leftists who had published those startling pictures.

"I don't know," said Miguel, partly to fool himself, to escape from the unexpected responsibility, "but I don't think they'd dare, if they are who I think they are."

"You bet they would," was Hercules' dry response.

"What could Haidée have done? She's not a Communist, never was!"

"That's her business."

"It's got to be some sort of settling of accounts. But it doesn't add up."

"Or revenge, maybe."

"Only she can say." Miguel needed to talk to Haidée, so he'd know what to do, if in fact all this were true and she wasn't already lying dead in her room upstairs.

"They threatened to rape her. They said they would drug her and then brutally rape her. They said they'd burn her alive."

Miguel tried to push away the very idea. Burning a person alive was an act of supreme barbarism, something only the twisted minds of the regime's executioners would be capable of dreaming up. Painful images came back to him. The secret dispatches that used to land on his desk, the closed-door meetings, the photographs in manila envelopes. Shocking scenes, which he had initially imagined were from the Vietnam War but soon discovered came from not all that far away. A nightmare: shattered bodies, rows of dead recruits, amputated heads, women with their skirts thrown up and bayonets between their legs. The photos came as proof that the rumors were not rumors but a truth to steal your sleep away.

"I know that M.O.," said Hercules coldly.

"What M.O.?" asked Miguel, caught up short.

"Burning people alive. You don't remember?"

"No," protested Miguel. He remembered nothing, he wanted no part of that memory.

"I'd just as soon forget it myself."

It struck Miguel that whenever he did manage to get out of there, by the time he got home he'd surely have a crick in his neck, because his head would be jerking from side to side as he drove through the streets with the constant sensation that he was being followed. He wasn't the type to feed paranoia, but a door had just opened into a room he had been avoiding for half of his life.

"Were you ever a cop, Hercules?"

"Nope, never. Although lots of people will swear the opposite. The way I look . . . you know how it is. But I worked in the State Department as a lower-level functionary, and Dona Haidèe's diplomat husband asked me to come work for him when he was sent to Guatemala. As a sort of a butler, you know, a little bit of everything. Then, after he died, I retired from the State Department and went on working for her."

"Yes, I remember."

Hercules looked around the office.

"It's almost as if this were my home."

Miguel sighed and ran his hand across his sweaty face. There had to be a move, a way out of this dead end.

"I can't take it anymore, Hercules. We have to do something."

Hercules rose to the bait.

"Well, let's go."

"Really?"

"She said you should drive her car."

"Where?"

"All you have to do is drive, I'll tell you the way."

"Not a chance!" Miguel exploded. "What the hell is this? I'm not going anywhere without knowing where I'm headed."

"I know how you feel."

"You don't know a thing. I feel like a complete idiot."

Hercules stuck his hand under his jacket and pulled out his gun.

"You take it," he said, before Miguel could react.

"What for?" said Miguel, furious.

"Just a precaution. Maybe you'll feel more secure."

"I don't want your fucking gun. And you can keep your phony

phone calls to yourself, too. I'm going home."

"I'm afraid that's no longer possible."

"What?"

"You're in this thing up to your neck."

"No way. I'm not in it one bit."

"Oh, but you are, Captain Gouveia."

The name struck Miguel like a blow to the head.

"What did you say?"

"You heard me, Captain."

It was as if Hercules were talking about someone Miguel had known years ago.

"I'm not a captain anymore," he protested.

"You never stop being a captain, you know that. Haven't you ever dreamed of getting revenge on the people who stole your rank?"

"No one stole my rank. I left because I wanted to."

"You're the only one who believes that."

"Besides, I'm not vengeful by nature."

"Everyone is, Captain."

"One day those butchers who dirtied the uniform will pay for what they did."

"Do you really believe that?" asked Hercules with a sarcastic smile.

"I'm leaving!"

Hercules grabbed him by the arm with a grip that paralyzed his muscles, controlling him like a puppeteer.

"There are all kinds of revenge, Captain. One of them would be to expose those people to the light of day. That's what they're afraid of, isn't it?"

Miguel didn't know what to do now. The hand on his arm hurt and the words in his ears terrified him. Even so, he no longer felt like leaving; he wanted to stay, it was as simple as that.

"Okay," said Miguel, thinking how crazy this was. "But don't get the idea that I like what's happening."

"Haidèe will be pleased," said Hercules, tossing Miguel the keys to her car.

The rain had stopped. The Dodge Dart was parked at the door, just in front of Miguel's Brasília.

The maid appeared at the door looking drowsy.

"You're leaving already?"

"Yes," said Hercules. "You can turn in. If the phone rings, don't answer it. Is that clear?"

"Why?"

"Because that's the way your boss wants it."

The girl shrugged and disappeared into the house.

Miguel crossed the wet grass, casting glances in every direction, as if someone might leap out at him at any moment. He got into the two-door Dart and waited for Hercules to do the same. The car glided smoothly down the driveway and out into the real world.

Following Hercules' instructions, they drove out Avenida Brasil to the Zona Norte. Miguel couldn't conceal his frequent glances in the rearview mirror, but at least there didn't seem to be anyone following them. It was already past midnight, but traffic was heavy. As they approached the Ilha do Fundão, where the Federal University was located, Hercules told him to pull over.

"You can get out here," he ordered.

"What?"

"Don't worry, it won't be hard to get a cab. Go home, get some sleep, you'll talk to her tomorrow."

Miguel got out of the car, exhausted from all the mystery.

"Be careful, Miguel. Not a word to anyone about this."

Miguel walked away before Hercules' warning could sink in. He passed a newsstand and scanned the headlines. The vendor was dozing; a couple of street kids lay wrapped in gunnysacks in the doorway of a lottery store. Keeping one eye on the car, Miguel slowly moved out of the brightly lit area near the newsstand and up the street toward the corner. From this vantage point he saw a woman step out of the darkness and into the Dart. It was Haidèe, he was absolutely sure of it. Miguel stood rooted in place, watching the car slowly pull away. He raised his arm mechanically for a taxi and a venerable VW stopped, brakes squawking.

"Where to?" asked the driver.

"See that Dodge Dart up ahead? Follow it, from a distance, but don't lose it."

The driver gave him a suspicious look but chose to take the fare. Miguel was beginning to feel ridiculous. And the driver did nothing to diminish his sense that he was acting like an idiot. The radio was turned low, and every few minutes the driver stole a look at him in the rearview mirror. At least Miguel wasn't the only one cursed with paranoia. The driver was thin and hungry-looking and had a three-day beard. He must have been down on his luck because the dirty shirt he was wearing was more patched and mended than the country's constitution.

The Dodge turned into the Ilha do Fundão and drove between the buildings of the university. The road was poorly lit, and the fog didn't help. The Dodge slowed as it approached a group of sheds beside the water. Miguel asked the driver to hang back; the driver grunted in response. Fifty meters further, the Dodge stopped.

"I'll get out here," said Miguel.

Clearly relieved, the cab driver pulled over.

Once Miguel had paid the man, the cabbie hardly waited long enough to hand over the change before speeding off. Up ahead, the Dodge remained parked, lights off. This was not a place for many passersby; even during the day it was probably deserted. The students and staff circulated on the other side where the classroom buildings were located. A cold wind blew off the bay, sweeping a dense fog over the filthy water. Off in the distance, the lights of the Rio-Niterói bridge sparkled and boats at their moorings bobbed on a domesticated sea. Behind Miguel stretched an open area full of mud, construction debris, and huge piles of scrap iron and trash.

Miguel shivered and crossed his arms, rubbing himself vigorously to keep warm. All quiet at the Dodge, no movement, no nothing. Time passed, and Miguel's heart pounded in his ears, disturbing him almost as much as his growing sense of embarrassment. He couldn't stop thinking he was acting like a fool. But if the choice was between the foolishness of standing there waiting and the foolishness of being used like a puppet, he preferred the first.

He checked his watch. A half hour had gone by already without anything happening. He thought of the taxi driver and felt even more embarrassed. He had acted like a clown and the guy had probably reported him to the police.

Both doors of the Dodge Dart opened; Haidèe got out from the driver's side. It was hard to see in the dark, but he recognized her hair and her red dress, both flapping in the wind, and slung over one shoulder was that enormous and eternally overflowing purse. Squinting into the darkness, he made out another figure. Not Hercules—he was still in the car, Miguel could see his legs sticking out of the front passenger door. It was another man standing beside Haidèe, though Miguel couldn't make out his features clearly or imagine where he had come from. And the two were talking; scraps of voices reaching Miguel's ears. The man gesticulated a lot and sometimes plunged one of his hands inside his dark wool jacket pocket. The man's face was covered with bandages, as if he had been badly burned. He was gesturing a little wildly with his hands, and he kept crossing and uncrossing his feet. Haidèe looked characteristically calm; she spoke and fell silent, listening to the response. The conversation was apparently going downhill, however, and Haidèe was clutching her pocketbook to her chest in self-protection. Hercules leaped from the car, but Haidèe reacted instantaneously, whipping her purse through the air to strike the man with all her strength. He tried to dodge, but she never missed. Two or three blows had him staggering; he almost lost his balance and fell to the ground. Haidèe seemed crazed, pounding the man with her bag and screaming, until finally he struggled to his feet and slapped her hard across the face. She slipped backwards, practically into Hercules' arms, as the man advanced to hit her again. Haidèe scrambled for the car, leaving Hercules to confront her attacker.

He was considerably smaller and less muscular than Hercules, but showed no sign of being intimidated. He stepped back to get elbow room and then flew at Hercules with a barrage of punches that were lost in the air. Their arms became a knotted tangle and Hercules began to get the upper hand, pummeling the attacker and subduing him easily. The fight seemed just about over when Miguel saw something glint and disappear into Hercules' clothing. Hercules let out a muffled cry and reeled backwards, flapping his hands in front of him for protection, but the man lunged at him again and again, until Hercules collapsed. Haidèe slammed the car door shut and hit the accelerator, speeding off in the direction of the mainland.

Miguel didn't dare react. He was an outsider, he rationalized, he had no right to get involved. The shock of what he had seen paralyzed him. A man was seriously hurt and Miguel was overcome with fear—terror, really, a panic of the kind that reduces a person to an invertebrate. Hercules lay motionless now, and the man still stood over him, alternately observing Haidèe's flight and his victim on the wet ground at his feet. Then he very calmly placed the knife back in his pocket and ran off in the direction of the dark sheds and disappeared.

A convulsive tremor began to replace the tingling sensation Miguel had been experiencing. The invertebrate he had turned into was trying to get out. Trying to forget. He had witnessed violence: it was repugnant. Miguel coughed, and felt a hot, acidic taste in his throat, and then retched a bitter, bilious vomit, which only increased his panic. Haidèe was mixed up with people who were not afraid of violence. The threats were real. And, without knowing exactly why, Miguel was also walking down the same road.

Heaving and gasping, not from exertion but anxiety, Miguel ventured out of the shadows, though he was trembling so much that it wasn't easy going. To make matters worse, he was flooded with feelings of frustration and cowardice. Looking around him, he saw only the university buildings and flashes of light on the bay, the bridge describing a curve on the horizon until merging with the night. Hercules' body lay in a puddle of muck and blood near a gravel pile. There were stab wounds all over his body and his face was unrecognizable. Miguel's glance froze on one of Hercules' eyes, still open, as if shining with a small gleam of life. But the eye no longer saw, and reflected only the bewilderment of meeting death so unexpectedly. Surely the killer had fled, was all Miguel could think.

He began examining the immediate area, a plot of maybe twenty meters from where he stood to the various outbuildings. Beyond lay another vacant lot, surrounded by barbed wire and filled with rubble and huge heaps of trash. The man had disappeared without a trace in the direction of the sheds. By the light of day footprints might have been visible, but no chance of that in the dim light now. Just an eerie silence broken occasionally by the sound of cars on the distant road. A well-fed rat slithered out of a paint can and into a pile of scrap wood on the other side of the barbed wire. Miguel shuddered and realized he ached all over. This was a truly desolate place. Not a car had passed since the fight began. It had only lasted some twenty minutes, but the university campus must have guards making night rounds who were bound to come by sometime soon, no matter how casual they were about the job. In addition, Miguel began worrying that his cab driver might actually have alerted the police. The last thing he wanted right now was to get involved with the police. The little he knew about the situation pointed to the advisability of keeping them out of it. If this was the work of the so-called radical but sincere hard-liners, it would be best for him to be as far away as possible when the body was found.

This train of thought helped him to pull himself together a little. He couldn't wait to see Ruth and tell her everything. Just as he was about to head for the access road in search of transport to the mainland, a car appeared. It took the curve at the far end of the island, an area without streetlights, at high speed. Miguel began running, trying to keep his face hidden, but the car accelerated and drove off the pavement across the vacant lot, barreling in his direction.

Miguel ran in the opposite direction, crossed the road, and headed for the barbed wire. He sprang forward and jumped the fence, rolling along the ground among the debris and gravel. His knees got cut up a bit, which only served to jolt him out of his stupor. The car did a half-turn and also crossed the road, its headlights illuminating the fence, which would pose no obstacle. Miguel got up and ran. First, deeper into the vacant lot and then on a diagonal toward the clump of classroom buildings. If he could make it that far, maybe he could escape these men and the fate of Hercules.

The car lunged at the barbed wire fence and spun a heap of wood chips into the air. It rattled and shook all over, and was forced to reduce speed on account of the broken terrain and all the obstructions. Braced by the idea that he might actually get away, Miguel turned on the speed, leaping over rubble and mud puddles.

But his pursuers had the same idea. The engine shut off and the lights went out. Miguel heard the noise of car doors opening and the voices of his pursuers. How many were there? He didn't want to wait and see. He concentrated on the rhythm of his running, lungs heaving and eyes fixed on the gray buildings ahead. Then he heard a crack and something whistled over his head. A chill down his spine: he knew that sound. They had guns and were using them. Even if he made it to the open area at the far end of the vacant lot, he'd still be a sitting duck. But there was no going back, either. There had to be another way out, there just had to be. And fast. Another bullet whizzed by, not terribly close, though he ducked by reflex. He could hear their footsteps clearly now, running in the night's silence.

He spotted a pile of rubble up ahead. Big and little stones and a heap of crushed rock. He headed that way, retracing his earlier route. The men were a long way off and wouldn't realize he'd changed course until the last minute, until he'd reached the pile of crushed rock and found a sure way to survive, to escape.

The pile of crushed rock was immense. Miguel circled it, hobbling over the slippery red stones. The car sat in the middle of a mud hole, its doors thrown open, abandoned in the hurry to finish him off. Because that was what they were trying to do: to kill him. No interrogation; they just wanted him dead. He crouched flat on the ground and inched in the direction of the car—maybe they had left the key in the ignition! But suddenly he saw that it wasn't going to be that easy. One had stayed behind with the car. These were no amateurs, they knew what they were doing.

The man was standing directly in front of the car holding a sawed-off shotgun. He was peering into the dark in the direction the others had gone. Miguel lay glued to the ground and considered his chances. Not good. Everything was stacked against him. The man held a serious weapon and doubtless knew how to use it. His muscles bulged under a tee-shirt emblazoned with a bank's logo.

Miguel looked around. Rocks of every shape and size, rusty metal, rotting paper, all kinds of trash. But nothing that could be used as a weapon. He couldn't stay here much longer; the others would no doubt come along soon and discover him. Miguel did not want to die in that desolate wasteland. His hand scraped across something cold and metallic. It was half-buried in the rocks, an iron bar, almost half a meter long and as wide as a finger. He worked it out of the pile as quietly as possible. Luckily, the man's attention seemed riveted in the direction they had all disappeared. Maybe they knew who they were after and considered him easy work, a peaceable guy, an adman who liked to play soccer on the weekends with his buddies, into Eastern meditation. Shouldn't present much of a problem.

The man pulled out a pack of cigarettes, casually tapped one into his free hand, and dug into his pocket for matches. He looked supremely self-confident, gazing off into the blackness, but the match's flare, when it came, struck Miguel as a kind of signal. He scrambled to his feet and rushed the man; before he could react, before he even turned to see what was going on, the iron bar came smashing down on his head. Miguel heard the terrible crunch of bones breaking, the nose and maybe the jaw, and forced himself to bring the metal bar down once more on the man's head. The man fell to the ground, writhing and holding his head between his hands. A few low moans rattled in his throat.

Miguel could have told himself this was merely a payback for what they had done to Haidèe's secretary (and so many others), but he felt only nausea, the fervency of vomit rising to his mouth. He dropped the metal bar and picked up the shotgun. Though he wasn't skilled with such a weapon, he knew it could inflict a certain amount of damage even if all you did was pull the trigger. He dove into the car, slammed the doors shut, and climbed behind the wheel. The car was a beat-up four-door Brasília, and the keys were dangling from the ignition—they weren't so careful or professional after all. They had underestimated him. Miguel put the car in reverse and peeled out onto the road, tires squealing.

Suddenly a blast knocked out the rear window and the engine died. Miguel grabbed the shotgun and stuck the barrel out the open window. The two men who had chased him off into the darkness emerged from behind the pile of crushed rock. One was wearing a leather jacket. They were both running toward him full tilt and they were clearly furious. Another bullet whizzed through the window and shattered the windshield. Miguel pointed the shotgun in their general direction and pulled the trigger. Startled, the men threw themselves to the ground. Miguel turned the ignition, the engine caught; he stepped hard on the accelerator and felt the car leap forward, gathering speed. With the jolt, the glove compartment fell open and a .38 dropped onto the muddy rubber floor mat. Miguel didn't even want to consider what else might be in that glove compartment. It was hard to see through the broken windshield, but the radiating lines, like spiderwebs, formed a design: a mandala.

Ruth waited up until the last late-night movie on TV ended. Finally, her weariness—she was always weary—won out, and she fell asleep on the couch, a magazine in her hand. Later, Luciano walked into the living room in his shorts and found his mother sleeping.

"Hey, Mom, are you going to sleep down here?"

Ruth startled awake, squinting, to see her son standing over her.

"What time is it?"

The boy shrugged.

"It's late. Where's Dad?"

Ruth sat up, alert now. She was still dressed and needed to wash her face.

"Your father had a meeting. He must have been delayed."

"Geez, until this hour?"

Luciano had taken to watching his father's every step recently. He was clearly intrigued by Miguel's talk of his weekly discoveries and the various mystical sects that had caught his fancy lately.

Ever since the painful process of leaving the army, Miguel had been feeling a little like an abandoned orphan. Not that he would have admitted it, but Ruth knew. And she knew that just as Luciano was entering adolescence, he was watching his father undergo a mid-life crisis. As a psychology professor, as well as a mother, Ruth was worried. She had a lot of sympathy for Miguel but she didn't want what he was going through to affect their maturing boy.

"What's going on, Mom?"

"Nothing, everything's fine. Your father must have been delayed, that's all. He had a meeting at Haidèe's. You know how those things drag on."

Luciano looked at his watch, a handsome digital model he was so attached to that he didn't even take it off to shower.

"Do you know what time it is? It's four-thirty!"

"And you should be asleep. You're going to have a heck of a time getting up tomorrow."

"I was asleep. But I woke up and went for a glass of water and noticed that you and Dad weren't in your room. I thought you went out or something."

"We wouldn't go out without telling you, Luciano."

The boy rolled his eyes.

"And besides, you're old enough to stay home alone."

"It's okay, I'm not complaining."

So he said, but Ruth knew that he'd become very dependent on them, perhaps because he was an only child and a bit unsettled. Only in the last two years had they managed to put down roots in Rio. It was the first time Luciano had gone to the same school and had the same friends for two years running. Miguel's constant transfers had made Luciano a solitary and very inward child. He was well-developed for his age—at thirteen he had the build of a fifteen-year-old and was quite a bit taller than she—but he still had both the childish timidity and the vital curiosity of boys who have not yet entered the problematic years of adolescence. And truly, Luciano wasn't the problem; if anyone it was Miguel.

"Why don't you go to bed?" Ruth didn't want him to see how anxious she was beginning to feel. Miguel didn't sleep well away from home; even when he was stationed at the barracks, on the rare occasions he had night duty, he always managed to come home to sleep. And he wasn't one to hang around with bohemians and stay up all night. He was really quite a homebody, spending his free time reading, doing little home repairs, and making model ships and airplanes with his son.

"Okay, good night."

Luciano went back to his room, though he obviously didn't feel much like sleeping. Ruth realized that he probably wanted to talk some more, but not long from now, at seven, she would have to drop him at school and be off to class herself. If she didn't get out of the house on time, her first class would be left waiting, and that wasn't right. To make matters worse, the Institute of Psychology was located in an old and imposing building on Avenida Pasteur, and morning traffic in and out of Urca was always heavy.

And Ruth was really very worried about Miguel. At six o'clock, just as she'd walked in the door from work, he'd called to tell her about his after-hours appointment. At least twice a month he went to Haidèe's for publicity meetings. Ruth knew Haidèe and knew how important these meetings were, lubricated with good liquor and much convivial conversation, until a plan for marketing the new line emerged. But they never lasted until four o'clock in the morning.

At around one A.M. she'd called Haidèe's, but no one had answered. Ruth imagined that meant the meeting was over, everyone gone, and Miguel on his way home. She fell asleep on the sofa and woke up to the crackling of the television because the programming was over for the night. It had been two-thirty. Ruth wasn't the alarmist type, but it seemed odd that Miguel hadn't come home yet. She had called Haidèe's again; still no answer. She had dozed off again reading a magazine, and now here it was almost daybreak and she still had no idea where he was.

Miguel was going through some changes, that much was clear. It was not uncommon for men rounding the bend into their forties to suffer a phase of acute self-scrutiny before really accepting the fact that they were about to become middle-aged. But it was a little more complicated with Miguel. He had undertaken some kind of quest, some reformulation of his very being, and this process was sparked by a traumatic experience that had come back to haunt him after years of relative tranquility and security. The issues he was wrestling with ranged from economic questions—which were not earthshaking, but real—to the need to construct a personal raison d'être, a new way of being in the world, something he could truly believe in and which would give him strength.

In the beginning Ruth hadn't realized how much this quest of Miguel's might affect her. To tell the truth, she had considered herself the alienated one until then. She liked to use the word *alienated*, because the concept seemed wide and rich enough to describe her life before the great rupture. And what had that life been like? Well, nothing terribly mysterious. She got her degree in psychology in 1963, but had never practiced her profession, marrying that same year, when Miguel was a first lieutenant and had just finished his studies at the Agulhas Negras Academy. As the daughter of reasonably well-to-do parents from Rio's fashionable Zona Sul, Ruth's sights were aimed well within the boundaries of her social class. Her father was an influential attorney and a political conservative; at the time of Ruth and Miguel's marriage he was a state representative from the UDN party. Her mother was a perfect housewife and probably Ruth's greatest role model. Ruth and Miguel had been going out as long as she could remember, and her family was very enthusiastic about the match. Miguel had surprised everyone by qualifying among the top applicants in the exam for the military academy. He proved to be a brilliant student, and in no time his superiors had to admit he was not the gate-crashing son of civilians that they had suspected him to be, but a talented, disciplined cadet who showed a special ability to lead. He did so without seeming brusque, without declaring his authority, and yet no one in his class made a major move without consulting him. To add to his success, he blended a penchant for the practical aspects of military life with an intellectual perceptiveness. He graduated from the academy with two medals and a prominent post with the commanding general of the Third Military Region in Porto Alegre, the outgoing director of the school. The general had carefully watched the progress of that competent and always elegant cadet, who read a lot, was a sharpshooter, and wouldn't hesitate to throw himself into a mud puddle if necessary.

And what about her? What was she doing meanwhile? For a long time all she was interested in was being with her boyfriend. That—he—was her life, as terribly anachronistic and even embarrassing as this seemed to her today. But that was who she had been. Her friends went to parties, traded boyfriends back and forth, and happily accepted rides on the motorbikes that hung out at lifeguard station #6 on Copacabana Beach. Ruth, however, was scared to death of those noisy, teetering things and didn't for one minute trust boys who wore plaid shirts and stiff pompadours. She preferred weekends in Teresópolis with a select group of family friends, where she would go horseback riding, drink iced tea, and go to bed early dreaming of Miguel's next leave.

Miguel came home twice a month—his short hair in stark contrast to those motorbikers' greasy manes—and Ruth would forget everything else. They'd go to the movies, walk on the beach, nuzzle on the living room couch. When finally they got married, it seemed part of a natural progression. And for the next ten years she knew no other life than Miguel's career in the army, moving from city to city, base to base, until the alarm signals began to sound, because something was very wrong.

The rupture didn't happen overnight, of course. It was a cumulative process, which at first went unnoticed because Ruth was so absorbed in the protective illusion of her life as wife and mother. Luciano was born in Brasília in 1965 on the cusp of another transfer, this time to Belém, at the mouth of the Amazon River in the state of Pará. Their furniture and household goods were packed up and shipped as she lay in the hospital, which produced a certain amount of anxiety, but their routine was reestablished immediately, because she arrived to find her new house all set up, almost identical to the old one, except that it was located in suffocatingly hot Belém.

Ruth never could have imagined how much her life would change during the years they lived in the Amazon. At first things went along pretty much the same in Belém; Miguel worked with the bureaucratic service of the Eighth Regiment and decided to buy a boat to explore the region. In 1969 they were transferred to the far-west outpost of Porto Velho, Rondônia, and it was there that the first serious shock waves hit.

Miguel didn't like Porto Velho, and Ruth couldn't blame him. It was a miserable city, dusty and only precariously linked to the rest of the country. Luciano got sick, and Miguel blamed it on the yellow tap water. In June, during the week Miguel became involved in the incident that would undermine his confidence in the army, he received confirmation that he had been accepted for a nine-month course at the Officers' Training School in Rio de Janeiro. The prospect of going to Rio, even if only for nine months, was the sort of news that should have shaken Miguel out of his constant bad mood.

When Miguel came home from work that afternoon, though, he looked a lot more than ill-humored. Luciano was doing better, eating well, and their problems seemed to have been solved by the impending transfer, but Ruth had never seen Miguel look the way he did that day. He walked in, changed his clothes without a word, and began watering the plants. He was completely silent and clearly wanted to be left alone. At dinner he hardly touched his food. And then he sat reading in the living room, on purpose, expecting Ruth to pad off to bed without so much as a question. But she couldn't simply disappear. Miguel had never been like this before; she had to knock down the wall he was constructing between them. Miguel looked up, expressionless, at her question. Then he set the book down beside him; he hadn't been able to read anyway. And he told her.

That afternoon two squatters had been taken into custody. Rondônia was a frontier territory, and land conflicts were intensifying, but the associated violence, assassinations, and expulsions of the poor were not reported in the newspapers. Little Porto Velho didn't even have its own newspaper; it didn't need one. News circulated freely and it was impossible to hide things. The two squatters had been dragged off to the barracks at the request of a politician from the governing party. Miguel saw the men, half-naked and bound with ropes, tossed out of a military van like sacks of potatoes. Their bodies were covered with hematomas and one of them had been shot in the leg.

Horrified, Miguel decided to have a little talk with the sergeant in charge of the group who had made the arrests. Exhibiting total disregard for Miguel's rank as captain, the sergeant responded by telling him to stay out of it.

"These men are not staying here in this barracks," insisted Miguel.

Instead of answering, the sergeant yelled to one of his men to take the squatters to the stockade.

"Sergeant!" shouted Miguel. "This is not a police station. I want these men released or turned over to the appropriate authorities."

A man in dusty street clothes emerged from the van that had delivered the prisoners. He was around fifty, needed a shave, and had an arrogant air about him. He walked directly to Miguel, saluted, and presented a document that showed him to be a colonel. Miguel saluted back but was not intimidated.

"I'd like to know what's going on here, Colonel."

"There's no problem at all with what's going on here, Captain, and I hope you aren't going to create one now."

"I'm not the one causing problems, sir. This is not a police station. I've already explained that to the sergeant, but it seems he is unfamiliar with military rank."

"The sergeant is following my orders."

"But I'm the officer in charge of this barracks, sir."

"This barracks is under the command of the Twelfth Region."

"Correct, sir. But I have had no instructions to turn this barracks into a public jail, much less to organize a patrol to arrest civilians."

"That's true, Captain, you haven't."

"Exactly. Which is why I am going to have to reestablish order here, Colonel."

Miguel called the officer on duty and ordered him to arrest the sergeant who had been disrespectful.

"I can't do that, Captain."

"This is a case of flagrant disregard for discipline, Colonel. The man knows very well he cannot leave this barracks on a patrol without orders from me. From what I can tell, he left with ten of my men, plus weapons and ammunition, without the necessary authorization and returned with two civilians tied up like animals and seriously wounded to boot."

"But the civilians in question are Communists, Captain. They were inciting the farmworkers. The patrol was set up at the last minute. There was no time to go through regular channels."

"We'll look into that, Colonel. I'm going to order an inquiry of this incident. In the meantime, the sergeant is under arrest and you, sir, can deliver these civilians to police headquarters." Miguel turned to the officer on duty. "Lieutenant, confiscate these men's weapons and escort them to the stockade."

The lieutenant on barracks duty nervously approached the patrol. The men hesitated, waiting for the colonel's reaction.

"Hand over your weapons," ordered the colonel.

The sergeant and his men placed their guns on the ground and were led off to the stockade. His own weapon in hand, the colonel assumed control of the prisoners, pulling them along by the rope that bound their wrists and ankles.

"We'll have to have a talk, Captain. I see you're a real stickler. I like that."

Miguel was still not satisfied.

"Are you going to leave these men tied up like livestock, Colonel?"

The colonel looked at the squatters with disgust and shot Miguel a smile.

"Of course not. I'm going to take them to police headquarters, where they belong. The barracks stockade is for soldiers; these vermin might contaminate it."

He yanked on the rope, as if to stroll off down the street, parading the prisoners behind him.

"Would you like the use of a vehicle, Colonel?"

"Thank you, Captain. Much better than walking these Commies through the streets. They're certainly not to be trusted and, the way they look, the common folk might be silly enough to feel sorry for them."

Miguel gave orders for the colonel and the two prisoners to be escorted to his private jeep, then returned to his desk. Later, he would give the hotheaded sergeant a good talking-to and then let him out. As for the others, they were innocent and he would have them released before the day was out.

Two hours later, when he had almost forgotten the incident, the officer on duty asked to speak with him. Sheet-white and trembling, the man stumbled to get his words out. Finally he said:

"Uh, Captain, the colonel came back."

"Really? Is he outside? Ask him to come in."

"No, sir. He, uh, brought your jeep back and left it in the courtyard."

"Yes, of course. He had to bring back my jeep. So?"

"Well, uh, it's not just your jeep, sir."

"Exactly what are you trying to tell me, Lieutenant?"

"You'd better come with me, Captain."

Miguel followed the lieutenant outside. His jeep was parked in the courtyard in his designated parking space right where it was supposed to be. But inside the jeep, slumped in the backseat, were the bodies of the two squatters. The sight of them, skinny and tattered, bloody and riddled with bullet holes, sent Miguel reeling. Now he understood why his lieutenant had been reduced to stuttering.

"Son of a bitch!" roared Miguel.

He spun and pounded his fists on the top of the jeep. Then he strode back to his office, followed by the terrified lieutenant.

Miguel grabbed the phone.

"I want Colonel Trindade at Central Command, right away . . . This is Captain Gouveia."

Once he had Colonel Trindade on the line, Miguel explained, practically shouting, what had happened. After listening to the whole story in silence, the colonel said to do nothing until he got there. He would make a few phone calls and come directly to the barracks.

Miguel had his men throw a tarpaulin over the bodies and waited, tense. He ordered the group of curious soldiers who had gathered around the jeep to disperse and assigned two men to stand guard. And he stood nearby himself as well, with the jeep in his line of sight at all times, because too many things had happened without his knowing.

The colonel arrived in a black Opala, accompanied by a major. Miguel retold the entire story, more in control now, and the two officers limited themselves to listening and discreetly observing the tarpaulin-covered jeep.

When Miguel had finished, the colonel exchanged glances with the major and shook his head.

"You've done well, Captain Gouveia. This was all quite irregular."

Miguel should have felt vindicated by these words from his superior, except they had been uttered so formally.

"Captain," continued the colonel, "this is a very extraordinary, very delicate situation. We're going to make it go away."

"What?" gasped Miguel, wounded to the core. "Make it go away? But Colonel . . ."

"I know, Captain. It was very irregular, I agree. And the sergeant certainly deserves to be punished. He's in the stockade now, am I right?"

Miguel nodded uneasily.

"There are certain larger things at stake here, if you know what I mean. In any case, we're going to have to accept the facts. Don't think I'm happy about it."

"I have no idea what you're talking about, Colonel."

"Don't worry. You won't be held responsible for what happened. Not in the least, I guarantee it. I've already ordered that the bodies be removed, and everything's going to be just fine."

"But a man showed up here calling himself Colonel . . ."

"He is a colonel."

"Where has he gone? Who is he?"

"It doesn't matter. I've checked it all out, there are no discrepancies, though our colleague is a bit of a screwball. Maybe he wanted to make his mark, but we're all professionals here, aren't we, Captain?"

Miguel couldn't believe his ears. Two men lay dead in his jeep. They had been rounded up by a military patrol. The mysterious colonel claimed they were Communists, but even so, you don't just go around blowing away Communists and dumping their bodies at military barracks.

"Captain," said Coronel Trindade, attempting an air of complicity and authority, "we're going to forget this whole thing happened. It was a mistake, but it's been dealt with appropriately. Go back to your work and think no more about it."

Miguel saluted and turned to leave. The colonel slapped him on the shoulder paternally and said with an uneasy smile:

"Captain, I understand how you feel. But sometimes we have to break the rules."

Miguel acquiesced, equally uneasy.

The colonel removed his hand from Miguel's shoulder and stood straight.

"What happened here today, Captain, must remain between us."

"I understand, sir. But there's not much I can do if the enlisted men start talking . . ."

"Enlisted men's talk is the same as nothing. I'm referring to the officers involved."

Miguel kept the secret, relatively speaking. He resisted confiding in Ruth as long as he could—to spare her, he explained—but finally told her the whole story. She was more shocked on his behalf than by the incident itself. She didn't fully understand all the implications, and, while she believed it was wrong to kill people, even Communists, she also knew that mistakes happen sometimes. Partly out of wisdom and partly out of respect for her husband's state of mind, she did no more than console him.

The following day was Wednesday, and Miguel was off duty. Generally, he played soccer on Wednesdays with a group of friends from the barracks. But that particular Wednesday he instructed Ruth to get dressed early, pack a sandwich lunch, and gather Luciano's things. Miguel borrowed a neighbor's car—he would never again use his jeep—and they drove off down a rutted dirt road. Though Ruth knew this was no regular picnic, she didn't feel like asking where they were going. After driving for almost an hour, they approached a clearing with a few shacks. Miguel got out of the car and went to talk with a few of the men who were building a kind of kiosk, very common in that region and generally used for a little store. The men seemed hostile and responded in monosyllables. It was not long before Miguel returned to the car, because he apparently did not get the information he was looking for.

"Why are we here, Miguel?"

Miguel started the engine and answered in a deliberate voice, as if expecting her to try to talk him out of what he had in mind.

"You know why, Ruth. I'm trying to find those squatters' families."

"But Miguel, why? We don't have anything to do with it."

That was when Ruth realized something had changed. Miguel pressed the accelerator gently, pulling out onto the road, and spoke with great tenderness. But beneath the tenderness, deep inside him, there was also a new bitterness, which would grow to unbearable proportions over the years.

"But of course we do. Ruth, don't you see? Two men were murdered. No matter who they were or what they had done, this is not a barbarian country we live in. We live by rule of law. I refuse to keep my mouth shut. We can't just keep our mouths shut."

Ruth didn't like the sound of this. Miguel was evading her influence, the same way he was rebelling against the orders of his superiors. Not that she could condone the killing of those two men, but at that point in her life it couldn't touch her, it simply wasn't part of her world. At the same time, her husband's indignation prevented her—for fear of a serious argument that would disturb the harmony of their life together—from taking a position that might lump her with those who were trying to cover up the crime.

In any case, she had to do something to make him come to his senses—if he had any left after that incident.

"Think about it, Miguel. Soon we'll be leaving Rondônia and we can forget all about this."

"Maybe I'm acting the fool, Ruth. But I can't help it. What happened yesterday at the barracks was no accident, any more than it was just the result of some colonel being in a hurry. You don't know what you're talking about."

"What don't I know, Miguel?"

"The things they're saying. The things people talk about in low voices. Rumors. But I'm not so sure anymore that they're rumors."

At this point Luciano began to cry. Ruth tried to soothe him, but the combination of the heat and his father's agitated voice seemed to be taking their toll.

"Let's go home, Miguel. Please."

Miguel turned his attention to the baby and said nothing to his wife. But he also turned back onto the highway toward the city, as if he had heard her plea. Luciano tired of crying and accepted a drink of water, then began playing with a toy. Ruth's apprehension abated to the point where she found herself actually enjoying the scenery.

Back in Porto Velho, Miguel parked in front of a church.

"I'll be right back," he promised.

Ruth watched him disappear inside. He emerged ten minutes later, accompanied by a priest and a young boy. The priest was talking earnestly and patting him on the back. Finally they said good-bye and Miguel returned to the car.

"Let's go home," said Miguel, as if all the pressure had lifted. "How about a game of cards?"

Ruth agreed and they drove home. But it was no good—Miguel kept misplaying his cards, and as Ruth won hand after hand she gradually lost interest.

"This is no fun, you're too distracted. You owe me a fortune already."

"I'll pay you in kisses," he said, leaning toward her.

Ruth pushed back from the table and slithered out of his grasp, hoping he would follow her, but Miguel slumped back into his chair.

"I talked to that priest, Ruth. He knows the families. Those men were picked up last night by an Air Force C-47. The priest has no idea where they were taken, and he's worried."

"My God, Miguel," cried Ruth, "I thought you'd put that behind you. What the hell were you doing talking to that priest?"

"Trying to get some information. And it turns out I went to the right person."

"And?"

"And he gave me the names of the two squatters. He told me they had come from Goiás. From a place called Trombas—ever heard of it?"

"No."

"Me either. But the priest said they were marked men, all right."

"You mean Communists?"

"Not exactly, but members of the Peasant Leagues."

"The what?"

"The Peasant Leagues—they date back to before '64. Subversive, but completely disorganized. Those two poor devils weren't part of any cohesive movement. They weren't doing anything but looking for a place to live and plant a garden."

"I don't know . . ." said Ruth, incredulous. "They must have been doing something illegal. No one would arrest people just because they're poor."

Instead of saying anything in return, Miguel just frowned and held his cards tightly, looking distant. Ruth wondered, since they had spent the morning on their search, whether to prepare a noontime dinner or to serve the sandwiches still waiting in the picnic basket. Miguel settled her quandary.

"Let's go out for some fish."

The conjured image of a popular restaurant in downtown Porto Velho that served delicious fish stew was comforting. But Miguel's invitation did not put Ruth completely at ease.

Months passed, and they were transferred to Rio. Miguel entered and completed the Officers' Training course, but without his usual enthusiasm. The rank of major, which he had hoped to attain after the course, would never come. Promotions were doled out, his colleagues won new jobs, but Miguel was consistently passed over. Ruth began to suspect that something had happened, but didn't have the courage to probe. Only then did Miguel tell her about the report he had sent to the military commander of

Amazonia denouncing the incident, and about the silence that followed.

Ruth stared out the apartment window. Day was breaking. Her body registered the torpor of a near-sleepless night and the anxiety about her husband's disappearance. The scenes going through her head were not encouraging. Miguel had been nurturing his silence and this made him unpredictable. But there was no indication that his past fears were materializing.

Ruth opened the window to get some air. The morning was dawning clear and serene, as if last night's rain had never happened. The clock struck six; she went into the kitchen. She needed to think. Mechanically she began making coffee. She didn't want to worry Miguel's parents, much less her own mother, a widow prone to drama. She refused to entertain the notion of checking hospitals or calling the police. After all, Miguel had merely stayed out all night, no reason to make a stir. Or was it? She simply didn't know, and the uncertainty was like a dead weight that made it impossible to think straight. Maybe the thing to do was to let the college know she wouldn't be able to teach today; she'd invent some illness, a cold or something. She'd take Luciano to school and be free to do whatever she needed.

The aroma of coffee lent a little normality to the breaking day. Ruth poured herself a cup and drank. She lit a cigarette and returned to the window. The street showed signs of life, people hurrying off to work. She left the window and went to wake her son. Twisted in his sheets, the boy showed no inclination to get out of bed, which was just what she expected. Ruth smiled and began tickling his feet, until Luciano stopped thrashing and wiggling and opened his eyes, grouchy, protesting.

"Time to get up, Luciano."

"Really? Already?"

"Yes, coffee's ready. Come on, go brush your teeth and take a shower."

She pushed the boy out of bed and practically carried him to the bathroom. In the morning Luciano seemed most like the little boy he no longer was. Sometimes she regretted his getting older, and other times she accepted it. This morning, with Miguel gone, she realized she regretted it. If only children could remain six years old. Spirited, full of curiosity and inexhaustible energy. A useless wish; Luciano was already full of willfulness, painfully building his personality and aspiring to be independent from her.

She closed the bathroom door and leaned against it. Any minute he would call her for something he needed, a towel, toilet paper, toothpaste.

"Mom!" yelled Luciano from behind the door.

Ruth smiled and went into the bathroom.

"What is it?"

"The water's cold."

"Good grief, Luciano, you just have to adjust it, it's no big mystery."

He had a towel wrapped around him; he didn't want her to see him naked anymore.

"That's too hot," he said, practically pushing her out of the bathroom. "It's okay, I can do it now."

A half hour later Ruth was sitting on the bus with Luciano sulking beside her. It was the same every morning. He wanted his father to drive him to school, but Miguel's schedule never coincided with the time school began. So Ruth would ride the bus with Luciano to Botafogo, and then go on to Voluntários da Pátria, where she caught another bus to Urca.

"You're not going to work today, are you, Mom?"

It was Luciano's subtle way to note the absence of his father. Ruth knew he was worried and, above all, intrigued.

"No."

"You're going out looking for Dad?"

"No! Where did you get that idea? Daddy is probably home by now. There's no reason to go out looking for him."

"Then why aren't you going to work?"

"Because I'm coming down with a cold."

Luciano made a face. He believed that excuse about as much as he believed in Santa Claus.

"I think you should go looking for Dad. Call Grandpa and check the hospitals. And call the police."

Children's incisiveness astounded her sometimes.

"No, Luciano, it's nothing like that. Dad's fine. Everything is fine. These things happen sometimes. Dad will be home when you get back from school this afternoon and he'll tell you exactly what happened."

"I hope so. But I doubt it."

"What do you mean? You father isn't hiding anything from you. We aren't hiding anything from you."

"I think Dad's been kidnapped."

Ruth looked at her son in disbelief, then threw her arms around him.

"Luciano, everything's going to be okay. Trust me. Daddy will be home when you come back from school. It's nothing like that. If something bad had happened, we'd have heard about it by now."

Apparently he accepted her explanation; at least he fell silent and began looking out the window. When they got to school, Ruth watched until he was safely inside. Soon this ritual would no longer be acceptable. It would embarrass him and he'd insist on arriving at school by himself. Ruth remembered how at thirteen she had felt humiliated because her mother wouldn't let her walk to school alone. As a girl, even finishing high school, she was never really allowed to go anywhere without at least a friend.

Ruth stood watching the children stream into the school until the sidewalk was empty. She walked back to the bus stop feeling alone, abandoned. A public telephone next to a newsstand caught her eye. She screwed up her courage and crossed the street. First, she called home: no answer. She placed the telephone back on the hook and fished around in her bag for her address book. She looked up Haidèe's number and dialed. It rang, but no answer there either. Impossible, there was always someone at Haidèe's, she had an enormous and expensive house staff. Ruth thumbed through the address book and found the number of the ad agency where Miguel worked, but it was still early, people wouldn't begin showing up until after nine. She returned to the bus stop and waited for a few minutes, then decided she was far too restless to stand there in the morning sun waiting for a bus. She hailed a cab and told the driver to take her to an address in the exclusive Botanical Garden neighborhood. She'd find out directly from Haidèe what was going on.

Ruth had never really liked Haidèe. She knew she was an old friend of Miguel's family, but Ruth didn't trust her, plain and simple. And not because of all the rumors. Ruth's antipathy was based on something visceral, and Haidèe felt the same way about her, she was sure of it.

They were, in any case, civilized people. Their mutual dislike was cloaked in false courtesy, formal gestures, and polite words. Ruth had been cultivating her negative feelings toward Haidèe for many years, long before she knew of the connection to Miguel's family. It all began at a party in the Hotel Quitandinha, around

1959. It was carnival, and Ruth's parents had brought her to her
first real carnival ball. For adults only. She had spent days trying
on dresses, choosing shoes, and negotiating with her mother
about how much makeup she could wear. When she walked
into the ballroom, the first person Ruth met was Haidèe, who
emphatically ignored her. It was as if she were invisible. Only later
did Ruth realize that she was wearing the exact same dress as
Haidèe, just a different color, which did nothing to diminish the
disaster. Haidèe, meanwhile, was at her shining best. Perhaps
the most dazzling woman at the ball, she caught everyone's
attention, standing beside her somber diplomat husband attracting
men and stares. Ruth hated Haidèe utterly for reducing her to a
cheap copy. Her first ball lost all its charm. Of course time did
bring perspective; she knew her rage was petty. She was just
a girl at the time, and Haidèe probably didn't even remember
the incident. Neither one ever mentioned it. Yet the antipathy
remained.

The cab pulled up to Haidèe's gate and Ruth asked the driver
to wait. She rang the bell. No answer, and the house truly did
look deserted. Not that much could be seen through the trees and
shrubs, but there seemed to be no movement anywhere. Haidèe
always had at least three gardeners at work and a security man
stationed in a kind of guard box near the gate. But the box was
as empty as the garden.

Ruth rang the bell insistently and craned her neck to see further
up the drive. She couldn't be sure, but she thought she saw
Miguel's car parked at the front door, half-hidden by a clump
of Indian cane. She couldn't see the license plate, but it looked
exactly like his car.

A woman appeared. Very young. She stood in the garden
absently, wearing only a bikini, as if she were a model waiting
to be photographed. The woman looked out toward the gate and
froze, except for her hands fidgeting with the bikini.

"Please!" shouted Ruth. "Please come here."

The woman didn't move.

"Please, it's urgent."

Ruth was beginning to feel annoyed. A rush of anger washed
over her, anger toward Miguel and toward this inane woman.

She also felt ridiculous. What the hell was she doing here? Why
should she be out looking for her husband, anyway, making an ass
of herself like this? She felt like going back to the taxi and the

hell with it, but then she saw the woman had decided to come closer to the gate.

"What do you want?" she asked.

"I want to talk to Haidèe."

"Who are you?"

"I'm the one who should be asking you that, miss." Ruth put the emphasis on *miss*, because up close the woman didn't look the least bit like a model. She looked more like one of Haidèe's maids out to get some sun.

"I work here."

"Then go call your boss."

"She's not in."

"Oh? Where is she?"

"I don't know. And I'll tell you, it's beginning to get to me. Everybody else took off. I'm here all by myself, stupid me. No one told me anything."

"Just a minute," said Ruth. "Open the gate so we can talk better."

"I don't have the key."

"How do you get out, then?"

"There's a service entrance. Over on the side street. Go on around if you want."

Ruth nodded and, after telling the cab driver he could go, headed around the corner. Her heart was pounding with curiosity and irritation.

The service entrance was at the far end of the garden wall, and the woman had already thrown a beach robe over her bikini and opened the iron gate.

"I'm sorry, ma'am. I think I've met you before . . ."

Ruth motioned that it didn't matter.

"You said everyone left. When was that?"

"Last night."

"I just want to check something."

Ruth walked around the house to the colorful awning out front. There, as she suspected, was Miguel's car.

"What about this car?"

"I don't know, ma'am. It's been here since last night. I don't know what's going on. They didn't tell me a thing. It's like they gave everyone time off and left me here alone. I thought about leaving, but I'm afraid if I go, and there's no one here, they'll hold me responsible if anything happens."

Ruth couldn't take her eyes off the car.

"Are you sure there's no one home?"

"Of course I'm sure."

"Can I go inside?"

"What for?"

"To see if it's really true."

The maid looked fearful, plainly unsure what to do. Then she decided.

"Okay. You've been here before, haven't you?"

"Yes, I'm a friend of your boss," lied Ruth.

The woman pushed the door open and the two went inside. As they passed through the kitchen Ruth noticed it looked as if only the maid had had breakfast that morning, but it was still early for people who went to bed in the wee hours.

They headed for the living room. The maid was clearly still nervous about having let her in the house.

"I guess it's okay," she was mumbling. "All they said was don't answer the phone. I don't even want to know what's going on."

Ruth felt a flash of her old weariness as she climbed the stairs. She would begin her inspection with the bedrooms. What was she doing in this place?

Miguel opened his eyes. A ray of sun shone in through a tear in the curtain, falling precisely on his face. He sat bolt upright and looked around. The walls were covered with mirrors. He was sitting on a round bed, and directly in front of him was a portable bar set up on a tea cart. The moth-eaten curtain covered the window only piecemeal, but the room was clean and smelled of disinfectant mixed with the sweat of a night's sleep. Where was he? What the hell had happened? He pushed back the covers and saw that he was naked. Both knees and one leg were covered with scrapes and cuts. Every muscle in his body ached. He climbed out of bed and pulled on his shorts. Then he went into the bathroom, washed his face, and dressed. His clothes were torn and filthy, he couldn't go out in the street looking like this. Running a comb through his hair, he remembered the car. Little by little his memory returned and with it a sinking feeling in the pit of his stomach.

He had made it to a hotel on the Dutra Highway. He remembered its neon sign blinking in the night. He had decided not to go home or to call Ruth, to lay low and avoid needlessly involving his family until he could figure out what was going on. To be ignorant was the worst way of showing yourself to be weak—that was what he had learned from his first Tae Kwon Do lessons. He had seen the motel sign: Flamingo. He needed rest, he needed sleep; later he would have a clear head to think.

A motel was the best choice. No one asks questions at motels. He'd be able to sleep all night without being disturbed. Suddenly he focused on the car again. The Brasília was theirs, they would be out looking for it. And the owner of the motel would certainly cooperate with the police; places like this had close ties with the police, they depended on the cops' goodwill.

He left the room and slowly walked down the hallway, the .38 that had fallen out of the glove compartment tucked into his belt. He had ditched the shotgun along the side of the road, and felt safer carrying a handgun. The motel was a one-story U-shaped construction, so this hallway connected all the rooms. Not the most discreet setup—anyone leaving a room had to walk the entire corridor to one tip of the horseshoe to get to the exit and parking area. Guests entering the motel at the other end of the U would use the same hallway. On a good day this hall must be the stage for some unforgettable scenes.

Arriving at the end of the hall, he peered out and saw the Brasília parked beside a Corcel and two Volkswagens. At the end of a ramp was a sort of sentry box, where an employee waited to check for proof of payment before letting down the chain across the exit. Miguel stood there a few seconds studying the scene. The clerk was sitting on a bench in the booth with his back to the ramp, listening to a portable radio. Miguel heard a door open down the hall and pictured an exhausted couple leaving their room. He had to act fast if he didn't want to be seen looking the way he did.

He walked over to the Brasília and let the air out of the two front tires. Then he took a one-hundred-cruzeiro bill out of his wallet and went to talk to the clerk. He flashed his receipt, and saw the guy's eyes narrow at his appearance.

"I've got a problem with my car," said Miguel before the clerk could ask him about his clothes.

"What's wrong?" asked the clerk, continuing to give him a suspicious once-over.

"My two front tires are flat. Is there a tire place around here?"

The man turned off his radio and came to the door of the booth.

"There is one, but it's not real close. I've got the number, I can call and ask them to come pick up your tires. It'll take a while, though."

It wasn't going to work. Miguel needed to get the guy out of the booth. One of the Volkswagens was coming up the ramp. The clerk returned to his booth and took the receipt from the driver.

"I have two spares," Miguel lied. "Think you could give me a hand?" He flashed the one-hundred-cruzeiro bill.

The man looked at the money and hesitated.

"I'm not really supposed to leave the booth."

"It won't take long," prodded Miguel.

The man took the money and followed him.

As they drew alongside the car, Miguel slapped himself on the forehead in mock dismay.

"The keys! I left them in the room. I'll just be a second."

He hurried off and threaded the U-shaped corridor to the opposite exit. He sailed up the ramp, hurdled over the chain, and hesitated for a few seconds on the shoulder of the highway, unsure which way to go. He decided to head back toward Rio, because last night he had noticed a gas station about three kilometers before the motel. He could hitch a ride with someone at the station; he'd say he'd been robbed, make up some kind of a story.

He sprinted off, trying to put some distance between him and the motel, but his muscles ached and the gashes on his knees throbbed. Then he realized the stupidity of what he had just done. He had paid the motel bill with his credit card! When they found the car, his identity would be handed to them on a silver platter. This thought made him run faster, as if to compensate for his mistake.

It had occurred to Miguel earlier that his pursuers might not know who he was. Maybe they thought he was Haidèe's bodyguard or something, or just an inadvertent witness in the wrong place at the wrong time. If they questioned Haidèe, she would deny the existence of a bodyguard. But they might suspect her of lying. And even if they thought he had only been there by chance, the question of his identity was important. It would give him a lot more room to move if they didn't know who he was. But if they did, and what had happened last night was just a clumsy way of getting him involved, then he was on shaky ground and must act with the greatest caution.

He arrived at the gas station panting for breath. The three attendants looked at him in alarm. A refrigerated truck was being gassed up and the driver climbed out to go to the bathroom.

"Help," gasped Miguel, "please—help me."

As two of the gas station attendants approached, Miguel crumpled to the ground. The bid to emphasize his desperation worked better than he'd planned; he let out an involuntary cry as his bloody knees hit the pavement.

The men pulled him to his feet.

"What happened to you, pal?" asked a compact black man, toothless and covered with grease. Miguel looked at him and took a deep breath.

"I got mugged. Some guys grabbed me . . . I stopped to take a piss and these guys came out of nowhere . . ."

"Shit, it's almost every day now. It's okay, man, you're safe now."

"I have to get to Rio."

"Don't worry, we'll call the cops and they'll come right down."

"No," protested Miguel. "I don't want any cops."

The men looked at each other, suspicious.

"I mean, not until I've talked to my lawyer. The cops always squeeze more money out of you. It's bad enough those thugs took what I had on me, and roughed me up besides."

The gas station attendants seemed satisfied with his explanation.

"Let me talk to the driver of that rig over here. Maybe he can give you a lift."

They took Miguel inside the station and offered him a drink of water.

"You want a cup of coffee instead? Or a shot of rum?" the black man asked. He was clearly the more communicative of the two.

"Coffee, please," said Miguel.

They brought him some coffee and he took a sip. It went down easily. He looked at his watch, it was seven o'clock. The sun was bright and the sky clear, almost cloudless. And it was hot. He thought of Ruth. She must be worried. Their comfortable routine had been broken once more, and she would not be prepared for the experiences ahead. But she was strong, she had already proven that.

Miguel finished his coffee and crumpled the plastic cup. Before it hit the trash can a small blue pickup truck screamed by on the highway with two men hanging out the window. It was a C-14 doing about eighty, and Miguel saw that it suddenly braked and was thrown into reverse. Something at the gas station had caught those men's attention and it wasn't gasoline. It was him, sitting there in a chair behind glass as if on display. Miguel made a mad dash for the refrigerated truck. The driver was still in the bathroom, and the door to the cab was hanging open.

The metallic-blue C-14 screeched into the gas station in reverse and the men piled out. Miguel was positive they were looking for him. He didn't wait to find out, he wasn't worried about being thought paranoid. After last night, anything was possible. He scrambled into the cab of the truck, relieved to see the key dangling in the ignition. This was the second time a careless or overconfident person would save his skin. Miguel had never driven a truck like this, but all vehicles were the same, at least under circumstances like this.

He managed to get the thing in gear just in time to see the men turn and run back to the C-14. They were after him, all right. He stepped on the accelerator and the truck surged forward, ripping out the hose that had been pouring diesel fuel into the tank. Miguel swerved around the gas pumps, scraping the post, and bore down on the C-14. They had no time to react; it was all too unexpected. The refrigerated truck smashed into the C-14 with enormous impact, throwing it backwards as if it were an old tin can.

The C-14 was totaled; it wasn't going anywhere without a tow truck. Miguel saw the gas station attendants run to try and pull the men out of the wreckage. He didn't want to think about what he'd just done. He had to escape. He leaned on the accelerator and roared onto the highway. The heavy truck drove like a tractor. At first he had trouble keeping it under control, but soon he was zooming along at eighty, in the midst of the intense tide of traffic, and had evaded the cluthes of fate once more. If nothing happened along the way to stop him, he would soon be in a position to sort out and extricate himself from this mess.

The small restaurant in Montmartre was artlessly decorated with framed documents issued by the Paris Commune. If they were authentic, which they probably were, that meant the restaurant must have existed since before the bloody clashes between the Paris masses and the Versailles troops in 1871, and been popular with some of the important figures of the time.

Carlos usually had lunch at Le Fouette at least once a month, because it was off the tourist track and because he liked to think he was dining in a place his beloved Louise Michel had frequented during the romantic and hope-filled days of the Paris Commune. He might well be one of the last to remember who Louise Michel was, but when you reach your sixties, it's not uncommon to see your dearest idols sink into oblivion.

The young woman across the small table from him, her back pressed up against the shabby wall with bricks showing through, had certainly never heard of Louise Michel. This young woman's name was Vivian, and she was tall, dark-haired, twenty-seven years old, and always sad, because she couldn't do what she most desired in life: get on a plane and return to Brazil. Carlos knew that at twenty-seven it was difficult to live with an unfulfilled desire. Vivian's skin longed for the sun at Ipanema, and she had a pair of amber eyes that he found enchanting. But he knew that Vivian despised frivolity and included in this imprecise category all references made by men to her beauty.

"What are you thinking?" she asked, wrenching him from his thoughts.

Carlos smiled and pushed back his plate.

"Didn't you like the rabbit?"

"It was excellent, but I'm not hungry," he said.

Vivian never felt entirely comfortable with him. Maybe no young person could feel comfortable in the presence of an old revolutionary with a checkered past and a history of mistakes. But to say she wasn't comfortable was not a criticism, it was actually a compliment. Carlos had never tried to appear conciliatory or wise, like certain activists his age who were finding themselves more and more isolated, embittered by an exile for which they were unprepared.

"Have you ever heard of Louise Michel?"

Vivian looked at him, expressionless.

"No. Should I have?"

"Whenever I come here I think of her," said Carlos, gazing around the overheated restaurant. "She was one of the leaders of the Paris Commune. A great woman, who preached socialism to the end of her life. I didn't expect you'd know who she was, she's not from your time."

"Nor from yours, Carlos. The Commune dates back quite a while, from the last century, no? You'd be something to reckon with if you went back that far."

"In a certain way I do."

Vivian dabbed her lips with the linen table napkin—this was one of those glorious Parisian restaurants, Carlos reflected, where the unseemly habit of using paper napkins had not yet arrived.

"What's on your mind, Carlos? You're acting a little strange today."

"I need to talk to you. You're the only person I really trust. You know that, Vivian."

Rather than rebuffing him she accepted his confession with unexpected grace, but then immediately changed the subject.

"Have you heard? There's some kind of split going on inside the military. I heard that some of the hard-line groups are refusing to accept Geisel as a candidate."

"Mmmm, the news is more and more confusing," he agreed. "It will amount to the same in the end, though. General Geisel's from the National Information Service; he'll give the hard-liners just what they want. I'm not even allowing myself to get excited, because this business of a split within the military always ends up hurting us."

Vivian was becoming a little less remote now. She put aside her persistent shell of self-defense and was allowing herself to dream about her most fervent desire: the prospect of coming out of exile.

"I talked to a journalist from the *Estado de São Paulo* yesterday, and he told me some good news. Want to hear?"

"Of course."

Her amber eyes flashed as she spoke. Vivian loved to speculate on the inside workings of the military regime.

"You know that series they've been doing on the exorbitant spending of some of the ministries?"

"I read a few of them—quite enlightening. I was particularly impressed by the amount of butter consumed by the minister of labor. I wouldn't be surprised if he claimed the whole thing was an ingenious plan to lower the unemployment index, because you'd need some incredible labor force to spread all that butter on bread."

Vivian laughed, relaxing even more.

"No kidding! The same journalist told me the owners of the paper received quite an irate phone call from the generals."

"I'm not surprised."

"So they instructed the press to work up something a little softer, a series on what the ministers do in their spare time, articles on their favorite hobbies and so on."

"Good God! Spare me . . ."

"Well, they got together a list of the each of the minister's favorite pastimes and their first choice was General Geisel, but it turns out he doesn't do interviews, you know, because of his position, et cetera. After the first rebuff they asked again, not terribly hopeful, and to everyone's surprise they got confirmation that the general would receive the designated reporter in his office in Brasília."

"You'd have to be one brave reporter to keep that appointment, don't you think?"

"The reporter showed up with his tape recorder and everything and practically before he got through the door he got the dressing-down of his life. I mean he really caught hell."

"Mmmm, I've heard the general is a very refined man."

"After hurling abuse at the reporter for ten minutes or so, the general finally decided to tell him his favorite hobby. Know what it is?"

"No, but I'm sure it's not overly wholesome."

"Come on, have you heard this story already?"

"No, I swear, it's just my years of experience."

"Well, the general said his favorite pastime was buggering."

"What?"

"You heard me, ass-fucking." Vivian blushed slightly.

"My God, Vivian, and he's going to want to do it to all of us."

"My thoughts exactly," she said, smiling.

"It can't be true," protested Carlos. "As crude as those guys might be, they still must keep up at least a facade of dignity."

"The reporter swore it was the truth."

"Then we better get ourselves some Vaseline . . ."

They fell silent as Vivian took another forkful of her *pavê-grille*. She chewed serenely, elegant as ever, and Carlos wondered once more what had led this sophisticated, bourgeois girl to the armed struggle.

Vivian had some questions of her own about Carlos. Not that she disliked him; over and above their differences, which did sometimes make her uneasy, Carlos always seemed to her a fascinating man, especially considering the age difference between them. He had a certain air about him, like that of an old-fashioned gentleman—the kind they don't make anymore. He cultivated certain urbane habits that she didn't find in friends of her own generation and convictions. This old man with white hair and gray eyes made no secret of his anachronistic manner. He was a perfect exemplar of the species of gentleman who would walk all the way around the car to open the door for a lady or incline himself toward any woman who tried to get his attention. Carlos could be counted on to volunteer a few flattering remarks whether or not a woman was pretty, and, though Vivian didn't believe in such things, she didn't always complain when he acted that way either. Plus, the man spoke perfect French and was utterly at home in Paris. This was his third exile here, and Vivian was not ashamed to seek in him the security that she often felt she lacked. Carlos considered himself an internationalist, and he was really a citizen of the world, above and beyond political considerations.

"So. What was it you were going to tell me, Carlos?"

He sighed and signaled he would wait until she finished her lunch. That was his way. He habitually waited until the cheese course to bring up a new subject.

Vivian concentrated on her plate. She had known Carlos for two years now, though of course she knew of him long before. Who hadn't? He was the lieutenant who had participated in the controversial movement of 1935, weapon in hand, and then turned up in Spain, and later accompanied Mao Tse-tung as he entered Shanghai. Carlos' biography was long and full of surprising turns of events. But once Vivian knew him, none of it seemed fantastic.

She herself had come to Paris in 1973, and by now was settled enough to take a philosophy course at the University of Vincennes. Life was not easy for a young Brazilian in Paris, but at least she wasn't too bad off financially; she received a stipend from UNESCO and her parents sometimes managed to send her a couple of dollars. Vivian lived well, really, by political-exile standards, but her nationality always left a bad taste in her mouth. There were more than ten thousand Brazilians in Paris, the majority of them political exiles of whatever stripe, people who were on the run from the military dictatorship. It was rare to meet one who had legal status in France, with the option of returning to Brazil whenever he wanted—the fundamental, and divisive, difference between exiles and non-exiles. To complicate the situation further, the exiles split up into partisan groups reflecting the diversity of the Brazilian left. All this, plus the fact that Vivian had a little money—which did not win her much popularity among the exiled leftists—meant that Vivian lived to a large degree outside the circles of her fellow countrymen. She maintained formal contacts with her old political group, but most of her friends were French or African. Only rarely did she attend gatherings of Brazilians, and when she did she steeled herself for the inevitable snide remarks and accusations typical of the idiotic paranoia that dominated certain cliques.

Vivian and Carlos' friendship, if their periodic encounters could be called that, had been a product of chance. She was halfway out the door of the Lojas Fnac in Montparnasse, her arms full of the books and records she had just bought with the first installment of her UNESCO stipend, when she tripped and all her purchases tumbled down the steps. A comic-book meeting, Carlos called it ironically. An older man had appeared out of nowhere and collected her packages, expressed genuine concern as to whether she had hurt herself, and was so solicitous that—without even knowing he was Brazilian—she invited him for a cup of coffee. They had been meeting regularly ever since, perhaps because it relieved his solitude and because she felt safe—if distant—beside him. And although they never discussed their personal lives when they met for lunch or a concert, Vivian found that little by little she was revealing her murky political situation, asking advice, debating, disagreeing, and almost always following his suggestions. It was Carlos who always initiated their meetings, but once they were together it was Vivian who set the agenda for conversation. Today, though, Carlos seemed to have something on his mind.

Vivian finished eating, and Carlos asked for the cheeses and another half-bottle of the good bordeaux they were drinking.

"I have something to ask you, Vivian," said Carlos, as soon as the waiter was gone.

"Go ahead."

"I'm not sure I should."

"Well then, decide, because I have an appointment at three and I'm going to have to run. I make the French crazy with my lateness."

Carlos took a sip of wine and spoke hesitantly.

"Vivian, what I'm about to ask you to do comes with a certain amount of risk. Serious risk. Can you accept that?"

Vivian was not alarmed; in a certain way she was used to risk, she had already experienced situations where her own life was a pawn in the larger game.

"If you trust me, then out with it. I can take care of myself."

"That's what I was hoping you'd say."

He stared off at an indefinite point in space, hesitating to reveal what was going through his head.

"I want to make it very clear," he continued, after a long pause, "that this is something that could be dangerous. Your life would be at risk."

Vivian began to get impatient.

"Okay, if you don't trust me, if you think I'm immature, then don't tell me."

"Don't get annoyed . . ."

"I'm not annoyed, I'm just stating what's true."

Carlos made his decision.

"I'm not going to tell you everything because I don't need to yet. Just a little, so I can breathe easier."

"Whatever you say."

"Vivian. If anything happens to me in the near future, I want you to take this key—" He pulled a key out of his pocket and placed it on the table. "—and go to Austerlitz Station. It's for a baggage locker. The number of the locker is on this tag attached to the key. In the locker you'll find an attaché case and inside it a folder. Read the papers inside very carefully and then follow the instructions. You must destroy the instructions after memorizing them—for security's sake, you understand."

"What's going on? Is someone threatening you?"

"I can't tell you more than that. And we won't be able to see each other for a while."

"How will I know you're all right?"

"Don't worry, you'll know. And if nothing happens in the next two months, we'll be able to go back to having lunch together and forget the whole thing. All right?"

Vivian agreed, but she was worried. For the first time she had shed her reticence, and she saw Carlos as simply a vulnerable person who believed she was his last hope.

"You're sure there's nothing else I can do? God, Carlos, now I really am concerned about you."

"I'm sorry, I knew you'd be upset, but there was no other way. I thought about this all day yesterday."

"Who is threatening you, Carlos?"

He shook his head, as if opening his mouth might lead to saying more than he wanted her to know.

"Take the key," he said gruffly. "And don't lose it."

She put the key in her purse. Lunch was over.

Once they had parted, Vivian walked along the Sacre Coeur esplanade because, though she was already almost late, she really needed to think. She didn't want anything to happen to the old man, it would be like losing a special uncle—or worse, like losing an intimate and irreplaceable friend. Vivian was only now beginning to realize how connected she felt to him. She gazed down at the city enshrouded in afternoon fog. The tower of Montparnasse stuck out above the slate roofs, and the air up above was clear and golden. The Forum commercial complex, a temple of consumerism, had sprung up on the spot where the Les Halles market had stood for centuries, and right nearby was Beaubourg, the arts center that looked like a refinery, the pinnacle of Gallic technology. Suddenly remembering the time, Vivian hurried to the closest *métro* entrance, willing herself to believe that it was all just hyperbole on old Carlos' part.

Carlos was on his way back to his study on Place Maubert, where the street was blocked off every Tuesday, Thursday, and Saturday by an outdoor market. He walked to Pigalle and went down into the *métro*. It was hot and there was a steady stream of passengers, most of them high school students and housewives out shopping. But as Carlos descended into the station he felt someone's eyes on him and turned to see a young man with Arab features, a person he could swear he had seen somewhere before. Carlos considered himself good with faces, but this one escaped him. The man was on the side of the platform for Porte de la Chapelle; Carlos would be heading in the opposite direction, toward Mairie D'Issy.

A train pulled into the station on the other side of the tracks, and Carlos tried as hard as he could not to lose sight of the young man, but when the train was gone he was no longer on the platform. Maybe he boarded the train, Carlos told himself, trying to allay the fear that he was being followed.

Carlos' train arrived and he stepped into the midst of smiling Vietnamese loaded down with plastic sacks. Listening to them, he thought they talked like birds, in small darting voices. Finally the *métro* arrived in Sèvres-Babylonne and he got off, wove his way through the looping underground corridors, and stood waiting for a train on the Austerlitz line.

Fifteen minutes later he was entering his building, a warm baguette in his hand, having completely forgotten the young man in the *métro*. He checked his mailbox, removed some newspapers, and prepared to climb the stairs to his third-floor apartment, noting, uneasily, that something was wrong with the lights. No matter how hard he pressed the switches, which were slightly phosphorescent in the dark, nothing happened. And the stairs were steep and dark. Carlos always climbed them slowly, resting as he went, because his old heart complained all the way to the last step. He steadied himself on the handrail and began the climb. The wine from lunch seemed to be making him feel woozy, a thought he discounted immediately. He climbed hesitantly, feeling for each worn, wooden step. As he reached the second landing, he suddenly imagined there was someone hiding in the dark. He thought he could hear the light, fatigued breathing of someone who had an adenoid problem and knew it, but didn't want to let the sound out into the darkness.

Carlos froze. His heartbeat quickened. He could almost smell someone hiding in the blackness. He didn't know how to explain it, but the image that came to mind was the young man with the Arab features. For a few seconds he just stood there, stock-still. Holding his breath. Then two strong hands came out of the dark to grab his throat; they shook him like a scrap of cloth, and threw him into the abyss. His cry as he fell vanished into the blackness eight meters below where his body landed, not far from the door behind which the concierge was huddled.

It was late before Vivian arrived home that night. She had been at a friend's house studying and wanted to go straight to bed. She had stared at the key Carlos had given her off and on all day long. It was small, silver-colored, and serrated, nothing out of the ordinary. Once home, she took the key from her purse and stuck it into a thick philosophy text on the bookshelf. Then

she peeled off her clothes and stepped into her tiny cubicle of a
bathroom. As soon as she was under the shower she heard the
telephone ring. Her hair dripped on the carpet as she picked up
the phone.

"Is this Vivian?" asked a man's voice in Spanish.

"Yes, who's calling?"

"I have a message for you."

"Who is this?"

"Never mind," said the voice gruffly. "Carlos had an accident."

"What? What happened? Is he okay?"

"It was serious. He's in the hospital, unconscious."

"What hospital?"

"You don't need to know that. But he's being taken care of."

"Is he going to recover?"

"We don't know yet. He fell down the stairs. It looks like the
lights in the hall weren't working and he slipped. He fractured
his pelvis, some ribs, and got a bad knock on the head."

The voice sounded hurried and cold. Vivian was having trouble
getting her questions out fast enough.

"I need to know what hospital he's in, he's my friend."

"We know. But not now. Later," said the voice.

And hung up.

Vivan collapsed on the bed, the phone still in her hand. The
dial tone filled the room and she began to cry. She didn't know
why she was crying; from a rational point of view, she shouldn't.
But all she could do was let the tears come, because she felt sorry
for the old man. And it wasn't just the sense of loss that made
her cry. She was frightened. She cried because she was afraid
for herself, because she had that key and was going to have to
read the papers that Carlos had placed in her trust.

Ruth was sitting in the office of the director of the Multimedia Advertising Agency, looking sullen. She felt offended
and betrayed by her husband's boss. The two federal police
agents sitting beside her were feigning a kindness and tolerance
they clearly did not feel.

"Ma'am, please try to understand!"

Ruth was not only indignant, she was incredulous. The accusations the police were making against Miguel were ridiculous.

"Just tell us where he is. We need to find him. He can't go on just wandering the streets. It's for his own good."

"You make it sound like he's crazy!" said Ruth sharply. She was determined not to be intimidated by these people. But she wasn't angry at the police; what really enraged her was the cowardly attitude of Miguel's boss. If it hadn't been for him and his treachery, she wouldn't be sitting here now being interrogated. And this whole scene only added to the humiliation she had endured during her preposterous inspection of Haidèe's house.

First, Haidèe's maid began making insinuations about her employer's private life, which was unpleasant enough. Then she began to treat Ruth with an irritating complicity, as if Ruth were motivated by jealousy, chasing after an unfaithful husband who had some sort of sexual relationship with Haidèe.

"So that's your husband's car out front, then," the maid had said. "He came by last night, but dona Haidèe wasn't here. He was in the office for a while talking to Hercules, that gorilla. Then they left together. I don't know where they were going, they didn't tell me."

Ruth said nothing. She had decided simply to ignore the damned maid. But the woman just wouldn't stop. Young and impressionable, she was clearly fascinated by the life her boss led.

"Dona Haidèe has several lovers who come here to see her," the maid continued, heedless of Ruth's silence. "It's the money, of course. And they're always a lot younger. Your husband visited pretty often."

Ruth felt a hotness rise through her body and an almost uncontrollable desire to slap the woman across the face. But she managed to swallow her ire. Of the various reasons that had prompted her to search Haidèe's house, jealousy was positively not one of them. The changes she had undergone in her life had helped her eliminate that feeling. She trusted Miguel and expected that he would never betray her. Their relationship was based on truthfulness; they talked things over, instead of hiding them from each other. The fact that the maid was mistaking her for a jealous wife made her furious.

"I've seen what there is to see," she said finally, after glancing into Haidèe's boudoir.

Downstairs, before leaving, she decided to call Miguel's office, just in case he had turned up there. She was so convinced that Miguel would answer that the nervousness of the receptionist took her by surprise.

"Don't hang up, dona Ruth. Mr. Nelson wants to talk with you."

She heard the click of the call being transferred and then the elegant voice of the agency's director was on the line.

"Dona Ruth, can you tell us where we can get in touch with Miguel?"

"I thought he was there," she answered, with genuine surprise and frustration.

"No, he hasn't come in today." The director's voice was tense. "Are you at the university by any chance?"

"No, I didn't go in to work today."

"Could you possibly stop by Multimedia?"

"What for?"

"So we can talk. It's important."

"What's going on, Mr. Nelson? Is there something you're not telling me?"

Miguel's boss stammered a bit, and his voice became shrill and anxious. This was not the self-confident advertising executive Ruth knew.

Finally he said, "Just please stop by the office, okay? I'll be expecting you. It's important to all of us."

Ruth hung up and practically sprinted out to the street. It wasn't going to be easy to find a cab. This was a high-income residential neighborhood, with winding, interweaving streets. Hurrying down Lopes Quintas, finally she got lucky. A taxi pulled to the curb at the far end of the street to let out some passengers.

Ruth knew something was definitely wrong as soon as she arrived at Multimedia. When the receptionist saw her step out of the elevator, she paled and jumped up from her desk to open the director's office door. The office was spacious, decorated with the usual élan of advertising agencies. It was on the eighth floor of one of those spiky-shaped black marble buildings with tinted windows. The view of Botafogo Beach was magnificent, but it was lost on Ruth. All she saw was the director hunkered down in his high-backed chair and two men on the sofa.

The men stood up as Mr. Nelson came to greet her. His hands were cold and clammy, and his dark eyes avoided hers.

"I hope you'll forgive me, dona Ruth, for the way I summoned you here."

"For the love of God, what is going on? What's happened to Miguel? He never came home last night."

"You haven't seen your husband then?" asked one of the men, who had posted himself beside the desk, waiting to be introduced.

"This is Dr. Castilho, and this is Detective Veloso," said the director. "They're from the federal police."

Ruth's mouth fell open, and her knees went rubbery. The men were watching her analytically, studying her reactions.

"Why don't you have a seat," suggested the director.

She sat down in slow motion, as if afraid she would fall. The presence of the two policemen removed Miguel's disappearance from the category of simply an escapade, the fruit of his eccentricities—and while she already suspected that something serious had prevented him from coming home last night, she had been working very hard not to think about it.

"Dona Ruth," said Dr. Castilho, "we're here to help. I want you to understand our position."

The man spoke with a studied calmness, but his eyes betrayed a thinly disguised arrogance. He was dark and oily-looking, with short, thinning hair. Ruth resolved to stay calm and not be taken in by his words. She no longer had any illusions about government agencies; like all smart Brazilians she had lost her once-unshakable ingenuousness and had learned instead to be alert and suspicious.

"All right, Mr. . . ."

"Castilho."

"All right, Mr. Castilho. Then can you tell me what's going on here?"

"When did you last see your husband?"

"Yesterday morning, before leaving for work."

"And you haven't seen him since? Or talked to him?"

"I talked to him on the phone late yesterday afternoon. Just after I got home from work Miguel called to tell me he had an after-hours meeting at a client's house."

"Did he tell you the name of the client he was going to see?"

"Yes, Haidèe Jaffet. He went there a lot, at least once a month. Miguel is responsible for her account. Mr. Nelson can confirm that."

"That's true," said the director dutifully.

The policeman made a note in his little notebook and stood studying what he had written.

"Does your husband often sleep away from home?"

"Not without letting me know. Since he didn't, I was worried and couldn't sleep myself. I waited up the whole night in the living room. My son didn't sleep right either."

"Did you call anyone? Ask for help?"

Ruth thought a minute and closed her eyes. The questions were beginning to irritate her.

"Dona Ruth, please!"

"Sorry," she said blankly. "I don't feel very well."

"That's understandable," said Castilho. "Would you like some coffee, or a glass of water?"

Ruth shook her head. She rubbed her eyes, trying to clear them. But the director ignored her refusal and ordered coffee and water over the intercom.

"Would you prefer to continue this conversation in my office downtown? We could set a time . . ."

"No, let's go on," said Ruth. "I'll answer your questions, but then you're going to have to answer a few of mine."

"Fine, whatever you'd like."

Ruth breathed deeply and looked straight into the man's face.

"No, I didn't talk to anyone last night, or ask for help."

"Why not? After all, your husband's behavior was out of the ordinary and it would be natural for you to be alarmed."

"I never get alarmed."

"Then you told no one?"

"Not yesterday, no, but I did today," Ruth lied. It was pure instinct. For some reason she knew this was a necessary lie.

"Who did you call?"

"A whole lot of people, friends, relatives. Lots of people. Miguel isn't alone in the world, you know."

"Of course not."

"That's why I didn't go to work this morning, so I could take care of this. How could I give a lecture when Miguel had disappeared? This is a violent city, Detective, badly policed and everything else . . ."

The policeman nodded and made another notation.

"Why didn't you call Multimedia?"

"I did, that's exactly why I called Mr. Nelson. Obviously I was hoping Miguel had come to work."

"Come to work? After staying out all night?"

Ruth decided to play it tough.

"He's a man, Detective, and we women have had to learn to expect anything and everything from our men."

The role of abandoned wife looked promising, judging from Castilho's face. He cleared his throat and wrote something else in his little book.

"Any more questions, Detective?"

"I'm not a detective, dona Ruth, I'm an inspector."

"Excuse me, Inspector. Maybe now you can answer a few questions for me."

"Of course!"

"Well, I'd just like to know what's happening here. It's already too much for me to handle. My husband disappears . . ." Her lips trembled and tears welled up in her eyes.

An office boy came in with coffee and water. Ruth regained her composure and downed a glass of water in one gulp. The policemen exchanged glances; Mr. Nelson was struggling to disappear into his armchair.

"Please, don't keep me in the dark," she begged, as soon as the office boy had gone.

The policeman sat forward on the sofa, leaning closer to Ruth.

"I should tell you first that everything I'm about to say is pure conjecture. This case landed on my desk only this morning and the investigation is just getting underway. So you shouldn't take anything we say as established fact. But we will get to the bottom of this, I assure you."

"For the love of God, Detective!"

"Try to stay calm, dona Ruth . . ."

"Just tell me: is Miguel all right? What has happened to him?"

"We think he's all right. We know he's alive . . ."

"Oh, God," said Ruth, truly terrified now.

"A crime was committed last night in the University district. You teach there, don't you? Does your husband go there often? I mean, does he drive you to work?"

"No, I don't teach at the Fundão. My classes meet at the campus in Urca. And as far as I know, Miguel's never even been to the Fundão. He hardly ever comes to my office at Urca, for that matter. Our schedules conflict."

"Interesting! Our investigation indicates that whoever chose the site of the crime was very familiar with the area. Well. I'll try to be as objective as I can, dona Ruth. A man was murdered last night. He was stabbed more than a dozen times. A patrol car that happened to be in the area almost caught the perpetrator, but he managed to flee after exchanging gunfire with the police and stealing a vehicle. The police were very careless, and the killer was much more clever than they expected. The motive for the crime was narcotics. The victim was a trafficker, we have a file on him." The inspector extended his hand theatrically to the other policeman, who handed him a photograph. "Can you by any chance identify this man?"

Ruth looked at the photograph. The man was middle-aged, well-dressed, and well-built. His features were not altogether unfamiliar to her, but she couldn't manage to place him.

"No. No, I can't," she said.

"Take as much time as you like."

He handed her the photograph and she examined it for several minutes. Nerves and fatigue precluded the clarity of thought she needed right then. Little by little the face looked more familiar. Ruth let out a gasp of surprise.

"Do you recognize him?"

"Yes, but this must be an old photo, right?"

"It's all we have."

"He's Haidèe's secretary . . . yes, of course. Is he the one who was killed, poor man?"

"He's a drug trafficker," said the policeman.

"But what does all this have to do with Miguel?"

"Well, ma'am, we have reason to believe it was your husband who stabbed this man a dozen or so times."

Ruth leapt from her chair screaming, "Liar! Liar! Miguel is not a violent man. He detests violence, he would never resolve his problems like this. I know my husband."

"Does your husband use drugs? Cocaine? Marijuana?"

She shook her head vehemently, though she knew that some time ago Miguel did smoke marijuana. Ruth had even tried it, but it made her sick to her stomach. In any case, she knew Miguel was not the one who had done this.

"Why are you so sure Miguel was there last night? Do you have pictures? Did the police find any evidence?"

Once again the inspector extended his hand to his assistant. This time he was given a white envelope. He opened it and removed a credit card receipt.

"Is this your husband's signature?" he asked, passing the receipt to Ruth.

She examined it. There was no way to explain Miguel's presence at the Flamingo Motel on the Via Dutra Highway.

"Yes," she said, perplexed. "But what in God's name does that prove?"

"As I said, the police pursued the killer for a half hour, but he eluded them. This morning, however, a clue led them to this motel, where the criminal, or suspect I should say, was careless enough to pay with his credit card."

"I don't believe it," protested Ruth. "It's a trick . . ."

"Maybe. But we can't establish that without your husband's cooperation. And it seems he's not interested in helping us."

Ruth bowed her head and began to weep. She didn't want to fall apart in front of these men, but there was simply no way not to. Her terror was immense. Maybe Miguel was hurt. Maybe the police had shot him or set an ambush. Her concern for Miguel's safety was logical and natural; what didn't figure was why all this was happening in the first place. Ruth knew she had to find Miguel. Before the police did.

"Just one more thing, ma'am. The press has caught wind of this and tomorrow the papers will be full of it. It's regrettable, but we do have freedom of the press and the reporters really go after these stories."

"Can I go now?" asked Ruth, regaining her composure and gathering together her pride.

"Of course. We only hope you will cooperate with the authorities. It will be better for your husband that way."

"Don't worry, Inspector, I know what to do."

Ruth stood up and turned to leave without any gesture of farewell. Miguel's boss ran to open the door for her and mumbled some words of sympathy. Ruth strode out the door and across the reception area, her head high, like a woman who knows who she is and has no intention of surrendering to adversity. Even if Miguel were guilty, it was her duty to prevent the consequences of his actions from damaging her and Luciano's future. But their story was hard to swallow. Even if Miguel had gone crazy, he would never do a thing like that. Just how much was human nature capable of changing? But, in point of fact, Miguel's history represented a total negation of the kind of violence in which he had now seemingly become involved. It was brutality and deception that had destroyed the world as Miguel knew it; there was no way, now, that he would stoop to the level of those he found most despicable.

The two officers followed Ruth out and took the same eleva-tor downstairs. They weren't following her, really; they merely wanted to make it clear that this was their job, their daily routine. Standing beside her, stiffly indifferent, holding their briefcases like any executive, the only thing that gave them away was the bulge of their weapons under their cheap polyester sports jackets.

Out on the street, they paused to say good-bye to Ruth and headed for the police vehicle parked ostentatiously on the side-walk. Noticing that Ruth had positioned herself on the curb to call a taxi, the inspector walked back in her direction.

"Excuse me, ma'am, but can we drop you somewhere?"

Ruth almost refused, but decided she should accept in order to show that they didn't intimidate her.

"Yes, thank you, Inspector."

"After you . . ."

He motioned her to go ahead, opened the door for her, and helped her climb in. It was a metallic-green C-14, with official plates, in reasonable shape. If not for the shield of the federal police on the door, it could have passed for any government vehicle.

"Where can we take you, ma'am?" asked the detective, all solicitude. He was obviously exerting himself to seem something he was not.

"I'd really appreciate it if you would drop me off at the courthouse."

Without comment, they delivered Ruth to the address she had requested.

The slow burn of the sun on Miguel's shoulders was com-forting. The serene afternoon air carried the subtle scent of the weeping willows swaying in the wind. The sense of peace was wondrous. Naked on a straw mat in lotus position, he intoned his mantra and concentrated on a point in his very center. The green lawn extending to the horizon looked like a golf course; the expanse of grass was smooth and uniform, rippling gracefully in all directions, interrupted only occasionally by weeping willows with thin, reedy trunks, their elongated leaves filling the air with that elusive scent.

Miguel was not alone; there were others meditating on their

straw mats. To his left, a woman repeated her mantra and let her thoughts fly into the emptiness. That was his goal, too, but it wasn't easy. The act of chanting the mantra had became mechanical, he felt restless, and knew this was not the path to the summits of meditation. He felt a shadow approaching from behind and turned to see who it was, proof that his concentration was still a prisoner of his surroundings.

There, framed against the sun, was Sabu-Maharishi, the guru, the master, the man of wisdom of the sect of Interior Illumination, an offshoot of Zen Buddhism. Like many masters who bring the light to the West, Sabu-Maharishi had a shaved head and dressed in red. But he was not Oriental and, while very highly developed spiritually, was only twenty-five years old.

"What is happening, my brother?" His voice was soft, slow velvet, demonstrating the patience that comes from years of meditation.

"I can't free myself, Sabu!"

"I couldn't help noticing when you arrived, Miguel. Your legs are all cut up. What happened?"

Miguel lowered his eyes to the puffy wounds that had been disrupting his attempt to meditate. But it wasn't just the cuts, there was also the violence he had witnessed and in which he had become embroiled.

"Do you want to talk about it?"

It was a tempting invitation, but Miguel wasn't sure he should accept. His intention in coming here had been to find the guru and talk, to tell him what had happened and ask his advice. But when Miguel considered the things he had seen and done in the last twenty-four hours . . . His dilemma was way beyond that of the usual devotee in need of the master's hand to overcome the obstacles in his life's path. And so Miguel decided instead to simply strip off his clothes and ask for a meditation mat. It wasn't his day for meditation, but that didn't matter. Every Saturday morning Miguel made the hour's drive out from Rio on the road to Cabo Frio. The sect's farm was an enormous, well-tended property in the beautiful lake district; some of the most advanced followers worked here planting wheat and greens and living communally. The farm had no name because the group didn't believe in naming things. All was part of nature and that was name enough. Miguel contributed ten percent of his salary to support the farm and the work of the sect in other cities in Brazil.

This was his fifth attempt to find a little peace and security in the tumult of his life. He had been coming here for only six months and was still learning about the group; Ruth had fought him at first because it ate up such a chunk of his salary, but in the end she accepted the idea and he was beginning to think he had finally found what he was looking for.

Sabu-Maharishi turned and walked away. The master was a man of few words and never tried to push anything on his followers. Miguel stood up, rolled the mat under his arm, and followed him.

They went into a building with modern lines which had been the original farmhouse. Now it was the Interior Illumination headquarters. The guru lived in a smaller cottage nearby, beside an Oriental garden, all stones, which had been flown in from Japan in crates.

The headquarters contained furniture, no decorations. The walls were painted gray and the floors were covered with Persian-style carpets. The windows were closed and draped with heavy curtains; the only light was a tall candle at the far end of the room.

They sat down on the carpet and the guru ran his fingers over Miguel's knees. It hurt, but Miguel tried not to show it.

"Well?"

The guru was short, thin, and very fragile-looking, with a long beard, faded blue eyes, and thick lips. His skin was not naturally dark but well-tanned. He had grown up in São Paulo, son of immigrant Italians. During the sixties he had been a militant leftist, but once armed resistance broke out he left the country to wander Europe aimlessly. He got involved with drugs, fell seriously ill, and one day boarded a bus in Amsterdam that took him to Nepal. Later, he went to India, where he entered a Zen monastery and became transformed, put his past behind him, changed his name, and returned to Brazil. The purpose of Interior Illumination was to bring to Westerners the Eastern liberation from material things, which was why the sect was self-supporting and obliged to send financial assistance to its supreme master, the guru Surphanandra, who was presently living in the United States.

Miguel told the master everything. All the details and all his suspicions. As always, Sabu-Maharishi showed no surprise, in fact no reaction at all. At the end of the story, he remained motionless, his faded blue eyes fixed on Miguel, looking completely absent. Faced with such immobility, Miguel began to ask himself if the guru had heard a word he had said.

Time passed. Miguel's anxiety increased with every passing moment of Sabu-Maharishi's lack of response. But Miguel had inner discipline. He had spoken and he knew that silence was sometimes a response.

The guru finally lifted his right hand from his lap and traced the cuts on Miguel's knees.

"Blood . . ." he said.

And he ran the same hand through his dark, silky beard.

"Even lies are true, because once said they become words and enter into existence. And that which exists is real and that which is real is true."

Miguel nodded, but could not assimilate the meaning of this. He needed something more direct, some practical advice, not a philosophical maze.

"Without words there would be no lies," continued the guru, "but the truth would also be difficult to recognize. One day a merchant came to Buddha full of questions and complaints about the harm he had suffered on account of a failed business deal. Buddha told him that it was all the result of intervention by the hand of King Wu, and the merchant left consoled and ready to enter into another dubious business transaction. That same day came a general, weeping bitterly over a battle in which he had lost a thousand men. Buddha wiped the general's tears and told him his defeat was due to the hand of King Wu. Looking much steadier, the general said farewell and returned to the battlefield for a new defeat. And thus, all day long, did Buddha speak of the hand of King Wu as a way of understanding men's troubles. The monks gathered around him as his disciples listened, intrigued, and at the end of the day decided to ask him the significance of his words, for they knew there had never been a King Wu and thus his hand could not be the cause for so many misfortunes. After listening to the monks' questions, the Buddha said: 'The hand of King Wu is the hand of each one of us, and is thus a solace to us because it is familiar and stands more in front of our bodies than our own consciences.' This said, he picked up his staff and walked off down the road."

The guru fell silent and went back to tracing Miguel's wounds. Finally he led Miguel back outside, spread his mat on the grass, and invited him to return to his meditation. It was sunset. The wind had come up and it was getting chilly. Most of the people who had been meditating had left. A small group was doing yoga in the yard beside the guru's cottage, and two or three people remained in a trance on the grass, oblivious to the cold.

Miguel sat down on his mat, crossed his legs in a half-lotus, and considered the guru's parable. He wasn't able to make much out of it. Maybe under other circumstances it would have impressed him, but right now it seemed awfully vague. Though of course it did suggest the immutability of destiny and the ease with which men let themselves be tricked by appearances.

Frustrated, Miguel abandoned the idea of meditating and rolled up his mat. The guru's path led only to passivity and what he needed now was the strength to survive. Unless the parable was a warning of some sort—that might be the way to read it. Considering this possibility, he arrived in the dressing room somewhat distracted. Even though he had not achieved a meditative state, simply sitting in the sun, breathing the perfume of the willows in the silence of afternoon, had helped him recover a little equilibrium.

What he really needed to do was to talk to Ruth. Together they would find a way out. The police must have made a little visit to the house by now, if for no other reason than because of the damage he'd done to the C-14 at the gas station on Via Dutra. But there had to be a way for him to talk to her.

The dressing room was empty. It was in a small annex to the house, adjacent to the office where devotees handled the sect's paperwork as well as the distribution of the farm's produce, a small yield of organic vegetables, which were just coming into fashion. Miguel had begun putting his clothes on when he heard voices in the office. The calm one he recognized as the guru's; the other sounded extremely agitated and shrill. A shiver ran down Miguel's spine when he heard the guru mention his name. He stopped dressing and tiptoed closer to the door.

Imagining Miguel was still meditating on the lawn, Sabu-Maharishi had not bothered to close the office door. He was repeating Miguel's story to a member, who, curiously, did not address the guru with the respect appropriate to a superior man. The devotee called him a jackass and insisted sharply that he didn't want problems with the police. Without raising his voice, the guru replied that Miguel trusted him and that maybe he was even exaggerating a little bit.

"Only you could believe a story like that," barked the devotee.

"It sounds to me like this guy Miguel is in up to his neck and I say we shouldn't get involved. Call the police now, man, and tell them he's here. Clear our name fast."

The guru said nothing, but Miguel heard a telephone being dialed. The man in whom he had put his trust was calling the police. They would be here in no time and there was nothing he could do. He'd left the truck at a gas station near the toll booth on the Via Dutra and taken a bus to Cabo Frio. The isolation of the farm made it a perfect trap. Miguel looked down at his torn, filthy clothes. Dressed like this, he wouldn't even be able to hitch a ride on the main road.

He rummaged through the few clothes still hanging in the dressing room, collecting car keys and looking for things that would fit. After putting on a pair of faded jeans, a print shirt, dark glasses, and rubber thongs, he stood and listened at the office door for a moment. Silence. He hurried to the parking lot. Most everyone had gone home already, and Miguel had managed to find only five sets of car keys. He would have to try them in each car until he found a match. That could take time, but he promised himself he would stay calm.

In the parking lot there were three Volkswagens, a Camaro, and a beat-up Corcel. He started with the Corcel and then went on to the Camaro. The key was easily identifiable; it dangled from a key chain with a Camaro insignia laminated in plastic. Just as Miguel was about to shift into reverse, a woman's face startled him at the driver's window, half smiling and half surprised.

"I think you're in the wrong car," she said. It was the woman who had been meditating next to him. "It happens all the time. People just seem to be drawn to this car."

Miguel flushed and opened the door to get out. The woman closed it again and went around to sit in the passenger seat beside him.

"Look, you don't have a car here, do you? I saw you arrive on the bus. So why not drive mine? We're going to the same place, aren't we?"

"I'm sorry," stammered Miguel. "I just wanted to try it out, it's a magnificent car."

"I know, it happens. Don't worry about it."

"My name is Miguel," he said, extending his hand.

The woman smiled, distant, as if she had not completely emerged from her meditative state.

"I'm Rosa," she replied, shaking his hand.

She was nearing forty, with a healthy face, but her solemn features didn't go with her bleached-blonde hair.

Suddenly Miguel caught sight of the guru crossing the parking lot, accompanied by the devotee he'd been talking to in the office. Miguel started the car and made for the gravel road that led to the main highway, completely ignoring the two men gesturing wildly in their direction.

"What do they want?" asked the woman.

"Who knows," lied Miguel. "They must be trying to get that guy's attention, over there." He pointed to a young man with a shaved head who was alternately pounding the door to the Corcel and frenetically searching through his pockets.

"Yeah, he does look a little crazed," said Rosa, waving good-bye to the guru and his companion.

Finally they were on the main road, headed for Rio. Traffic was light and Rosa curled up in her seat, as if to go to sleep. Miguel remembered that he still had the keys to the other cars in his lap. With one quick movement, he tossed them out the window. The woman sat bolt upright in her seat.

"What did you just throw out the window?"

"Nothing."

She accepted this reply with a vague murmur and shoved a cassette into the tape deck. As the Camaro streamed down the highway, the sound system began to fill with the always startling chords of a raga played by Ravi Shankar. The sun was sinking behind the mountains and soon they would be in Rio. Miguel had to find a way to talk to Ruth. The police had surely gotten to her by now and would be waiting for him at home and in all the places he habitually frequented.

Meanwhile, where had Haidèe gone? Would she have gone home? And what about his parents, would they have been notified? He wasn't worried about his father, the old man was tough as nails, but his mother had been sick and he didn't want to give her a shock.

"Where do you live?" asked Rosa.

"Ipanema."

"Are you married?"

"Yes."

"But things aren't going too well, am I right?"

Miguel shrugged.

"I could tell," she said casually.

"I haven't been home since yesterday morning," he confessed, thinking it was perfect for her to think he had marital problems. Maybe she'd inadvertently end up helping him.

"Where did you sleep—at a hotel?"

"No, I hate hotels. I just wandered around. Had a few drinks."

He felt bad about lying, but figured that a little fantasy couldn't hurt anyone. If he managed to get himself invited home with her, then he'd have a safe place for a time and even a telephone, who knows? He took a deep breath and looked at the woman beside him.

"I've been going through a lot of changes . . ."

She nodded her head sympathetically. "I went through the same thing, after I joined the Illumination."

"It wasn't the Illumination," said Miguel, partly to provoke her and partly because of his recent disillusionment with the guru.

"No?" She was surprised, but still had a distant and weary air about her. "It was devastating for me. I was going through a separation too, and feeling this enormous emptiness. That was six months ago. Now it's all beginning to make sense."

"That's what I thought, too, in the beginning."

"But you haven't been a member for long, have you?"

"No, not too long, but I'm just not sure what I think anymore. I had to pay twenty thousand just to get my private mantra. And I give them ten percent of my salary."

"But that's exactly what inspires confidence. Pledging a percentage of my income makes me feel like a more responsible person. Finally I'm really building something, and my greed is just melting away. I'm simply not attached to money the way I used to be."

Miguel was silent. They were already in Niterói and heading for the bridge over the bay. The chords of the raga filled the car with a note of despair, and Miguel was thinking how the moment was coming when he would have to leave this woman and go back to being a wanderer. Rosa went on about her complete surrender to the sect and how her life was now full of significance.

They crossed the bridge to Rio and headed down the coast. Rosa lived in Santa Tereza; he had said he would drive her home and then return by streetcar.

"Or maybe I'll stay in one of the hotels up in your neighborhood. The ones full of old folks."

Once they had turned up the hill to Santa Tereza, she pointed out an enormous house jutting out from the top of the hill, surrounded by jackfruit trees, eucalyptus, and mango trees.

"You live there alone?"

"Right now I do. I turned the ground floor into a studio and I live upstairs. I'm a painter."

"A painter, how interesting."

"Really? Do you do some kind of art yourself?"

"No, no, I'm no artist. I'm in advertising."

Miguel got out of the car and walked Rosa to the gate. Several flights of stairs led to the outcropping on which the house had been constructed, probably during the previous century. Miguel held out the keys.

"Well, I guess I'll be going. Maybe we'll see each other around."

Rosa tugged his arm and closed the wrought-iron Art Nouveau gate behind them.

"Let's go up and have a glass of wine. You're in no hurry, are you?"

"Not in the least," said Miguel.

They climbed the stairs to a courtyard made of Portuguese tiles, with a wrought-iron arbor over which a luxuriant maracujá spread out its wide, faded leaves. In the background, the last rays of the sun glinted on Guanabara Bay. The city was already beginning to light its lights and prepare for nightfall. The air was damp and fragrant with eucalyptus, and the dark house looked like a romantic ruin in the middle of a forest.

Rosa opened the door and Miguel saw a spacious living room with an ultra-high ceiling, full of easels and canvasses leaned against the walls. On one of the easels, still half-finished, stood one of her paintings. Miguel knew very little about art, but the piece looked strangely familiar, even with part of the canvas still blank.

"*Voilà:* my problem in living color," said Rosa, throwing her canvas bag on a leather easy chair overflowing with pillows. "I'm not really an artist."

"What do you mean?"

"Don't you recognize it? It's a Miró. I paint forgeries. It's a talent I have, I can imitate just about any artist's technique. I just can't manage to be myself."

"But why do you do this?"

"Because it pays. People lay out a lot for my canvasses. I told you I was very attached to money."

She began to prop up a series of already completed paintings as she went on talking.

"See, here are some of the masters: Portinari, Di Cavalcanti, Djanira. There's also Degas, Rebolo. A friend of mine who's an expert forger takes care of authentication and sells them to filthy-rich ignoramuses. You wouldn't believe what people are like in this country. They pay with their eyes closed, they pay any amount of money to have a painting with a famous name on it hanging on their wall, who cares if the origin is suspect. Sometimes I even get the feeling they know they're buying a fake."

"That's incredible." Miguel was truly dumbfounded.

"I stopped painting when I joined the Illumination. I haven't worked on any of these pieces for a long time. And I don't really want to sell the finished ones anymore, but I can't bring myself to destroy them either."

Rosa wandered off into the kitchen. Miguel looked at canvas after canvas, amazed at how they seemed to evoke the same air of reverence as the originals. A Di Cavalcanti mulatto woman gazing sensually at a sailor was executed in colors as carnal as the master's, with the same luxuriant, tropical atmosphere and ethnic bite. The Djanira forgery rang true as well: children flying kites in a delicately colored shantytown where poverty and promiscuity didn't exist.

"Shit, there's nothing in the house," said Rosa, returning from the kitchen. "I thought there was still some wine, but I guess somebody drank it last night."

"I'll go get some, if you want," offered Miguel.

"Will you? I'm so tired."

"Sure. There must be a bar or something nearby."

"Just up the street. The wines aren't the best, but they go down easy."

"I'd like to make a call first, though. Do you have a phone?"

"Yeah, but I had it disconnected. It annoyed me. But there's a phone in the bar."

"Okay, I'll call from there."

Miguel went down the steps and opened the gate. The old-style cobblestone street was deserted, the few houses dark. He headed for the lights of the bar up ahead on the corner. As he walked he felt the bulge of something in his pocket and remembered that he still had the keys to the Camaro. He made a mental note to leave them somewhere in the studio when he returned.

The bar turned out to be more like a little grocery, with a group of regular customers sitting at two tables playing dominoes and drinking shots of rum. He asked about the phone and bought three bottles of wine. If things didn't work out, he figured he'd go on a bender and forget everything. Not that he was much of a drinker, really, but under the circumstances he couldn't think of anything better to do.

He called home. Someone picked up the phone.

"Hello," said Miguel.

There was a silence at the other end, and then Ruth's voice, nervous and feigning calmness.

"Miguel, is that you? For the love of God, are you all right? Tell me that, before anything else."

"Yes, I'm fine, but Ruth, I just want to explain—"

"No, don't explain anything," she interrupted. "You're in trouble, Miguel. I talked to your father this afternoon. I had to call him, I didn't know what else to do. He said the best thing for you to do now is to turn yourself in. Where are you, anyway? Your father's really worried and said to remind you that the stability of the government comes before everything else."

"Okay, Ruth, don't worry. I'm going to follow Papa's advice."

Miguel hung up the phone and felt his heart pounding. Ruth was under pressure, the police may have even been standing right beside her as they talked. She'd obviously been given instructions to tell him to turn himself in. It almost made sense that Ruth would want him to go to the police; she had no idea what was going on and the authorities were surely giving her a slanted story. But Ruth was clever. She had found a way to send him a sign, a warning. And the sign was clear. Maybe she actually had gone to her father-in-law for help, but what she'd quoted him as saying didn't fit the old man's line of thinking. A Catholic with strong liberal leanings, Miguel's father was a criminal lawyer who had gained some notoriety in cases against the death squads. Miguel's choice of a military career had been a disappointment to him, especially in the beginning. He really only accepted the idea once Miguel proved himself to be a competent student and, later, a respected military man. He would never claim that the government's stability came first, he of all people, who was always saying that almost every initiative of the administration was a cover for darker motives.

So what to do? Ruth was besieged. It made sense that the police would make her the focus of their plan to capture him. But he couldn't give himself up. Even if Ruth and his father really did think he should, Miguel knew this alternative didn't exist. He'd be an immediate target for an "accident" and probably turn up stabbed to death in jail by some marginal who needed points with the police.

He would pay for the wine and go back to his painter of forgeries. If he could draw any meaning from the guru's parable, it was that at least so far he was not personally responsible for the clumsy intervention of the hand of King Wu in his fate. Miguel climbed the stairs in the certainty that, at least for the night, the wine would have the power to free him from his nightmare.

Inspector Castilho hung up the extension and nodded approvingly at Ruth. He was sitting comfortably in the living room of the Ipanema apartment that Miguel would be paying off for the next fifteen years. In the hallway outside stood another armed cop, while downstairs near the entrance, discreetly seated on the stairs, out of view of anyone entering the building, yet another kept watch. Ruth's only consolation was that she had followed her father-in-law's advice and taken Luciano to his place. The police presence would have embarrassed him terribly. She hadn't told him anything yet; she was waiting for something more definitive, waiting to get Miguel's version of the story, which she believed would be more accurate. It wasn't the first time they had tried to play her against her husband, and once more she hoped to find out what he knew, both to comfort her and to get her life back on solid ground.

Arriving at the courthouse, she had found her father-in-law deeply absorbed in a case, an especially difficult one, he said, because his client was poor and had confessed under torture. He was struggling to build a case for the man's conditional release, and fell silent, ashen, as if he were about to asphyxiate, when Ruth blurted out what was going on. But, typically, he regained his cool immediately and swung into action. They went to his office on rua Debret, where he asked her to repeat everything that had happened, down to the last detail. Old Dr. Gouveia was famous for his meticulousness and competence, in addition to a rare fearlessness in confronting a legal system that was almost always corrupt and hopelessly logjammed.

"There's something wrong here," he said when she had finished.

He was seventy-two, but still possessed a vigor and charm that Ruth found captivating. He was one of the few people she trusted unconditionally, and he treated her with a tenderness and paternal warmth that had grown over the many years they had known each other. Ruth knew this man as well as she knew her own father, perhaps even better, because her father had been a skillful politician with an artful, chameleonlike personality that she didn't like very much.

"What are we going to do, Dr. Gouveia?" She called him this not out of formality, but as an affectionate way to show respect and because the title fit her father-in-law like a second skin.

"I'm going to make a phone call and then we'll see."

As he dialed, Ruth saw that his hands were shaking. Emotion, however controlled, was evident. The old man really loved his son, and she could well imagine how worried and perplexed he was.

After a few minutes on the phone, he pushed back from his desk and picked up his hat.

"Let's go."

"Where are we going?"

"To talk to a friend of mine."

On the way out the door he put on his hat, which completed the picture of an ancient and hard-boiled fighter. They got a cab and headed for the northern section of the city. Miguel's father was having trouble breathing. Ruth began to worry about him, too.

"Are you okay?"

"Yes, my dear. You know this is not going to be easy."

Ruth nodded. It already wasn't easy and it could get much worse. When the taxi finally pulled to the curb she saw, startled, that they had stopped at a police precinct.

"Don't be alarmed, my dear. An old friend of mine works here. He may be able to help us."

It was a small, dirty neighborhood precinct with two deteriorating police cars parked outside. One of them had no tires, and in the other two cops were relaxing to the sound of radio static. A fat man with white hair and a gun on his hip trudged out the door to greet his visitors.

"So you still haven't retired, you old fox," he chuckled, embracing Dr. Gouveia and clapping him on the back.

"I'm just like you, Fonseca, I won't quit until the Grim Reaper himself takes me off the case."

The two men laughed and Gouveia introduced Ruth.

"Let's go into my office," said Lieutenant Fonseca. "It's not a lot better than out here, but at least it doesn't smell."

The office was crammed with stacks of papers and cardboard boxes. Two wooden chairs faced a table; on the other side sat an exhausted desk chair, its vinyl upholstery so tattered that the stuffing seemed to be bubbling out of it.

"I see you're as hard on chairs as ever," said Miguel's father.

"And you're just as busy putting criminals back on the streets," replied his friend.

This exchange marked the end, apparently, of amenities and the start of serious matters.

"What can I do for you?" asked Fonseca.

Gouveia repeated what Ruth had told him, pointing out some of the contradictions in the facts as related by the federal police, and presenting some of his own conclusions.

"Give me a minute to see what I can find out on the radio."

"Be discreet," advised the lawyer.

Ruth couldn't seem to get comfortable in her chair; her anxiety was growing by the minute. She did not expect to hear good news from this man. Her father-in-law, on the other hand, seemed calm and sure of himself.

They sat waiting for a half hour. It was late afternoon by now, and Ruth remembered she hadn't eaten lunch. But she didn't feel hungry, just weary and unbearably anxious.

Lieutenant Fonseca returned scratching his head.

"Yes, my friend, there are a lot of things in this story that don't add up."

"Tell me everything you know," demanded Gouveia.

"One thing at a time, my friend. I talked to the district where the incident ocurred. They don't know a thing about it."

Gouveia sat bolt upright in his chair and Ruth's mouth fell open.

"Exactly. None of their patrols pursued or exchanged fire with a suspect last night. Neither did they find a body. So, next I called the commissioner's office and talked to Moura—you know him, his brother went to school with us. Palito—remember? The one who died of cancer last year."

Gouveia nodded.

"Well, Moura put his ear to the ground and found out that it's all with the feds. An incident did occur, a body was found, it's at the morgue and hasn't been released to the family yet. He was told that the killing was drug-related and that a suspect has been identified from documents found by investigators, just like you told me. But even Moura said there's something fishy about the case. The dead man had no police record and was a retiree from the State Department. He worked for a women's clothing company. Moura said the thing reeks of politics. And it's the political section of the federal police that's on the case. This Inspector Castilho who interrogated your daughter-in-law is linked to DOI-CODI."

"DOI-CODI!" Gouveia almost leaped from his chair. "That's not even police, that's army—and a completely extralegal operation. My God, then Miguel really is in danger."

"That's all Moura could come up with. The feds are keeping the lid on, which is nothing new. And there's something else doesn't make sense. The guy was stabbed to death, right—but apparently the killer had a gun because he exchanged fire with the nonexistent police patrol."

"What do you suggest we do?"

"In all honesty, I'd say you'd better keep him out of sight and wait to see if the smoke clears. I know that's illegal and I shouldn't be telling you this, but this thing smells pretty bad to me. The feds think they're untouchable. Once they get their hands on him it'll be pretty tough to get him back. They can tell you any story they like."

"I know my son had nothing to do with all this."

"I believe you. You're an honest man, Gouveia. Do everything in your power to keep the feds away from him. You've got excellent connections, it's time to use them."

"But what can we do?" asked Ruth.

Without waiting for an answer, Gouveia picked up the hat that was resting on his knee, rose to his feet, and extended his hand.

"I don't know how to thank you," he said.

The lieutenant returned his handshake warmly.

"You know I'm always here for you."

In the cab on the way back Gouveia began setting out their strategy. His analytical mind, his depth of experience, and his self-assurance were holding him together, giving him the strength to think coherently.

"First, my dear, we're going to Luciano's school. We'll pick him up and bring him back to my house for a couple of days. The police are no doubt parked at your door with a search warrant by now. Or maybe they didn't even bother—under Act 5 no warrant is needed in political cases. It would be best to keep the boy as far away from all this as possible."

"I don't want to lie to Luciano, Dr. Gouveia."

"I'm not saying you should. Tell him what we know. He's perfectly capable of understanding."

Children were already pouring out of the school when they arrived. The sidewalk was filled with boys in uniform, and cars were lined up at the curb waiting for them. Luciano was in the oldest group, the last group to leave, sweaty and disheveled, their shirts untucked and their sneakers filthy. He saw his mother and grandfather waiting for him in the taxi. Since his father had not been exceptionally steady lately, Luciano's grandfather had become a kind of model of continuity. He sincerely liked his grandfather, and one of his favorite things was to sleep over at his grandparents' house, though even this had changed somewhat with the onset of puberty.

Luciano ran to the taxi, worried. "Dad hasn't come home yet, has he?"

Ruth shook her head and opened the door for him to get in.

"You're going to spend a few days at Grandma and Grandpa's. We're taking you over there now."

"Right now? But I have to pick up some stuff at home."

"You just tell me what you need and I'll bring it over."

"Why can't I go home first?"

"We'll talk about it when we get to Grandpa's."

Luciano settled into his seat without protesting further, as he usually would have. The faces of his mother and grandfather were enough to convey the seriousness of the situation. All three remained silent until they arrived at the ancient Moorish building on Flamengo Beach where Luciano's grandparents had lived for more than thirty years.

Upstairs in the apartment, dona Rita looked anxious.

"God in heaven, Gouveia, what's going on? The phone hasn't stopped ringing. Where have you been? Why haven't you been in your office?"

She fell silent and looked at Ruth and Luciano. Her intuition, so alert to family crises, was now like an exposed nerve. Ruth was clutching Luciano's book bag and struggling to hide her fear and exhaustion.

"Ruth—say something," begged dona Rita.

Dr. Gouveia took her by the waist and led her to the couch. He stroked her white hair, which was pulled back and tied with a silk ribbon. Dona Rita's thick glasses gave her eyes a perpetually alarmed look, but now she was truly terrified, almost to the point of asking them not to tell her what they were about to tell her. She knew deep inside that something terrible had happened to Miguel.

Ruth and Luciano sat down beside them and Gouveia began to speak, slowly and haltingly bringing his wife and grandson up to date on the situation. Luciano listened intently and watched for his mother's reactions. Once finished, the old attorney sighed.

"Now, my dear, who all have been calling here?"

Dona Rita took off her glasses, dabbed at her myopic eyes, and regained her composure.

"All kinds of reporters, with questions about Miguel. Finally I started hanging up as soon as they said who they were. Then someone from the federal police wanted to talk to you. I told him to call back at dinnertime. What an afternoon."

Luciano pressed his book bag to his chest and sank down into the armchair. He hadn't opened his mouth; he was acting as though it were all unreal, far beyond his imagination and comprehension. All he could do was share the adults' sense of fear, and it was an uncomfortable and frightening sensation.

"How about a nice hot shower, Luciano?" suggested dona Rita, as a way of getting him out of the living room. She knew that Ruth and Gouveia had a lot of planning to do.

For the first time in his life Luciano did as his grandmother asked without a complaint. He followed her out of the room like a small, frightened animal. Touched by this sight, Ruth swore that she would let no one break his pride or challenge his integrity.

She turned to her father-in-law.

"He's very scared."

"Of course, but he's a strong boy, and smart. He knows how to cope. Maybe better than we do, my dear."

Ruth agreed.

"You should go home, Ruth. Stay there and keep in touch with us. Let's agree that you'll call three more times today. Call as soon as you get home, and then at ten o'clock tonight, and again at midnight. After that, try to get some sleep—take a sleeping pill or something if you need to. You're really beat and you've got to keep your strength up. Call me again first thing in the morning and then go to work. It's very important to maintain your normal routine. Miguel might try to contact you. If the police show up at the apartment to wait for Miguel to get in touch, do as they ask, as long as it doesn't give him away. If Miguel does call, don't make a date to see him unless you're very creative. Our phones are probably bugged, they've learned how to do that now."

"I don't know if I can do it, Dr. Gouveia!"

"Of course you can, my dear."

Ruth got up and went to look for Luciano. He was in the shower and refused to open the stall door, but called out a list of what he needed from home. She said good-bye and thought to herself it was better that way, because she was crying and didn't want Luciano to see.

Arriving home to an empty apartment, Ruth gathered the mail that had been slipped under the door and hurried out of her clothes to take a bath. Everything looked so normal. The doorman had greeted her as always, and in the elevator a neighbor from the floor above, who had emigrated from Iran ten years earlier to become owner of a luncheonette in Ipanema, remarked on the critical situation in Iran.

As Ruth came out of the bathroom, more relaxed and in clean clothes, her body feeling lighter and the fatigue less insistent, the doorbell rang. She looked at her watch and saw that it was seven o'clock already. A quick look through the peephole made her spirits fall from the pleasant relaxation of the moment back to the tension that had been with her all day long. It was the presumptuous Inspector Castilho. She opened the door and he shoved her aside, with none of the ceremony of their meeting that morning.

"What's going on here?" Ruth protested.

Two other men, who had been out of the peephole's range, barged past her, guns drawn, and disappeared into the apartment.

"There's no one here but me," said Ruth, feeling humiliated but steeling herself to stand up to these cops and put them in their places.

The men dashed from room to room. Finally they returned to the living room where Ruth was still leaning against the wall beside the door, practically pinned in position by the inspector.

"There's no one here, sir," one reported.

"What right do you have to invade my home like this?" Ruth spoke firmly, and though she didn't raise her voice, her jugular vein was practically jumping out of her neck. "I want to see a warrant."

The inspector smiled—it was a grin, really—and grunted.

"Take it easy," he warned, closing the apartment door. He turned to his men. "You, park yourself out there in the hall, and you go down to the vestibule."

The men obeyed.

Ruth picked up the telephone and the inspector's hand clamped down on hers.

"What do you think you're doing?"

"I'm calling my father-in-law to let him know what's going on."

The inspector removed his hand.

"Go ahead," he said disdainfully and sat down on the sofa. He crossed one leg over the other, placed his hands on his knees, and waited for her to finish her call. Once she hung up, trembling, he filled the room with his harsh voice. The message was intimidation. The specifics were that he was not going anywhere fast, he would wait for Miguel to show up or to call. Ruth promised to cooperate and prayed to God Miguel would do neither.

Miguel's call, meanwhile, came soon after. And Ruth apparently passed the inspector's test.

"He's going to turn himself in," she assured him.

"It will be better for him that way. Your husband's been acting crazy. Completely totaled one of our pickups with a refrigerated truck."

"Where did that happen?" asked Ruth, going pale. This damned cop had a special talent for freezing her blood.

"On the Dutra Highway, this morning."

"Why didn't you mention it before?"

"It wasn't important."

He stood up, slapping his knees with satisfaction and, to Ruth's relief, made for the door.

"Don't worry about a thing. My boys will stay at their posts."

Ruth hurried to open the door. The inspector had returned to his polite mode.

"Good night, ma'am. My best to your father-in-law. He's a very famous man, one of the best lawyers in the country."

Ruth said nothing. She closed the door and stood in the middle of the living room like a statue.

Carlos lay in a public ward in the hospital l'Hôtel Dieu, an ancient building on the plaza of the Cathedral of Notre-Dame. His condition was critical, but the doctor held out the hope that he would at least regain consciousness. It had not been easy for Vivian to locate him among all the hospitals and clinics in Paris. She spent a whole day checking hospitals in and around the 5th arrondissement where he lived, starting in the 7th and ending up in the 4th, at the hospital where he had been taken after his accident, if it had in fact been an accident. Carlos was hanging on, at least for the time being, and Vivian decided to give their agreement a more flexible interpretation. As long as Carlos was alive, she would say nothing to anyone; she would wait and hope for the moment she would be able to talk with her old friend.

She walked down the double row of beds, accompanied by two African friends, her faithful companions ever since the terrible news. Nurses bustled around them; the ward was clean and silent. The high windows gave a view of the Seine and the d'Arcole bridge.

Carlos had tubes coming out of his mouth and nose; his breathing was measured and slow. He looked like a mummy with his wrinkled face and sparse white beard. One side of his face was swollen, the eye half-closed by a hematoma. Both legs were in plaster casts, part of his trunk was hidden beneath a chain mail of bandages and gauze.

He was strong, she knew that, but the doctor said he would never walk again. A fractured pelvis did not set easily at his age; the bones would decalcify rapidly. Old age and a Parisian staircase were finally doing to him what two dictatorships and two revolutions had not managed to do.

Vivian couldn't imagine Carlos in a wheelchair, dependent on someone else for his most intimate needs. He was a proud and independent man, and in a way death might be preferable to living as a prisoner to the whims of others. But Vivian didn't want him to die, not now. She wanted to talk to him one more time, hoping he would tell her a little more about his strange request.

A surly-looking nurse approached Carlos' bed. She changed his IV, examined the monitors, and gave him an injection.

"Your grandfather?" she asked brusquely.

Vivian shook her head no.

"You people are Portuguese then?" she asked, after a glance at the name tag at the bottom of the bed.

Instead of responding, Vivian moved off to gaze out the window, her two friends close behind her like black guardian angels.

"He's in bad shape, Vivian," said one. "I think you should prepare yourself for the worst."

"He'll be better off," assured the other. "He's suffering now, with all the medications, injections, all the pain. And he's lived a full life."

Once they left the hospital, Vivian found herself staring at the schoolboys chasing pigeons in the gardens surrounding Notre-Dame. When the boys rushed them, the pigeons would flap up into the trees and dart in and out among the gargoyles. On the bench closest to the hospital sat a young man who looked Middle Eastern. Thick, coarse hair, a thin mustache, and light olive skin. He seemed to be staring at her intently, but that was not unusual behavior for an Arab. Maybe he wasn't even looking at her, but at one of her African companions. The Arab was wearing a blue vinyl jacket and pinstripe pants. He had a small leather purse in his hand.

Vivian lost interest in the young man as they crossed the street, heading for the Latin Quarter. She was thinking about sitting in a café on Boulevard Saint Michel and drinking a beer. She felt terribly sad. It was as if the person lying in that hospital bed near death were a very close relative—and suddenly this didn't seem so far from the truth. Carlos had become family to her, though only now was she realizing how much that meant.

She remembered a conversation she'd had with another Brazilian exile soon after meeting Carlos for the first time. He told her about Carlos' 1969 arrest by the Rio DOPS, how badly he'd been beaten, suffering broken fingers and ribs, without uttering a single word. Vivian asked Carlos about it later, but didn't get much out of him; he didn't like to talk about such things.

"It's very disturbing," he had said. "The human animal is very debased in a torture chamber, Vivian. The torturer included, of course."

They never brought up the subject again, except after they heard about Frei Tito's suicide. Carlos arrived looking utterly disconsolate and hardly ate at thing.

"These things are a disgrace," he remarked, "a disgrace to the human species. When a young priest of Frei Tito's stature is pushed to such extremes, it means that something in our culture has become diseased."

That was what impressed Vivian—Carlos was of a time when the word *culture* still existed. The word itself sounded intriguing coming out of his mouth. He never used leftist jargon himself, claiming with an ironic smile as he read some group's manifesto, full of shopworn phrases and ready-made blather, that rhetoric was simply not his forte.

Vivian and her friends sat down at a sidewalk café on the corner of Boulevard Saint Michel and rue St. Severin. Vivian barely followed the conversation as the two men talked and sipped their beers, but her friends understood. The café was packed, and vendors selling books and records at curbside tables squeezed the pedestrian traffic closer to the café. A familiar figure caught Vivian's eye. It was the Arab-looking young man who had been staring at her outside the hospital. He was absently flipping through a pile of posters at a nearby stall, stopping every now and then to glance at their table. It was a good thing she had two men with her. Arabs were aggressive when it came to women and didn't think twice about making a scene as they followed someone through the streets. Vivian herself had had trouble more than once with infatuated Arabs. A year ago the excessive zeal of an Algerian had cost her an expensive trip to the dentist. The man had followed her all over town until finally she took refuge at a newsstand; when he sidled up to her there and she rebuffed him, he socked her in the jaw, knocking out one tooth and loosening several others. The damage required several stitches, and her mouth was a mess for over a month.

"Do you see that guy over there?" she asked, pointing ostentatiously. "I think he's following me."

"You're a magnet for Arabs," said one of her friends.

"Careful you don't lose another tooth," said the other.

Laughing and staring at him as a threesome made Vivian feel more relaxed. They would stay at her side until she was safe at home behind locked doors and the apparently obsessed boy would have no opportunity to approach her.

Once the three tired of sitting in the café, they paid the bill and strolled down Boulevard St. Germain. Vivian lived in a building on rue Monsieur le Prince and the Africans in Carrefour de l'Odeon. Not the least bit intimidated by Vivian's escorts, the Arab followed the whole way. He no longer even bothered to be discreet, throwing her meaningful glances and at one point even blowing her a kiss. Vivian was beginning to think it was funny, and her friends kept turning around making angry faces and holding up clenched fists.

While they were upstairs in Vivian's apartment, the Arab skulked around the courtyard beside the empty trash cans. Eventually Vivian's friends went home. The first thing she did after closing the door behind them was to run to the bookcase to check that the key Carlos had entrusted to her was still there. It was. She sat and stared at it for a few minutes.

Then she changed clothes, turned on the TV (picture, no sound), and wandered around the apartment, collecting the clothing strewn about and considering whether or not she should wash the dishes in the sink. When she heard something outside her door, she stopped what she was doing. It sounded like footsteps, but when she looked through the peephole all she saw was the dark hallway. As she crossed the room to turn on the TV's sound, there was an enormous bang and crash and the door flew open. The young man who had been following her stood in her doorway with a knife, looking drug-crazed and capable of anything.

Vivian screamed as he hurled himself at her, and kept screaming as she darted sideways, catching him in the groin with her leg and desperately grabbing for a pillow off the bed. He snarled with rage and lunged repeatedly with his knife, slashing the pillow she held in front of her. She picked up a heavy metal vase and threw it at him. It missed but distracted him long enough for her to grab a long steel straightedge a classmate had left on her desk. Brandishing it like a sword, she made a horizontal thrust that caught him at neck level. He let out a yell and lost his balance, dropping the knife. Vivian was shaking, but her survival instinct told her to strike him again. This time she hit him in the back, slicing his blue jacket open, revealing a bloody gash. Dragging himself across the floor like an eel, he made it to the door and struggled to his feet. Vivian stood frozen in place while her attacker stumbled down the stairs and disappeared.

The knife lay on the floor among the wreckage. Gripping the

steel rule tightly, Vivian ran and closed the door. The locks were bent and broken, completely useless. She dragged a chair over and wedged it against the door. Then she leaned up against it herself, sobbing and trembling. She was by nature the kind of person who coolly confronts adversity and falls to pieces once it was all over. But she coudn't fall apart now. That man was no overaggressive, would-be lover; he wanted to kill her. He knew something.

Feeling lightheaded, Vivian bent down and picked up the knife. The blade was long and sharp, the kind used in the military. She stared at it for a long time and shivered: made in Brazil. She threw it on the bed and ran to the bookshelf, opened the book, and lifted out the key. She slipped on a dress and grabbed her purse.

She strode through the hall and down to the ground floor with the steel rule gripped firmly in her right hand. She could wait no longer. She must go to the Austerlitz Station. What happened to Carlos had happened. And if she were also already on the list, it was essential to know what was in that file folder in the baggage locker.

Vivian hurried out into the night to find her African friends. She truly needed them now. And they would know how to protect her.

Miguel opened his eyes. The light stabbed his pupils like a thousand needles. His mouth was fuzzy and his head hurt. He was lying on a bare, seemingly ancient mattress in a room with not one other piece of furniture. But he did dimly remember the night before. Knowing he had a low tolerance for alcohol, he figured he must have passed out soon after the first bottle of wine.

He was fully dressed but shoeless. When he stood up everything began to spin. He needed a cold shower and some aspirin. Struggling not to fall or to throw up, he went looking for Rosa. He remembered her saying that the master bedroom was at the end of the hall.

Finding nothing but a rumpled bed and windows open to the breeze, he stumbled downstairs. Rosa was in the kitchen, sitting at the table drinking wine.

"What time is it?" Miguel asked.

Rosa smiled and took a sip of wine.

"I don't know, I don't wear a watch. There looks to be one on your wrist, though. Why not have a peek?"

Miguel mock-hit himself on the head and then held his wrist up to eye level: it was eleven A.M.

"I need a shower and some aspirin."

"Got a headache?"

"Splitting."

"I have some upstairs, I'll get you some."

Miguel sat at the table holding his head in his hands to stop the world from spinning so fast. There on the table in front on him, among the bottles and wine glasses and other debris, was the morning paper. He picked it up and tried to read. The letters danced before his eyes; nothing made sense. It was *O Dia*, full of crime stories from the sleaziest neighborhoods—not a paper Miguel generally read—and he was about to put it down when his eyes caught on a photograph in the bottom left-hand corner of the page. It was him, Miguel, his driver's license picture. As if by magic, his hangover disappeared, his eyes were clear and his mind lucid. Miguel read the story under the picture, hoping it was a dream but knowing he was wide awake. He felt Rosa's eyes on him from the kitchen doorway. She was holding a bottle of aspirin.

"I'm addicted to *O Dia*," she said.

Miguel wondered whether she had already seen the picture and called the police.

"You still want aspirin?"

Rosa's voice was calm. She didn't seem the least bit frightened.

"Have you read this morning's paper?"

She nodded.

"It's all a bunch of lies, you have to know that," he said, without sounding very convincing.

"It's okay, Miguel. I know you're okay, I just feel it. If you weren't, you wouldn't have told me your real name."

"I wish I could explain all this to you," he said, dispirited, "but the hell of it is I'm not even sure what's going on."

"Like I said, it's okay. There's nothing to be afraid of here. My door is closed to everyone else. As long as you're here, you're safe. Your karma agrees with mine!"

Miguel didn't know what to say. He wasn't even sure he should accept the reassurance. It could be dangerous for Rosa, no matter how good her karma was.

"I want to help you, Miguel."

"Why?"

"I don't know, we'll think about it later, okay? The guru told me that what matters is not the path of the arrow but the cord taut and ready on the bow."

Miguel nodded his head in agreement, without understanding the maxim, while Rosa filled a glass with water. She handed it to him with the aspirin.

"Take these, they'll take care of the headache. And use the upstairs bathroom, the shower head's better."

"Thanks."

Rosa walked up to him, her eyes shining, and kissed him on the cheek.

"You poor thing," she whispered in his ear.

Rosa took him by the hand and led him upstairs to the bathroom. She turned on the shower and tested the water.

"It's pretty cold."

"That's what I need."

She showed him where to find a towel and stood at the door, watching him in a maternal sort of way. Miguel slowly unbuttoned his shirt. Finally she left him to his shower, the comforting jetting of cold water on his body.

When Miguel came out of the bathroom, Rosa was in her studio arranging her forgeries in a pile.

"I'm going to burn them."

"No, don't," he said. "They're so beautiful."

"But they don't exist, they're lies. And they're dangerous to my true self."

Rosa motioned to Miguel to help her carry the stack out into the yard, where she gathered sticks and dry leaves and laid a fire. After sprinkling the canvasses with rubbing alcohol, she lit a match and the flames took over.

They stood and watched a billow of white smoke rise to the tops of the jackfruit trees. Rosa smiled, suddenly less distant and weary. Since they first met she had maintained a certain distance, as if to discourage physical contact. Now, as she watched many months of work go up in flames, she seemed more accessible, even vulnerable.

"So what really did happen to you, Miguel?"

The question took him by surprise. Rosa's smile was full of warmth and complicity.

"It was the hand of King Wu," he replied.

Part 2

Ancient Wisdom

A single forty-watt bulb lit the entrance to the tent. The Friday evening performance had gone well, the audience responding enthusiastically to the artists' improvisations. The Shangri-la Circus Theater had been in town for two weeks. The canvas tent was small, accommodating only a hundred seats and a semicircular stage where the cast of eight performed dramas, comedies, and religious pageants. Whenever things weren't going well, there was always some duo of country music players willing to put on a show and liven up the house. But the pride of the Shangri-la Circus Theater was the staging, complete with sumptuous costumes, of the Passion Play during Holy Week. To add to the appeal, people for nonspeaking roles were chosen from among the most talented in the area. And it always was a hit. Presented only five times a year, the Passion Play represented the lion's share of the circus' income.

But the pleasure of a full house on Friday night didn't last long for the owner of the circus, a frail sixty-year-old Spaniard who had made his first appearance in the ring, beside his juggler parents, at age five. When Pepe walked onstage that night and saw the woman sitting in the front row he almost drew a complete blank. If he weren't such a veteran, he certainly would have blown the scene, and his fellow actors would have thought he was becoming senile. But Pepe was scrupulous when it came to his work; he simply put the woman out of his field of vision and let his comedic talent flow into the role he had played enough times to lose count. Pepe was well aware that, of all the varieties of circus, circus theater was the only one in full decline. Movies, radio, and now television were putting it out of business. But that didn't bother him, the Shangri-la Circus Theater would be around for a long, long time. It would put food on his family's table even after he was gone. The Shangri-la was a family business

89

in the fullest sense of the word—always had been and always
would be.

A year earlier, Pepe's wife had wasted away of lung cancer,
getting thinner and thinner before their eyes, but she had remained
on the stage until her illness worsened to the point that she could
hardly talk. She left a gaping hole in the troupe and in Pepe's
heart. But when finally she died, their daughter took on her female
comedic roles. The daughter and her husband Arturo, an Italian
already too old to be the leading man he invariably played, had
produced a pair of grandchildren, also actors, restless adolescents
who no longer saw the circus as an ideal way of life. Now, the
curtain down for the evening, Pepe sat gazing at the yellowed
photograph of his wife that was taped to his dressing room
mirror, enjoying a sweet nostalgia for the past. In the picture
she was wearing an Arab outfit from a Portuguese play that had
been a big hit in the thirties. As Pepe looked at the photograph,
his nostalgia was displaced by a wave of anxiety. Soon a visitor
would be knocking on his dressing room door—a rare enough
occurrence in itself—but he was not looking forward to this
particular encounter in the least. The spectator in the first row
whose presence had disturbed him carried with her unpleasant
memories.

The trailer door opened and there she was. The well-preserved
face was a startling reminder of his wife.

"I think it's time," she said, without entering the dressing room.

A cold shiver ran up Pepe's spine. Not just the voice, so much
like his wife's, but the phrase itself hung in the air like a doleful
portent. It was as if he had made a pact with the devil and the
moment of reckoning had arrived.

But this was not exactly an emissary of the devil, this was his
rich sister-in-law, Haidèe Jaffet, and the pact that he'd made with
her eight years ago had brought him no gain.

Now she had come back, as she promised she would.

"My God, Haidèe, you look so much like her."

Haidèe came inside and sat down on an old trunk. The resemblance, he reminded himself, ended there; in every other way
the two sisters were utterly different. His wife had renounced
everything to be an actress; Haidèe had renounced nothing and
had more all the time.

"It was a stroke of fate," she said, "that you saw what you saw,
Pepe. I told you that one day it would be our insurance."

"Your insurance. I'd just as soon forget about it."

"Have you forgotten?"

Pepe shook his head. He would never forget that night. He couldn't imagine anyone who would.

"So, what do you think we're going to do?" asked Pepe. "They still hold all the cards."

"Not like before. And they're desperate."

"Which makes them even more dangerous."

"That's true, theoretically. But less power means less danger."

"I'm not so sure."

"You still have doubts?"

Pepe shrugged and went back to taking off his makeup. The dingy mirror gave back the figure of Haidèe sitting in the shadows, and her remarkable resemblance to her dead sister made all kinds of emotions well up inside. Pepe was not a man with many friends—his nomadic life as a two-bit player touring the interior of Brazil had not left much time for that. The friends he did have were all members of the circus. If not for her relationship to his wife, Haidèe would be considered an intruder. And the resemblance was disturbing. She had the same energy, the same audacity that had inspired his wife to remain on the stage to the end, the same vibrancy and beauty that shone through her very first performance, in 1952, when she won over the audience immediately. Like Haidèe, Pepe's wife had always been immoderate in all she did, and Pepe liked that. She had fled the family and nothing anyone said was enough to make her change her mind. Faced with her father's implacable objection, she had threatened to take her own life.

The circus didn't have much to call its own, but Pepe's wife wasn't after riches—*that* was the difference between her and Haidèe. Happiness was simply having enough money to go on mounting plays. She adored the tent, the colorful stage lights, the wooden benches, the collection of old backdrops Pepe had acquired from the municipal theater of São Paulo in 1953, and the rickety old trailers that served as living quarters. Of all their belongings, Pepe was most proud of the backdrops, which had been done in oil by a scene painter in the twenties: a forest of poplars, a castle beside a lake, and a street scene with elegant store windows. The audience's eyes always grew wide when the curtain opened on peasants working the fields in front of a fairy-tale castle. Thinking about all this was like remembering a past that was gone forever, while Haidèe's face in the mirror almost made him believe the past wasn't gone.

The events of that night in 1972 had destroyed the serenity of Pepe's life. He would never forget it. The Shangri-la had camped in a large field of low scrub on the outskirts of Guadalupe, a district of Rio de Janeiro. It wasn't the first time they had set up their tent in that neighborhood. Guadalupeans were working-class folk, who had not yet been totally enslaved by television and who appreciated a good play. Those were profitable engagements, and Guadalupe had the advantage of being quite close to Camboatá, another populous neighborhood, which happened to be full of emigrants from the northeast. It was the end of their repertory, and they would be leaving soon.

There was a paved road nearby, and stops for the major bus lines also, making for easy public access. The settlement itself was across a main highway, about two kilometers straight south. This road was poorly lit and very dangerous at any time of day, but especially at night. Almost every week there was a fatal accident involving daredevil pedestrians.

Pepe was arranging some cardboard mannequins in a wooden trunk and was feeling sleepy. This task was keeping his brain awake, though, and he was thinking about their next date. He'd had a good dinner, roast chicken, and even drained a bottle of beer with his son-in-law.

Pepe left the cutouts in the open trunk and stepped outside, where he stood watching the road. Trailer trucks and semis thundered by in both directions, spitting smoke and filling the air with an infernal roar. But in between there was silence, the kind of silence familiar to those who suffer insomnia, interrupted only by the barking of dogs in the distance and the chirping of crickets. Pepe turned and headed out back behind the tent. He had to find a quiet place to relieve himself of last night's dinner. Somewhere far enough away so that he wouldn't smell up the site. He crossed an empty lot and headed for some clumps of grass and weeds, an area littered with rusty cans and broken bottles. His nostrils filled with an awful smell, but he went on some fifty meters, leaving the circus far behind. The night had turned cold and cloudy. Not a single star, nothing. Only the modest glow of Guadalupe in the distance, and, further, the amazing glare of Rio. Pepe could barely see where he was going; the stink of garbage and the wiry branches of shrubs were the only indications he was still in the clearing. Looking behind him, he could see the dark blob of the tent and the highway lit by each passing car or truck. But the noise was deadened by distance, and what had been the roar of engines was reduced to the weak rumble of remote thunder. In between he listened to the apparent calm of the clearing, the almost inaudible rustling of small creatures who swarmed in the trash.

Pepe felt like turning back, but the urgency in his bowels was a fact. He edged a bit further, looking for a spot that was a little less foul, and discovered a line of low bushes that hid a small area of relatively bare ground. He let down his pants and squatted.

Pepe was not a philosopher in such situations; his aim was to get the job done quickly and get out of there. But before he was finished, a car that had been thundering up the highway from the direction of Rio suddenly swerved off the road and began speeding toward him across the wasteland, plowing through the brush and raising clouds of dust.

There was nowhere to run, and no time. Terrified, Pepe considered his fate if this wild man were a criminal running from the police or, worse, someone from the death squad dropping off a "ham." There was nothing to do but crouch behind a bush and pray. The car came zigzagging through the low brush and screeched to a stop about ten meters from where he was hiding. The radio was blasting and all the lights had been turned off. Behind the raucous and insistent music he could hear a woman's voice, clearly begging; he could tell from the tone and because her entreaties alternated with screams for help. Pepe realized he was about to witness a rape. His best bet was to stay extremely quiet until it was over. Things like this were not uncommon in this neck of the woods.

Music blared from the car radio. He would never forget it. A bouncy tune, written for lovers, but in Pepe's ears it would always sound like the background music for a nightmare.

A car door opened and a girl scrambled out. The darkness was immediately broken by headlights and Pepe saw that she was no more than a child, around thirteen or so, still in that shy phase of early adolescence. Tall and pretty, with shoulder-length hair. Dark shorts, a knit top, and bare feet. The girl looked desperate and completely disoriented, as if drunk or on drugs. And she was staggering toward his hiding place. Pepe felt a shiver; his throat was so dry he could hardly breathe. Then the man jumped out of the car and lurched after her, catching her by the waist. She tried to fight him with a flurry of kicks and punches, until finally he smacked her, hard, across the face. The girl let out a howl and rolled to the ground, but the man didn't stop there, he began kicking at her and shouting insults.

Everything happened so fast, to the sound of that fluttery love song. The man got down on the ground and straddled the girl. He ripped off her shirt and shorts, tore her undies to ribbons, and pinned back her wrists. Her naked body wriggled on the filthy ground like a beached fish refusing to die. But she tired quickly, and the man spread out on top of her, pushing her thighs open. She seemed to have no resistance left and just lay there sobbing softly. Once he had raped her, the man took a handkerchief out of his pocket, wiped himself, and then doused it with liquid from a flask and placed it under the girl's nose. She seemed to fall asleep, or lose consciousness. Pepe thought to himself that it must have been some kind of powerful sedative, because she just lay there, lifeless, even when the man returned from the car with a can of gasoline and sprinkled the contents all over her. Once the can was empty, he struck a match. Flames exploded in the darkness and enveloped her body. The man returned to his car, turned the ignition, and bolted the same way he had come.

Pepe was aghast. He had seen a lot in his time; he was no stranger to death, or violence. But this was beyond comprehension. One drunken night a friend of his had been stabbed and died in his arms, bleeding and calling for help. A senseless death, but at least it had an explanation. Not so the killing he had just witnessed. A young girl had been dragged out to the middle of nowhere, raped, and then savagely murdered. And the killer had acted as if he had every right to do what he did. As the flames flared up around the body, Pepe got a good look at him. He was in his twenties, tan and athletic, naked from the waist up, wearing vaguely military pants. His face remained expressionless the entire time, even when he was yelling.

The car was long gone and the fire reduced to a smolder when Pepe finally emerged from his hiding place. He stumbled off toward the tent, unable to bring himself even to look at the girl's half-charred body. But halfway there, halfway to safety, Pepe decided to turn around and go back, and he had been wondering why ever since. If he had just kept on walking, many of the problems that came later, including this visit from Haidèe, would never have happened. But Pepe did go back, and he would never forget the mix of terror and revulsion that overwhelmed him when he looked at the girl's body. The fire was dead and the clearing was being battered by a cold wind that would make the circus tent flap and the bushes dance the whole night long.

An acrid smoke hovered over the body, and later seemed to have impregnated his clothing and even his skin. Pepe sat and wept, contemplating what remained of the girl, his stomach clenching and tears rolling down his face. He thought he was going to black out, but he just sat there crying, his conscience demanding the response he had been too terrified to submit to at the moment of the tragedy. What would have happened if he had stepped from the bushes? Common sense told him that maybe the girl would still be alive. Now there was nothing he could do but feel the remorse that would be with him forever. As he turned to go back to the circus, Pepe noticed something on the ground near where the car had parked. It was an expensive leather wallet. Inside were two ten-cruzeiro notes and a school I.D. He decided to keep the wallet, but swore never to show it to anyone. There was no doubt in his mind that the picture on the I.D. was of the rapist, but Pepe had been around long enough to know that it would cause him and the troupe nothing but trouble if he tried to do something about it.

But Pepe didn't keep his promise. He told his wife, because she knew something was wrong when he tossed and turned, unable to sleep. He also told her because he simply couldn't bear the weight of it alone. And his wife ended up telling her sister because, though she was not close to Haidèe, she knew her brother-in-law Ambassador Jaffet had high-level connections in the regime. Meanwhile, the killer remained at large and Pepe's life went on as before.

"You know what I think?" Pepe's bare face wore a tired expression. "It's the troupe that will get hurt. And you were the first to squelch the whole thing way back then."

"Things were different then."

"I don't see how."

"Come on, Pepe, you're not stupid. I hate it when you play the victim. In those days the press was under heavy censorship."

"That's true. I mean, we found out the guy killed five girls, and nothing ever came out in the papers, it was one big cover-up. The families must have been pressured into keeping quiet."

"But now the press can afford to print the story. They're thirsty for a scandal like this."

"What do you want from me?"

"The I.D. and a statement for the press."

"Why now?"

"Because someone's on my tail, and threatening to go public is the perfect way to get rid of them."

"I don't have anything to do with your problems, Haidèe. We're from two different worlds. I have my life, you have yours. And I know if I get mixed up in this I'm going to pay dearly for it."

"If you don't help, they're going to kill me."

Pepe silently considered this. He could find no pressing reason to help Haidèe, but there was the pact. She had given financial support to the troupe back then, in exchange for his silence. She had paid for her sister's costly medical treatments, even knowing that she was a lost cause. And beyond these debts was the main reason, the promise made to his wife on her deathbed. She had made him swear that if Haidèe came to him he would help her, he would give her the I.D., and do whatever she asked. And Pepe loved his wife. He would do as he had promised even if it destroyed him.

"Okay, Haidèe," he said sadly. "I'll do it for her."

Haidèe opened her purse and removed a sheaf of documents.

"I have here the investigative reports on all the crimes. The only one he slipped up on was the one you witnessed. They're coming after me now because they think I have nothing to hold over them. When they find out about this, they'll have to give up."

Ruth walked down the hall toward her classroom carrying an armload of books. An animated circle of students was gathered outside the door, but conversation ceased as she approached. She warily made her way through the group, sure they had been talking about her. Miguel's picture was on every newsstand, and the story, if not an out-and-out scandal, was no doubt being talked about all over campus.

At the department office, she thought her colleagues had greeted her with forced cheer. It was not going to be easy to keep up her routine, as her father-in-law had advised her to do. The doorman in their building had averted his eyes to avoid saying hello, and when

Luciano saw his father's picture in the paper he had refused to go to school because he dreaded having to face his classmates.

Once in the classroom, though, Ruth realized her imagination had been working overtime. These students hardly ever looked at the newspaper; they probably would only hear about the incident when and if it were reported on television. She went through the motions of teaching her class and when it was over headed to the cafeteria for lunch. Just outside the lunchroom doors, a woman rushed forward and threw her arms around her.

"Hug me," the woman whispered in her ear. "Act like we're old friends."

She did as the woman asked, but the fear she had temporarily left behind flooded back.

"Who are you?"

"A friend of Miguel's."

Ruth looked at her, hard.

"My name is Rosa," the woman whispered.

"I'm Miguel's wife," said Ruth, convinced she was talking to a policewoman.

"I know. I want to talk with you."

"Okay, but it has to be right now. I've got two more classes after lunch."

Once they had filled their trays, they found an isolated table and sat down.

"Miguel is at my house," said Rosa. "Since yesterday. He had nowhere else to go."

This revelation was so totally unexpected that Ruth looked down at her food and realized she was no longer hungry. What was Miguel's relationship with this otherworldly creature, dressed like a bohemian in her orange and purple Oriental wrap tied at the waist with a green satin scarf? She certainly didn't look like a cop, but Ruth knew she shouldn't really trust her intuition. Measuring the woman anew, she realized she must be well into her forties.

"You're not sure if you should trust me, right?" said Rosa, taking Ruth's growing hostility in stride. "I understand. This must be a hard time for you."

"Why did Miguel turn to you?"

"Actually, he didn't, we didn't even know each other. I found him in a parking lot yesterday trying to steal my car."

"My God," said Ruth. "Where?"

"I was at the Illumination farm and he was too. When I went to leave, I found Miguel sitting behind the wheel of my car with a pile of key rings in his lap, looking very nervous."

"So, what did you do?"

"Well, I was a little scared at first. But I could tell he was okay, I could trust him. I don't know why, maybe it was his karma I felt, who knows. We ended up coming back to Rio together and I let him stay with me."

"And what has he told you?"

"Nothing. I sensed he was going through a tough time, but he didn't seem to want to open up, so I let it go. Until yesterday I saw in the paper that he's wanted by the police."

"What did he do then?"

"When Miguel saw the paper, he got upset, but I told him I wanted to help him."

"But—why?"

"He asked me the same thing, and to be honest with you I don't really know. All I know is that Miguel radiates good energy and the police always radiate bad energy."

Ruth was desperate for more information, so she asked if she could see Miguel, even though she still suspected this was all an elaborate trap prepared by the oily Inspector Castilho.

Rosa opened her purse and took out a photograph.

"Miguel knew you would be suspicious of me, so he gave me this to show you."

It was an old picture of Ruth and a very young Luciano on Mosqueiro Beach in Pará. The edges were crinkled because Miguel had been carrying it in his wallet all these years.

"Where do you live? I want to talk to Miguel. Take me there. Right now."

Rosa put the photo back in her purse.

"I can't do that," she said stiffly.

"I have to talk to him. Don't you understand? I was afraid you were with the police, but now I know you're telling the truth. I know you want to help us. That's why you have to take me to him."

"Miguel doesn't think that's a good idea right now. You're probably being followed by the police. He could tell when he called you that something was going on, the police listening in or whatever. And he understood the message you sent him."

"Oh, Rosa, thank God," said Ruth, her voice full of gratitude as she pronounced for the first time the name of this woman who for some reason wanted to help them. "What does Miguel want me to do? Did he send a message for me, or some kind of instructions?"

Rosa looked at the ceiling, as if trying to remember Miguel's message verbatim, and spoke haltingly, like a student reciting a lesson, the true significance of which she did not fully understand.

"First, Miguel asked me to tell you that he's okay. His knees were a little cut up, but they're already healing. And Miguel did not kill the man who was murdered that night, although he was there, and saw the killer. But he can't figure out what's going down and why they want him to take the rap. Second: he doesn't want you or his father to get drawn any deeper into this. At least not until after he tries his next move."

"And what is his next move?" asked Ruth, tense again, because she knew that Miguel wasn't equipped for this kind of thing.

"Well, he said he's going to begin at the beginning."

"What does that mean?"

"Finding a woman named Haidèe. It all started with her."

"She disappeared—I went to her house and talked to her maid," said Ruth. "How is he going to find Haidèe?"

"He didn't say, but he must have a plan. After all he's gone through, he thinks Haidèe will be able to explain this madness. What else can he do, really?"

"Oh, God, we can't just sit on our hands," said Ruth. "I'll go crazy. These people obviously have absolutely no respect for human life . . ."

Rosa stood up, her tray in hand, the food practically untouched.

"Look, I have to go. I'll come back on Monday. If you need to contact me, in an emergency or something, go to Bob's in the Avenida Central building on Rio Branco at five P.M."

"Okay." Ruth nodded, thinking her life had turned into one big emergency.

Rosa took her tray back to the counter and left. Ruth just sat there and let her mind wander, unsure what to think. Later she would stop by her father-in-law's to see if there was any news. Her courage had limits, and now there was no denying that Miguel was in a very delicate position. If his pursuers were who she thought they were, they could nab him at any moment.

Trying to put the idea out of her head, she recalled the day Miguel had his first run-in with the military hierarchy.

It was October 1972. Miguel was stationed in Belém, at a bureaucratic post. Confidential orders landed on his desk daily authorizing the release of tons of provisions and munitions that would be loaded onto trucks arriving at the barracks through the night. The unit was on alert, like an army, but neither operational reviews nor extensive training were underway. But something was up. The rumors flying around the barracks were not to be believed—and, choosing not to believe them, Miguel habitually came home from work depressed. One day a friend of his, a major, was hospitalized. When Miguel went to the hospital to see him, he was told the major had been accidentally wounded by a grenade and was in critical condition, unable to receive visitors. Two days later the man died and his body was quickly dispatched to his relatives in Minas. As soon as Miguel heard the news, he went to the military hospital for further information, but they claimed they had none. As he was leaving, frustrated and irritated by the bad humor of the medical officer who had practically had him thrown out of the place, Miguel ran into a sergeant with whom he had served in Porto Alegre. The sergeant had come to visit the major and had just been informed of his death. He was in his late forties, a straightforward kind of guy from the interior of Goiás, an old-style military man, very attached to his troops, who had dedicated his whole life to his soldiers. He announced to Miguel that he was leaving the army.

"But you, Silva! You don't know how to do anything else!"

The two spent the afternoon at a bar, where the sergeant went on a bender and said some terrifying things. From that day on, Miguel began to give more credence to the rumors.

"The major's death was no accident," said the sergeant.

"How do you know?" asked Miguel. "They said a grenade went off accidentally during a training session. He was standing nearby and got hit. Lost an arm and part of his intestines."

"That's where the grenade got him, all right," said the sergeant, "but it wasn't any training session. I was there, man."

"What are you talking about?"

The sergeant had polished off half a bottle of cane liquor by this time and had left his inhibitions behind. His face looked positively tortured, which was particularly striking because he was a simple man, unaccustomed to reflections on the intrigues of his profession, especially about the sinister side of things.

"You ever heard of Xambioá?"

Miguel shook his head, but deep inside he already knew that whatever he was about to be told would only confirm his suspicions.

A cloud of cigarette smoke encircled the sergeant's head.

"Well, there's a battle going on . . ."

"Battle?" Miguel was shocked. He knew that was the purpose of an army, to be ready to fight, but serving in the army of a peaceful, nonaggressive country had given him the apparently mistaken impression that he would never find himself involved in a war. He had truly never considered the possibility seriously, even though a good part of his time was spent preparing for it. Not that he had moral scruples. He wasn't a pacifist, he saw nothing wrong with picking up a weapon and using it, because if there were a war—which was only a remote possibility—he would be killing his country's enemies. Granted, this was a simplistic view of things, but Miguel had until then not run up against any reason to elaborate further on the subject.

"Well, a bunch of kids from the south went out to that part of Araguaia and started some kind of guerrilla movement. Probably thirty or forty of them, all around twenty years old. They're Communists and seem pretty organized. Some have already been killed or captured. But what's going on down there, I'm telling you it would make your hair stand on end."

Miguel shuddered at the connection between what he was hearing and what was crossing his desk.

"They're really Communists?"

"Yes, definitely. They belong to the Communist party of Brazil. But for me the shocker was how our guys decided to do the job. They went over the heads of the regional Military Command and everybody. There's no unity whatsoever, it's chaos. I've been there the last two months with a unit of paratroopers, and everything went wrong, everything. They've mobilized something like twenty thousand men. I'm not kidding. To fight thirty kids with no leadership half-lost in the jungle. Our friend the major was just one of the many victims of the idiocy going on out there. He died in an ambush set by our own guys—yeah, think about it, you're commanding a night patrol and you get attacked by your own paratroopers. The major and a local guide were the only ones to come out alive, all the enlisted men bit it right there and then. Last month, too, a detachment of twenty men was hit by friendly fire."

"When did this all begin?"

"The operation began in April, but the Communists have been working the area for two years or something. Not that they've gotten anywhere. People down there are real suspicious by nature."

"So why are they taking the guerrillas so seriously?"

"Because, well, they're a bunch of ass-kissers, brown-nosers to power, trying to make a name for themselves. It's their golden opportunity, and meanwhile they're turning it into a swordfight in the dark. Everybody showing off and trying to be the hero, and who gets fucked but the men in the middle."

"Thirty guerrillas, you say?"

"That's right. And isolated. All they'd need to do is send in one platoon of the Pará military police. These Commies are goners already, they can hardly come by enough flour to trick their bellies into thinking they're eating. Logistics? Nonexistent. Anyone can see that, except our top brass. And meanwhile, the troops just wipe their feet on the local population, so people tremble at the sight of olive-green—how does that debasement of our uniform strike you? Oh, I wish you could have seen some of the great acts of courage: I saw quite a few colonels out in the jungle shit their pants at the sound of a rifle report or a monkey's scream. But when they're safe in base camp or they've got good coverage, like the day a whole contingent of them picked up three Communists, then they turn into real animals. It's enough to make you sick. I never thought I'd live to see this."

The sergeant's macabre report went on, but Miguel could hardly listen anymore. He'd had nothing hard to drink, just one beer, while the sergeant was swilling cane liquor like there was no tomorrow. And, sure enough, a week later, the sergeant was dead. He was found naked in his apartment, apparently the victim of heart failure while bathing. Miguel didn't believe a word of it. A heart attack. The sergeant had been in excellent health, very athletic, he was from strong peasant stock—he should have lived another thirty years. There was a very small turnout at the funeral, just a couple of fellow sergeants, the widow, a fifteen-year-old son, and a niece who had lived with them. The son looked like his emotions were in deep freeze. A good kid, energetic and likable, thought Miguel, remembering him from the time they were stationed in Porto Alegre. Occasionally they had taken him to the zoo or to a soccer game, because he had become very attached to Ruth. Now, at fifteen, he was letting his hair grow, had the beginnings of a beard, wore thick steel-rimmed glasses, was a member of an amateur theater group, and was active in the student movement.

For what seemed like a long time Miguel stood there in the chapel of Santa Casa arm-in-arm with this boy, who was clearly shaky but also very rebellious. None of which would have seemed surprising if the boy hadn't decided to talk.

At times like these, Miguel lost his tongue completely. He knew that words of consolation sounded false and were of no help to anyone, so he wasn't even sure why he suggested they walk outside. The boy, meanwhile, seemed to understand Miguel intuitively, and perhaps welcomed his discomfort.

"Is there anything I can do?" asked Miguel.

The boy shook his head.

"You know, some pretty strange things happened," said the boy. "I wouldn't even know where to begin." Only his innate shyness and confusion at his father's death were keeping him from cracking wide open.

"What do you mean? You can tell me."

"Well, I know I've got to accept that my old man is dead, but it was so strange the way it happened . . ." The tears he'd been holding back began running down his face. "I mean, it was really unexpected, you know?"

"What happened? He didn't have any sense of it beforehand?"

"No, he was feeling fine." The boy paused. "Oh, shit," he said in despair. "When I try to talk about it, nothing makes any sense."

"Go on, son, you can tell me. We go way back, the two of us."

"It's just that I don't think my father died of natural causes like they say," he blurted.

"Why?" Miguel's heart was pounding.

"Well, first, because he was in great shape. He had a complete physical just recently, when he signed up for some new life insurance. He wanted to make sure we were taken care of, but I know he wasn't afraid he was going to die anytime soon, I'm sure of that. And the examination and all the test results were great. That's why I just can't buy this heart-attack stuff."

"Tell me what happened the day he died."

"He came home, took a shower, and sat down in the living room to watch TV. Me and Mom went to pick up a few things at the supermarket. We weren't gone more than half an hour. When we came back, he wasn't in the living room and we heard the shower running. Right away, I thought that was pretty strange because he'd already taken a shower. Well, after a while when he didn't come out my mom got worried and started pounding on the door, but he didn't answer so we had to kick it in. We found him in the shower stall with the water running. And he was dead by then."

Miguel was listening quietly to the boy's story.

"My old man was going through some kind of crisis when he died," he continued. "Not that he talked about it much, but you could tell. And things between him and me had gotten pretty bad lately. Everything got worse after he came home from his last trip. He was grouchy all the time and he got on my back for the least little thing."

Miguel shared the boy's perplexity. He had been a good friend of the dead man, and everything the boy said made sense. And this was the second friend he'd lost under cloudy circumstances in a week. But Miguel had learned something from his experience in Porto Velho. He would not pursue this through official channels or take any legal action—not that he was thinking of doing anything illegal, either. He would restrict himself to making use of the small and irritating power he had at hand: bureaucracy. From that day on, he would do everything in his power to delay, confuse, and confound the progress of the papers that crossed his desk, especially those relating to middle-of-the-night shipments out of the barracks.

A month after he had put his new tactic into practice, he was called in by his commanding officer. After being subjected to some senseless double-talk that didn't even contain the veiled threat he had been expecting, Miguel was invited to take his accumulated vacation time. He accepted the offer without blinking.

Ruth had a very clear memory of what Miguel's life had been like during the month following his friends' deaths. He was tense all the time, lost weight, and began to develop an allergic reaction to the fabric of his uniform. Whenever he had to wear it, various parts of his body itched and burned terribly. He took to wearing street clothes whenever possible, which only seemed to aggravate his rising torment.

The family did take a vacation, visiting several cities in Venezuela, followed by a quick trip to Colombia. As his vacation time neared an end, Miguel decided they should go back to Caracas, where a Caribbean music festival was being held. Ruth didn't understand this sudden interest in *cumbias* and boleros, but she humored him. He was tense in the Belém airport the day they returned, and soon that tension had its justification. Miguel was arrested and was held incommunicado for five days. After waiting for a promotion since 1969, it was clear now he would never get one.

On his release, Miguel was given orders to appear at the CMA in Manaus. Ruth said good-bye to her husband, certain he would be invited to request retirement. Her premonition was only wrong in degree—the "invitation" was actually more drastic.

Miguel returned from Manaus relieved of his command. February 1973: the beginning of their most difficult period. Miguel was brought before his commanding officer in Manaus who behaved like a reform school director gone mad. He called Miguel irresponsible, together with a slew of other insults, and even insinuated that he was in league with the reported minority of officers of leftist tendencies working to undermine the efficiency of the army.

At first, Miguel tried to explain. He insisted that he was not a saboteur, had no connection to and should not be lumped with the others, whatever they were up to. But as he got more worked up he began making accusations about the leadership and questioning the current role of the nation's armed forces. The general lost his composure completely and began thrashing and twirling about in his chair, letting loose a barrage of swear words and, finally, the ultimate accusation: Communist.

Miguel's response was to slug him in the mouth. Ruth knew her husband was not a violent man. Such a breach of conduct could only have been provoked by extremely offensive behavior. In any case, the sixty-two-year-old general lost his dentures and was hospitalized after falling senseless in his swivel chair.

Miguel was once again arrested and had to answer to the IPM and a subpoena to appear before the war tribunal. He was found guilty of insubordination and discharged without benefits. As far as the army was concerned he was dead, and Ruth was offered a widow's pension, which she refused. The judicial inquiry and Miguel's fall from grace were the prelude, and a little more than three months later—a very accelerated rate for the military bureaucracy—he was out on his ear.

It had been a nightmare, having to pack up and leave Belém and reconstruct their lives.

Someone called Ruth's name and jolted her from her thoughts. The cafeteria was almost empty; two students were looking down at her, smiling, their papers clutched to their chests.

"Aren't you coming to class today?"

Ruth grabbed her tray and stood up.

"Of course. Let's go," she said, concealing the intense emotion her memories had evoked.

The students were unaware of what was going on in her life, but that wouldn't last long. She left her tray at the counter and followed them to class. If her students began staring at her the way her colleagues had today, Ruth wasn't sure she'd have the courage to show up for class.

The doorman was asleep at his post. The small table and chair in the reception area were not exactly ideal for taking a snooze, but there he was snoring to the accompaniment of a tiny portable radio tuned to a popular radio station. It was an ancient and pretentious building in the Gloria district, which had seen better days and now served as refuge for prostitutes and civil servants of the lowest level.

A brutal slap woke the doorman with a cry, and he fell to the floor, scraping his arm on the edge of the glass tabletop. At the same instant a man slammed the table with the butt of an INA machine gun, producing an intricate spiderweb of fractures.

"Where does this bitch live?" he bellowed at the stupefied doorman, pushing a photograph in his face.

The lobby was swarming with heavily armed, wild-eyed men. Several residents who happened to walk in were roughly pulled aside and searched.

"So, is the bitch upstairs or what?" shouted the man.

The doorman trembled and struggled to speak. The man grabbed him by the tie and fairly dragged him out from behind the table. Then he kicked him several times, shouting all the while.

"What are you, some kind of wise guy? Start talking, you son of a bitch!"

Then the man burst out laughing and said to the others, "This guy's as good as they get!" And kicked him a dozen more times. The doorman lost consciousness.

"He passed out," said one of the other men matter-of-factly.

"Doesn't matter," said the leader. "She's on the eighth floor. Let's go."

Five men took the elevator and two the stairs. The others guarded the lobby and the service entrance. A large number of residents and curious onlookers had gathered, but no one dared say a word. Police brutality was no news in this neighborhood.

Up on the eighth floor, the men broke down the apartment door and stormed in, striking those ridiculous poses they had learned in police training classes. The woman they were looking for greeted them with an indignant look. She was sitting at an enormous antique desk. The apartment was set up like an office.

"Relax, gentlemen," said Haidèe, without the tiniest wobble in her voice.

"Relax, my ass," shouted the cop who seemed to be in charge.

The men had their weapons trained on the woman as if an entire army were sitting behind the desk.

Haidèe slowly closed the book she was reading and looked carefully from face to face. Their guns were cocked as if they expected some violent reaction.

The man in charge took the photo out of his pocket, compared it to the woman in front of him, and yelled: "Are you Haidèe Jaffet?"

"There's no need to shout," protested Haidèe.

The cop became infuriated and hurled a string of dirty names in her direction.

"Are you finished?" she asked. "Do you feel better now?"

"Answer my question," he grunted.

"Yes, I am Haidèe Jaffet, in person. And you fellows . . . I don't suppose you're from the interior decorator's . . ."

The cop put the photo back in his pocket and signaled the others to lower their guns.

"Let's take a little walk, shall we?" he suggested sarcastically.

"So they took the bait, did they," said Haidèe.

"Are you going to come peacefully or would you like us to slap you around a little to get you moving?"

Haidèe stood up and placed the book in a desk drawer. She was wearing a gray jacket and matching pants, complete with a tie.

Her self-assurance bordered on contempt, as if the cops should be scared of *her*.

"You really should cooperate, ma'am," said the leader, without raising his voice but clearly impatient. "I'd hate to have to mess up your face."

Haidèe looked him straight in the eye.

"And I'd hate to see you gentlemen get your asses fried."

The leader lost his patience and tried to grab hold of her arm. Haidèe jerked free so unexpectedly that the man momentarily lost his balance.

The other men raised their weapons.

Haidèe heard the clicks of the guns being cocked.

"You guys really have your heads screwed on straight, don't you." Her confidence was impressive. "Of course you don't, you're probably all high, right? Doped up, that's the only way to do your kind of dirty work. So, who's going to pay to fix my door, huh? You nobodies going to take care of that?"

"Come on, let's beat the crap out of her," said one of the men, his eyes glazed. "I'm going to bloody your nasty mouth, bitch."

Haidèe drilled him with a look of defiance and he seemed to wince.

"It's not blood the boss wants from her," said the leader, "at least not yet."

"Fine," said Haidèe, a sliver of alarm just beginning to work its way into her self-confidence. "So where are we headed?"

"Not far, ma'am. Don't you worry about the route."

"You boys are behaving awfully well," said Haidèe, arrogantly striding to the door. "Going for some extra points?"

Instead of answering, the men took their places and escorted her to the black Opala waiting outside. She was blindfolded and handcuffed and told to lie down in the backseat. The drive seemed interminable. Haidèe's thoughts were racing. The die was cast; she'd flushed them out, but her life wasn't worth a damn if things didn't go according to plan. After the meeting with her brother-in-law the night before, she had set in motion the second part of her plan. The patient, expectant wait behind the desk in the apartment rented on a moment's notice from a company that did such things without asking questions marked the end of its first phase. Now she was counting on two other kinds of bait. One was out running around wreaking havoc among the enemy: Miguel. The other was contained in the innocent-looking envelope she had left that morning in the mailbox of a certain multinational corporation at an imposing downtown office building.

At last the car stopped; Haidèe was led inside, where her blindfold and handcuffs were removed and she was left in a room without windows or furniture. The walls and ceiling were painted gray, a single light bulb hanging from the ceiling. The silence was total; the room had been soundproofed.

Soon the door opened and two men came in.

"It's you, darlings!" said Haidèe sarcastically. "I could start charging for this talent of mine for guessing things."

Her greeting clearly took the men by surprise. They were both middle-aged, in need of a shave, wearing olive-green tee-shirts and camouflage pants. They were unarmed and seemed neither as spacey nor as uneasy as the team that had brought her in.

Haidèe looked at them cynically. They were well-built, sweating heavily, and watched her with an apprehensiveness she would try to use to her advantage.

"You're looking well, ma'am," said one.

"You too, Major Portugal!"

The major gave her an insinuating, almost shy smile, but it was just his game. Major Portugal was one of the best-known hatchet men of the repressive regime; his name occupied a prominent place on all the lists, published by Amnesty International and others, of those involved in the torture of political prisoners during the prior ten years in Brazil. In 1971 he had been accused of mistreating political prisoners and raping two Frenchwomen during an interrogation. The French government made a fuss and he was discharged from active duty. His violent character and complete lack of scruples made him a permanent headache to the military. If he were ever to fall into justice's net, his case would be as controversial as the Nazi war criminals'. But Haidèe knew this was unlikely; Major Portugal was now an upper-echelon executive in a powerful São Paulo electronics firm.

"You have a good memory, dona Haidèe," said Major Portugal. "We only met once, and briefly."

"You're quite famous, Major."

He smiled the same shy and misleading smile, that of a tender-hearted man unaccustomed to dealing with strangers.

"Not as famous as my friend here," said the major, indicating the man beside him.

"You haven't even introduced us yet!" complained Haidèe. "Your manners are slipping, Major."

"Forgive me. This is my colleague Dr. X."

Haidèe raised her eyebrows and looked the man over.

"Dr. X! Yes, of course. What an honor! This is too much all in one day! Your name is all over the place these days."

The man flushed.

"It's the Communists," he said, irritated. "Forever trying to get their revenge."

His voice was grave, almost unnatural. A theatrical whisper.

"Captain Maurício, I presume?"

The man's mouth quivered ever so slightly. Clearly he did not expect to be recognized.

"You're a very well-informed woman, dona Haidèe," said the major.

"It's a matter of survival, gentlemen," she explained, examining the surroundings. "I see you've got quite a setup here. And a team in proper form. What is this place, anyway? A nostalgia club for old fans of some extinct sport? Oh, my dears, it's touching, really! For men cut down to size after those two unfortunate on-the-job 'accidents' in 1976!"

The men remained silent. They hadn't stirred from their spots since they walked in.

"And all because of that damned German, wasn't it? But let's be fair, the work you did on the Jewish journalist and the metalworker was primitive, even amateurish."

Haidèe's provocations were beginning to get to them. The major was lacing and unlacing his hands vigorously and the captain was practically hyperventilating in his effort not to explode.

"Don't get nervous or anything," said Haidèe.

"Shut up," snapped Captain Maurício.

Haidèe curtsied shamelessly and placed her hands over her lips as if to seal them.

"We'd like to have a little chat with you, dona Haidèe," said the major.

Her lips remained sealed.

"Don't play the great lady with us. We know you don't have any great clout. To the regime you're as much a pariah as we are."

Haidèe burst out laughing.

"Pariahs!" she said, guffawing. "Now that's a word! Is that the way you heroes are feeling these days?"

Major Portugal stepped forward and leaned his body into hers. Haidèe inhaled the unpleasant odor of sweat and cigarettes. But the major apparently changed his mind.

"Enough," he said. "You know why we're here, so why don't we just cut the crap and get to the point?"

"The point? What's the point?"

Haidèe crossed her arms and stepped backwards to lean against the wall and escape his disagreeable smell. She needed to keep both her sarcasm and her reasoning sharp and not let herself be intimidated. But the danger was real, these two had already been exposed to so many extreme situations that they no longer possessed moral restraints. Captain Maurício, for example, had been described in two Amnesty International reports as a torturer whose specialty was slowly castrating his victims, including a young physics student who was now in an asylum in Sweden, and was not expected to recover.

"Listen," hissed the captain. "I'm not as patient as my friend here. I've never been genteel and I'm not about to start now . . ."

"No, *you* listen," Haidèe cut in. "I don't have anything to say to you two. I was expecting someone else."

"Then you were wrong," said the major.

"All right," she said, "but not here. I'll talk to you someplace more . . . more neutral, shall we say."

The two men smiled.

"Put this back on," said Major Portugal, producing the cloth that had been used as a blindfold.

Haidèe placed it over her eyes and the major tied it tightly behind her head.

Haidèe thought finally she'd gone up a rung and was being taken to the man she wanted to see, but it was only a short walk to another room. Along the way she heard typical country noises: birds chirping, roosters, a dog. She imagined they were on the outskirts of Rio, Baixada Fluminense maybe, at one of the old farms used to hide political prisoners and where many killings had taken place. The fact that they had not left the house baffled her a little, and her confidence was beginning to slip.

When they took off the blindfold Haidèe saw that she was in a kind of office. Two simple chairs, a small desk, an empty steel bookshelf, and a map of Brazil covered with colored pushpins.

The one window was closed, and the office had fluorescent lighting.

"Sit down," said the major, indicating the chair nearest the door.

Haidèe sat, her legs crossed in a studied pose that said she was calm and unafraid. Inside, her pulse was accelerating and her nerves beginning to spark. The two men, experienced at this, knew very well that Haidèe's posture betrayed a defensive attitude.

"All right, then," said Haidèe. "Let's talk."

The major sat in the chair beside her and the captain sat down at the table, resting his elbows on the back of his chair.

Major Portugal took the initiative.

"Between 1970 and 1972 you made frequent trips to Europe, correct?"

"I still do," said Haidèe.

"We know that, but we're not interested in your more recent travels. We'd like to talk about the trips you made during the years I mentioned." He removed a piece of paper from his pocket, unfolded it, and read aloud: "One trip in February of 1970, to Geneva, with a stop in Paris. Another in July of the same year, same itinerary. Then, let's see, both March and September 1971, and, finally, August and November 1972. Seems you were pretty wild about Geneva back then."

"Yes, as a matter of fact I was," said Haidèe. "I was quite taken by the Swiss culture. But then I tired of it."

The two men glared at her until she felt as if the intense hatred they radiated was beginning to surround her, threatening to pin her to her chair.

"What? What is it?" she prompted.

They merely kept glaring.

Haidèe stood up.

"Sit the fuck down," barked the major.

Haidèe obeyed. She knew that they would kill her if they could. The desire to kill her was almost palpable, but they were disciplined, they needed her right where she was—that is, they needed her to lead them where they wanted to go.

"My dear woman." Major Portugal's voice was calm now. "We know everything. And it won't hurt you a bit to give us what we want. Word of honor. Because it doesn't even belong to you personally, far from it."

Haidèe frowned.

"I'll just throw out a number—maybe it'll jog your memory," said the major. "Say . . . three million dollars?"

Haidèe felt the blood drain from her face. These two knew more than she thought. They were not simply emissaries sent to frighten her.

"I'll take it one step further," he said. "The money was deposited in the honest hands of the executives of Geneva's Caisse d'Epargne."

"If you know so much, why did you bring me here?" Haidèe needed to play for time. The money they were talking about had, in fact, passed through her hands, but the hell of it was that she hadn't the slightest idea what had happened to it. She suspected that it was gone, spent during the years of the repression, but she wasn't sure. She had sent a signal to Carlos, her last contact in Europe. He would know what had happened to the money. But she had heard nothing from Carlos, maybe he was dead.

"We brought you here because you have something we want. Something Swiss executives value very highly—the sequence of letters or numbers that identify the account in which that money was deposited."

Haidèe shook her head.

"The person with that information is dead. You people killed him in 1971 and he took the secret to his grave."

The major let loose one of his sinister laughs.

"Lamarca wasn't the only one who knew. Whoever made the deposits had to know the number."

"Then all I can say is you're knocking on the wrong door, because I don't know a thing. And if I had to guess who might, I'd bet on a member of Larmaca's group—just bring somebody in and interrogate him. Lamarca's people must be easy pickings nowadays on the streets of Paris, or any other European city for that matter."

"You're not thinking of keeping all that money for yourself now, are you, Haidèe?"

"You boys are stirring up a real hornet's nest here—you better watch out or you might end up getting your little fingers stung."

"Or your pretty little butt," retorted Major Portugal.

"I'm not saying another word," said Haidèe.

The two men exchanged looks.

"Consider our situation. We jumped head-first into the shit and destroyed the subversive elements in this country. What did we get for it? We got labeled as torturers and murderers. And the officers who formulated tactics and commanded the operations against the armed struggle, who came and made beautiful speeches to us, today they turn their backs on us and pose as democrats."

The major looked to the captain as he spoke, as if he were summarizing a bill of particulars they had worked and reworked over hours of discussion.

"Is anybody talking about anything else these days?" he asked. "Amnesty for the leftists, reprisals for the torturers. They're treating us like lepers. The administration will pardon the exiles and they'll come flying back. They'll come back rich and organized, and we'll be surrounded, abandoned and defenseless. They're going to want revenge; it's going to start all over again. All we want is to be ready when it happens."

"*If* it happens," added Captain Maurício.

Haidèe's interest was piqued.

"Just what are you plotting?"

Major Portugal smiled.

"Thank heavens you decided to start talking again. I wondered if we were going to have to resort to other methods. But I knew you'd have the wisdom to understand our situation."

"Answer me!" demanded Haidèe.

"We're not plotting anything," said the major. "We just have a few matters of principle to defend."

"Naturally," she said. "But you're also refusing to tell me anything I don't already know. I'll wait for someone higher in the ranks to fill me in on what's going on. How can you expect me to collaborate on something I know nothing about?"

"There is no one higher in the ranks," declared Major Portugal.

"We're running the show," added Captain Maurício.

"I don't believe you. You're the brave young men, you like the front lines. You're not familiar with tactical matters and what have you. I need to talk to the directors of the operation . . ."

"You're looking at them," said the captain.

The major went to the desk, opened a drawer, and took out an envelope, which he held up triumphantly.

"If you're thinking of the person to whom this envelope is addressed, you're dead wrong."

Haidèe's heart lurched. It was the envelope she had sent to a certain address that morning, confident she was planting a small bomb in the beast's lair.

"I see that my suspicions have been confirmed," she said, hoping the opposite was true. Surely they had simply been handed the envelope, surely the addressee had simply opted to put the screws to her without making a personal appearance. But no.

Major Portugal opened the envelope and dumped the contents in her lap.

"Have a look—it's all there!"

Some of the papers fell to the floor, but without even looking she knew it was true. It was all there. Even the Xerox copies of the I.D.s.

"Gosh, this stuff might have given the old man a heart attack," said the major, shaking his head disapprovingly. "It's a good thing we monitor his correspondence. That would have been very mean . . ."

Haidèe's jaw went slack.

"The old man's still our great role model, of course, but he's retired now. Sits behind that desk earning loose change from the gringos. He doesn't even suspect we're here, in fact, but deep down he'd be pleased to know we haven't given up the fight."

"You're lying," said Haidèe, tremulous, all her arrogance reduced to nothing. "He's the only one who knew about the deposits in Switzerland. And he wouldn't tell you about it and stay on the sidelines. No, I want to talk to Lyra. I refuse to negotiate without him."

"We're not here to negotiate," said Major Portugal.

Haidèe couldn't believe her ears. Lyra wasn't stupid enough to give information like this to a couple of dissatisfied extremists for nothing. Especially since their secret was a lot bigger than these two cretins could imagine. What she and Lyra had done meant a lot more than three million dollars of the left's money. General Lyra was neither a cheap opportunist nor a withered old man who could be manipulated like this. The idea that he had no part in this confrontation was as improbable as expecting charity from these two butchers.

"Well, I'm not here to negotiate, either."

They were on top of her in an instant. Haidèe fell off her chair trying to shield herself from their blows. Actually, merely slapping her around a bit was tantamount to cordiality, considering what those walls had seen.

"Enough," ordered the major. "Let's not hurt the old bitch too bad."

Haidèe was coughing and trying to hold back tears. Her lip was split open. A trickle of blood ran down her chin and onto her collar. She wiped it away with the back of her hand and tried to regain her composure.

"You're going to pay dearly for this," she threatened.

They dissolved into raucous laughter.

"You going to complain to General Lyra?"

"You going to denounce us to Amnesty?"

Haidèe stood up and lunged at them. They caught hold of her easily. Struggling in Major Portugal's arms, she screamed and clawed the air.

"I'm going to knock this bitch's teeth down her throat!" yelled Captain Maurício.

"No, you're not," said Major Portugal, tightening his grip around her waist. "I just know she's going to cooperate with us."

"Never!" screamed Haidèe.

Captain Maurício seized her fists, which were still pounding the air, and leaned in, almost nose to nose.

"Your witness has no doubt met his maker by now," he said. "And without him, these papers mean nothing. Where did you hide the originals?"

Haidèe went limp. She was short of breath and too exhausted to think straight.

"Miguel will do the job for me if I can't," she said, still struggling to get her breath.

Major Portugal threw her to the floor. She fell forward with a dull thump and lay there as if unconscious.

"Your little renegade is surrounded," thundered Captain Maurício.

Haidèe, meanwhile, remained motionless. Major Portugal turned her onto her back. He checked her pulse to see if she were all right. She was breathing more easily now and her eyes were closed.

"She's out cold. Let's take her back to the cell. A little solitude might help her get her head together."

"We don't have a lot of time," protested Captain Maurício.

"What can we do? Without her we're back to zero."

"But we're not going to give up, even if she doesn't talk."

Major Portugal nodded.

"You're right. It'll be harder, but not impossible."

They carried Haidèe out of the office and locked her in the room she had been taken to earlier. There were many ways to break the resistance of obstinate people.

Miguel had been sitting behind the wheel of the red Camaro since very early morning. He was parked in the Jardim Botânico district observing Haidèe's imposing mansion and walled garden. The place looked vacant. No servants, no deliveries, nothing. It was a quiet street; the rare passersby were either wealthy joggers from the neighborhood or servants out walking dogs. The only suspicious thing in the area was an ice-cream vendor who apparently lacked all business sense, having set up his cart much too early in the day and on a corner that was unlikely to yield many customers. If it hadn't been for him, Miguel would have already done some exploring at Haidèe's. But he imagined if he did, the ice-cream man would reveal his true identity and the place would suddenly be swarming with police. Miguel's certainty that the man was on a stakeout was confirmed with the changing of the guard in mid-morning.

An electric company truck drove up and parked on the corner nearest the house. Two men got out and began climbing in and out of a manhole; whatever they were doing looked so pointless and confused that it had to be sham. And as soon as the electric company workers showed up, the ice-cream man and his cart disappeared without having sold so much as a Popsicle.

Around noon Miguel unwrapped a sandwich and began to eat. The instinct for self-preservation was now his main stimulus, along with a growing desire to identify the forces responsible for knocking him off-balance. Nothing else mattered; he had come to accept his present condition and didn't expect to be able to go back to being what he was before. Ruth and Luciano seemed very distant already, as if they belonged to another dimension, one that was fading with the passage of days and the acceleration of events. He found this distancing a consolation of sorts. Maybe now his wife and son would get free of him, maybe they would be able to get their lives in order without his disturbing presence. He had caused them far too many problems already. It had taken all of the last two years to achieve a certain equilibrium and financial stability for the family, and now all had been lost in one evening.

After eating the sandwich, Miguel felt sleepy. The silence of the street tempted him to take a nap, but he couldn't let down his guard. It was dangerous enough just being there, in the middle of a police stakeout, armed only with a .38 and a handful of bullets. He had studied a map of the neighborhood and carefully noted all the possible escape routes. But he didn't intend to peel out of there with the cops on his heels, bullets flying through city streets, like an American cop show. And he certainly wasn't there to confront his pursuers; he intuitively knew that the men on the stakeout would never imagine him stupid enough to come back there. They, like him, were looking for Haidèe herself, or some clue that would lead them to her.

Around two o'clock there was movement at the servants' entrance. The small iron gate opened and out came the young maid from the night of his meeting with Hercules, a plastic sack dangling from her hand. The girl descended the sloping street, swinging her hips as she walked. Miguel noticed one of the ostensible electric company workers watching her and talking into a walkie-talkie. The maid continued on toward rua Jardim Botânico. As she stepped into a bakery, Miguel noticed a man who had been walking behind her stop and stand casually outside, waiting while she made her purchases. A pretty routine tail, Miguel thought to himself—they weren't going to much trouble to conceal what they were doing. The girl didn't seem to notice, though. She walked on, hips swaying, without looking back once.

Miguel hesitated. He couldn't start the car and dash off in pursuit without attracting the attention of the electric company workers. But if he didn't do something fast, he was going to lose sight of the girl. Of course she might just be going home for the day, or off to a rendezvous with her boyfriend, but the fact the cops were tailing her meant they didn't discount the possibility she might tip them off to the whereabouts of her disappeared boss. Or so he imagined.

Miguel started the engine. He'd take a cross street to rua Jardim Botânico and wait. If she changed direction during this maneuver he'd be back at square one. But at least now he knew someone was staying at the house.

He darted around the block and parked near the corner. Then he set out on foot toward where he thought the woman would emerge. He had guessed right. She walked another half block and then stood at a bus stop. Two buses came by; she boarded the third, the cop on her heels. Miguel sprinted back to his car and took off after the bus.

They went through the Dois Irmãos tunnel and came out in São Conrado. The girl got off at the stop near the Hotel Nacional and headed for the Rocinha *favela*, a collection of shacks and hovels that sprawled over the towering hillside. The cop seemed to be letting the distance between them increase, as if unsure what to do or how far to follow her.

Miguel parked in front of a supermarket and walked to the steep staircase leading up the hillside. The girl had already disappeared above, the cop nervously in pursuit.

The shantytown was immense and swarmed with half-naked children playing in open trenches of fetid water clogged with garbage. The stench was overwhelming. It was Miguel's first time in a *favela* and he sensed suspicion, curiosity, hostility from all sides. The gun bulging under his shirt didn't make him feel the least bit secure. An intricate web of alleys and narrow footpaths made the place a veritable labyrinth. A person could go in there and never come out.

They walked for about half an hour. Miguel was sweating heavily. His shoes were caked with mud and animal feces. Up ahead, the girl walked on with unnerving calm, greeting acquaintances, embracing friends, stopping to chat with someone at an open window, and waving to the groups of men who whistled as she passed. She was in her element.

Finally she simply stepped into a wood shack. The cop stopped in his tracks, about thirty feet from the shack, and examined it carefully. Miguel took a seat on a wooden bench beside an old man smoking a cigarette. He was tired, nauseated by the stink, and intimidated by the aggressiveness of the locals.

The cop decided to approach the shack. As he stepped forward, two black men emerged from an adjacent alley and ran past him, laughing. Miguel looked up, intrigued by their laughter, just in time to see the cop begin reeling and lurching like a drunk.

The two men had vanished. Miguel's heart was racing. Unable to steady himself, the cop fell to his knees in a puddle, clutching a rickety fence post to keep from collapsing entirely. Finally he toppled sideways and lay motionless. After a few seconds he stirred again, his legs kicking spasmodically, and then he lay still, face-down in the puddle.

The old man next to Miguel had not even looked up. His dark glasses had deep scratches across the lenses, and the stub of his cigarette dangled from his withered lips.

Miguel stood up and looked around nervously. He walked over to the cop and bent down to get a better look. The man's throat had been cleanly slit by a blade sharp enough to slice through the cartilage of the larynx and leave nothing but a red gash. Blood still throbbed from the wound. Miguel felt dizzy. The heat was unbearable, and the sight of that neat red line and the yellow fatty tissue beneath struck him like a blow. He knelt there, watching the blood seep into the mud and the flies begin to swarm.

"Help! Somebody help!" he yelled, forgetting for a moment that the victim was a cop.

Still yelling, he ran and pounded on the door of the shack, but no one answered. He pounded so hard that the flimsy thing fell off its hinges. The place was empty, just a few old cartons and a ragged mattress flung in one corner. It was a single room with another door onto one of the *favela*'s many narrow alleys. The girl had escaped. Miguel flung open the back door and stood paralyzed, trying to imagine where she had gone. The *favela* spread out before him in every direction, anonymous and terrifyingly empty. It was as if the people had simply evaporated.

Just as he began to despair of finding the girl and decided instead to return to his car, Miguel saw it would not be so easy. In the door frame of the shack, all smiles, stood the men who had so cleanly dispatched the cop. One of them held a gleaming razor and the other a steel chain.

"I'm not with him, I'm not a cop," Miguel stammered.

The men looked at him, expressionless.

"We know," said one, after a few long seconds.

Miguel was careful to keep his hands as far away from his gun as possible; he didn't want any of his gestures to be misinterpreted.

"Hand over the piece," demanded the other.

Anxious to show his cooperation, Miguel reached under his shirt for the gun.

"Slow," warned the man, "real slow. Bring it out by the barrel and throw it on the floor."

Miguel did as he was told. The gun clattered to the floor and he nudged it forward with his foot. The man with the chain picked it up, examined it, and stuck it in his belt.

"We're going for a little walk," said the one with the razor.

"Where to?" asked Miguel.

"There's some people want to talk to you," said the man, placing the razor in his pocket. "Just come with us and every-thing'll be cool."

"Who? What people? The girl, the one who ran in here and disappeared?"

"You don't know them," said the man. "But they must know you. Let's get moving."

"Okay," said Miguel.

They stepped out the back door of the shack and climbed a steep hill. It was still as quiet as a tomb. All the doors were closed, windows shuttered, children rounded up inside. A half hour later they came to a house in a clearing surrounded by a high wall with gaps every few feet just as wide as the muzzle of a gun. The place was a veritable fortress. It was also a whimsical two-story structure, with two Doric columns supporting a veranda and a large crop of sophisticated-looking radio antennas.

Miguel's escorts knocked on an enormous iron gate and a peephole opened.

"We've got him."

The peephole closed and the gate swung open. Inside was a parking area with two Veraneios and a Mercedes. At the front door, wearing a pair of shorts and a blouse rolled up at the waist, stood Haidèe's maid and a fat, aging mulatto holding a Panama hat in his hand.

The mulatto stepped forward, extending his free hand.

"We've been expecting you, Mr. Gouveia."

Miguel shook his hand and looked at the girl, as if for an explanation.

"Don't worry," the mulatto assured him. "You're among friends. Please, let's go inside."

Miguel was ushered into a large living room full of splashy furniture. The place struck him as utterly kitsch. At the back of the room was an altar loaded with candles and ribbons and featuring a statue of Saint George plus another smaller piece of sculpture that looked like some kind of smiling demon.

"I am Dico, Dico of Rocinha," said the mulatto. "And this is my goddaughter, Mariazinha. I'm a very good friend of Senhora Haidèe."

At these words Miguel felt a wave of relief. The room was cold, with two air conditioners silently working away in their niches high on the walls.

"Please, sit down," said Dico. "I have been waiting for you since yesterday. Our mutual friend assured me you would come."

Miguel eased into a leather armchair, relishing the coolness that seeped through his clothes to his sweaty skin.

"How could Haidèe be so sure I would come?"

Dico and his goddaughter sat down on the sofa and an old woman brought a tray of espressos.

"Coffee first. Wakes you right up. Perhaps you'd prefer a shot of *cachaça*, my friend, but I don't permit alcoholic beverages here."

Miguel accepted an espresso without taking his eyes off these two unexpected friends of Haidèe. Unfortunately for him, that woman was an inexhaustible source of surprises.

Miguel drained the tiny porcelain cup, placed it on the tray, and crossed his legs, settling into his chair.

"Do you know where she is?"

Dico shook his head.

"Dona Haidèe is in trouble, my friend. Deep trouble. I've been friends with Haidèe since 1962, and with her husband, the late ambassador. They were both very kind to me, they were always there for me when I needed them. Even during the worst times of my life. I have the greatest respect for dona Haidèe, and for the memory of her late husband."

"Just what kind of trouble is she in?"

"You don't know?" Dico looked shocked.

"I don't know anything. My story is so complicated at this point that even I'm beginning to doubt that it's true. I showed up for a meeting at Haidèe's and—"

"I know," Dico cut in. "My goddaughter told me. That was a dark day for dona Haidèe, as you know, with those phone calls. But she didn't want to ask for help, she didn't even tell Mariazinha what was going on. Luckily, though, my goddaughter is no fool. She listened in on one of the phone calls and got a message to me. I went to see Haidèe right away, but she refused to tell me what was going on. She said there really wasn't any way I could help and that for my own good I shouldn't get involved. I kept insisting, and finally she agreed there was one thing I could do for her. And that was to watch out for you, Miguel, and to give you something."

"What?" said Miguel, intrigued.

"I'll be back in a minute," said Dico, leaping up and striding out of the room.

"You've heard of my godfather before, haven't you?"

Mariazinha's question sounded as if it came from underwater.

"Your godfather? Dico, yes, I'm sure . . ." lied Miguel.

Mariazinha smiled as she got up and went over to a massive rustic wooden table and opened the attaché case sitting on top. It was full of neat packets of money, all five-thousand-cruzeiro notes.

"He controls the numbers game from Rocinha to Pepino Beach. And he owns lots and lots of apartments in Nova Ipanema. He's a very rich man, maybe even richer than dona Haidèe."

"I don't doubt it," said Miguel.

Dico came back and handed Miguel a thick envelope.

"She asked me to give you this."

Inside the envelope Miguel found a handwritten letter from Haidèe and a stack of hundred-dollar bills. He did a quick count and saw that it amounted to something like ten thousand U.S. dollars.

It was a laconic letter. She asked him to fly to Paris and follow the enclosed instructions.

"Is there any way I can help?" asked Dico.

"I'm still in the dark," complained Miguel. "But there's one thing you may be able to explain. Why was Haidèe so sure that I would show up to get this envelope?"

"Dona Haidèe said she's known you since you were a child," said Mariazinha. "She just knew you would find a way to make contact. That's why I stayed at the house. Dico said it was the only way for you to find us. He knew you'd come around, even with the police watching the place. This morning I noticed a different car parked down the street. I looked out dona Haidèe's bedroom window upstairs with binoculars and recognized you. So I waited until after lunch and then left the house. I knew the police would follow me. They've been doing that ever since dona Haidèe disappeared, but I just play dumb. I go to the supermarket or the bakery, chat with the other girls that work in the neighborhood, and just pretend I have no idea there's somebody watching my every move. But today I tricked them."

"If I may ask, what does the letter say?"

Miguel handed the letter to Dico, who read it attentively and handed it back.

"She doesn't say a whole lot," he remarked. "So, Miguel. Are you going to do it?"

"I don't know. My name must be on the Galeão airport's computer honor roll by now. And I don't have a passport."

"If you did, would you go?"

Miguel thought for a few seconds.

"Yes, I think so. I don't have much choice. It may be the only way to find the answers I'm looking for."

Dico nodded.

"If you want, I can hit up a couple of my contacts for a passport, that's no big deal. Of course you won't travel under your real name, but these things can be done very carefully. No slipups. All you have to do is ask."

Before Miguel could open his mouth to answer, a man burst into the room yelling, "There's some men on their way up here, and they don't look like cops."

"How many are they?" Dico wanted to know.

"About twenty, with machine guns," said the man, his eyes flashing nervously.

Dico slapped his fat knee. "Shit, today of all days, when most of my men are gone."

"It's no regular police raid," said the man who had brought the news. "The radio guys talked to our contacts and they said the cops don't know anything about it."

"If it was a police raid we'd have known about it twenty-four hours in advance," said Dico.

There was a burst of machine-gun fire and five more of Dico's men ran through the living room with carbines and 9.5-mm automatic rifles. The house was apparently surrounded and a real battle underway. Already the shooting was intense. Miguel sat frozen in his armchair, white as a sheet, his sweaty hand clutching the packet of dollars.

"You've got to get out of here, Miguel," said Dico.

"How?"

"Come on, Mariazinha will show you."

"But what about the passport?" Miguel was convinced, now more than ever, that he had to go to Paris and follow Haidée's instructions.

Dico was too busy fumbling with the padlocks on a large gate to answer Miguel's question. The gunfire outside was fierce, and suddenly the house was shaken by an explosion.

"My God!" exclaimed Dico. "They've got grenades! The sons of bitches are using grenades!"

He flung open the gate and pushed Miguel and Mariazinha toward a stone stairway. There was no light, but Dico grabbed two lanterns from a cupboard near the entrance.

"Go," he said, handing them the lanterns and shooing them down the stairs. "Follow the tunnel and you'll come out far from here. Do what Mariazinha tells you. And be careful . . ." Dico's eyes widened as he turned back toward the living room and coughed as three bullets tore open his chest and tumbled him down the stairs to their feet.

"No!" screamed Mariazinha.

Another explosion shook the house and the stairway began to fill with smoke, falling mortar, and a blast of heat. Miguel was thrown to a stone landing below, where he landed hard on his back. He struggled to his feet and began heading down toward the tunnel, but then remembered the girl. He found her still kneeling over her godfather's body, cradling his head in her hands and weeping.

"We have to get out of here," Miguel gasped. "Come on, come with me!"

She wouldn't listen, so Miguel grabbed her by the arm. But it was too late: two men had emerged from down below and stood pointing machine guns at them.

"Hold it," shouted one of the men. "Hands behind your head. Come on, this way, nice and slow, unless you want to eat some lead."

Miguel felt the envelope of money slip down inside his pants leg to the floor.

"Upstairs, now," ordered the man, beckoning with his machine gun.

Mariazinha flew at the men, screaming. She got smacked in the head with a rifle butt and fell to the floor, blood streaming from her face. One of the man yanked her by the arm and slung her over his shoulder like a sack of potatoes. They climbed the stairs and returned to the living room. Miguel had lost hope entirely; the envelope of money was lying somewhere on the stairs and would surely be found. And his pursuers finally had what they wanted: him.

The living room was in a complete uproar. Only Saint George's altar remained intact. One entire wall had been destroyed by a grenade and a number of Dico's men lay stretched out on the floor under the watchful machine guns. The bodies of men who had been hit lay wherever they had fallen.

They dumped Mariazinha on what was left of one of the sofas and shoved Miguel down on the floor beside the other prisoners. Miguel craned his neck to see the man directing the operation. He was well-built, needed a shave, and wore a black leather jacket. An automatic pistol hung from his belt in a leather holster with silver studs. But the most striking thing about him was how arrogantly he treated not only the prisoners but his own subordinates.

"You find him?" he demanded.

"Over there, Major," said one of the men, pointing to Dico's lifeless body.

"No, not him. The other one."

"We haven't made the identification yet."

The man in the leather jacket strolled down the line of prisoners laid out on the floor and stopped right next to Miguel's head. He yanked Miguel's hair savagely. Miguel yelled out in pain.

"I'd say it's this one. He's the only white, at least."

He pulled Miguel by the hair until he was upright and then struck him in the face with the back of his hand. Miguel's vision clouded and his ears rang.

"This is him, all right," said the man, furiously shaking Miguel by the hair.

He pulled Miguel aside, separating him from the others. Miguel felt as if his scalp was about to rip right off the top of his head.

"What do we do with the rest of them?" someone asked.

"Take off their pants," said the man in charge. "Strip them down to just their shorts and tell them to get the hell out of here. We've got what we came for, they're nothing to us. Poor fuckers lost their boss, now they're out of a job!"

The men laughed and began stripping down the prisoners, lining them up at what was left of the door. Dico's men stood there awkwardly, chins on their chests, humiliated, trying to hide with their hands what little clothing was left to them.

Finally one of the major's men shouted: "Okay, beat it, all of you. Don't look back, just run on home and hide under your mothers' skirts!"

The prisoners didn't wait for him to change his mind. They were out of there in one wave, disappearing into the *favela*'s narrow alleyways. Meanwhile, the twenty intruders out in the parking area stood around in small groups yipping it up like a victorious army. The Mercedes had been reduced to a pile of twisted scrap metal and the Veraneios were riddled with bullet holes on the outside and pretty well scorched inside.

The man in the leather jacket walked up to Miguel.

"I am Major Portugal—not that you're going to live long enough to do much with that piece of information."

Miguel was still dizzy, his ears ringing and his vision fuzzy. The man's voice sounded hollow, as if arriving from a long way off. The pain Miguel was feeling made his bravado seem small.

"Wake up," said the major, slapping Miguel across the face. "The war's over for you."

"What war?" mumbled Miguel.

Major Portugal laughed, and so did the men circling around to get a look at Miguel, as if he were some kind of dangerous subversive.

"Why did you come here?" He hit Miguel in the face again, the slaps turning to blows and growing in intensity. "Some company you keep, huh!"

The few words Miguel got out were unintelligible.

Someone appeared with the envelope Miguel had dropped on the stairs.

"I found it on the stairs back there," he said. "Must be numbers money. There's five thousand dollars and a letter inside."

He handed the envelope to the major and waited for him to count the money. The major turned away from Miguel for the moment.

"Liar!" he bellowed.

"What do you mean, Major?"

"Hand over the rest. I know you bastards."

"I'm no thief . . ."

The major drew his gun, pointed it at the man's chest, and stuck his other hand in the man's pants pocket. He drew out several one-hundred-dollar bills.

"Yeah, so what's this? Won it on the numbers, did you?"

The man paled and began babbling excuses.

"Shut up!" ordered Major Portugal. "And give back the rest. This money belongs to the operation, no one's laying a finger on it. Anything else in the house you can divvy up."

Looking sullen, the man pulled more hundred-dollar bills out of every conceivable hiding place on his body, while the major looked on and counted.

"There's still three hundred missing."

The man stuck his hand inside his shorts and produced the last three. Major Portugal yanked them out of his hand.

"Now get out of my face. Shit, what a bunch of scumbags. If you don't keep on top of things, they'll steal the beard off your chin."

The other men laughed.

"What are you laughing at?" yelled the major.

The men fell silent and began to disperse.

Miguel was rising to consciousness little by little. He didn't feel nervous or scared; he was observing everything as if a mere spectator.

"We're out of here," said Major Portugal. "This has been a very productive day."

He turned back to Miguel and then paused to read the letter.

"Paris! Well, isn't that fabulous! Plus ten thousand dollars in pocket money, not bad. And just when did you plan on leaving, pal?"

Miguel didn't answer. The provocation couldn't reach him; nothing could reach him at that moment. Not only was his fear gone, but his will, too. A part of him hoped, with some fervor, that they'd just kill him, without even an explanation.

"Let's go," said the major, pulling Miguel by the arm.

Miguel allowed himself to be led out of the room.

"Aren't you just a little bit interested in where we're taking you?"

Miguel didn't even look up. The pain in his back was so unbearable that he was working hard not to pass out. But a ray of hope shot through him when Major Portugal delivered the next provocation:

"Well, I'll tell you. You and I are about to take a little jaunt to Paris."

*   *   *

One of the few exiles Vivian had any ongoing contact with wired her an invitation to a party. Vivian had not gone back to her apartment since the incident; her two African friends had insisted, and she had agreed, to stay at their chaotic apartment on Carrefour de l'Odeon and let them stop by her place every day to pick up her mail. The last thing on Vivian's mind was a party. Carlos still lay in the hospital in a coma; the doctors offered no hope for his recovery. His condition was complicated by pneumonia, presently under control, but the doctors considered it more dangerous than all his many fractures. While Vivian was trying to gather the courage to do as Carlos had asked, she spent her time in the apartment protected by her friends. They were brothers, philosophy students from a middle-class family. Their father held an upper-level cabinet post in Yaounde, Cameroon's capital; his work occasionally brought him to Paris. The older brother, who wore thick eyeglasses, was called Sanga Ekokot, and the younger, lighter-skinned brother's name was Kouma.

Kouma loved parties, and Vivian had promised to bring him to a Brazilian party someday.

"You're not going?" he asked.

"I'm in no mood for a party, Kouma, you know that."

"But you can't stay like this forever," he insisted. "You never leave the apartment, you didn't go to class today. Forget about that Arab, Vivian, you'll never see him again."

Sanga picked up the telegram.

"This must be some rich Brazilian," he remarked. "He lives in the 16th arrondissment."

Vivian had to laugh. Her exile friend was quite a character. A small-framed mulatto from Pernambuco, Rogério was edging toward fifty; he was soft-spoken and neatly manicured, and always dressed in jacket and tie. In the winter he wore a big sheepskin coat with a fluffy white collar.

"Oh, come on, let's go to the party. They'll probably have *feijão, feijoada*," said Kouma, exaggerating the pronunciation of the Brazilian national dish of black beans.

"But the whole frustrated bunch of them will be there," moaned Vivian. "And with Carlos hanging on by a thread, I just don't feel like a party."

Kouma and Sanga knew how Vivian felt about the Brazilian exile community, but still they couldn't understand her reasons completely. She obviously felt guilty somehow that she had more resources than the majority of them, but the brothers saw this as only natural, given that she was such an attractive young woman. What they didn't know was that Vivian simply couldn't stand to listen to the fanciful explanations of those who were in exile more by choice than from necessity and who wore their status like a second skin so completely they were intolerable.

"Do you know this guy pretty well?" asked Kouma, not about to give up.

"Rogério? Sure, he left Brazil in '64, part of the first wave, as we call it. I think he went to Uruguay originally, but was expelled or invited to leave, I don't know the whole story. He's been here in Paris a long time, much longer than most of the Brazilian exiles."

Vivian was not too clear about the Pernambucano's life previous to leaving Brazil, but then it wasn't her style to pry into anyone's background. He had helped her when she was trying to get a student stipend; he had connections in the French Socialist party and was friends with some unionists.

In the end, the persistence of Vivian's friends finally won out. Sanga wore a formal navy-blue suit and Kouma a very American-looking slacks-and-blazer outfit. And though Vivian didn't primp the way her friends did, their excitement was a little bit contagious.

They arrived at the elegant and imposing building on Kleber Avenue and went upstairs in a complicated, ancient elevator. The apartment took up the entire third floor. It was luxurious, somber, and richly decorated with enormous Persian rugs, crystal, fine china, floor-to-ceiling damask, eighteenth-century paintings, and glassed-in shelves full of leather and velvet-bound books. Two middle-aged Frenchwomen, dressed in black and dripping jewels, flanked Rogério in the doorway. There were few guests, and those who had shown up were lamenting the absence of the others, because the buffet and the array of wines were out of this world.

"I'm so glad you came, and brought some friends along, Vivian," said Rogério, smiling and embracing her warmly. "Half the people I invited haven't shown up."

"A lot of them must have been scared off by the address," said Vivian, trying to cheer him. "This place is incredible, Rogério. My congratulations."

Rogério accepted the praise but looked resigned.

"They're fools, the bunch of them," he grumbled. "And when they hear what a fabulous party it was they'll start snubbing me on the street. Well. I'd like you to meet Ninete and Sylvie," he added, indicating the women beside him. "They don't speak Portuguese."

Vivian introduced Kouma and Sanga, whom Ninete and Sylvie seemed to devour with their eyes. Both women were gaunt, as if they had been sculpted from wax, and had graying blonde hair and lusterless cobalt-blue eyes. They looked like twins.

"Make yourselves comfortable," said Rogério.

"We went to Cameroon once," said Sylvie. "It's a beautiful country. Now we're thinking about getting to know Brazil, but we're going to wait for the dictatorship to fall."

Rogério laughed awkwardly and shook his head.

"They sound like aristocrats, don't they?" he said to Vivian in Portuguese. "But they're solid middle class. Inherited an old factory that makes casks for wine and olive oil."

The women didn't blink, though they seemed to know he was talking about them. Rogério would be seen around town with those two strange creatures for the rest of the summer. They affectionately called him their "third world."

"How's our friend Carlos doing?" asked Rogério, returning to heavily accented French. "What a terrible thing. Did he have health insurance?"

"I'm afraid the doctors have just about given up on him," said Vivian. "Only a miracle . . . They say it could be a matter of hours."

"You two were very close, weren't you?"

"Yes. Carlos was a real loner here. His accident was a terrible shock."

Lapsing into Portuguese, Rogério said, "I heard a rumor that it wasn't an accident."

Vivian raised her eyebrows. "I don't know anything about that. What did you hear?"

Rogério shrugged.

"Probably just paranoia. You know how most of the group is— they see agents under every bed."

"I just don't have much patience anymore for that kind of paranoia," said Vivian, heading for the living room. About twenty people were gathered in three circles of conversation. Three

distinct political lines, she was willing to bet. The group from
the Brazilian Communist party was standing beside the fireplace
drinking wine. They were easy to identify, the men in light-
colored sports jackets and fashionable silk ties and the women
in dresses from the Rue de Rivoli and costume jewelry. At the
opposite extreme, gathered around a small gold table laden with
canapés and wine, stood the circle of Trotskyites. They were
substantially younger, dressed more informally, and the men had
disheveled hair. The young women wore counterculture clothing
and looked undernourished. The third group, settled into a set
of brocade sofas and armchairs, seemed aligned with Rogério:
fiftyish, former high-level federal bureaucrats who, after falling
off the ladder of success, refused the charity of the European
left, but still dreamed of the advantages of a genuine solidarity.
Two lonely and displaced Frenchmen circulated from one group
to another in search of acceptance.

"It looks like another one of those parties," said Vivian.

Without waiting for further commentary, Kouma headed for the
buffet. Not that he really liked Western food, quite the contrary—
he thought it insipid and lacking imagination—but he loved to
try anything new and claimed this helped him to get to know
people's souls. Sanga stuck close to Vivian, the two of them
adrift like the Frenchmen. Brazilian music played discreetly in
the background.

Having apparently given up hope that more guests would arrive,
Rogério left his post at the door. The two Frenchwomen had
disappeared. Suddenly Sylvie was back, looking worried.

"I think he did too much," she whispered to Rogério. "I'm
scared. He's hardly breathing."

Vivian picked up a canapé and, for lack of anything else to do,
listened to the woman's weak and tremulous voice and watched
Rogério's growing concern.

"You shouldn't have let him," she complained. "The boy is
out of control."

"He knows what he's doing," insisted Rogério. "What am I
supposed to do—throw him out?"

"Isn't he a friend of yours?" asked Sylvie.

"I hardly know him, he's new here. And he doesn't talk much,
just acts crazy most of the time. The type that simply can't
adjust." He paused. "The regime made a lot of us like that."

Sylvie left the room without another word.

"I couldn't help overhearing," said Vivian. "Anything wrong?"
Rogério shrugged his bony shoulders.

"No, it's okay. No great secret. Just an acquaintance who did
too much coke, apparently. You know how it is."

Vivian accepted his explanation, because Rogério was legend-
ary in the Brazilian exile community. It was said that he had been
First Lady Maria Tereza Goulart's valet, escaping with the presidential family to Uruguay during the last hours of the '64 coup.
Another well-known rumor had him leader of the Peasant Leagues
in Recife, fleeing on a Norwegian cargo ship with a large sum of
money in U.S. dollars, donated on the eve of the coup by certain
North American political groups. Rogério never denied any of the
myths that circulated about him; he seemed to get a kick out of
such improbable stories. Meanwhile, it was clear he was surviving
his exile in Paris with a large dose of imagination and had never
been known to lack the basic comforts. At the moment he was
the privileged recipient of a grant from an international Buddhist
organization with headquarters in Japan. No one could explain
how he had managed this feat, since Buddhists were very rigorous
by nature and generally only granted aid to needy students from
their own part of the world—except to speculate that he had
convinced them that being from Pernambuco was the next best
thing to being Asian. But Rogério's talent for survival didn't stop
there; he was the only Brazilian exile who could come and go in
the Brazilian Embassy without arousing suspicion. And he had
used his position to help a lot of people out of a lot of jams.

Rogério left for a few minutes and returned, clearly concerned.
He refilled his wineglass. The party was not going according
to plan.

"Who is this guy, Rogério? Is he really bad off?" asked Vivian.
Rogério's slanty eyes were inflamed.

"He's just a guy I met on the *métro* one day on his way back
from the embassy. He'd lost all his documents. I felt sorry for
him, so I invited him to the party. He got here early and did a lot
of coke. Just when everyone was due to arrive, I found him lying
here catatonic in the living room. I took him into the bedroom to
lie down and now he's completely out of it."

"I feel sorry for him," said Vivian. She herself was terrified
of losing her papers. It was the Brazilian regime's policy to
make it as difficult as possible, even for simple tourists, to get
new passports. And for an exile this would mean going without

papers entirely or asking the U.N. to help obtain a yellow expatriate card.

"The guy's a lost soul," Rogério went on. "I think that's why he's running from everything and going overboard with the coke."

Vivian could well imagine what he was going through. His plight struck her as emblematic of a new malaise in the Brazilian community in Paris. More and more people—exiled or not—were either simply giving up hope or realizing that the old ideological certainties no longer applied. They searched for escape through LSD, cocaine, and angel dust. A good number of the old partisans were being labeled as examples of the painful ambivalence of the exile, vehemently repudiated by those who considered their compromises either an appalling deviation or a cowardly betrayal or both.

"He got into a fight or something in Marais and his documents disappeared. So he goes to the embassy looking like hell, no money, no papers, nothing. You know how it is these days, they didn't even let him talk to the consul."

"Is he a political exile?"

"No, he's just flipped out. Here on a tourist visa, I think. He's only been here a week, if that. But he speaks good French."

"So what's he going to do?"

"Who knows. Rumor has it he's always on drugs, lots of coke, lots of acid."

"He's going to have to reenter Brazil with some paper from the consulate or something. He won't get a passport, that's for sure," said Vivian.

"The worst of it is that nobody wants anything to do with him. There's even a rumor that he's an agent, which I don't believe. They'd have to be really nuts to hire a guy like that."

Vivian smiled gently at her friend, who was clearly upset by the way his party was going.

"You're a good person, Rogério," she said. "You believe in everyone."

"No, it's not that," protested Rogério. "It's just that he's a fellow countryman in trouble. We can't just throw him to the dogs like the bureaucrats at the consulate."

One of the other guests, a thirtyish Communist party member with graying sideburns, drew near after listening for a while. At the far end of the room, Kouma had found himself a big-breasted

Brazilian who came up to his shoulder. Sanga was just sipping his wine and gazing wearily around the room. This would definitely be his last Brazilian party.

"I think you're being much too charitable," said the party member. "It's fashionable these days to call anyone concerned with security paranoid. Security died of old age, and you know that as well as anybody, Rogério."

Rogério raised the palm of his hand, like an ancient prophet.

"All right, my friend, so maybe I did let down my guard. But so what? We're screwed already, anyway."

"The guy's father is a general," said the man. "We have that from a dependable source. And we're almost positive he's no innocent member of the counterculture. Three days from now we'll have a more complete report on him."

"Why all the interest in this guy, anyway?" asked Vivian.

"Because he's destroying more than his own nasal membranes," answered the party member.

"What do you mean?" Vivian learned forward intently, the image of the knife flashing MADE IN BRAZIL fresh in her memory.

"Well, you know what happened to the *Brasil Insurgente* people, don't you?"

The *Brasil Insurgente* was a mimeographed newsletter published sporadically by a group of exiled CP members, precariously financed by some French intellectuals who called themselves the Bresil Solidarité Committee. The newsletter ran articles on the Brazilian repression; it was printed in French and targeted for European journalists.

"No. What happened?" asked Vivian, startled. The last issue had run an ill-advised interview with Carlos.

"They were all called in by the police."

This was not staggering news to anyone, since the French police were always harassing members of the exile community, dragging them in for hours and hours of questioning. There was a rumor going around that the French police had a secret pact with the Brazilian repressive forces, and no one doubted it was true. Several well-known torturers had been seen parading through the streets of Paris in French police cars.

"The *Insurgente* people made the stupid mistake of putting together the last number at Mirian's house," the guest went on. "You know Mirian—the chunky girl from Dissidence who drags

home any man she meets on the street. Well, that day she'd picked
up your friend with the lost papers and there he was, pretending
to be out of it, the whole time they worked on the paper. He
heard everything. Two days later, before the issue even hit the
streets, they were all called in and interrogated. The police knew
everything they'd said and even had Xeroxes of the articles that
were to appear."

"But it's not an underground paper," argued Rogério. "It's
sold openly, the police know that. Anyone can buy a copy at
Maspero."

"True enough, but how did the police know everything they'd
talked about, can you tell me that?"

"Who was at the meeting?"

The man looked at Rogério in disgust.

"The regular group. Trustworthy to a person, except for that
one guy. The problem is that we're getting lax about security,
blinded by the possibility of amnesty and of being able to go
home. But the regime hasn't been toppled yet—it's still very
much in power."

"It couldn't have been him," said Rogério. "He's too doped
up all the time. If he's here to infiltrate he's doing one lousy
job of it."

The man was becoming more indignant by the minute.

"If we had known he was going to be here, we wouldn't have
come. You have no right to endanger us all like this, Rogério."

A heated discussion ensued, with Rogério trying to play down
the dangers some of his guests saw in the undesired visitor. Not
inclined in the least to participate in this kind of argument, Vivian
decided it was time to leave. She scanned the room for her friends.
Kouma was nowhere to be seen—he had no doubt gone off with
the busty Brazilian. The Frenchman talking to Sanga looked so
earnestly committed to his monologue that Vivian didn't want
to break in. She was on the verge of leaving without saying
good-bye to anyone when her eyes lit on the door through which
the two Frenchwomen had disappeared, the door she imagined led
to the room where the controversial guest was lying in a stupor.
Vivian headed down the long brocaded hallway. The walls were
covered with oil paintings, and she counted six doors. She opened
them one by one and finally found the suspicious visitor.

He was stretched out on the bed, fully dressed, his dirty shoes
lying on a priceless embroidered coverlet from the Madeira.

Except for the little light that shone in from the hall, the room was dark, so that Vivian couldn't distinguish the features of the sleeping man.

She was filled with a morbid curiosity. She wanted to see the young man's face, to know who he was, to satisfy her own paranoia and perhaps avoid him in the future. She tiptoed into the room and approached the bed. She could hear his light breathing and smell the mustiness of a room that got little air.

Standing at the head of the bed, her eyes finally accustomed to the dimness, Vivian froze with her hand over her mouth, unable to scream. She knew that face, she would never forget that sickly, dark-skinned face, attractive under other circumstances, the sloping eyes that gave him a Levantine look. Awake, those eyes would be dominated by something disturbing floating in the brown, bloodshot pupils: it was the "Arab" who had tried to kill her with a Brazilian-made knife. The barely healed scars of the wounds she had inflicted on him were there to prove it.

Trembling, Vivian turned to go, to find Sanga, and to tell Rogério the whole story. But a pair of cold hands grabbed her wrists from behind. She screamed, letting all her terror escape at full voice, until one of the hands clamped over her mouth. Vivian gasped for air, her body bucked and struggled, but the man sat braced against the bed and held her firmly.

Vivian could think of nothing but escape; reduced to the most primal of instincts, she kept thrashing wildly.

"It's no use," the man hissed in her ear. "You might as well save your strength."

He let go of her wrist. She felt a clammy hand run across her breasts. She tried unsuccessfully to bite it. The hand began fondling her more insistently and she writhed and squirmed, humiliated and revolted.

"If you promise not to scream, I won't have to hold your mouth shut."

She nodded her head in agreement.

Still pawing her breasts with one hand, he slowly removed the other from her mouth. Vivian took a deep breath.

"Who are you? What do you want from me? Why do you want to kill me?"

He grasped her right wrist again and twisted her arm behind her back in a typical police move. He lurched from the bed, dragging her along with him, and closed the door. The room disappeared in darkness.

Vivian screamed and felt a terrible burning as her arm was twisted sharply upward.

"You want me to break your fucking arm? Just go on yelling."

"Who are you?" Vivian gasped. Drops of sweat were beginning to run down her forehead and panic was scattering her thoughts.

"I am the enemy," he said. "My name isn't important."

"What do you want from me?"

"Your life!"

A bitter knot rose in her throat and her heart pounded wildly. "But why? What will you get out of killing me?"

"I like to kill," he said.

This dialogue in the pitch-darkness was going to drive her mad. Unable to see her attacker or to defend herself in any way, she felt lost in a nightmare from which she would never awaken.

"But first you're going to do something for me. Two things, actually."

"What do you want me to do?" She might as well talk to him. Maybe it was all a mistake, a misunderstanding. Maybe the man was only an infatuated druggie after all.

"First, you're going to screw me."

"No, not here."

"Why not?"

"Someone might come in."

"I closed the door, no one's going to come in. No one even uses this room. Those two French bitches told me."

He stuck his hand under her dress and yanked on her panties. She began trying to twist and squirm away from him again, but he bent her arm upward until she could no longer bear the pain.

"What's the other thing you want me to do?"

He removed his hand from between her legs. Vivian breathed a sigh of relief but knew it was no victory.

"We're going to take a little stroll to Austerlitz Station."

Vivian broke into sobs. No one would come to save her, they were all in the living room absorbed in their infernal discussions. She was easy prey for this lunatic.

"Okay, I'll go there with you. But what for?"

His answer was to bend her arm even more.

"My arm, for God's sake, it's going to break off."

The pressure on her arm slackened.

"We'd better go now," she said. "It might not be possible later."

There was a laugh in the dark.

"How do you intend to get me out of here?" she asked.

"This apartment has three exits," said the man. "No one will see us leave. Let's go. We'll save the other for later."

Vivian felt herself pushed through the blackness. He opened the door, looked into the hall, and then pulled her after him, her arm still doubled behind her back. They headed the opposite direction from the way she had come. He seemed very familiar with the layout of the apartment.

"Through the kitchen and down the stairs. My car's parked at the corner."

"You can let me go, I won't try to escape."

"No way, baby. You almost did me in the other day."

"Not much chance of that now."

"Okay, but just try something and you'll be very sorry."

Vivian's arm still tingled and burned. She stumbled along haltingly, pushed from behind.

They left by the servants' entrance and descended an iron staircase into an internal courtyard full of trash cans and cartons. The man took her elbow firmly and opened a door. Once out on the street, he led her to a van with dirty windows and a psychedelic paint job that was a bit out of date.

"You're the one who pushed Carlos down the stairs, aren't you," said Vivian.

"The old man tripped. I didn't wish him any harm."

Vivian looked at him with revulsion and held back the desire to spit in his face.

"You don't believe me," he said. "Okay. All I did was help nature along a little. He was already falling apart."

The van rumbled toward the station. Vivian put her head in her hands and cried. Poor Carlos had survived all that he had in Brazil, only to have a deadly assassin throw him down the stairs in Paris.

"The old man was a Communist," said the man, "and you are too, right? I just don't get it—a good-looking, smart girl like you, from a well-placed family, getting mixed up with subversives. It pisses me off just thinking about it, you hear me? Makes me feel like beating the shit out of you, you disgusting bitch."

"I feel sorry for you," replied Vivian, but it wasn't true. She felt like killing him.

"You Commies think you're going to go back to Brazil and start all over again, don't you. Well, you're wrong, you hear me? You think you're being pardoned. You can wear the fucking flag if you want and they still won't forgive you."

Vivian didn't rise to the bait. They had just passed the Jardin des Plantes and she knew he was looking for a parking space. Finally he found one, pulled into it, and turned off the engine.

"Now we're going to get out and do everything just right," he said. "Afterward I might even change my mind about the other thing."

He came around to open her door. They headed into the station and straight for the baggage lockers. An elderly clerk pointed the way without raising his eyes from his magazine. The lockers were on the first floor, near the doors to the train platforms.

"Now I want you to open the old man's locker and hand me what's inside."

He gave her a nudge and she began fumbling around in her purse, stalling for time. She had to think fast or all Carlos' work—whatever it was inside that locker—would be lost. He was getting impatient. She took out the key, checked the number on the card attached to it, and slowly scanned the lockers for the matching number.

"Come on, hurry up," bellowed the man.

His bellowing unnerved her; without thinking she angrily pushed away the hand at her elbow. Surprised, he grabbed for her arm. Vivian pushed him again and ran for the door marked DEPARTURES, where two policemen stood talking.

"Please, Officers," said Vivian, gasping for breath, "that man is bothering me."

He stopped chasing after her and stood uneasily watching the policemen.

"Who?" one of them asked. "That one over there?"

"Yes, that's him. He grabbed my arm and said he was going to rape me."

The policeman raised a whistle to his lips and blew. He and his partner took off across the station, yelling for Vivian's attacker to stop.

He turned and ran back toward the lockers, but there was nowhere to go. He was surrounded. Other policemen appeared and began questioning Vivian.

"I think he's an Arab. You know how they are," Vivian explained, taking advantage of the French's well-known prejudice against Arabs. "He was following me on the street and when I ducked in here to try and lose him, he came after me . . ."

The two original policemen approached with the man in handcuffs.

"Is this the one, miss?" asked the policeman with the whistle.

"Yes, that's him," confirmed Vivian.

The man tried to leap at her.

"You're a dead woman, you bitch!" he hissed in Portuguese.

"What did he say?" asked the policeman.

"I don't know, I don't understand Arabic," said Vivian.

"I'm not an Arab, I'm Brazilian," shouted the man in French.

The police looked at him, then at Vivian, intrigued.

"I'm the one who's Brazilian, officers," said Vivian, "and this man is not speaking Portuguese."

"She's lying," shouted the man.

One of the policemen searched the suspect.

"No I.D.," he reported, "but take a look at this."

He held up a knife found in the suspect's right boot.

"Typical," said his partner.

"Would you like to make a complaint at the precinct, miss?"

Vivian thought for a minute, then decided.

"No," she said. "He didn't actually harm me, since you officers were on hand to come to my rescue. But I hope, since he doesn't have any papers, that he'll have to spend the night in jail. That might teach him a little respect for women."

"As you wish, miss," said the policeman, giving her a little bow.

"May I go, then?" asked Vivian.

"Of course, miss. This one won't be bothering you anymore."

Vivian looked into her attacker's eyes and saw that he was measuring her with hate and murderous intent. But she also could see fear; he was probably wondering how in the world he was going to get out of this fix. Picked up by the police as an underground Arab immigrant with no papers, he could spend months in jail.

   The police pushed the man along toward an annex to the station where the day's prisoners waited to be escorted to the precinct station. Her thoughts rushing in all directions, Vivian headed back to the locker. Inside lay an elegant, executive-style leather attaché case with a handle. She walked out of Austerlitz Station with the briefcase in her hand and practically ran all the way back to Kouma and Sanga's apartment.

   Haidèe opened her eyes. She saw that she was still in the clutches of the paramilitary group. Sitting in a chair near the bed, watching her, was Captain Maurício.
   "Where am I?" she asked in a thin voice, feigning disorientation.
   The captain smiled.
   "The Hilton Hotel."
   Haidèe ran her hand across her face and felt the blood that had crusted on her scalp and hair and down her cheek all the way to the collar of her gray suit.
   "We'll take care of that later," said the captain dryly.
   Haidèe struggled to her feet. She was dizzy and had a throbbing headache.
   Someone pounded on the door. The captain opened it and an agent stuck his head into the cell.
   "There's a message for you in the communications room."
   "Shit," said the captain. "Okay, I'll be right there."
   "Hurry," the agent insisted.
   The captain opened the door a little further and turned back to Haidèe.
   "Very shortly a friend of yours will be arriving—a certain Captain Miguel Gouveia, remember him?"
   Haidèe's throat made a grating sound. She threw him a look filled with loathing.
   Once Captain Maurício followed the agent down the hallway, Haidèe reluctantly sat down in his chair. When the captain returned he no longer seemed so arrogant or sure of himself.
   "We have to leave," he said.
   "Leave? For where? I'm not leaving unless it's to go home."
   "I said we're leaving, damn it!" bellowed the captain, shoving Haidèe out the door.
   He grabbed her arm and pulled her down the hallway. They hadn't even bothered to blindfold her this time. Though somewhat

fuzzy from her headache, Haidèe noted that this must be some kind of farm or estate. And when they reached the parking area, she saw they were not very far from Rio. It was a kind of country house with a large tract of land in one of the neighborhoods near the central station. The house must have originally stood isolated on its plot, but now was surrounded by factories and a burgeoning *favela*. The tracks ran only about two hundred meters behind the back property line.

Haidèe was pushed into a Volkswagen Bug, but they never even got past the entrance to the estate, where several sentries armed with INA machine guns waited to wave them through. Two army vehicles had pulled up and stopped just outside the gate and a small detachment of elite troops armed with automatic rifles climbed out. An elderly man in civilian clothes stepped out of the driver's seat of one of the vehicles. The men on guard inside the gate readied their weapons, but the white-haired man didn't even deign to look at them.

The elite troops approached the gate. Haidèe scrunched down because it looked like a shoot-out was imminent. But as the elderly man got closer the guards began to look indecisive.

From the Volkswagen where she was a prisoner Haidèe yelled, "Lyra! My God, Lyra, it's you!"

The man squinted toward the Volkswagen to see who was calling to him. Captain Maurício looked as if he wanted to slip down beneath the dashboard, like a boy caught red-handed in some prank.

The guards lowered their guns and saluted as General Lyra passed through the gate.

"Lyra!" yelled Haidèe again.

The general recognized her voice and looked worried. He practically ran to the car, drawing his .45 automatic pistol as he did. Frightened, the captain leaped from the driver's seat.

"It's me, General, don't worry, everything's okay," he shouted.

"Get over here, you idiot," ordered the general.

The captain threw his weapon on the ground and obeyed. The general put his pistol away. He turned to the gate and signaled his men. The guards were surrounded and disarmed.

The general strode past Captain Maurício, opened the door to the car, and helped Haidèe step out. Her hair a mess, dried blood on her face, she was in a deplorable state.

"My God, what have these animals done to you?"

All of Haidèe's fear and anxiety rose to the surface, transformed into rage. She flew at the general and began pounding his chest with clenched fists. He dodged her blows, then deftly caught her wrists. Haidèe crumpled and fell to her knees.

"Traitor! Traitor!" she cried hoarsely, over and over.

"Now, no hysterics," blustered the general, shaking her vigorously by the arms.

"Why did you betray me, Lyra? I don't understand."

The general let her fall back again. Tears streaming down her face, she looked up at him wide-eyed and imploring.

"Captain!" shouted the general.

The captain came running and stood at attention, spine straight, his arms glued to his sides.

"So you men think I'm going senile, is that it?"

"No, sir!"

"Why did you bring this woman here?"

"Well, General, it's, um . . . it was just that . . ." stammered the captain.

"Just what are you up to?"

"Nothing, sir. Everything's in order, sir."

The general shook his index finger in Captain Maurício's face.

"I want the whole story, do you understand? All of it. Do you think I was born yesterday?"

The captain remained silent, white as a sheet, his eyes fixed and impassive before the finger dancing in front of him.

"I have my sources, you fool. What do you think, you think I spend the whole day in that office playing around with my secretary or scratching my balls? I'll get to the bottom of this. Times have changed, you cretins."

"I don't agree," said the captain, in a somber voice.

"What did you say?"

"Nothing, sir."

"I asked you what you said, Captain!" thundered the general.

Captain Maurício faced the general squarely.

"I said that I don't agree."

"You don't agree because your head is full of shit," said Lyra, turning away.

The captain stood red-faced now, his mouth trembling with rage. His hands curled against his thighs. He would have physically attacked the general but his sense of discipline and hierarchy were out-shouting his anger.

"Let's get out of here," said the general, pulling Haidèe to her feet. "You'll be grateful to this traitor yet."

Lyra ordered his troops back to the two vehicles and motioned Haidèe into the front seat with him. Maurício's men watched all this like rabid dogs straining at their chains. As humiliated as their captain, they had done nothing only because they remained reluctant to fire against men in olive-green uniforms.

"Just what is going on?" asked Haidèe, tired enough by now of the same question but unsure how else to open the conversation.

The tension was beginning to get to Lyra. He was a thickset man, firmly muscled, with a square jaw and amber eyes that gave him a reptilian look.

"Those boys have gone mad," he said. "We have a lot to talk about, Haidèe. They're going to screw up a few things and burn their own tails in the process."

"How did you manage to get all these soldiers?"

"A favor."

"You military men have all gone completely insane."

The general paled at her frankness.

"It's not insanity, from one point of view. They're well-trained boys, good boys, who love Brazil. And, unfortunately, politics don't always take the country in the direction we think is right. Especially when it's the disastrous politics of a half dozen corrupt men who don't want to share the bone. These boys are actually our healthy side, but they're going to be sacrificed so that the traitors to the Revolution of '64 can go on sucking at the tits of the nation."

"I don't know what you're talking about, Lyra," protested Haidèe. "That song's been sung for an awfully long time. It's time to change the record."

The general fixed her with his hard and furious amber eyes, and spoke from between his teeth.

"I should have left you there, so they could knock a little of the brass out of you."

"Oh, would you really do a thing like that?" she asked, playfully twirling a strand of his white hair.

"Stop that," he said.

Haidèe put her hand in her lap and shifted in her seat; she was squeezed between the general and the corporal who was driving.

"Are you taking me home?" asked Haidèe.

"No, I'm taking you to my house. You'll be safer there. I still don't know what those mad dogs are planning."

Retired since 1976, General Jovelino Lyra was currently president of the Brazilian subsidiary of Life Chemicals, Inc., a Canadian multinational that produced fertilizers and petrochemicals. As a career military man, he had held a string of important posts: chief of the General Staff of the Third Army, commander of the Fourth Army, and chief of staff to the director of the National Information Service—SNI—from 1967 to 1971. His final years of active duty were spent on the bench of the Supreme Military Court, irritating the regime with his hard-line conservative positions. The press accused him of leading an extreme-right paramilitary group, and of having gone to the Geisel administration's deposed minister of the army with a destabilization plan that included kidnappings and assassinations. Lyra never admitted to these activities but never bothered to deny the accusations, either. Haidèe had known him since 1955, when he was a colonel involved in the conspiracy to prevent Juscelino Kubitschek from taking office. But her relationship with Lyra changed drastically in 1970, during the kidnapping of her husband, Ambassador Hugo Jaffet.

It had been Lyra's idea to divert the money collected in a national campaign to ransom her husband from the Tupamaros, a Uruguayan terrorist group, and instead, with the help of the SNI, deposit it in a numbered Swiss bank account. His arguments had been very convincing: he reminded her that her marriage had been over for some time and insisted that, since the terrorists were going to kill the ambassador anyway, she would only end up fattening the coffers of the Uruguayan guerrillas, who were demanding two hundred and fifty thousand dollars (a third of the price asked for the two North American technicians abducted the same day that the ambassador's car was surrounded on a quiet Montevideo street).

General Lyra lived in a spacious apartment in Tijuca and enjoyed his position as a man from the fashionable Zona Norte. He had been widowed since 1975 and lived alone. Lyra's chief concern, after the Communists, was his son Aldo. He hadn't mentioned his son to Haidèe in years; she surmised that he had been committed to a psychiatric hospital. Aldo had always been a troubled boy and had inherited, in the extreme, the anticommunist obsessions of his father, which had led to serious maladjustment and involvement with hard drugs. In recent years, Aldo had been moved from one clinic to another. His mother, an insecure woman of humble origins, blamed herself for her son's state and ended up committing suicide with an overdose of tranquilizers. Lyra had faced his family problems like a tractor plunging ahead blindly over uneven terrain.

An elderly maid met the general and his guest at the door.

"You don't need to make such a face, Matilde," said Lyra on seeing the maid's shocked expression. "My friend was assaulted on the street, but she's fine now."

"Dona Haidèe, come in, come with me and wash your face," said Matilde, ceremoniously taking Haidèe by the arm. "This city, it's just terrible. The other day a mugger yanked the gold chain off my neck, right here in Saens Peña Plaza."

"Now I don't want you scaring her any more than she already is," warned the general. "When Matilde gets started on her litany of tragedies, there's no stopping her."

Grumbling, the maid led Haidèe to the bathroom.

"Let me get you some hydrogen peroxide."

"Thank you, Matilde, but it's just a small cut on my lip."

"What about your head?"

"That's just blood from my lip. I fell down . . ."

"How awful. Did they steal much?"

"Just my bravado!"

"What?"

"Nothing."

After washing up and disinfecting the wound, Haidèe returned to the living room. The drapes were drawn and the apartment plunged into shadow. Though the room was filled with expensive antique furniture, a venerable black-and-white TV perched on a table littered with magazines, and everything smelled of Pine-Sol. Somehow it did not look like a rich man's home.

"When did they get you?" asked Lyra as soon as Haidèe sat down.

She told him about the phone calls and the packet she had sent as a lure, omitting only the details about the contents of the envelope. Lyra listened attentively.

"And you thought I betrayed you," he said when she had finished.

"It was the logical conclusion. You're the only one who knew. They were quite well-informed, they knew things that only you could have told them."

The general nodded and stared at the dusky drapes fluttering in the wind.

"They came to me last October. They were worried about the way the presidential succession was headed. The ousting of General Frota was like a warning signal. Here was a respected leader being treated like a laborer you dismiss with a gesture—and they were frustrated by the lack of support in the high command. It was as if Communist infiltrators had reached the inner sanctum of the military. And the confirmation of General Figueiredo was proof they were being displaced, so that later they could be handed over to the Communists on a platter. I tried to talk them out of it, but they were bent on resisting. I told them it would be no easy battle, that they would be dogged by basic problems such as the total lack of resources and the limitations of working underground. They came to see me twice more and then I heard nothing. But I kept an eye out."

"As far as I can tell, they still have appreciable resources."

"That's all appearances. They're getting something from the governor-elect of São Paulo, organizing a parallel security force for him—that's the seed money for their movement, but it's precarious. Their weapons are outdated, their logistics are weak, and their mobility has been seriously reduced. People who used to have it all at their fingertips have a hard time pinching pennies and still functioning with any efficiency."

"Which is why they want the left's three million dollars."

"That and more."

"I thought so. They laid a few cards on the table, so they could play some others later. I just don't understand how they came by the information."

"I'm investigating that. But meanwhile we have to neutralize them. They're running scared and might do something crazy. They think there's an amnesty program for the terrorists in the works, to be signed after Geisel kills Institutional Act 5. They're afraid the terrorists will use that money to come back and orchestrate their revenge."

"I'd be surprised if the money was still there."

"Me too. But they're convinced it's there for the taking, since Lamarca died before he could use it to buy weapons in Czechoslovakia and Cuba."

"That's crazy. The left had heavy expenses—three million dollars is nothing under those circumstances. I asked a contact

in Paris to check on it, but I haven't heard anything yet. I'm
worried that they've done something to my contact."

"What difference does it make, if the boys have found the map
to the mine, as it were? Even if the left's dollars are spent by now,
which is likely, they'll stumble on the other money and we won't
be able to say a thing."

"Just look what you got me into," complained Haidèe.

"Taking a long view, they're right, you know."

"You're nuts, Lyra."

"No, think about it: the Communists have had time in exile to
cool off and get reorganized. One of these days they'll step off
a plane like persecuted heroes, maybe even with money in their
pockets. Our boys want to pull the rug out from under them as
well as to get back the money that the left raised illegally here,
through assaults and other illicit acts. That way the lefties will
come home with their pockets empty and their hands tied. They'll
have to have charity teas to raise funds for subversion."

"Except that while the left is holding charity teas we'll be
subsidizing a band of malcontents to wreck the country."

Haidèe ran her fingers over her cut lip and looked at Lyra.
During the two years after she deposited her husband's ransom
money in a Swiss bank, Haidèe had received fat commissions for
making other deposits, all in the name of General Lyra. Several
times she had handled cash from prominent figures in the regime,
always under the protection of the federal security apparatus. By
the time the money stopped flowing, after an incident in Geneva
when French treasury agents mistook Haidèe for a specialist in
evasion of foreign exchange from France, she had amassed more
than six million dollars in her own personal account. At the
general's request, she maintained access to his account, since
she had mobility and he didn't want to arouse suspicion. The
other accounts had been given new numbers, and their owners
arranged other agents or personally assumed control. But only
she, General Lyra, and three leftist activists knew about the
original account holding the deposit of the left's money. Two
of the leftists had died in 1971; the remaining one retired from
activism and was living in exile in Paris.

Lyra had always considered Haidèe's assistance to the leftist
group an unnecessary risk, accepting the accomplished fact out
of pragmatism, she imagined, because he needed her for his
own deposits. Haidèe, for her part, did what she did out of

sympathy and friendship for one of the activists. Her friend had been transformed by the hardship of underground life into a tense, suspicious, beaten-down creature, begging her to help his cause in exchange for a small fee. Haidèe accepted the commission because she was professional, but she entertained the initial entreaty out of pure sentimentality. In his younger years— handsome, revolutionary, and virile—Carlos de Almeida Souza Lima had been her first lover.

Haidèe had never trusted Lyra completely. Convinced that she had better protect herself, she tried to keep her financial relationship with him clearly defined, and she slowly and carefully gathered a dossier on the general, which she considered her main security against surprises. The papers she had sent to Lyra at the multinational were a small and explosive part of this dossier. Now it was in the hands of those madmen.

"But how did they find out?" she asked again. "I guarantee it wasn't the leftists who told them. You yourself said there wasn't a word of it in any of their depositions. And I never said a word."

"I don't know. I never told anyone, not even my wife. The documents are in my safe—" He gestured toward the bookcase. "—and I'm the only one who knows the combination."

"What about Aldo?"

"Aldo doesn't know anything, I assure you. And he certainly doesn't know how to open the safe. He tried to break it open once, but he didn't even come close. It's British, utterly dependable. You'd need a blowtorch or a stick of dynamite. And my son is a lost soul."

"Where *is* Aldo these days?"

"At a clinic in Petrópolis. He's been there six months now, in a padded cell, isolated from the other patients. His last attack was truly terrifying. He came at me with a knife—you know how Aldo was always fascinated by knives, ever since he was a child. He collected them for a while."

"Are you absolutely sure he's still at the clinic?"

"Yes, I visit once a month. Not that it's pleasant . . ."

"And you've seen him."

Lyra looked pensive.

"He's not walking too well, he couldn't come out of his cell. The last two months I only watched him through the window. He's doped up all the time because the doctors are afraid he'll kill himself like his mother did."

Haidèe shook her head and noted that Lyra betrayed no sadness, only a sort of mild indignation, as if Aldo had chosen his fate deliberately, just to spite him.

"I'd like to go visit Aldo," she said.

"Whatever for?"

"No reason. I'd just like to see him. You know he used to come visit me years ago. I don't know exactly why he trusted me, called me Aunt Haidèe, but he'd show up at the office. Remember?"

Lyra waved his hand as if to dismiss such memories. Haidèe's eyes were fixed on the dependable English safe.

"You have to find out who's onto our secret," she said. "And stop them before it's too late."

"They don't stand a chance. You're the only link . . ."

Haidèe looked alarmed.

"Not anymore."

"What are you saying?" asked Lyra, forcing himself to seem surprised.

"After the threatening phone calls began, I baited a few hooks. One of them drew a friend of mine into the whole mess."

"For God's sake, who?"

"Captain Miguel Gouveia, the son of that liberal lawyer."

"How the hell did he get involved?"

"He was pushed, actually, without even knowing where he was headed. He's an impulsive young man, very upright, I knew he'd be drawn in if I could just whet his appetite. I left him an envelope with money and instructions for him to get in contact with a certain person in Paris."

"Damn," grunted the general. "He's a dead man."

"Maybe," said Haidèe thoughtfully. "Maybe it was a mistake. This afternoon, just before you arrived, Maurício told me they'd gotten to him. They really are mad dogs, Lyra, you have to get Miguel out of there."

"That'll be almost impossible now. They'll take extra security measures." Lyra's fist pounded the air. "And through him they'll get exactly where they want to go. What a blunder!"

"So what do we do?"

"How should I know? You're the one who screwed up—now you've got to fix it."

"I hope you're not saying I have to get back into things."

"Precisely. You have to get there before they do. Those boys are specialists. They'll sort it out in no time."

Lyra got up and shepherded her to the door.

"Good luck," he said fiercely. "Just pretend you don't know me if everything goes wrong."

Haidèe was staggered.

"But . . . but how can I fight them alone?"

"Why don't you ask your Commie friends for some help?" he asked sarcastically, as if he had just tripped someone up and was enjoying their fall.

Haidèe shot a withering look toward the general and stalked out the door.

It was perhaps the filthiest bar in Lapa, and its Portuguese proprietors didn't even have to work very hard to maintain this distinction. The doors remained open year-round, with the exception of Good Friday, and the grimy imitation marble bar was permanently stained and streaked with dirt. A couple of grubby platters behind cloudy glass offered strange-looking, and perhaps lethal, food to the unwary. Business was scant during the daytime, just a few drunks in the last stages of the D.T.'s, chasing after pink elephants at the only table, until the nocturnal fauna arrived to displace them. Then the bar belonged to the most boisterous, agitated patrons, miserable, loud-talking, loud-dressing prostitutes waging an old war with the drag queens. These regulars would come into the bar, down a shot, and go back outside to the traffic island where they pedaled their merchandise.

An elderly man in a dark suit and hat was clearly out of place there, but no one dared bother him because on the next stool sat an overweight cop, also well along in years, who was not looking too favorably on the women dashing in for a quick drink and then back out to the street, hiking up their skirts for the passing cars.

The elderly man in the suit was visibly uncomfortable.

"Why on earth did you choose this place? It's depressing, to say the least."

The cop spat out the wooden matchstick he had been chewing on and adjusted the gun in his holster.

"This is a good spot, Gouveia. I have to be careful."

"Okay. You said on the phone you had news. Have you heard something about Miguel?"

"Well, I put my dogs on the scent, as you know. And I've got a start on cracking the mystery—your son was picked up this afternoon."

Gouveia almost fell off his bar stool.

"Where is he? What precinct? Is it the federal police?"

Lieutenant Fonseca shook his head.

"Nope. No police involvement at all, in fact. It's what I suspected from the beginning. You have no idea the risk I'm taking."

Gouveia took a deep breath.

"And I don't know how to thank you, my friend."

"Do you have any connections in the Ministry of the Army? That would really help."

"It's DOI-CODI, isn't it? You suggested it yourself the other day. But now you have proof?"

"That's what I thought at first, but it's even more complicated than that. Your son's involved with people a lot worse than the DOI-CODI. It looks as if there's some kind of knife fight going on in the cellars of the military. A lot of people are unhappy with President Geisel's so-called slow and gradual political 'opening.' Miguel's mixed up in this somehow. He's a military man himself, isn't he?"

Gouveia nodded.

"So, do you have any contacts in the military?"

"Not a one," replied Gouveia. "My relationship with this administration has been difficult, as you know. As an attorney representing political prisoners, my relations with the military are adversarial." He stopped to think and lowered his gaze when a near-naked prostitute swaggered in, gyrating her plastic miniskirt scandalously. "Wait. Maybe there is someone, though he's not on active duty anymore. He was Miguel's commanding officer, I met him when I visited Pará. He might still have some influence."

"If I were you, I'd look him up immediately."

Gouveia stood up and extended his hand to his friend.

"Thank you for everything."

"Do you want a lift? Safer than taking one of these taxis."

"I think I'll take you up on that."

"Where does this guy live?"

"The last I heard, he was living in Urca."

"Okay, I'll drop you off."

Gouveia took his friend's arm.

"Maybe it would be better if you came in with me." Fonseca did not look pleased with the idea. "Would you do me that one more favor? It's just that the word of a police officer would carry more weight. And this is a serious matter."

Fonseca shook his head and furrowed his brow, as if he had taken a swallow of something bitter. Then he gestured toward the door and said, "What we won't do for friendship's sake."

As far as Gouveia could remember, the man they were looking for lived in a small four-story building on avenida Marechal Cantuaria. A doorman opened the door, looking shocked to see the police car parked out front.

"Good evening," said Gouveia, removing his hat. "I wonder if you could help me . . ."

The doorman mumbled something that Gouveia chose to take as consent.

"Does General Barros live here?"

"Second floor," said the doorman.

"Is he at home?"

"Probably. He hasn't been able to get out at all lately, with his sore foot. Twisted it playing tennis."

"Then we'll go up and talk with him," said Gouveia, motioning to his friend, who had remained in the police car.

After scrutinizing them through the peephole, General Barros' wife answered the door.

"Good evening, ma'am," said Gouveia stiffly, his hat in his hand. "We'd like a word with your husband. We know he's laid up, but this is urgent."

The woman didn't know what to do. Gouveia looked eminently trustworthy, but she knew her husband was in no mood to receive unexpected visitors. Having his foot in a cast had transformed him into an extremely touchy creature, apt to explode over the tiniest thing.

"I'm sorry, but I'll have to ask you to wait out here in the hall. If you give me your names, I'll tell him you're here."

Gouveia tried to act calm and understanding, but he was anxious and flushed.

"I am Dr. Edmundo Gouveia," he said, handing her his card. "Please tell your husband it's in regard to my son, Captain Miguel Gouveia, whom I'm sure he'll remember."

"Just a minute," said the woman, closing the door.

They waited a few tortuous seconds before she came back and escorted them into the living room. An obese man in blue pajamas, his leg in a cast propped up on the coffee table, sat watching television with the sound off.

"Good evening, gentlemen. Please, sit down," he said. "What can I do for you?"

"It's my son," said Gouveia. "Miguel is in great danger . . ." He fell silent, looking for signals that the general's interest was piqued. "This is an awkward situation. I'm not sure where to begin."

The general picked up the remote control and clicked off the TV.

"Begin at the beginning," he said. "I've been following the reports about Miguel in the papers. What's really going on?"

Gouveia summarized the events with his customary precision, holding back nothing, and the general listened attentively. General Barros had been very understanding during Miguel's difficult time in Belém, but he had not moved a muscle to prevent his young officer from leaving the army. He had limited himself to a kind of formal expression of solidarity, as if going any further would have meant venturing into mined territory. Once Gouveia had finished his story, he was no longer sure that approaching the general would produce a solution. But perhaps he'd be proven wrong.

"This is a very serious situation," admitted Barros, his pale eyes filled with concern.

"There are a couple more details," offered the weary old cop who had remained silent and unobtrusive, sitting in a chair near the TV.

"I told him everything you told me," said Gouveia, surprised. "Unless there's something you've been keeping to yourself."

"There are a few twists I've been trying to corroborate, without much success so far. If the general is interested . . ." Gouveia looked extremely nonplussed. "Forgive me, Gouveia, but there are certain things that a police officer shouldn't even tell a friend."

"Miguel has a short fuse," said the general. "But he was right, God knows he was right. I've always been against using the army for these things. It's the police's job to combat subversion. In the instance we're referring to, anyone could see that there would be excesses and that the armed forces would be called in. Excess corrupts and, by God, I never thought I'd see the day the armed forces of Caxias and Rondon would torture prisoners like the Haitian *tontons macoute*. But what can you do? Like it or not, I had to keep silent, I had to swallow it. And now we see the result."

Gouveia and his friend nodded soberly. The general's words were heavy with bitterness and guilt.

"Miguel was one of the officers who saw the absurdity of it all. The misusing of the military hit him very deeply because he was a professional. But his hands were tied, like everyone else's." Barros sat in silence for a moment. Then he turned to Fonseca, indicating for him to resume his story.

The lieutenant shifted nervously in his chair.

"Two incidents were reported today. A numbers game fortress was attacked in Rocinha, with an unknown number of dead and injured. The official line is that it was part of a bookies' war, but I know a little about the racket and I talked to some of my people on the street. They swear there's no such war and they're scared. One guy told me it was army troops who stormed the Rocinha fortress. He couldn't figure the motive, but suspected the military was instigating some sort of showdown."

"And the second incident?" asked the general tersely.

"The second occurred out near the central station. Two army vehicles stormed some country estate. The First Army not only denies the operation but insists it didn't happen. The estate belongs to a major by the name of Henrique Portugal, formerly of the DOI-CODI, now retired. We'd been keeping tabs on the place because we suspected it had become a base for a group of hired guns who do commercial work, protection services, stuff like that, and sometimes just eliminate the suspected thief. The investigation never got very far, and we never even came close to busting the place, because all our efforts were shut down from higher up, from the commissioner's office itself. But I have a feeling that these two incidents are somehow linked to Miguel's situation. I think there's even a chance that the estate near Central is where he's being held."

"These groups obviously have strong backing," said the general, "but there must be something we can do. Miguel could easily be killed. And if he's mixed up in this, it can only be because he discovered something terrible."

"I don't understand," said Gouveia. "Miguel was never interested in politics. He's no longer connected to the military, he had a good job . . ." Gouveia shook his head and fell silent.

"Miguel is an idealist," said the general. "His rebellion was a lesson to me. I think you'll understand when I confess that I never had the kind of courage he did. When you're in the middle of a thing it's very difficult to judge what's best. There were times I condemned Miguel's attitude, but it was just to quiet my conscience. The truth is that what happened to him laid me low for a long time. I'd had confidence in him, I'd expected him to have a brilliant career. But the times were wrong."

"There's one more thing," said Fonseca.

Both General Barros and Gouveia looked at him expectantly.

"The group on the estate has ties to General Lyra."

"Lyra! That doesn't surprise me," exclaimed the general. "It's men like Lyra who are standing in the way of President Geisel's cleanup program. Just as I feared. When it's time for a major housecleaning they disappear into the woodwork like roaches. It's not going to be easy to neutralize that bunch."

The general pulled a small table with a telephone toward him.

"I'm going to make an appointment to see the commander of the First Army. He's a Geisel man and should be very interested in this story. Let's see if we can save Miguel and prevent God knows what else those malcontents have up their sleeves."

He dialed the phone and exchanged a few words with the person who answered. "It's his wife," he said, with his hand over the mouthpiece.

The commander came to the phone and the general asked for an appointment as soon as possible about an urgent matter, tomorrow if possible. He didn't specify what he wanted, but indicated that it had to do with irregularities in the area of security.

"Tomorrow, nine-thirty," the general passed along to his visitors. "I'll meet you there. I may be retired, but I'm not dead."

"Forgive us for troubling you," said Gouveia. "With your foot in a cast and everything . . ."

"It's no problem, believe me. I'd get up and go after those radicals even if I had only one foot."

They said good night. The general turned the TV back on as his wife accompanied them to the door. Gouveia bowed to her in parting. Lieutenant Fonseca walked on ahead compulsively fingering the gun in his holster.

"I'm done for, Gouveia," he said as soon as they were in the elevator. "I'm going to end up with my mouth full of ants for sure. Do you really think we can trust this guy?"

"I don't know. We have to. Speaking of which, why didn't you tell me about those other two incidents?"

The elevator door opened and the cop coughed, avoiding a response.

"Really. I don't understand. Why?" insisted Gouveia.

"Because you're crazy, my friend. I thought if you knew about that estate, you'd storm the place with a band of shysters, the penal code in your right hand and the Constitution in your left."

"Of course I'd do something. I can't just leave my son in the hands of those butchers."

They got into the police car and the cop looked at his friend sitting haughtily beside him.

"I'm taking you home, Gouveia. This is no time of night for an old man like you to be wandering the streets."

One of the routes out of Urca was a bridge over an arm of sea. The two rode in silence. Gouveia gazed out at the bay full of pleasure boats bobbing on the glassy water. He was thinking about Miguel, about the boat his son had bought when he lived in Pará. A small boat, four-hundred-horsepower, used for cruising around the twists and turns of the Amazon's tributaries. Miguel had been forced to sell the boat, among other things, when money got tight after he left the army. And Gouveia also thought of his grandson, who was showing signs of insecurity, no doubt in large part due to Miguel's sudden changes in fortune. But that was life, and Gouveia really didn't have anything to complain about. Miguel was an honest man, he didn't let himself be humbled easily, and he had chosen a woman with a lot of personality.

"Damn! We're in serious trouble now, Gouveia."

A car was parked sideways up ahead, blocking their lane, its lights out.

Fonseca shifted into reverse, but another car materialized to close off their retreat. He turned off the ignition and grabbed his revolver.

"Do these bastards really think they can hold up a police car?"

Three men armed with machine guns surrounded the car.

"Don't try anything foolish," one of them shouted. "Throw your weapons out of the car."

"Shit!" grunted Fonseca, tossing his gun out the window. "That's the only one," he shouted back. "My friend is unarmed, he's a lawyer!"

One of the men approached and peered in the window on the driver's side.

"Good evening, Officer," said the man. "Aren't you a long way from your precinct?"

Fonseca didn't answer. He knew who these guys were, even though he'd never seen them before. His cop's instinct never failed him.

"It's them, all right," yelled the man to the others.

The other two approached.

"You were pretty well-behaved today. But the illustrious attorney just didn't look right in that bar in Lapa."

Fonseca opened his mouth to speak but decided against it.

"Right. You're better off keeping it buttoned up," said the man.

Gouveia was in a state of shock. He felt his body stiffen and his heartbeat become slow and erratic. When he saw the men had machine guns, he knew this was no ordinary assault. These were a different breed, for which it was no daring feat to intercept a police car. In their case, the barriers that for centuries had separated bandit from police simply didn't exist.

"How was your little talk with that lame general in pj's?" asked the man, smiling. "Did he show you a bellyful of bravado?"

Little by little Gouveia was emerging from his state of shock, reaching a level of alarming indignation, which was prodding him to act, to confront these butchers who were keeping his son prisoner somewhere.

"You're going to be sorry," he said, unable to contain his rage. "You are the shame of the country . . ."

"Well, well, well," chuckled the man. "If it's not the illustrious Dr. Gouveia, defender of Communists. Did you complain to the general too?"

"I'll live to see you and your accomplices sentenced in court."

The man laughed tauntingly.

"I hate to disappoint you, Dr. Gouveia, but your career as a defender of subversives seems to have come to an end."

Fonseca shifted behind the wheel.

"And yours, too, Lieutenant," the man added.

"You're not about to do anything that foolish," said Fonseca, cold, emotionless. "It wouldn't make sense. You're professionals and you know that as well as I do."

"Smart thinking, Lieutenant. Relax, we're just here to give you a warning."

"I'm listening."

"We're on our way to have our own little chat with General Barros, who, by the way, happens to have a tail made of straw that he's not about to let catch fire, but first we want to set you straight about something. Forget your little plan, whatever it was. It won't work. And you might just get hurt." He paused to note the effect and went on. "Come to think of it, I'd like to know exactly what you three cooked up. What was the plan?"

Fonseca remained silent.

"You'd rather not say?" roared the man, nudging the cop with the barrel of his machine gun. "These suckers drill holes in people with the greatest of ease—they're made in Brazil, after all."

"Do you have Miguel?" asked Gouveia.

"Answer my question, Detective! What did you set up with Barros?"

Fonseca let out a sigh.

"He made an appointment to see the commander of the First Army. Tomorrow, at nine-thirty. We're supposed to meet him there."

"That won't be necessary. Barros is going to cancel. You can sleep in tomorrow."

The men withdrew to their own cars, but then the one who had done all the talking returned and planted himself at the window once more.

"Oh, I almost forgot! Your son is fine, Dr. Gouveia. But his health depends on you now. Do as I say and it's quite possible that Miguel will be able to tell this adventure to his grandchildren someday. Play it smart, and everything will work out fine. But I have to say: if that meeting takes place tomorrow, or any other day, it's a good bet you'll lose not only a son but a grandson also."

"You scum!" shouted Gouveia, as the man walked off to his car and sped away. Fonseca started the engine and headed across the bridge. They traveled in silence all the way to Gouveia's house. They were crushed, powerless, and looked as if they had aged several years.

As Gouveia walked into his apartment building, his friend's parting words echoed in his ears: "Don't do anything without talking to me. I haven't given up either."

Ruth was getting tired of pacing back and forth in front of Bob's Luncheonette with a cup of orange juice in her hand.

She thought it was unlikely that Rosa would show up, since they had just met earlier that day and maybe Bob's wouldn't begin functioning as a meeting place until tomorrow. But Rosa had been clear that this was the place to come if the need for contact was urgent. Not that Ruth had any new news or any specific urgency, but she was feeling vulnerable and so at a loss for ideas that when she left campus she decided to come to Bob's on the off chance that Rosa would turn up. At least she might hear something concrete about Miguel and feel closer to him that way.

Office workers from the various businesses in the building were getting off work and the sidewalk was thronged with people. Ruth was on the verge of giving up when a young, dark-haired woman who looked vaguely familiar walked up to the counter. Finally she said something to the cashier, throwing what looked like urgent glances at Ruth all the while, clearly not the least bit interested in the food she'd ordered.

Ruth studied the girl, wracking her brain, and then it hit her. It was Haidèe's maid, the one who had annoyed her so much that morning in her bikini with her insinuations and idiotic remarks. Her arm was bandaged, and she was limping. Ruth had just decided to approach the girl when Rosa appeared. She was wearing the same clothes she had on at the university, and she was very sweaty, as if she had walked a long, long way.

"Thank God you came," said Ruth. "I thought maybe the plan to meet here didn't start until tomorrow."

Rosa looked as if she were on the brink of bursting into tears.

"Have you heard anything about Miguel?" asked Rosa. "Has he been in touch with you?"

"No, I haven't talked with him since the phone call last night. Did something happen?"

Rosa held back the tears. "Well, he took my car this morning. He said he was going to try to contact that woman Haidèe, and he promised to call me twice, at ten and three. But he only called at ten. I waited and waited for the second call, but nothing. I just felt so scared I decided to run over here."

"Did he tell you how he was going to try to get in touch with Haidèe?" Ruth barely had enough voice to get the question out; she was on the verge of nervous exhaustion.

Rosa shook her head. "No. He didn't tell me anything, which makes it pretty hard for us to help him."

Ruth's eyes wandered nervously from Rosa to scan the crowd in the luncheonette.

"What is it?" asked Rosa.

"I saw someone here, a woman. She works for Haidèe. She kept staring at me while I was standing here waiting for you."

"Is she still here?"

Ruth nodded. "See the girl over there with the bandage on her arm?"

"Let's go talk to her," said Rosa impulsively.

"Do you think we should?" Ruth was looking all around now, examining the passersby and carefully registering each face. She thought it odd that the police seemed to have suddenly lost all interest in following her.

Rosa hesitated a minute, then decided to follow the impulse.

"Let's go. What the hell."

The girl looked panicked when she saw the two women striding decisively toward her. She threw what was left of her food in a trash basket and limped out onto rua 7 de Setembro. But it wasn't hard for the two to catch up with her.

"Wait a minute," said Ruth, grabbing the girl's arm.

Mariazinha whirled to face them.

"Let go of me," she said, jerking away. "I don't know you!"

"You're Haidèe's maid," said Ruth. "Why were you standing there staring at me?"

"I don't know what you're talking about . . ."

Ruth was about to explain, but two large black men appeared and towered meaningfully over them. Passing pedestrians squeezed by the group without paying any attention to what was happening.

"Leave her alone," warned one of the men.

Mariazinha heaved a sigh of relief.

"It's okay, Tico. They didn't do anything."

The other women noticed that Tico and his friend had more in their jacket pockets than their hands: they were armed.

Rosa began trembling and leaned against Ruth for support.

"Who are they?" Tico asked the girl.

"That one's the guy's wife—and the other one I don't know."

"Yes, I'm Miguel's wife," said Ruth, but this information didn't seem to make a dent in the man's aggressive manner. She decided to concentrate on the girl. "Why are you here, at the exact same place I arranged to meet my friend?"

Mariazinha lowered her eyes and displayed none of the arrogance of that morning at Haidèe's.

"Just chance. I didn't know anything about you or your meeting. My cousin here does security for one of the offices in the building. I came to see him."

"Where is Haidèe?"

Mariazinha shrugged her shoulders.

Ruth grabbed her by the collar. "Where is she? If you don't tell me, I'm going to make a real scene. Your cousins can shoot me if they want, I couldn't care less."

Mariazinha just stared at her, dumbfounded, and the two men remained frozen in place. Passersby were beginning to turn their heads to see what was going on.

"All right," said Mariazinha. "I know where she is. You can come with us."

"This is not part of the plan," protested the cousin.

"Haidèe knows her," explained the girl, "it won't be a problem." She turned to Ruth. "But it really was chance I was here, I swear it. I've been through so much today. If I'd known what was going to happen, I wouldn't have promised to help my godfather and none of this would have happened."

"Let's go if we're going," said Ruth. Still leaning on Ruth for support, Rosa was shaking so hard her legs hardly held her up.

The men led them across avenida Rio Branco. It was a strange group: two tall black men leading a limping girl and two women, one of whom seemed to be dragging the other along by the waist. But no one they passed seemed to bat an eyelash.

They piled into a light-blue, extremely well-preserved Galaxy, the men up front and the women in back. The driver was a smiling mulatto, who had been waiting behind the wheel. They crossed the street and headed for Vidigal. A half hour later they arrived at one of Dico's fortresses, an uninhabited condominium. Haidèe met them at the door, accompanied by a middle-aged man, almost an exact duplicate of the deceased numbers king. The man was silent the entire time, though it was no secret to anyone that he was in charge. Mariazinha began to cry and Haidèe embraced her warmly.

"Try to calm down, it's all over now," she said, patting the girl's back. "Come on, let's stop crying." Haidèe looked up at the other women, who were watching the scene in bewilderment. "Forgive me. Please sit down. We have a lot to talk about."

Ruth led Rosa to a chair and sat down beside her. She was speechless, at a complete loss to understand what she was seeing. The two men having disappeared into another part of the building, Haidèe settled Mariazinha into a chair and remained standing herself.

"How did it happen, Mariazinha? Tell me everything," ordered Haidèe.

Mariazinha stifled her tears and began talking. The more of the story she heard, the paler Ruth became. Rosa seemed to be lost in a swoon, her head tilted to one side, her eyes wild. The man who looked like Dico's double watched and listened impassively.

"Thank God you got away," said Haidèe, relieved.

"The only person they wanted was your friend Miguel. They left me in Jacarepaguá. They sent all my godfather's men off half-naked, just to humiliate them. I called Jamelão right away, because I knew things would get crazy."

Dico's double nodded knowingly.

"Jamelão knew how to handle it," said Haidèe, pride in her voice. "And I don't know how to thank him."

He shrugged off her praise.

"Jamelão told me to get in touch with my cousin Tico, who would know what was going on and would bring me here to see you. You have no idea how awful it was . . ." Mariazinha looked at Haidèe, and controlled her tears. "And then when I was waiting for Tico I ran into Miguel's wife and her friend."

"It's okay, my dear. You did what you had to." Haidèe removed an envelope from her purse. "Now you're going to take some time off, a little vacation away from all this. Tico is going to take you to the interior of Minas, where you'll stay until I send for you."

Mariazinha nodded and accepted the envelope. Tico appeared in the living room and took his cousin by the arm, as if even the timing had been prearranged.

"Have a good trip," called Haidèe. "I won't forget what you did for me, my dear. Your godfather would be very proud of you."

Mariazinha left in a torrent of tears set off by the reference to her godfather.

Haidèe sat down at the desk and looked at Ruth.

"I'm all alone now, my friend. Depending on the friendship of some very brave people."

Ruth shook her head as if trying to put her thoughts in order. Her mouth was dry and her tongue thick.

"I understand how you must be feeling," said Haidèe, her voice softening and an expression of sympathy spreading across her face. "I'm sure it's been very difficult for you."

"They're going to kill Miguel," said Ruth, hardly recognizing her own voice it sounded so shrill.

"No. No, they won't do that, at least not for a few days. He's only useful to them alive. He's the one link they have to what they want. Or at least that's what they think."

Ruth opened her mouth to say something, but Haidèe went on.

"I'm going to tell you everything," she said. "But first, come in the bedroom. I want to show you something."

Rosa sat stock-still in her chair as Ruth followed Haidèe into the bedroom. What Ruth saw almost knocked her over. She closed her eyes and turned her back, her hands hiding her face.

A man lay stretched out in his underpants, handcuffed to the bed. Five armed black men stood guard. The man was breathing hard, his face distorted by multiple hematomas, his chest covered with cigarette burns.

"Ironic, isn't it?" said Haidèe. "He's made a career of doing precisely this to political prisoners. And when the tables were turned he showed what a true coward he is—he started talking at the first blow. But I just couldn't control the boys, they were out of their minds after what happened to their boss."

"Who is he?" asked Ruth.

"Corporal Farias. He works with Major Portugal, the man who is keeping Miguel prisoner."

"God in heaven . . ." Ruth's voice was hushed and fragile now. "Why is all this happening?"

Haidèe explained what she knew, from the threatening phone calls to the attack on her friend Dico's gambling fortress. She told how she had been captured and then rescued.

"Now those madmen are organizing something called the New Brazil Brigade. They want to provoke a series of riots, to create a difficult climate for the government in this transitional period."

"What does Miguel have to do with all this?"

"Nothing, directly," replied Haidèe.

"Then why . . ." Ruth stopped. She didn't want to hear the answer. It didn't matter anymore. All she wanted was to be able to think clearly about how to proceed, what to do without irreversibly compromising Miguel, who was caught in the middle of all this madness.

"Miguel is doing me a very big favor. And I'm sure he'll continue doing himself proud."

Ruth turned to confront Haidèe. Her small eyes radiated hate. "It was you, wasn't it. You're the one who got him mixed up in this. You lured him into a trap!"

"I had no choice," said Haidèe, not the least bit fazed by Ruth's attack. "And I read the situation correctly. I just didn't think they would take things this far. I've already lost two close friends." She sat down, pensive, and then added: "But they'll be sorry."

"But what do they want from you? That's the one thing you haven't told me, Haidèe. Why did they want to get to you in the first place?"

Haidèe's lips twisted into a scowl.

"Money," she said coldly. "Money, my dear."

"Don't call me dear."

Haidèe accepted the rebuff with a wave of the hand, as if to chase away the words.

"We haven't got much time," she said. "Corporal Farias told us some interesting things. It seems that Geisel is planning to revoke Act 5 in a matter of weeks, as part of the beginning of an ongoing liberalization of the regime. Major Portugal and his men are preparing a series of provocative actions in the next few days to try to subvert the Geisel plan. I don't know all the details; this poor devil didn't have that kind of access. But within five days they plan to assassinate ten well-known figures—politicians, businessmen, and a couple of cabinet ministers. The wheels have already been set in motion and we're going to have to run to keep up. If they succeed, the president will have to change his course and get tougher instead of more liberal. It's utter madness . . ."

Ruth said nothing. Haidèe words were difficult to digest and she herself felt too shaky to think straight. All she could think about was Miguel, trapped in his own powerlessness and facing down that crazed machine.

"You should talk to your father-in-law. He's a man of wide experience, he probably already knows a lot of what's going on. You need to mobilize well-known friends and acquaintances, put the respectable sectors of society on alert."

"And what about you?" said Ruth, almost shouting. "Why don't you come along with me and explain all this to Dr. Gouveia?"

"Because I don't have time. There's something that must be done which only I can do." She looked at her watch and shook her head. "If I fail, Miguel's life will be worth nothing, and they will win."

Ruth's back stiffened and her voice came out a harsh murmur: "Someday I'm going to make you pay for this."

"Perhaps," replied Haidèe, indulging her. "But it couldn't be avoided. Miguel is my margin of error. And he's worked out better than I ever could have imagined."

Haidèe waved her hand as if to shoo Ruth away.

"Go on, what are you waiting for? Drag your friend out of here and go straight to see your father-in-law. Leave the rest to me."

Ruth left, promising herself that one day she would smash the face of that amoral woman who manipulated people without the slightest scruple. In Ruth's mind, Haidèe's actions were as obscene as those that took place in the cellars of the military regime.

Miguel's parents' apartment had never seen as much traffic as it did that night. Sedated, still in a state of shock, Rosa was resting, at dona Rita's insistence, in the couple's own bed. She had aroused a great deal of curiosity in Luciano. The boy had spent the day under the strict supervision of his grandmother, forbidden to leave the house, and he was grumpy and sullen. He had, in the past, demonstrated certain traces of his grandfather's obstinance, and Miguel took pride in this, but Ruth didn't have the same patience and frequently found herself flying off the handle. Given present circumstances, his obstinance was only natural. He wanted to help, he was struggling to participate in the adult world, to share the responsibilities however he could, but he was being pushed aside and treated like a child. Although the grown-ups weren't hiding anything from him, the facts in their complexity eluded him, and he took this as a veiled way of keeping him safely removed from what was going on. It had been clear since he was very little that Luciano was not born to be a mere spectator, which was precisely why his grandmother had redoubled her vigilance, fearing some impulsive action on his part.

Ruth had arrived at the apartment, dragging Rosa along with her, before her father-in-law got home. Luciano was in the living room and had come grudgingly to offer his help. Dona Rita was on edge because Gouveia had left his office in the middle of the afternoon without telling her where he was going and she had heard nothing from him since. Ruth gave vague reassurances to her mother-in-law, but she could see that Luciano wasn't buying a word of it. Once dona Rita had busied herself with Rosa, settling her into the bedroom and calling a neighbor who was a doctor, Ruth took the opportunity to level with her son. She gave him a less optimistic and abbreviated view than she had Miguel's mother, omitting only the most violent and repellent details. Luciano listened intently, asking no questions. When she had finished, he refused to let her give him a hug.

"Don't you have anything to say?" asked Ruth.

"What can I say?" he answered, frowning.

Tired and anxious as she was, Ruth was short on patience, but she could feel the fear and confusion emanating from her son.

"It's always Dad," he said.

"This isn't your father's fault."

"He's always getting mixed up in stuff like this. And who's that lady? Where did he meet her?"

"At the meditation center in the country. It was just a chance meeting."

"You mean he really didn't know her before?" he asked, incredulous.

"I don't think so, but she was a big help to him. I'm very grateful to her."

Luciano's lips narrowed. "Dad's some piece of work . . ."

"What do you mean by that?"

"Nothing . . . I was just thinking about some things."

"What things?"

"Dad's not . . . well, he's not mixed up in the drug business, is he?"

Ruth's heart clenched. For the past three years Miguel had been smoking pot every once in a while. She'd actually tried it too, but felt foolish and decided never again. And she had disapproved of his doing it openly at first, lighting up in front of the boy, acting ridiculous, giggling at the slightest provocation. When she complained that it made Luciano nervous as well as intrigued, Miguel got mad and called her a square, a conservative, accused her of wanting to raise the boy under a bell jar. Luciano was ten years old at the time and of course understood what was going on, though his father refused to accept the possibility. Now she had proof.

"Of course not, Luciano. What an idea!"

"Well, he used to smoke pot—did you think I didn't know?"

"He was just experimenting, Luciano, he wanted to know what it's like." It upset Ruth to have to defend Miguel this way. "If he were really mixed up with drugs, I wouldn't hide it from you. I've never lied to you."

"Does that lady smoke pot?"

"Her name is Rosa, and I don't know anything about what she does and doesn't do."

Luciano apparently accepted his mother's explanation and, as if to avoid prolonging an awkward scene, got up and headed for his grandparents' bedroom.

"I'm going to check on how she is. She dresses like the people at the hippie craft fair in Ipanema. I think it's cool."

Around one A.M., when dona Rita was beginning to think about calling hospitals and police stations, Gouveia arrived home, looking simultaneously indignant and down in the mouth.

He walked in, took off his jacket, and loosened his tie, which under ordinary circumstances he never did in front of his daughter-in-law, much less in the living room. Noticing how worried the two women looked, he assured them he was perfectly fine and then launched right into what had happened and why he was so late getting home. His life generally followed a rigid daily routine: he rose at six, showered, shaved, and read the newspapers over coffee. Then he worked on his cases until ten, when he left for the office. For thirty years he'd lunched at the same downtown restaurant; by six o'clock he was invariably at home reading or talking with his wife. This routine was only broken when he was invited to lecture at the law school or at the Order of Attorneys of Brazil, the OAB, of which he was a member of the executive board.

When Gouveia had finished with his story, Ruth told him about her unexpected and surprising meeting with Haidèe and the numbers racket people.

"I'm not giving up," insisted the old lawyer. "Tomorrow I'm going to drag that general out of his house if I have to. There's no way I'm going to miss that appointment with the commander of the First Army. And I want you to come with me, Ruth."

Gouveia stumped off to his book-lined study. Ruth followed, because she was worried about him.

"They're not going to let us keep that appointment," she said. "They already threatened to use violence."

"They don't have the moral stature to stop us."

"I don't know, Dr. Gouveia. I'm afraid for you."

"None of that, my dear. Right now I'm going to sit at my typewriter and get everything I know down on paper. I could use your help; we don't want to leave out a single detail. This document must be as complete as possible, including every name we heard and everything Haidèe told you. I'll make copies. In addition to handing this to the commander in person, we'll send copies to the president of the OAB, the president of the National Congress, the minister of justice, the minister of the army, and to President Geisel himself."

"Do you think your document will really get to those people? And if it is delivered, will it be taken seriously?"

"Yes and yes. Because we'll send copies to the press. I'm going to call the president of the Brazilian Press Association and a couple of journalist friends. And we'll have the others hand-delivered as well, by OAB board members."

They worked through the night. The day dawned cloudy, and the document, flawlessly typed, leaving out not a shred of information, turned out eighteen pages long. At six A.M. Ruth went to the kitchen and found her mother-in-law and Rosa chatting and making coffee.

"How are you feeling?" Ruth asked Rosa, noticing that she was pale and had dark circles under her eyes.

"I'm fine," said Rosa. "God, I haven't slept like that in a long, long time. It was all the tension, it starts to get to me and then I just fall apart."

"And all because she wanted to help Miguel," said dona Rita, smoothing back Rosa's hair.

"I'm going to bring Dr. Gouveia some coffee," said Ruth, setting up a tray. "He's probably reading that document over for the ninety-ninth time."

"I'm worried about him," murmured dona Rita. "He's too old for all this. But you just try and tell him that!"

Ruth returned to the study and found a space for the tray on the table piled high with papers.

"Take a break and have some coffee, Dr. Gouveia."

"Of course, my dear. I could smell it coming." He pointed to a folder. "There it is, all ready. We're going to have to stop and get it photocopied. But I finished all the cover letters, they're in that envelope."

"You need to take a shower and change."

"Right away. We have to leave as soon as we can. While you were in the kitchen, I called General Barros. Old people get up early, you know. Sure enough, his wife picked up after the first ring, but when I identified myself she said the general had gone out and was not expected back. Strange, don't you think?"

"He must be terrified. Now how are we planning to get to the commander's?"

"With General Barros."

"But if he's gone . . ."

"I don't think so, his foot is in a cast. They threatened him and he's playing invisible, is all. But I told you I'll drag him to that appointment if I have to."

Gouveia downed his coffee and left the study. Fifteen minutes later he was showered, shaved, and changed. Ruth had not been able to summon up the energy to do the same. She was still wearing her clothes from the day before.

Gouveia called his friend the policeman to say they were leaving for General Barros' apartment.

"He's going to meet us there," Gouveia told Ruth. "And he'll bring police support." He picked up the folder with the document, grabbed his hat, and said: "Let's go."

Dona Rita walked them to the door, wringing her hands and instructing him to be careful.

For the very first time Ruth felt she was part of the counterattack. It was a comforting feeling, a counterbalance to her physical exhaustion. The dull morning light brought no signs of hope, however. She knew theirs was the weaker side and their adversaries were like animals whose trainer got careless one day and let them attack another animal or eat raw meat. If they really meant to stop that meeting from taking place, Ruth knew that Gouveia didn't stand a chance, even with police backup.

In the taxi on the way to Urca, Gouveia noticed his daughter-in-law's worried expression.

"Scared?"

She nodded.

"I am too, my dear," he said tenderly.

Ruth squeezed the old man's arm and leaned her head on his chest. Dr. Gouveia patted her head.

"Be brave," he said. "It doesn't do any good to think about the enemy. We're not like them, we are very, very different."

Ashamed of herself, Ruth sat up and looked out the window. He was right, of course, but still it was hard to find the courage to confront such adversaries.

"You know, my dear, when Miguel first got interested in Oriental philosophy, I borrowed a couple of his books on the subject and read them myself. I'm Catholic, of course, and I look to the Gospels for truth, but that ancient wisdom, or perhaps its poetic essence, ended up giving me a few themes for my own contemplation."

Ruth shook her head and sighed. She didn't have much patience for those philosophies that so impressed Miguel, but she listened carefully to what her father-in-law was saying.

"I'm thinking of . . ." he went on. "I forget the name of the philosopher, but he was describing a lovely dream in which he turned from a bird into a bee and finally to a butterfly. When he woke up he began to doubt the value of being anything other than oneself. And felt enlightened. That's what I mean, my dear, we are who we are, no matter what we dream. And there's no way to run away from it."

Part 3

Heavenly Handwriting

Even in summer Le Bourget was not the busiest airport in Paris. The Air France Caravel pulled up to the gate at the international terminal. Passengers began disembarking, leather carryons and raincoats in hand, and hurried toward the building with large, dirt-streaked windows. The passengers on the afternoon flights from London all looked alike: reserved, middle-aged gentlemen with severe gray suits, mustaches, and hats. Haidèe cut a contrasting figure in their midst. She wore a fluttering yellow poplin cape, a champagne-beige knit dress that clung to her still-shapely figure, and a glittering array of jewelry. None of the British gentlemen so much as raised an eyebrow as she passed, balancing elegantly on her high-heeled lizard pumps.

An immigration official gruffly stamped her passport; a customs agent took one look at her two suitcases and, smiling a discreet, gallant smile, told her to go on through. Haidèe discreetly smiled back into the agent's brown eyes, which were fixed on her sparkling bosom. She wagged her finger in mock admonition and picked up her bags. A representative of the Brazilian Embassy was waiting on the other side of the glass exit door. She handed him her luggage and they walked out to the parking lot.

"My goodness, the island was completely socked in," she said. "It was raining so hard over the channel the plane shook. I don't know why they still insist on using those old Caravels."

The young diplomat smiled. "Are you afraid of flying?"

Haidèe smiled back.

"Not in the least. But I don't trust those Caravels."

He opened the door of a Citröen that looked like it wanted to bury its front bumper in the ground. Haidèe climbed in as the young man loaded her bags and slid in behind the steering wheel.

"It's been one hell of a summer," he remarked, starting the car. "No sun at all! I'm as white as wax."

175

"Do you miss the beach?"

"Oh, a beach would sound pretty good right about now."

"Summer here is just a ruse," said Haidèe. "It's not Paris' best season."

"And it's rained a lot, which is a drag."

The car purred onto the highway, heading for Villete bridge. Traffic was heavy but moving along at a pretty good clip. The young man turned on the tape deck low, and soft music completely blocked out the muffled noise of the engine.

"You're really having an attack of nostalgia, aren't you," said Haidèe, recognizing an orchestrated version of a Vinícius de Morais tune.

"How was your trip?" asked the young man. "The ambassador was very worried."

"Tiring, of course—I'm not twenty years old anymore. But it was fine. I took a night flight out from Galeão, no surprises. In London I didn't even have to pass customs. A guy from the consulate was waiting for me at immigration. There are still a few advantages to being an ambassador's widow."

"I'm glad everything went so smoothly," said the young man. "The ambassador was very nervous; your visit was so unexpected."

"Oh, he's like that. If my trip had been on his calendar a year in advance he would have been just as rattled."

"But he's not that way about anything else—just you. He's quite levelheaded otherwise and very much in control, you know that. It's very rare for him to let his anxiety show."

"He's extraordinary, really. And not even a career diplomat!"

"Last year, when he heard you were coming, he suggested me specifically."

"And I didn't forget to sing your praises afterward, my friend. You were a great help to me. A shame I was only here two days, it's just that Europe bores me. I used to be in love with this city. But now I prefer my Rio de Janeiro, beggars and all."

"Will you be staying longer this time?"

"I don't know yet, it depends how things go. Probably less than a week, which will seem like an eternity. I have very few friends in Paris these days, it's like an alien city to me."

"Nonsense, you're an inspiration the way you move effortlessly among all the different circles."

"So, how is the ambassador? That man is indefatigable."

"Nothing out of the ordinary, but we have been very busy. He knows he'll be leaving, with the turnover of administrations and all the changes going on at home. He expects a cabinet post in the new government."

Haidèe looked at the young man beside her. She knew he came from an important family from Minas Gerais—his father was a ruling party senator—and that he'd entered the diplomatic service at a very young age. But with his looks, it was clear he'd needed no special string-pulling to be hired by the ambassador. He was athletic yet graceful, with a well-sculpted face, green eyes, and just a few signs of precocious aging that gave him a serious and intellectual air. His voice, too, was an asset, because it was clear and deep, with a certain appealing gruffness around the edges. A few wrinkles at the corners of his mouth completed the picture, adding a touch of determination. Perhaps he was really nothing like he looked—Haidèe knew this to be true—but he was cut perfectly to the ambassador's taste.

"And your father?"

"I think he's doing well, though I haven't spoken with him much lately. He was here, visiting, in the spring. Having him around was a full-time job, as usual. He's such a hypochondriac. He went to see half the doctors in Paris and just about drove me crazy. He decided he had cancer."

Haidèe laughed; she knew the senator well. The son had apparently broken tradition, because all the men in the family ended up conservative, government-party senators.

They rode in silence for a while. They were coming into Paris proper on rue de Flandre, heading in the direction of the Gare de l'Est. Traffic was heavy because it was the end of the workday, and people were scurrying into the *métro*. A group of cyclists kept pace alongside the car.

"Where are we going?"

The young diplomat turned onto rue de La Fayette and they hit a tie-up on the viaduct over the railroad tracks.

"The ambassador made reservations for you at a hotel on Boulevard Strasbourg. I don't know the place, I've never been there before. If you don't like it, we'll move you somewhere else."

"That's sweet of you, but the ambassador usually knows what he's doing."

"I expect he does," said the young man, "but he's put me in a couple of tight spots. Not long ago he had me make reservations for a group of colonels at a hotel on rue de La Harpe. Can you imagine the scene when they got there, surrounded by the fauna of the Latin Quarter? I was at the embassy when they stomped in, furious. They accused the ambassador of negligence."

"I am not a colonel," said Haidèe.

"Of course not, that wasn't the implication."

In addition to being handsome, the boy was irony-proof, pure sugar-coating. Maybe his arrogant self-importance could be chalked up to his living abroad. Under other circumstances he would simply be an affected young man taking advantage of family perquisites.

The hotel was squeezed between a jewelry store and a tobacco shop with racks of posters and magazines on the sidewalk out front. Haidèe thought it looked inviting, like one of the many spots in Paris intended for those who wanted privacy.

The diplomat signaled the bellhops to take charge of the bags and helped Haidèe out of the car. The place had a very discreet feel to it and was impeccably decorated. They went to the reception desk. behind a varnished wood counter stood an old and enigmatic clerk.

"Madame Jaffet," announced the diplomat. "Reservations were made by the Brazilian ambassador."

The old man examined Haidèe, jewels and all, nodded his head slightly, and consulted an index card.

"Ah, yes! Very good." He tapped a bell on the counter and an adolescent in uniform appeared. The old man handed him the keys. "You're in 319, madame." He consulted his cards again and looked solemnly at the diplomat. "Yours, sir, is number 320." The boy in uniform was waiting primly, blinking his eyes continuously.

Haidèe looked up in surprise.

"I forgot to tell you—the ambassador has appointed me your escort. I am to be at your disposal, just a knock away, at all times, that's what he told me."

Haidèe wasn't sure whether to be grateful or to protest. But the ambassador must know what he was doing.

"All right," said Haidèe, "let's go on up. I'll decide when I see him whether to thank him for his graciousness or slap him around a little."

They laughed and boarded an ancient, baroque elevator, which was in no hurry to go anywhere, dragging itself up floor by floor with unnerving tranquility.

The young diplomat stood at the back of the elevator, distracted by some detail in the metallic braid trimming. Haidèe applied herself to speculating on the ambassador's motives for choosing this hotel. She usually stayed on rue Marbeuf, at a place that was much more centrally located and where she already knew all the staff. But it was not uncommon there to run into well-known Brazilians passing through Paris. Possibly this was why the ambassador had chosen instead a luxurious dump which, judging from the specimens in the lobby, was frequented only by rich businessmen from the provinces.

The room itself was spacious, situated at the back of the building, with windows that opened out over a landscaped area, three apple trees planted in a triangle, each surrounded by forget-me-nots. Haidèe unpacked, chose a dress to wear, and placed all her jewelry in a black case. Then she tapped on the door dividing her room from her young companion's.

"Yes?" The diplomat opened the door. "Is your room all right?"

"Quite pleasant, don't you think?" She handed him the black case. "Would you take this down and have it put in the hotel safe? I don't want to take any chances."

"Of course, only take me a minute," he replied, closing the door behind him. "Don't worry, I won't make off with your jewels."

Haidèe laughed a fake laugh and stood with her ear to the door, waiting to hear the outside door to his room open and close. When she was sure he was no longer in his room, she dashed to the phone and dialed. No answer. She let it ring several times, but somehow she knew there would be no answer. She'd been dialing that number for days from Brazil and it had done nothing but ring and ring. She had asked that the line be checked for trouble, but was told it worked perfectly, the only and obvious explanation being that the party was not at home.

She got a new dial tone and put her hand out to make another call, then stopped, suddenly indecisive. Finally she made up her mind and dialed, slowly this time, as if hesitant to complete the number she was calling.

The telephone rang and someone answered.

"Hello, I'd like to speak with Rogério, please," said Haidée in French. She made a face at the reply. "And he didn't leave a

number or an address? All right, no, it's not that important, just
an old friend passing through. Thank you."

She hung up the phone and ran to listen at the door between
rooms. Not a sound. But then there were two knocks at her
main door.

"Who is it?" she asked.

"Room service," called a man's voice.

"Come back later," shouted Haidèe.

"But madame . . ." the voice grumbled.

Haidèe was nonplussed to hear a key being turned in the
lock. As the door swung open, she staggered backwards, taking
a defensive posture.

It was the Brazilian ambassador himself.

"Damn you!" exclaimed Haidèe, gasping for breath.

The man laughed, enjoying her reaction, and casually strolled
into the room. He looked around, examining the interior decora-
tion, the quality of the bed linens, the open suitcases, the view,
and even the flowers in a small vase on the nightstand.

"So, what do you think? I only discovered this place recently myself. The clientele is mostly entrepreneurs from southern
France and German businessmen. It has the distinction of being
the lair preferred by the most discreet gentlemen of the Common
Market."

"I'd like to know why that little queer is supposed to follow
me everywhere I go."

The ambassador let out another deep chortle.

"And I'd like to know who Rogério is."

Haidèe stiffened. "Listening behind closed doors now, are
you?"

"I learned it all from you, my dear." His face clouded. "Who
is he?"

"An acquaintance," said Haidèe casually. "Nobody important."

The ambassador grabbed her by the wrist and twisted her arm
back painfully.

"Liar!"

Haidèe yelped and he let her go.

"You're a fast learner," she said, rubbing her sore wrist.
"Already taking on the qualities of your military employers."

"Who is he, Haidèe?"

"An exile, some poor devil. We lost contact, now he's moved
and didn't leave an address. That's life, isn't it."

"What did you want from him?"

"I have a letter," she said. "His family asked me to deliver it."

"How touching," said the ambassador. "You haven't changed a bit. Still lying through your teeth."

"Why are you so on edge?"

The ambassador ran his hands over his face and sagged onto the bed, one leg bent behind him on the mattress, the other dangling to the floor.

"You couldn't have shown up at a worse moment."

"What's going on?"

The ambassador looked at her.

"The embassy is worse right now than the White House during World War Two. A nest of spies."

Haidèe's jaw dropped.

"A nest of spies . . ." she said, not sure whether to laugh or to take him at his word. "Could you be a little more specific?"

"There's been a colonel looking over my shoulder for two months now. Prying into everything, creating incredible confusion. He's installed himself on the second floor of the embassy, where he sits typing reports for the SNI. I offered him a secretary but the fanatic refused. And as if that's not enough, there's that awful man in London . . ."

"Your colleague the ambassador there . . ." said Haidèe.

"Right, the one who's already had at least five plastic surgeries. A pathetic little man. And, get this, he sent some skirt to spy on me. She hangs all over the colonel and generally makes a fool of herself. Little does he know that foolish woman is one of the miracles of Swedish medicine, a product of the scalpel, a transsexual. In the not-so-distant past *she* was a *he*—a banker from outside São Paulo with an existential problem. A hard dish for an ex-seminarian to swallow."

"You're really low, do you know that?" said Haidèe charitably.

"No, I'm serious. The embassy is impossible. Spies having shoving matches in the halls. The other day I caught a guy in my bedroom . . ."

"That's nothing new!"

"Except he was in the process of bugging the place. I kicked the jerk out." The ambassador's shoulders drooped as he looked at her, resignation written all over his face. "And now, to complete the picture, you show up on a moment's notice."

"There wasn't more than a moment's notice to give. There's something terrible going on. There are probably more spies in the embassy than you think. If I were you, I'd call your colleague in London and thank him. If he hadn't sent that 'woman' to spy on you, and if the colonel weren't tied up with his reports, maybe it wouldn't even have occurred to you to set me up in this hotel."

The ambassador looked more anxious than ever.

"I think you'd better tell me what's going on."

Haidèe pushed her suitcases aside and sat down next to him on the bed.

"Besides the extra traffic in the halls, you haven't noticed anything else different?"

The ambassador thought for a moment and shook his head. "How could I, with the place in an uproar? But what, may I ask, would you expect me to notice?"

"Oh, maybe a couple of holdovers from the cellars, if you get my drift."

"Oh, them. No, it's been a long time since we've seen any of them around here."

"Well, I'm sure there's somebody snooping around. Not as openly as before, perhaps, and much less concerned with you or embassy business than previously. They don't think you know anything about what they're after."

"You don't mean . . ."

"Exactly! The money in Switzerland."

"How did they find out?"

"I don't know yet, but I have my suspicions."

"Don't tell me Lyra betrayed us!"

"No, it wasn't him."

"Then who?"

Haidèe raised her eyes and stared at the delicate glass chandelier shaped like a bower of green leaves.

"Lyra's son."

"Aldo? That lunatic?"

"Lyra swears that Aldo doesn't know anything, that he's in some clinic in Petrópolis. But I don't think so. For the last two months, Lyra hasn't been able to actually visit with him. He contented himself with a glance at a person tied down in a padded cell. Always was a terrible father."

"So you think Aldo is behind this?"

"I think he's in front of it, to be more precise. He's capable of anything, my friend, there's not a moral bone in his body. At first I suspected Lyra himself, and I put together a dossier to blackmail him."

The ambassador lowered his head and furrowed his brow.

"Do you remember that series of crimes in Rio around 1972? The papers didn't go anywhere near the story, but the rumor mill was full of it, remember?" Haidèe's voice was hard and cold and she was watching the ambassador closely for his reaction.

He gave no sign of recognition.

"Five girls were murdered. Drugged, raped, and then burned alive."

The ambassador's eyes widened as he finally remembered and anticipated the revelation Haidèe was about to make.

"It was him," said Haidèe. "I have proof. But it would only be valuable if his father was the one betraying us. Aldo is incapable of feeling threatened. All these years of impunity have perverted him completely. It wouldn't matter if the victims' bodies came up from their graves to accuse him."

"So where is he now?"

"I don't know yet, but I'm pretty sure he's not in the sanatorium where Lyra thinks he is. But I'll know soon."

The ambassador mopped his brow and squirmed on the bed. "The hell of it is I don't have many trustworthy people here."

"The little queer you set up in the next room isn't good for much."

"That's what you think," said the ambassador. "He's Machiavellian."

"But if he hears footsteps behind him, he'll head for the hills."

"That's true. Physical bravery isn't one of his strong points."

The ambassador sighed. It was getting dark, and Haidèe switched on the chandelier.

"You have to get to Geneva before they do," he said. "Why are you even here?"

"I would have gone directly to Geneva—and I'm going to, as soon as I can. But they're bringing someone here. They think he's the link they've been looking for."

"Who?"

"A friend. I roped him into this mess. Suffice it to say he was supposed to be a decoy to keep them away from me. But I underestimated their reach, and once my friend had the information on my contacts in Paris, they grabbed him."

"How could you do such a thing?"

"I was afraid I wouldn't be able to get out of Brazil. I was afraid they'd surround me and wring the information out of me. I was hoping he'd be able to do the job if I couldn't."

"I still don't understand why you're here," said the ambassador. "You should be in Geneva. From what you've told me, they're probably taking him around to local exile get-togethers right now. Or trying to get in touch with the contacts you so generously shared with him. I certainly wouldn't want to be in his shoes."

Haidèe stared at the glass branches overhead. The calm of the hotel seemed to exaggerate the silence.

"I can't just throw my friend to the wolves."

"You're out of your mind." He was both enraged and terrified. "How could you risk everything for such a petty consideration? That's not at all you, Haidèe."

"There are certain things a person just can't ignore."

"Guilty conscience," the ambassador retorted, rising to his feet and pacing the room, hands in his pockets. "You of all people, who never had a conscience before, suddenly find one now."

"Hey, I also want my revenge!"

"That's a lie! I don't believe you for a minute. There's something you're not telling me."

Haidèe looked at the ambassador with the proud expression of anticipated triumph.

"It's the absolute truth. They crossed the line. They need to be taught a lesson or we'll never have peace. If I don't do this, they'll keep rising from the dead, coming back to haunt us like ghosts."

"What are their plans for the money?"

"Oh, they'll give courses in paranoia, as always. They think the left has had too much time to cool down and get their heads together in exile and will come back not only organized but rich, with this money. They want to pull the rug out from under them and at the same time fund their own movement. Expropriating what the left expropriated. Their own spigot has been shut off, so now they have to do odd jobs. Free-lance repression: think of it. Only in Brazil. And that's exactly what those bastards have been up to. A small job here, another there, but now even that well has gone dry."

The ambassador nodded his head in agreement.

"Just recently I was talking to a businessman from São Paulo who has been a big source of financial support to the repression. And he told me they'd come to him several times lately but he refused to cooperate."

"And many others like him," said Haidèe. "Brazil is changing, but they can't accept that. What's worse," she added, "is that they won't stop with the leftists' money. There's a lot more to be had and you know it."

The ambassador stopped pacing. If he had been someone else he would have blushed.

Pepe sat in a line of people on a wooden bench, holding a bag of fruit from the supermarket. The bench was on the porch of a once-grand country house surrounded by gardens and footpaths where sick people strolled in their white clothes, accompanied by vigilant orderlies. The landscape itself was restful, untouched Atlantic forest climbing mountain hillsides, typical of Petrópolis. This mental hospital must charge dearly for its services, thought Pepe, it was so calm and clean, a far cry from the sordidness so common in places like this.

That the people waiting beside Pepe on the bench were friends and relatives of patients was clear from their serious faces and their air of perplexed melancholy. Pepe, on the other hand, was frightened and tense. He was pretending to be Aldo Lyra's uncle. When the nurse told Pepe that Aldo was seriously disturbed and unable to have visitors, he had insisted, claiming he lived in the country's interior and this was his only opportunity to visit his nephew. The nurse told him he would have to wait if he wanted to talk to the doctor, but that was two hours ago. While the other waiting visitors each took their turn going in and coming back out, he just sat there waiting.

Finally the nurse stuck her head out the door. "You can come in now, sir. Dr. Rocha is ready to see you."

Pepe thanked her meekly and went through the door she indicated, where the doctor stood waiting.

"So you're Aldo's uncle?"

Pepe shook the doctor's hand and tried to look even meeker, playing the role of a wealthy hayseed visiting a troubled relative.

"I live in Uberaba," said Pepe, affecting the appropriate back-country accent. "And, well, I was visiting in Rio, so I decided to come see my nephew."

"You're the general's brother, then?"

"No, his brother-in-law. What my sister went through with that boy, a terrible thing. And then we lost her. I'd really like to see him, Doctor."

"I don't think that will be possible."

Pepe lowered his eyes and looked profoundly disappointed.

"But . . . I've come from so far away, Doctor. And I haven't seen the boy for ten years. We were so close when he was a child, I thought it might help if I came."

"The patient is going through a very difficult phase. He cannot be left alone and he's been receiving strong drug treatment. I'm afraid he's not a pretty sight. During this kind of treatment we don't allow relatives to visit the patients. It's very grim. I can assure you the very rationale for this policy is to spare people like you."

"I understand." Pepe made as if to leave with a shy bow of thanks, but changed his mind halfway to the door. "Would you please give this fruit to the boy, then? That is, if he can . . ."

"Of course," said the doctor, placing the bag on the table. "Sometimes he improves for a time and can take solid food. I'm sure he'll be delighted. And if possible I'll tell him who brought it."

Pepe bowed again, but didn't move.

"His father told me that sometimes he's allowed to look at the boy through the window of his room. Couldn't I just have a glimpse of him?"

The doctor shook his head.

"That's strictly reserved for immediate family, like Aldo's father. I'm sorry, we can't make any exceptions."

"I understand," said Pepe, his eyes on the floor, "but no harm in asking, right? I'm a sprirtualist and I wanted so to see the boy, I have a great deal of faith and . . ." His hand hovered in the air, then fell limp as he turned to the door.

"I'll see that he gets the fruit."

"Thank you, Doctor."

Pepe headed down through the garden toward the parking lot, which lay outside a high wire fence. He walked slowly, haltingly, like an old man for whom it had taken a supreme effort just to be there. But his attention was on the orderlies alongside each patient. He nodded to each, and occasionally received a smile back. None of them seemed terribly approachable. They limited themselves to watching the patients, pushing their wheelchairs, or supporting those who had difficulty walking. Pepe saw the gate looming closer and knew that once he reached the parking lot there would be nothing more he could do. In his pocket was a stack of bills Haidèe had given him and instructions for carrying out the investigation.

Near the gate he saw an orderly standing beside a very old woman whose wheelchair was parked beneath a fig tree. He gave his customary nod and the orderly responded with distant courtesy. Pepe decided to take a chance.

"How is she doing today?" he asked, maintaining the humble posture and fake Mineiro accent.

"Pretty good. You know her?"

"We used to be neighbors," he said. "Life's full of surprises, isn't it? She was the most cheerful person I ever met."

"She was?" said the orderly, surprised.

"You'd never guess it now, would you."

"I guess anything's possible. She's been here nearly ten years. She was one of the first patients."

"My God, how time flies," said Pepe, sitting down on the grass. The woman was apparently oblivious to their conversation. "Have you worked here all that time?"

"Almost," said the orderly, beginning to tire of Pepe's presence.

"Your job must demand a lot of patience and goodwill," said Pepe, looking to lead the conversation in a particular direction.

"I've never seen you here before," said the orderly.

"This is my first time. I don't live in Rio, I'm from Minas. I came to see a relative."

The orderly grunted.

"I'm Aldo's uncle—do you know Aldo, Aldo Lyra?"

"Aldo? No, there are a lot of patients here, more than a hundred and fifty. It's impossible to know them all."

"My nephew's on the ward for the ones who are worst off."

"Oh, really."

"And the doctor won't let me see him. I'm really disappointed, because I came such a long way."

The orderly looked at him as if he knew what Pepe was about to propose.

"Couldn't you help me?"

The orderly smiled, understanding.

"No, we get this kind of request all the time, but I'd lose my job."

"But there must be a way. I just want to see the boy, just for a minute. I don't even need to talk to him. For an old man?"

"I'm sorry, I really can't."

"What if I made it worth your while?"

"No way," protested the orderly.

"I just have to see the boy. Please, you won't be sorry."

"You've got the wrong person. I can't help you."

Pepe pulled the wad of money out of his pocket and showed it to the orderly.

"There's 100,000 cruzeiros there. It may seem strange, but that's what old age does to you. I just can't leave here without at least seeing my nephew's face."

The orderly hesitated, eyes fixed on the wad of bills. It represented practically six months' salary.

"Wait here a minute," he said and walked away, disappearing behind some bushes. He returned almost immediately, a smile on his face. "Let's see if we can't make an old man happy. Come with me."

Another orderly appeared out of nowhere to care for the woman in the wheelchair, and Pepe followed the first one along a straight dirt path to a square, two-story building in a different style than the one where Pepe had talked with the doctor.

They circled the building and arrived at a large wooden door wide enough for an ambulance, or even a truck.

"Wait here," the orderly told Pepe.

He disappeared inside the building. Pepe's heart pounded wildly. When the orderly reappeared he handed Pepe a white lab coat like the one he was wearing.

"Just stick with me and let me do the talking."

They went down a hall and up a stairway. A man sat behind a table at the top of the stairs, and Pepe began to see why they wouldn't let people visit the ward where the most seriously ill patients were confined. The place reeked of urine and feces, the walls were stained and dingy, and the cells had barred windows like a prison.

"How's it going, man," said the orderly to the man at the table. "All quiet?"

The man responded with a snarl and then sank back into his former pose, legs sprawled open, hands linked behind his head on the chair back.

"I think he's down there," said the orderly to Pepe, pointing to the fifth cell from the end of the hall.

Pepe's step quickened and the orderly followed along behind. When they reached the door, the orderly took out a small key and inserted it in the small window set at face level in the door.

"This only opens the window," he warned.

"That's all I need," said Pepe.

The metal plate slid aside, and the orderly was the first to look in. He gasped aloud.

"What is it?" asked Pepe, his heart pounding.

"There's no one in there!" said the orderly.

"Maybe he improved," suggested Pepe, tremulous. "Maybe he was transferred to another ward."

The orderly shook his head.

"No way, this patient has been here for ages. I checked his file before we came up. He's supposed to be here."

The orderly went back to the man at the desk and said: "Hey, cell number five is empty, what gives?"

The man leaped up from his table. "What the hell are you two doing here, anyway?"

"I'm telling you a patient has . . . has disappeared!" stammered the orderly.

Pepe stood peering into the cell, which showed no trace of being inhabited lately.

"Where did you get that key?" demanded the man, pointing an accusing finger at the orderly. "Something isn't right here." He looked at Pepe trembling, heaving with emotion. "And who's he?"

"What difference does it make?" said Pepe. "My nephew is not where he's supposed to be!"

The man ran off toward a phone on the wall.

"I'm going to call the supervisor."

"No, wait," shouted Pepe.

The man stopped and looked at him.

"Don't report it," said Pepe, breathless with anxiety. "Not yet."

He yanked the money out of his pocket and waved it at the orderly.

"You can split it with him," he said. "Just give me enough time to get out of here."

The orderly took the stack of bills and looked at the other man, perplexed, as if to say: *It's news to me!*

Pepe didn't wait for an answer. He ran down the stairs and headed for the parking lot without once looking back.

The parking lot sat at least some 100 meters from the building. Pepe wished he were thirty years younger and able to go the distance at a full run, but his legs were prisoners of arthritis and his lungs the captives of age.

He was going as fast as he could, but he saw that the doctor he had spoken with and two security guards were making their way down the porch steps. He tried to lose himself among the patients, latching onto a thin man with a lost look who was walking along gesturing as if conducting an invisible orchestra. He led the man, who seemed not to even notice, in the direction of the gate. The doctor and the security men ran past on their way to the other building.

Pepe darted off the footpath and onto the grass without letting go of the patient, then decided on a shortcut. The man was stumbling and Pepe could barely support him. But he saw the gate was already being closed by a group of men armed with billy clubs.

"Shit," moaned Pepe, releasing his human shield.

He turned and walked parallel to the wire fence, hoping to find another means of escape. Haidèe's warnings about what would happen to him if he were caught had been horrific. He cursed his sister-in-law for everything she had made him do all those years. The enforced silence, the original promise, the fear, all of it.

The wire fence seemed to encircle the sanatorium totally. Pepe was beginning to think he would never find a way out. They would have no mercy, she had said. He was a dead man, and he didn't want to die, not now, not before telling someone what he had discovered.

He had left the area immediately surrounding the hospital and was entering denser vegetation. He saw a large stand of eucalyptus trees on a hillside that dropped off to a gully at the fence. He heard voices and dogs barking. Now they had the dogs after him. His legs barely supporting his tired body, Pepe scrambled down the ravine more out of momentum than any act of will.

Erosion had carved away at the earth, leaving a strip of bare sand beneath the fence. The fury of the water must have twisted the wire a little, so that the support was coming unearthed. He was a slender man and, with a little effort, perhaps he'd be able to squeeze through. It was worth a try, because the barking was drawing closer by the minute.

Pepe got down on his belly and began trying to inch himself under the fence. Finally, with much difficulty, he managed to slip through to the other side. His white jacket covered with dirt and his shoes full of sand, he crawled to a clump of bushes and collapsed on the ground to rest. But time was short. If the dogs led the search party to the fence, men younger and more agile than he would easily capture him.

He stumbled in a direction perpendicular to the fence, using it as a guide back to the parking lot. A siren sounded, shrill, mournful, insistent, making him feel more pressed than ever. The parking lot had to be close now. If his car was being watched, he would try to take one belonging to another visitor. It wouldn't be easy, but it was the only way out. He banged his head on a low-hanging branch, tripped in a hole, and fell to the ground. His head throbbed and his ankle was twisted, though not badly. He got up and limped off, gasping for breath and trying to ignore his fear and fatigue.

Finally the parking lot came into view. It didn't look as though his car was under surveillance, and the security men at the gate were facing the other way, scanning the area inside of the fence. He wound his way among the cars and made it to his Volkswagen. As he climbed behind the wheel and dug in his pocket for the keys he felt something cold and metallic against his neck.

Turning to the window, he saw the doctor, and the gun.

"People from Minas are curious by nature," said Dr. Rocha, "and curiosity can be a very dangerous thing."

Pepe was paralyzed.

"Get out of the car," the doctor ordered, waving his gun.

Pepe obeyed, moving very slowly, his hands over his head, just like he'd seen in shoot-'em-up movies.

"Let's go," said the doctor.

They began walking between the line of parked cars toward the gate. As they approached a light-blue Galaxy, a large black man leaped out. Pepe heard a muffled crack and froze in his tracks. Dr. Rocha slumped sideways onto Pepe's shoulder and then fell to the ground. Pepe began shaking; his eyes blurred. He turned to look down where the doctor lay, eyes wide, a singed red hole in the middle of his forehead where the bullet passed through. Pepe felt someone grab his arm, thrusting him into the Galaxy. The car sped off just as his head hit the backseat and the process of disintegration was complete: he blacked out.

When Pepe opened his eyes, he was lying in his own bed, his daughter's face hovering over him.

"Daddy, please, for the love of God, talk to me." She was shaking him by the shoulders and weeping.

Pepe moaned and his vision cleared. It was true, he was in his own bed and he could hear the circus tent flapping in the wind.

"Daddy? Daddy, are you okay?"

"I'm fine now, honey, I'm just thirsty."

His daughter lifted his head and held a cup of water to his lips.

Pepe smiled, as if reborn.

"Who brought me here?"

"Two men. They said you collapsed on the street."

"They didn't say who they were?"

"No. They just brought you in and left." Pepe's daughter frowned. "What happened to you, Daddy? You've been acting strange ever since Haidèe showed up here. Tell me what's going on."

"Don't you worry about it, sweetheart."

"Those men were so weird and nasty-looking. They looked like criminals. What's going on? You're hiding something from me and I want to know why."

"Because it's better that way. Don't ask me any more questions."

Pepe attempted to get out of bed and felt his head begin to spin.

"We'll have none of that," protested his daughter. "You're not going anywhere."

"I have to."

"Have to what? Tell me and I'll do it."

"I have to make a phone call."

"A phone call?"

"It's important. I need to do it right away or it might be too late."

With his daughter's help, Pepe managed to sit up.

"Does it really have to be right now? The only telephone around is the one in the restaurant on the other side of the highway."

"No, that's no good. I have to go to the long-distance office downtown. Call your husband, he can take me."

She shook her head at his obstinance.

"All right. If it's that important."

The couple helped him into the old circus van and they headed for the Telerj office. Pepe's head still throbbed and his twisted ankle was swollen. At the phone office, when he said he wanted to make an overseas call to Paris, the clerk looked at him, incredulous, but noted the number on a form and pointed to the booth where he should wait for the call to be completed.

Pepe sat down in the booth and slumped against the wall, the receiver at his ear. Finally a voice said: "Brazilian Embassy, may I help you?"

"Hello, yes! I'm calling from Brazil, and I'd like to leave a message for Mrs. Haidèe Jaffet, in care of the ambassador. This is her brother-in-law."

"All right, sir, just a moment." There was a pause, then, "Go ahead."

"Just tell her that the fruit was not delivered as she requested. The party was not there to accept the gift, so it was passed along to others."

"That's it?"

"That's it. She'll understand."

"Okay, sir. But I can't guarantee that she'll get the message. Dona Haidèe hasn't come to the embassy. Are you sure she's in Paris?"

"She's there," said Pepe. "Just give the message to the ambassador, miss. I'm going to hang up now. Thank you."

Pepe placed the phone back on the hook and opened the door to the booth. "We can go home now," he said to his daughter and son-in-law.

Pepe knew that his life was no longer worth a dime. When Haidèe asked him to investigate the sanatorium, he knew that meant he was no longer valuable as a witness. Not that she said anything about it, but Pepe had enough experience in life and wasn't about to ask questions. Ever since he had witnessed the crime and identified the criminal, Haidèe had carefully protected him, so that at any moment he could be brought forward and the perverted murderer of that girl would be convicted on the basis of Pepe's testimony and related proof. But now, though he didn't understand how, the criminal was free, loose in the world and apparently beyond the reach of the law. On his way to the hospital in Petrópolis, Pepe had played and replayed the image of the man whose brutal acts he had witnessed in the vacant lot that night in 1972. He remembered how young the attacker was, barely twenty, if that. And Pepe had tried to imagine what he would look like now: sick, addicted, prematurely aged by a dissipated life.

Haidèe's instructions had not been very detailed. She had simply asked him to use any means possible to get to see the boy. She suspected that the sanatorium was merely a subterfuge to hide his real whereabouts. Pepe had been working on the case for years. Son of General Lyra, a high-ranking member of the administration, Aldo was effectively beyond the reach of justice, but Pepe worked discreetly to build a dossier on his activities. He had managed to link Aldo to other similar crimes that occurred in different locales but shared the same barbarous details. Later, he learned that Aldo was a volunteer with DOI-CODI, known for his brutal interrogations of political prisoners. Apparently Aldo had still other deaths on his head.

Recently, when the Shangri-la Circus played Contagem, Minas Gerais, Pepe had met the father of a young military man who had disappeared in Rio. According to the boy's father, he had fallen into the hands of the repression in late June 1973, during a raid on an apartment where a political meeting was being held. The boy and his friends were taken to an estate in Baixada Fluminense and brutalized by a torturer known as J.C.—and the person who went by these apparently innocent initials was none other than Aldo Lyra. The heartbroken father had but one hope: to recover his son's body. One of the boy's friends had managed to escape and lived in exile in Mexico; some years ago he had revealed to the father the identity of the person responsible for his son's death.

When Haidèe came looking for proof, Pepe imagined the time had come. He still harbored a small hope of seeing the criminal get his reward, but the old certainty that had kept him going during the long years of waiting had vanished.

Back at the circus, Pepe's daughter tucked him into bed. Time was a tricky thing, this he knew. He remembered Haidèe, young, beautiful, smiling out from the box seat at the big circus where he worked in the beginning of his career. And seated beside her, the girl he would marry. Time had not betrayed him as it had Haidèe, but it was being especially hard on him in regard to the event that he had witnessed involuntarily.

Pepe waited for his daughter to leave his bedside. Then he got up, went to a small metal cabinet, and removed a vial of tranquilizers. He dumped the blue pills onto the bed, poured a glass of water, and swallowed them one by one. When he was finished, he carefully set the glass and the empty vial on the nightstand, laid down in bed, and waited. He had had enough.

Ruth got out of the elevator first, the ever-chivalrous Dr. Gouveia motioning her on ahead. General Barros' apartment building seemed quiet enough, except for the steady stream of maids heading out to buy the morning's bread. After waiting outside for fifteen minutes, Ruth and her father-in-law had finally decided to go up and speak with the general.

When they rang the bell his wife came to the door, looking nervous. She opened it only a crack.

"Good morning, ma'am," said Gouveia. "We'd like to see your husband. I was here last night, remember?"

The woman made an almost imperceptible movement with her head and her eyes darted back toward the interior of the apartment. Then she looked at Ruth and Gouveia.

"He's not here. He had an early appointment at the ministry."

"The appointment was for nine-thirty," said Gouveia.

"He didn't tell me anything," said the woman, trying to close the door.

Dr. Gouveia shrewdly put his foot in the crack. The woman looked at them, frightened, and sighed.

"My husband's not home," she said, almost pleading, without much conviction. "Why don't you come back later? He should be here around lunchtime."

"You say he went to the ministry?" Gouveia was trying to prolong the conversation any way he could.

"I think so."

"You think he did or he actually did go to the ministry?"

"He didn't tell me exactly. I don't have anything to do with his work," exclaimed the woman, becoming upset.

"Well, I think he's here," said Gouveia.

Ruth took hold of his arm. "Let it go . . ."

"Absolutely not, my dear. Don't forget that Miguel's life is at stake here. General Barros promised to help us. I understand how he's feeling, they put the pressure on him too."

The wife was impatient, but Gouveia's foot was preventing her from closing the door and getting free of them.

"Forgive me, ma'am, but we really must come in." And he pushed the door forcefully and ushered Ruth inside.

"You can't do this . . ." protested the woman. "I'll call security."

"Call anyone you want," said the old attorney, striding into the living room.

Stiff and red-faced, General Barros was sitting in the same chair, his cast propped on a footstool, as if he hadn't moved since the night before.

"You're a courageous man, Dr. Gouveia," said the general, his hand clutching a wooden cane, admiration written all over his face.

Gouveia stood gazing at the general, unsure how to proceed. Intuition and knowledge of human nature had gotten him this far, but now he felt lost, dumbfounded.

"Forgive the invasion," he stammered. "I didn't mean to upset your wife. But under the circumstances . . ."

"Have a seat," said the general, pointing his cane at a chair.

Gouveia sat down and lowered his eyes. Fatigue and tension seemed to be taking over again. The general extended a hand to Ruth.

"Good morning, dona Ruth. Please, sit down. I haven't seen you for so long, it's a shame to meet under these circumstances."

Ruth shook his hand and took a seat.

"Why didn't you wait for me at the commander's office, as we'd planned?" asked the general.

"I was afraid you wouldn't show up," explained Gouveia, more in control again. "I couldn't take that chance. I've been up all night preparing a document about the case, which I intend to deliver to the commander in person. And without you, we wouldn't get a foot in the door."

"Do you have the document with you?"

"Right here," said Gouveia, waving the file.

"Some strange things happened last night, Dr. Gouveia."

"Maybe you think what happened last night was strange, General, but things like that have unfortunately become routine in our sad country."

"Never mind!" said General Barros, an edge in his voice. "You came to see me with your police friend. I listened to your story and, since I've always admired Miguel, I promised to help. But things have changed."

"What do you mean?" asked Ruth.

"Simply that now I've heard another version of the story."

"What version?" Gouveia's voice seemed to leap. "What did those butchers tell you?"

"Butchers? I don't know what you're talking about."

"Yes, you do, General, you know very well. Last night, after we left here, our car was intercepted by a paramilitary group. We were threatened, and warned not to keep our appointment with the commander of the First Army. You must have received a similar visit."

"I was not visited by any paramilitary group, nor did I receive any kind of threat. I simply received an unexpected visit from the commander of the First Army himself."

Devastated, Ruth and her father-in-law exchanged looks. Gouveia sank back down into his chair.

"The commander was intrigued by my phone call," the general went on. "And, though it was late, he decided to drop over and talk with me. He lives nearby and didn't even bother to call a car. The commander and I have been friends for many years. We served together at various places and share many points of view. When I told him what was going on, and why I had asked for an urgent appointment, he informed me that he knew all about it already. Except that it's not the same story you told me, Dr. Gouveia, you were misled. Which is perfectly understandable, of course, since he's your son."

Gouveia fixed his eyes on the general, who was waving his cane and adjusting and readjusting his foot on the footstool. Ruth knew she would not be able to hold back her tears much longer.

"The commander received a report several days ago from the Army Intelligence Center. I'm going to reveal the contents of this report to you, because I have affection and respect for your family. But I must warn you that this is a secret document. What I'm about to say must not go beyond these four walls. The commander authorized me to fill you in, if you agree to keep silent about it."

The general looked at the two and waited. He had not been exactly belligerent, but there was a certain grudging tone to his words.

Gouveia nodded agreement. Ruth rubbed her eyes with the back of her hand.

"The Intelligence Center uncovered important facts about a Communist conspiracy that has been developing over the last months. It's amazing, the left just won't stop." The general paused to relish the effect of his words, and then continued. "Communists in exile are banding together to take advantage of President Geisel's liberalization plans. There are two centers of activity, one here in Rio, and the other in Paris. Funding is to be provided by the proceeds from their criminal activities prior to exile, which was deposited in a Swiss bank account. When Lamarca died, we thought this money had been lost. But apparently they've found a way to gain access to the account, and, according to the report, will soon have recouped these funds." The general's eyes widened and he spoke slowly, emphasizing each word. "We don't know yet exactly how much is in the account, but it's an enormous sum. We estimate that thousands and thousands of dollars will be made available for subversive projects: political assassinations, financing for various leftist candidates in the coming elections, money to corrupt the media, to accelerate the fall of the regime. Just to give you an idea of the danger, they'll be able to buy modern weapons in Europe and the Middle East. There wasn't anywhere near this much money at work in Paraguay. If our men fail, that's it, that's the end of the country. It's a terrifying thought, and proof once more that we must not underestimate the Communist threat."

"But what does Miguel have to do with all this?" asked Ruth, trembling, tears running down her face.

"I'm sorry to tell you that Miguel's situation is not a pretty one. He was apparently recruited by the left in 1972. From what we know, he participated in several subversive activities that year, but then there was a change of strategy and he had to sit tight for a while, until his problems with the army cooled off. Early this year he was finally reactivated. He's the link the Communists needed to get to that money. As we know, he's well-trained and terrifically professional, and his recruitment only goes to show how smart the subversives are."

"I don't believe it," Ruth shouted.

"Get hold of yourself, dona Ruth," warned the general. "I'm sure you had no idea what was going on. Miguel didn't bring this home with him, the report is very clear about that. But he didn't stint on his physical preparation and always kept his true objectives hidden. Miguel is really something. He's already killed one man and wounded four others."

"Are you saying that Miguel is being held by the Secret Service?" asked Gouveia.

"Miguel is not being held by anyone."

"I'm certain he was picked up yesterday," insisted Gouveia.

"No, Miguel is still out there, actively involved," said the general. "I should have realized something like this was going on back in 1972 when he began to have problems. Now I believe he must have been undergoing some kind of brainwashing."

"I don't believe a word of this paranoid story," said Gouveia. "This thing smells worse, from a legal standpoint, than it did before. Not only because a man's being held without due process, but also because they're fabricating a fantastic story to conceal some kind of scandal that I intend to uncover. The facts I've gathered point in an entirely different direction. In any event, you've helped me without intending to."

"You'd better not stick your nose in where you don't belong," warned the general, shaking his cane. "I told you all this out of friendship, but I'm quite clear which side I'm on. I will not lend support to any kind of dubious judicial maneuver aimed at obstructing the process of an army investigation."

"That's exactly the problem," said Gouveia, looking the general straight in the eyes. "You people feel that you're above everything in this country, above the laws, above the Constitution, above we common mortals. You're incapable of admitting that you make mistakes or are manipulated by forces you least expect. You abuse your position, secure in the knowledge that you have the weapons at your disposal. But you forget who pays your salaries and buys you your guns."

General Barros shifted in his chair and played impatiently with his cane.

"I have nothing more to say to you," he said. "I'd like you to leave now, I think I've been patient long enough."

Ruth stood up, but Gouveia remained in his chair.

"You have your version of the story," he said, "and I have mine. It's right here. You can do as you wish with yours, and I am at liberty to do as I wish with mine." An expression of sadness crossed his face. "It's unfortunate that this country has been reduced to such an impasse. You with your fabricated versions and we citizens with our factual ones. But the nation is waking up. I woke up a long time ago."

Gouveia rose to his feet and took his daughter-in-law by the arm.

"Let's go, my dear, we have a lot to do."

The bedroom door flew open. Captain Maurício and five men with machine guns burst into the living room.

"I was only trying to help," stammered General Barros.

"It was a serious mistake to ignore the warning we gave you last night, Dr. Gouveia," shouted Captain Maurício.

Ruth screamed and ran for the door. One of the men dragged her back into the living room, but not before she saw General Barros' wife cowering in a corner of the entryway, crying silently.

"How about we take a little ride," said Captain Maurício. "I'm sure that Captain Miguel will be more than willing to help us now."

"Where is he?" demanded Ruth, struggling in her captor's arms.

"What difference does it make? All you need to know is that for the time being he's in very good health," answered the captain.

The men escorted Ruth and her father-in-law out the service entrance and down the back stairs. An hour and a half had gone by, and Lieutenant Fonseca had not shown up. Had he been intercepted? Not that his presence would have made a difference, except to give Maurício and his men an excuse to use their weapons and extinguish Dr. Gouveia's last hope.

The group left in two unmarked vans. Ruth and Gouveia were handcuffed and thrown onto a pile of inner tubes, with two men watching over them.

"Are you all right?" asked Ruth, too terrified now even to cry. She was afraid for her father-in-law, her son, and herself, and felt utterly miserable, a complete nonentity.

Gouveia responded with a grunt. He was lying on the inner tubes, his eyes closed, breathing with difficulty.

"No talking," barked one of the guards.

They traveled for more than an hour. The windows were shaded, and they had no idea what route they were taking or where they were headed. When finally the van stopped and the doors were flung open, they saw they were in a large garage, with a cement staircase leading to another level. The garage was piled high with boxes and gunnysacks and smelled of urine and feces.

They were pulled out of the van, marched upstairs, and thrown into separate cells. The walls and floor were padded, filthy, smelly. The place reminded Ruth of an old-fashioned insane asylum.

She looked around for the least dirty spot to sit down and dissolved into tears. Ruth wasn't the weepy type, but lately her resistance had been stretched to the limit. Nothing she had endured before had prepared her for a day like today. The general's accusations against Miguel still echoed in her ears. But his story had no substance, it was a gross fabrication to turn things against Miguel. Ruth had felt certain misgivings when Miguel first showed signs of becoming disillusioned with the military, but had immediately rejected the idea that he was being influenced by the left. Marxist ideology had never appealed to him, he was more intuitive—methodical but not very rational, in the Marxist sense of the word. He was more inclined toward mysticism and alternative philosophies, and he condemned the violence of the left as readily as that of the military.

The day he left the barracks after serving his disciplinary suspension, he took off his uniform for the last time. He folded it neatly and laid it in a cardboard box, taped it shut, and never again opened it. But he could clearly never throw it away. The box sat in the utility room on top of the wardrobe; when they lived in a very cramped apartment, he stored it at his parents' house.

Ruth would have understood if Miguel had become a rebel after first leaving the military. But instead he put his years in the army to rest, which must have been no easy task, and concentrated on finding new ways to make ends meet. Their style of life changed radically. Ordered to vacate their house within a week, they packed up their belongings and shipped them to a storage facility in Rio while they tied up the loose ends in Belém.

Once in Rio, life was very hard. No job, no friends, too proud to ask for help from his parents. Miguel supported his family by selling off the possessions they had acquired over the years. First the boat, then the car, a plot of land in Saquarema, Ruth's jewelry, until there was nothing left to sell.

One day near the end of 1974, after unsuccessfully looking for work for three months, Miguel arrived home, his chin on his chest.

"I got a job," he said sadly.

"So why do you look so glum? Is it something awful, something you can't imagine doing?"

Miguel shook his head.

"No," he said. "In a way, it's perfect for me."

"Well, what kind of job is it?"

"A factory. In personnel. It's only three minimum salaries, hardly enough to pay the rent."

"I told you I was going to look for a job too."

"No, you don't have to do that. You've never worked in your life, Ruth. And what about Luciano—I don't want the boy raised in daycare."

"Why not? I have my degree and we need the income. It's not fair for you to be the only one to sacrifice. I want to help too, I've already had my quota of the good life. Everything that's happened to us, Miguel, it's opened my eyes. I've learned a lot through all this."

Miguel looked at her, too tired to argue.

"It sounds to me like you've already got something all lined up."

Ruth smiled and held up a piece of paper.

"I entered a job competition at the Federal University and look!"

He took the paper.

"I got the job!" Ruth was beaming. Up until now she had been nothing but passive, pessimistic, about their plight. Then she'd seen the ad in the paper and entered the competition without telling Miguel. She'd borrowed the entrance fee from her father, who was still alive at that time. After years away from the books she had studied earnestly, and it had paid off.

Miguel put his arms around her and kissed her.

"Then I'm going to tell that factory to go fuck itself!"

They laughed together, happy for the first time in a long while.

"And I promise you, Miguel, that Luciano is not going to complain about going to daycare. He'd be a lot worse off with two down-at-the-mouth parents."

"Yeah, you're right."

"I start next week. It's a three-year contract! I always liked the idea of teaching, but you spoiled me, Miguel. You gave me the good life."

"Was it good, really?" he asked.

Ruth smiled and nodded.

"Well, as far as material things go, of course it was, but now I see how having everything so easy made me dependent on you. It's been almost two years since you left the army and our life changed, and it's been really hard for me. I mean it, Miguel."

"I know. Selling off our possessions, no money for anything . . ."

"But we're no fools, we're learning how to turn things around. We're learning how to grow."

Miguel kissed her again.

"Have you found a place for Luciano yet?"

"Nothing but bad news on that score. I've been looking, but they're all too expensive. We aren't going to have the money for it at first."

"So what do we do?"

"You can take care of him."

"Me?"

"Well, you'll be at home . . ."

"But if I'm stuck at home, how can I look for work?"

"And I haven't been stuck at home?"

"Sure, but you're his mother."

"And you're his father, Miguel. What are you saying?"

"Well, there's no way I'm going to be tied down to a crying child. I've been tied down long enough. I'll talk to my parents, maybe they can take Luciano during the day."

Ruth was no longer smiling.

"No, Miguel," she said firmly. "We've avoided asking for their help up till now and that's not going to change just because you won't accept your role as Luciano's father. Your parents have their own lives, and Luciano would upset that entirely. And don't even consider my folks."

Miguel ended up staying home with Luciano for almost a year. He took advantage of the time to finish his degree in business administration, taking classes at night, and joined a Reichian therapy group, which was the beginning of his interest in alternative philosophies. Eventually Ruth's father got Miguel a job on a project for the Ministry of Communications. The old politician still enjoyed some prestige, but by late 1974 he was having his own financial difficulties. The Banco Halles, in which he had invested heavily, was showing signs of failing, and he saw himself on the brink of economic collapse. The old man had a

cerebral hemorrhage talking with friends in Copacabana. He was
dead by the time they got him to the hospital. The family's assets
continued to decline, and Ruth's mother was forced to move into a
one-bedroom apartment on São Salvador Square, where she lived
alienated and isolated from the world.

In 1974 also Ruth and Miguel ran into Haidèe, an old family
friend, at a party thrown by the Rio section of the OAB for Dr.
Gouveia in recognition of his legal assistance to political prisoners. Not long after, Haidèe convinced Miguel to take a position
in advertising, publicity for her clothing business—much less
restrictive work, and better-paying, than his government job.

Ruth heard voices outside the cell. She got up and pressed her
ear to the door to see if she could tell what was going on, but the
cell was too well-insulated. Next she tried the peephole through
which the guard observed the cell without unlocking the door.
The metal plate slipped aside easily. Ruth put her face right up
to the hole, standing on tiptoe to get a better view.

She began to scream desperately when she saw her father-in-
law on a stretcher, unconscious, being carrying off by two men.
Her screams were of no use; one of the guards simply closed the
opening in her door and padlocked it. Ruth went on screaming
until she had no voice left to scream.

Red-eyed, hollow-cheeked, and with deep circles under her
eyes, Vivian sat on a metal bench beside the slab where Carlos'
body lay wrapped in a sheet. He had died the night before and
would have received a pauper's burial if she hadn't appeared
when she did. She had had to come up with almost five hundred
francs, but that was the least she could do for the old revolutionary. Kouma and Sanga stood guard beside the entrance to the
hospital morgue. Vivian had no tears left to cry. She felt only
revulsion.

At ten A.M. two men around Carlos' age showed up. Under the
vigilant eyes of the two Cameroonians, they sat down respectfully
beside the body. Finally, after a long silence, one of the men
looked at Vivian.

"Were you a relative?" he asked in heavily accented French.

"A friend," answered Vivian.

"My name is Rafael Contreras," said the old man, "a veteran
of the Spanish Civil War, just like dear Carlos. This is Lopez
Duran, a Republican colonel and also Carlos' friend."

Vivian nodded.

"We understand you've already made the arrangements," said Colonel Duran. As thin and stooped as he was, with his hard, reddened face covered with dark splotches, his gray eyes were bright and alive. "But we'd like to help in any way we can."

"We were very upset to hear what happened to our comrade, miss," said Contreras, a stocky man, modestly dressed in a worsted suit, with a deep voice and a face that looked as if it had been carved from an ornery hunk of wood. "Carlos was a loyal defender of the Spanish republic and proved himself a true hero during our escape from Irún. My friend and I owe him our lives. If we can be of any help at all . . ."

The old man's sonorous Spanish struck a chord in Vivian. But it was too late to help Carlos.

Coronel Duran bent down, stiffly, until his face was beside hers.

"We know he didn't die a natural death," he whispered.

Vivian sighed and her lips began to tremble.

"We were the ones who called to tell you about his 'accident.' Carlos came to us recently and asked us to keep an eye on him. He didn't want to get us involved in his problem, but he did say some faction of the Brazilian military regime was after him. Apparently he told you a lot more, which is understandable, you're young and full of energy and we're two old men who can hardly put one foot in front of the other anymore. But after what he did for us, the least we can do now is offer whatever help we can to you. We may be over the hill, but there are still a lot of things we can do. We're trained professionals, señorita, and we will never surrender to fascism."

Vivian put her arms around the old Spaniard.

"Carlos would be happy to know that you came," she said, embracing the other man as well. "The burial is tomorrow morning."

"We want to do more than just help with the funeral," protested Duran.

Contreras nodded his head vigorously.

"We know there's work to be done," the colonel went on. "And we don't want you to shoulder it alone."

Vivian pointed to her two friends at the door.

"I'm well-protected," she said.

"Why not accept our help as well?" asked Duran.

Vivian couldn't refuse their offer. These were two ghosts from the past, living reminders of Carlos, bringing him back to life at that difficult time. Duran's determined eyes and Contreras' sober expression were proof enough that they would be useful.

"Come with me," said Vivian. "I'm sure you'll be interested in what I have to show you."

The five of them left the morgue and drove around for a long time in Colonel Duran's car to make sure they weren't being followed. Finally, they parked the car near the Carrefour Odeon.

Once upstairs in Kouma and Sanga's apartment, Vivian produced the leather attaché case she had retrieved from the locker in Austerlitz Station. She opened a file folder, removed a thick envelope, and unfolded the contents, several pages written in Carlos' hand.

"Do you read Portuguese?"

"Yes, of course," said Duran. "Reading's no problem. It's understanding you Brazilians when you talk that's hard."

Vivian handed him the papers. As the two bent over the document attentively, she removed a cassette tape from the envelope and set it in her lap.

TRANSCRIPT OF THE TAPE MADE IN FEBRUARY 1978 AT THE ANNEX TO THE SÃO LUCAS SANATORIUM, PETRÓPOLIS, RIO DE JANEIRO, BRAZIL

Source of tape: *This tape was made by Dr. Marcos Azancoth during a night shift at the aforementioned sanatorium. A psychiatrist who worked at the sanatorium twice a week, Dr. Azancoth was a staunch supporter of O from 1968 until 1972. He stumbled on the meeting-in-progress and, realizing its importance, managed to get approximately half an hour of it on tape. Azancoth made a copy of the tape and sent it to O. He was apparently discovered because two weeks later he was shot while jogging on Avenida Atlântica. The police registered the murder as an attempted assault. The tape came to me in April.*

Contents of tape: *A conversation between four unidentified males. I have given each voice in the transcript a number.*

1: . . . That's right (pause), so I opened the safe . . .

2: Then he left it open, on purpose. He's no dummy.

1: No way, man. It was locked, secret code and all. But I knew the code. I looked over her shoulder a couple of times.

3: He's going to find out.

1: No, he won't, I left everything exactly the way it was. I just made copies of what we need. He'll never know . . .

2: I don't want to be too optimistic, but if we pull this off we'll be able to begin the operation in October.

4: Just in time for the amnesty.

1: And they think we're sitting around on our hands!

3: Sure, sure, but what's this about October? You don't mean . . .

2: You got it: Operation Hades.

4: You guys are out of your minds.

1: Not with three million bucks we're not.

2: Three million? Shit, those Commies were set for life.

1: They were stupid, man. They let that money sit there getting moldy.

4: So what's the plan?

1: Simple. Only three people had access to the money. One had sole access, that was Lamarca, who we already took out. He gets fucked, which they figured, while two others can get to it, but only working together. They each have half the digits of the numbered account.

3: Who are they?

1: Hold on! I only know who one of them is. The other's referred to by a code name in the papers in the safe.

3: So, who's the one you know? Spit it out, for Christ's sake, don't keep us in suspense, you asshole.

1: This sucks, you guys are out of line. What's your problem? Don't you trust me?

(Altercation, all of them talking at the same time)

4: Quiet! Shit, one at a time, or we'll never fucking get out of here today.

1: Yeah!

3: But no more games, no more keeping things from us.

1: Nobody's keeping anything from anyone.

(Another altercation between 1 and 3—they trade insults)

4: Hey look, you assholes, this sucks. I'm out of here.

(The argument subsides)

4: That's better. Let's be cool.

1: Okay, this is the deal: what you need to do is put the squeeze on the one we know—which is Haidèe Jaffet.

(Murmurs)

1: I can't show my face, not till later anyway. But she has to know who's got the other half of the account number.

4: I'll take care of her.

1: She'll talk, I guarantee it. She'll want to save her skin. If I know Haidèe, she'll give us what we need, after she does a little kicking to keep up appearances.

3. And then?

1: Then I'll make the connection. I'll be the go-between, but remember, I stay behind the scenes. That bitch has got one hell of a file on me.

3: That wouldn't take much imagination, now would it?

1: Fuck off, man. Shit, this guy just won't get off my case.

3: Hey, doing business with you is worse than sleeping with a rattlesnake.

4: Okay, guys, let's not start . . .

3: My lips are sealed . . .

2: How much time do you think the . . . well, the *persuasion* phase will take?

1: Two or three days, I think. She's not going to have much choice.

2: And how long to get our hands on the cash?

1: The way I figure it, two more weeks.

2: So, Operation Hades can get started in May and peak in

October. I'd like to see them try to get amnesty for a saint after that.

4: The last phase is going to cost a bundle, at least four hundred and fifty thousand dollars. Almost half of it just for payoffs.

3: Corrupt sons of bitches in that administration.

4: No kidding.

1: But we're going to have all we need, while the Commies are going to be standing there in their undershorts.

3: How do you see the final phase?

4: We get together a dozen experienced hit men. For what we offer to pay them, they'll practically be willing to be kamikazes. We check them all out first, real carefully. And hell, we really will turn them into kamikazes—their pockets will be stuffed with subversive material. These twelve guys will be the front line of the attack, they'll be our commandos. (There is laughter) But we have to agree on the list of who to target.

2: I don't think any military guys should be included at all. Just the craphead politicians.

4: But we already agreed that it's important to have a few military targets. It's not enough to off two or three politicians and a few cabinet ministers. Some of our guys have to be in there too.

3: I think twenty-five is too many hits to begin with. Shit! We could lose control of the thing.

1: Control, what control? What the hell are we in control of now? The Commies are running around scot-free, publishing newspapers and everything.

4: Anyway, we do still have to work on the list . . .

1: And fast, because . . .

(end of tape)

Instructions: With O destroyed and disbanded, I'm alone now. Whoever gains access to this document should follow these instructions to the letter.

Once these emergency measures have been set in motion, the bearer of these instructions should appear twice a week, on Tuesday and Thursday, at 1:00 P.M., counting from zero hour, October 21, 1978, at the restaurant La Coupole, ground floor, with the leather briefcase containing these papers, until being contacted.

Contact will be made by a woman approximately 60 years of age named Haidèe Jaffet—her real identity—or by someone she sends in her place. The bearer will present the paper bearing half the account number and access code and demand the other series of numbers in exchange.

All care should be taken with the aforementioned sheet on which the number is recorded. It's the only copy. If it's erased or lost, the game is over.

Once the series is complete, it should immediately be taken to the CAISSE D'EPARGNE DE GENEVE and presented to the clerk in charge of the account, M. Jean-Pierre Grunt, who will initiate the appropriate procedures at that time.

Steps should be taken with due regard to the following contingencies:

a) the possibility of the funds being absorbed by the Swiss treasury.

b) the possibility of the funds falling into the hands of the extreme right.

Since O no longer exists, the ultimate disposition of the funds is left to the judgment of the bearer and the contact.

Colonel Duran handed the papers back to Vivian, his expression grave. It wasn't the first time he had been faced with something like this—the spoils of a leftist coalition destroyed by the powerful forces of authoritarian repression. These days his life consisted of almost nothing else—old libertarian dreams, all toppled into the same common grave of impossibility, unfeasibility. His friend Carlos hadn't escaped this fate either; here was the living proof. Even in death he was trapped by a piece of paper, a series of numbers.

Duran extended his thin hand and took the paper once again. He reexamined the code in Carlos' handwriting:

NEUFNEUFCINQDOUZEDOUZEUNE

"Have you followed the instructions?" he asked.

Vivian shook her head.

"What are you waiting for?"

"Courage."

The two Spaniards exchanged looks, understanding.

"You can count on us," said the colonel. "We'll figure out a way to make contact safely. There's less than twenty-four hours until the next scheduled contact."

Colonel Duran walked to the window and stood watching the traffic below. A ray of sun shone into the apartment, yellow, timid, indecisive. Sometimes the Paris sun made Vivian feel utterly forlorn, because it didn't heat anything, didn't burn anything, it was too polite to the skin. At such times she would dream of Brazil, of Rio, of the blazing promiscuity of her homeland. And her despair would increase; she wasn't cut out to live in exile. Perhaps that was true of Brazilians in general. Even Carlos, a citizen of the world, had surprised her sometimes with his nostalgia for home. It was very odd, and painful.

At the window, Colonel Duran was brooding, his thoughts wandering back to another time and place. A certain moment outside Barcelona in the middle of the night. He was in a convoy of prisoners under the guard of German and Falangist troops. It was February 1939, Catalonia was already in the hands of the Francoists, the partisans of General Miaja were negotiating the Republicans' surrender, and four hundred thousand defeated troops were crossing the French border as they could. He was determined to be shot trying to escape rather than remain captured. The convoy of trucks stopped in the middle of the night and Duran saw they were on the outskirts of Granollers, a small city near Barcelona. One of his fellow prisoners asked him to lean aside so he could look through the hole in the tarpaulin. It was Carlos, the restless young Brazilian from one of the international brigades. Carlos proved to have extraordinary courage, jumping out of the truck with Duran, escaping the guards' rain of bullets, disappearing into the sparse woods that bordered the road. As luck would have it, Duran was shot in the thigh. Not a serious wound, but it would slow his flight through an area infested with Fascists and terrified peasants. And so Carlos dragged him across the fields of Catalonia, heading north. They were almost captured in the Canelles swamp, but they skirted the village of Benabarre, and a month after escaping from the convoy made it to the border town of Irún and finally across the French border to Bayonne, accompanied by Rafael Contreras and a dozen other Republicans. If it hadn't been for Carlos' somewhat reckless style, they would never have staged an unarmed attack on a Falangist car, which they then used to cross the border. Once in France, they split up. Duran didn't see Carlos again until 1954, in Paris, when the Brazilian was returning from a trip to the Soviet Union. Perhaps this was the way dreams end, thought Duran, in a simple exchange of kindness. What was set in motion by ideals would end in the return of a personal favor, plain and simple. Shaken down to the individual level, between him and Carlos, no longer a question of grand hopes or ecstatic utopias.

"Carlos was an odd person," said Contreras.

Jolted out of memory, Duran nodded.

"Odd? How do you mean?" asked Vivian.

Contreras flushed. He was less extroverted than Duran, but resolved to explain himself.

"Well, he didn't seem like a Communist at all—I mean, we thought he was an anarchist at first. He never adhered to party discipline. He did risky things, acted on impulse, like an adventurer or something. I remember more than once he put everything on the line . . ." He paused and broke into a smile.

Vivian watched and waited, intrigued.

"He was thirty years old at the time," Contreras continued. "The youngest in the group, I think. Maybe that explains it, but it wasn't youth alone. Carlos was impulsive, extreme by nature. And that's what saved us."

Kouma appeared with a tray of tea. Contreras fell silent, and the Spaniards looked somewhat relieved to be freed of the weight of the past. Vivian thought she understood what they meant about Carlos, his informal, undogmatic character. The truth was that Carlos really liked being alive—of this she was certain—and life for him had meaning only when it was full of surprises.

Vivian was learning that she didn't like surprises. She sipped her tea and wondered if the unexpected legacy Carlos had left her might not somehow abbreviate her exile there.

Luciano was at the window watching the cars fly by in the high-speed lane, a schoolbook open in his lap, when he noticed a suspicious movement at the main entrance to the building. A dark blue station wagon had just pulled onto the sidewalk down below. Several men got out carrying machine guns.

It was noon. His mother and grandfather had left well before he woke up, and had been gone for hours. A strange sense of foreboding made him jump out of his chair and run to the other room where dona Rita was reading the newspaper.

"Luciano, what's wrong?" Dona Rita's paper dropped to the floor. Her nerves were on edge, and she was grateful for how Luciano had been behaving. Normally he would not last long studying quietly at the window, but would be running from room to room, pretending to be one of his favorite super-heroes.

"Grandma, there are some men downstairs. They have guns. I think they're coming up here."

"What are you talking about, my boy?" she said, clearly taking his warning no more seriously than one of his games.

Luciano became impatient.

"Grandma, I'm telling you they're on their way up here. If you don't believe me, that's your problem, but I'm not going to surrender, not me."

"Enough, Luciano, enough."

"But Grandma . . ."

The doorbell rang. Dona Rita felt her legs go tingly and the blood drain from her face.

She walked to the door in slow motion; the bell was ringing insistently. Luciano hid behind the bookcase, positioned so that he could watch the door.

Rosa appeared in the living room.

"Who is it?" asked dona Rita.

"Open up," yelled a gruff masculine voice. "It's the police."

"Just a minute," answered dona Rita, her voice thinning to a thread of sound. "I have to get the key."

She tried to close the peephole but the man wouldn't let her.

"Leave it open, ma'am," he ordered.

Rosa overcame her own fear and grabbed Luciano by the arm.

"We're getting out of here," she said.

The boy didn't answer but followed along. They went through the kitchen to the service entrance, but opened the door to find two men holding machine guns.

Rosa screamed. Luciano studied the dark metal of the guns, fascinated.

"Back inside," barked one of the men.

The other pushed Rosa up against the wall and began to frisk her.

"What do you think you're doing?" she protested as he ran his hands up and down her body with a zeal that was more about abuse and humiliation than a mere search for weapons.

"Shut up," said the man.

Luciano suddenly dodged around the man and ran down the hall and up the stairs. Caught off guard, the man was slow to react, even though they had express orders to come in cleanly and snatch the boy, unharmed.

"Shit, the kid!" his partner yelled. "Fuck, you let him get away!"

The other hurried off after Luciano. Taking advantage of the moment, Rosa followed the boy's example, dashing out of the apartment. She headed downstairs instead of up, hoping to draw the second man after her.

But he didn't take the bait; both men were already climbing the stairs in pursuit of Luciano. Rosa hesitated a moment, then hurried down the stairs. Though Luciano's initial instinct had been shrewd, he had chosen a route that held little chance of escape. She had to find a way to stop him from being kidnapped.

Rosa slowed when she heard voices. She was almost at the ground floor, and the voices were coming closer. It was incredible the knack she had lately for getting herself into jams like this. Guns seemed to be pointing at her from every which way, angry men threatening her freedom. Her karma was very strange—maybe in another life she had brandished guns in other people's faces and now she was paying for it. No way to be sure, but it made sense. The idea of reincarnation seemed very plausible; it offered a certain explanation for the troubled existence of someone who was by nature a calm, peaceful, nonviolent creature.

Rosa ran down the hall and rang the bell at the servants' entrance of the first apartment she came to.

"Who is it?" called a woman's voice from inside.

"Your neighbor from upstairs."

She could hear the men drawing closer. The door opened a crack, the chain still in place. That's the way it was nowadays, everyone was afraid, locked in behind bolts and chains.

"Please, I need help," begged Rosa. "Let me in."

A woman's face, perhaps the maid's, looked at her with visible apprehension.

"What's wrong? Who are you?"

"I live upstairs," said Rosa, trembling. "There are some men . . . I think we're being robbed."

The lie came easily, and elicited the desired result. The woman's mouth fell open and she peered into the hall nervously.

"My God," she said, fumbling with the chain. "Quick, come inside."

"I think the whole building's being robbed," said Rosa breathlessly. "Our apartment was overrun by men with guns. I ran out the back way . . . I'm so afraid . . ."

Rosa leaned full-body against the door, as if to prevent an imminent invasion.

"How many of them are there?" asked the woman.

"I don't know. When they do something like this there's usually a whole bunch."

The woman nodded assent.

"I'm alone here," she said. "I'm the maid. They all went out."

"We have to do something, fast. They're probably cleaning the place out, floor by floor."

"What can we do?"

"Call the police!" said Rosa. It seemed a ridiculous idea, to call the police on the police. But Rosa knew those men were not regular cops. Old Gouveia had been right. The boy was in danger, it was Luciano they wanted. And the presence of some real police might just confuse things long enough for the boy to escape.

"The phone's over there," said the woman.

"What number do I call? Check the phone book."

The woman found the list of emergency numbers and as Rosa dialed, called out each digit, but the line was busy.

"Shit," said Rosa. "That's the way it is when you need them."

"Try again," insisted the woman.

"You try," said Rosa, handing her the phone. "And keep trying. I'm going to see what's happening out there."

"Be careful!" warned the woman.

Rosa slipped out the kitchen door and up the stairs. The apartment was empty, everything in place. No sign of a struggle.

"Dona Rita," called Rosa.

No answer.

God, they had acted fast. And now they had Luciano, just as Dr. Gouveia had feared.

Rosa felt useless. But she didn't give up altogether. She took the elevator downstairs to find the lobby in an uproar. The doorman was trying to explain what was going on to a small group of indignant tenants who had been locked in the cleaning closet.

Two military police vans pulled up and parked at the curb.

No sooner were they in the front door than the police were barraged with questions from the furious crowd.

A sergeant stepped forward. "One at a time," he shouted.

Silence momentarily reigned.

"Someone called and reported a robbery in progress," said the sergeant.

"A robbery!" yelled one of the tenants who had been locked in the closet. "Those men said they were cops!"

"What?" said the sergeant.

Rosa pushed through the crowd and stood facing the sergeant.

"I'm the one who called. The men said they were police, but obviously they weren't. They abducted the grandson of Dr. Gouveia, who lives here in the building."

"Who are you?" asked the sergeant, trying to digest this information.

"I'm a friend of the family. I was there when it happened. They took the boy's grandmother, too."

Tense, struggling to overcome his fear, the doorman stepped forward. He was about to do something uncommon; usually people just kept quiet about such things and pretended to know nothing. But he was friendly with Dr. Gouveia.

"I noticed the license plate on one of the cars," he said. "6790. I don't know what letters it had on it, but it said 6790. They were two dark blue station wagons. One parked here at the entrance and the other one way over there, under those trees."

The sergeant rubbed his chin and went outside to his Patamo. It didn't take long to confirm that there had been no police activity at that address. It was just as he suspected, a snake he would now have to skin. He gave headquarters the license number so all patrol cars could be alerted, then returned to the building.

"Which way did they go?" he asked the doorman.

"They skidded up over the divider and headed downtown."

The sergeant ordered two men to stay in the lobby and collect as much information about the incident as possible and walked back to his car. Rosa ran out to talk to him.

"Can I go with you?" she asked. "I got a good look at two of them . . ."

Before he could refuse, she pleaded, "Please, Sergeant, I might be useful."

The sergeant relented.

The police van headed off in the direction indicated by the doorman, siren screaming. The sergeant was in constant communication with headquarters, but Rosa was at a loss to understand the police lingo he spoke in, especially with all the static.

As they approached the Marinheiros viaduct, something came over the radio. The sergeant requested confirmation and the message was repeated. Rosa felt his uneasiness and saw him exchange looks with the driver.

"What's going on?" asked Rosa.

"Nothing," said the sergeant. But he was a bad liar.

"For God's sake, tell me what's going on."

Neither cop said a word. The driver pulled to a stop in front of the Candelaria church.

"This is where you get out," said the sergeant.

"What?"

"You heard me," he shouted. "Get out."

And he opened the door and pushed her, hard, so that she almost landed in the gutter.

Rosa fell to her knees and the van took off like a shot. People on the sidewalk stepped back, afraid. But Rosa was not giving up. A more powerful force had ordered the cops off the trail. Rosa rose to her feet, wiped her scraped knees, and took a deep breath. She was not defeated yet. If all this was some kind of provocation, fine—she knew how to endure her karma. She looked around at the frightened passersby and shook her head, feeling sorry for them, slaves to their small fears.

The stone house, rustic and ancient, sat beneath a leafy woods in Combault, far outside Paris. There was virtually no furniture; the place looked abandoned. The entire ground floor was empty with the exception of one table, three chairs, and a gas range used to heat water for coffee. His food arrived on tin plates and there was no running water. Two lamps lit the whole house, one downstairs and the other in one of the upstairs bedrooms. Miguel lay on a mattress on the floor feeling grateful it was summer; as cold as it was, he could imagine what winter would be like here. Three men guarded him in shifts. This one didn't talk much. But then Miguel hadn't been too voluble himself lately.

Their arrival in France, on a regular Varig flight, had gone without a hitch. Major Portugal directed the operation with self-assurance. Miguel's fake passport didn't arouse an ounce of interest in the immigration clerk. A car was waiting for them at Orly airport, the driver just one more of his guard dogs. There were three of them: the arrogant Major Portugal, the other guy on the flight with them, whose qualifications were apparent from his build and his crooked boxer's nose, and the hairy driver who looked as if he were on drugs. Escape was out of the question, his captors had made that quite clear: if he didn't behave, the lives of his wife and son weren't worth a damn.

Miguel was more than a little disoriented, not just from the change in time zones, but because he had been kept in a small, dark, freezing-cold cell ever since his capture. They had left him alone entirely until just a few hours before the trip, and then made the threats against his family, handed him a passport, and told him to follow Major Portugal's orders to the letter. Famished, exhausted, and completely demoralized, he hadn't been able to sleep at all during the nine-hour nonstop flight from Rio to Paris. The on-flight food revived him slightly, but mainly he felt drained and uncomfortable. The man with the broken nose stuck to him like glue, even when he went to the toilet. Arriving in a foreign country where he didn't speak the language simply added to his sense of powerlessness. The only one who spoke French was Major Portugal, who made all the necessary contacts and arrangements.

The woods surrounding the house were mangy, full of garbage, sawed-down trees that lay where they fell, and several hopeless, rusty cars. The starkness of the house itself didn't help much, either. But once Miguel had been handcuffed to the metal ring on the wall above the mattress, he began to feel the need to react, to shake off his disorientation and despair and concentrate on some possibility, any possiblity. He resolved not to go on making life easy for his captors.

Miguel sat down on the mattress and studied the man guarding him, who was armed with a .45-caliber automatic pistol and sat nervously chewing a wooden matchstick.

"My arms and legs are asleep," said Miguel. "Can't I at least stretch a little?"

"I can't take the cuffs off, if that's what you're thinking," said the guard, clearly irritated and feeling almost as much a prisoner as Miguel.

"Sure you could," insisted Miguel. "Just long enough for me to stretch out a little, or run around the room. You've got a gun—I wouldn't stand a chance if I tried something, and I'm not stupid."

"Neither am I," said the guard.

"Come on, man. You don't have to be so inflexible."

"Are you crazy? You think I'd trust a Commie?"

"I'm not a Commie."

"No—and I am, right?"

"I'm a captain. And I bet you're—what? A sergeant?"

"Yeah, and you're a captain? Really?" asked the man, incredulous but intrigued.

"Really. They haven't let you in on anything, have they," Miguel said sympathetically. "Of course not, you're only a sergeant."

"You can forget it, I'm not taking the cuffs off you," said the man, but Miguel could tell he'd hit a nerve. The other two clearly treated this one with contempt.

"Okay, so follow the major's orders to the letter. But you know, the rope always breaks at the weakest point. And you know what happens to someone who shows disrespect to a superior."

"You're no captain, no way!"

"Want to bet? Just ask the major, he'll tell you."

The man sat with his legs crossed, bouncing the top one nervously as he studied Miguel. Then he examined the gun in his holster, stood up, and stretched.

"Hey, that's all I'm asking for," said Miguel, "just one good stretch."

The man walked a few steps toward Miguel and stopped. He scratched his head doubtfully and changed his mind.

"Shit, man," said Miguel. "I told you I'm not stupid enough to try anything. Look at me, you wouldn't even need your gun. If you gave me a good left hook, I wouldn't know what hit me."

The man just stood there.

"You're no flyweight, Captain," he said finally.

"Go ahead, make fun of me. But don't say I didn't warn you."

The man scratched his head again and looked at the metal ring on the wall. Miguel's right hand was free, but the left hung limply from the wrist, which the handcuff had reduced to raw meat.

"Okay, I'll let you stretch a little. But I mean it, if you try anything, you'll be sorry."

Miguel smiled. "I won't forget this."

"No more lip," said the man. "I still say you're nothing but a fucking Communist."

Miguel held his free hand up in a peace sign and waited for the man to release his wrist. After he had done so, the man stood poised, gun at the ready.

"Now you can stretch to your heart's content."

"When are they due back?"

"There's time," said the man, consulting his watch.

"Have you noticed that they spend less time on guard duty than you do?"

The man shrugged.

"Just do your thing, because I'm not waiting for them to come back to put the cuff back on. You have ten minutes."

"Thanks," said Miguel, beginning to shake his arms and legs, flexing and unflexing, still standing right beside the mattress.

The man watched him, jittery, his hand on his holster.

"Would it be okay if I run around the room a little?"

"Go on, but remember, you don't have a lot of time."

Miguel stretched a few more times and then began running around the room, slowly at first, the enforced inertia of the past days having left his muscles stiff and reflexes slow. Gradually he accelerated, without varying his circuit, keeping close to the wall with the man in the center of the circle. Five more times around and he began to slow; he was beginning to tire and didn't want to be short of breath. A crazy idea was brewing in his head, and he couldn't stop thinking that it was worth trying. He began kicking his legs up as he ran in circles, then tried a few hops. His guard continued to watch, still looking nervous but slightly less attentive.

Bounding about the room, Miguel decided it was time. If it worked, great, and if it didn't, he would be dead. The man followed him with his eyes from the middle of the room. Miguel stopped hopping, began running again, and suddenly jumped up onto the chair the man had been sitting on. From there, he catapulted through the air, aiming his feet to hit the man in the head full-force. The man's hand darted to the holster and he tried to dodge, but he wasn't fast enough. Miguel felt his heels slam the man's chin, hard, so that he fell backwards and Miguel landed on his feet, crashing against the near wall. He steadied himself and ran to the man, whose jaw was dislocated in a sinister smile, threads of blood streaming from his nose. He was unconscious, breathing heavily, his arms flung wide.

As if accustomed to violence, Miguel merely removed the .45 from its holster and began looking through the man's pockets. He found a billfold with two thousand francs, a hundred-dollar bill, and I.D.'s confirming that the man was a sergeant. Miguel stuffed the money in his pocket and threw the wallet on the floor. Then he began looking around the room for his fake passport. It was nowhere to be seen, so he went downstairs.

Before searching the ground floor, Miguel opened the back door and peered out. The woods were dense with low-hanging trees, but there was a path to the right. Miguel walked around the house looking for other escape routes. There was a narrow dirt driveway lined with boulders leading away from the house that ended at a low wooden gate with a simple sliding latch. On the other side of the gate was a quiet, seemingly deserted paved road. No neighbors. What to do? How could he take his chances with the inhabitants of a country whose language he didn't speak? Much less without drawing attention to himself. And how could he find his way? There were too many questions. He returned to the house to search for his documents or anything else that might be of use.

The others would be back soon, he had to hurry. Where did they put the suitcases? He found a built-in closet in the living room. Locked. He broke the door down and found the suitcases and a few packages. He pulled everything out. The wrapped packages contained bottles of sugarcane liquor. In the suitcases, among the clothes, he found his fake passport and the envelope with the letter from Haidèe that had contained the dollars. The money wasn't there, of course, but the instructions were still readable, though battered from so much handling. He put the paper and the passport in his pocket and stuffed everything else back in the closet. He went to the kitchen and opened the door. But where should he go? He didn't have the slightest idea how to get to the place indicated in Haidèe's letter and, besides, according to the instructions, he'd have to wait almost twenty-four hours. Where could he wait that long without looking suspicious? Right here, he thought. He didn't even have to leave the house. He'd wait for the others to return and surprise them. Then he would force the major to take him to the rendezvous.

Miguel went back upstairs. His guard was still grinning his disquieting grin. Miguel removed the man's holster and buckled

it around his own waist. He went and got the handcuffs, to secure
the man before he came to. But the weight of his arm! Miguel
bent over, his ear to the man's chest. Nothing, no heartbeat.
No pulse. Desperate, he shook the man, slapping his face. No
reaction. Gradually, bleakly, Miguel accepted the fact that he had
killed someone. Just a slam to the head in a wild effort to escape!
He hadn't meant to kill him, only to knock him out. But there
was no time for regret. He dragged the body to the mattress and
laid him down as if he were sleeping. Then, sweating heavily, he
went downstairs to await the others.

It was late afternoon before Miguel heard the sound of the car
arriving and the clang of the gate at the end of the driveway being
opened. He would wait until after they came up the drive and
parked the car out front and were getting out, distracted, maybe
even carrying packages. He opened the door a crack and watched
the car pass through the gate and pause for the man to close it.
Major Portugal was at the wheel.

"Okay," shouted Miguel the moment they stepped out of the
car, their arms full of groceries, "lie down on the ground with
your arms and legs spread."

The younger one dropped his grocery bags in midair and hit the
dirt just as Miguel had ordered. The major's reaction, however,
was to turn, heave his packages at Miguel, pull his gun, and shoot,
all in a split second.

But Miguel's reflexes were equally quick. He instinctively
dodged the groceries and ducked. As the bullet whistled over
his head, he squeezed the trigger of his automatic. The shot
reverberated much louder than the other one, and the kick threw
Miguel backwards. The slug opened a hole in Major Portugal's
chest and threw him onto the hood of the car. He slid down to a
sitting position on the ground, his back against a tire, his mouth
agape and eyes wild.

Miguel leaped to his feet, breathless and trembling, as the
major leaned slowly forward until his forehead rested on the dirt
between his legs. The other man, whose name he didn't know,
lay curled in a fetal position, as if waiting for his turn.

"You there," called Miguel, his voice a little unsteady, "don't
move, do you hear me? Don't move or you'll get it too."

The man curled tighter. Miguel approached and searched him
carefully. Instead of a gun, he found an enormous knife in a
sheath bound to his leg. Miguel held the tip against his back,

poking with just enough pressure to draw blood and instill terror. The man returned to a curled position and began moaning.

"What's your name?"

Instead of answering he went on moaning.

"I said, what's your name? Speak up!"

The back of the man's shirt was beginning to darken with blood.

"Get up," ordered Miguel, shouting. "Come on, on your feet!"

The man got up.

"Get your friend over there," ordered Miguel, pointing to the major. "Haul him inside. Let's go!"

The man grasped the major's lifeless body under the armpits and began dragging him toward the door. It was a difficult task—a heavy load under any circumstances, now literally dead weight.

"Keep moving," shouted Miguel.

The man didn't even dare look up.

"Come on, faster. Get him inside . . ."

Once over the threshold, the man left the major in a heap on the floor beside the door and collapsed, breathless and exhausted, beside him. The bullet had left a charred hole in the back of the major's leather jacket. Miguel looked at the cadaver and felt sick to his stomach. He wondered about the fate of the man's soul and about what sort of moral compensation he himself would have to pay. This was a strange way of fulfilling his individual karma, through violence and destruction.

Miguel quickly got hold of himself and kicked the door closed. He waved his gun, signaling the man to move away from the body.

"Now you're going to answer a few questions," he said.

The man stood up and in one leap hurled himself at Miguel. His move was so quick and unexpected that Miguel's attempt to dive out of the way was only partially successful. Knocked hard against the wall, he struggled to regain his balance and raised the gun. But the man had turned and sprinted for the back door, and the bullet smashed into the plaster instead. Miguel ran to the back door in time to see the man take off up the path into the woods. Clearly he knew the terrain, which gave him an advantage. Maybe he hoped Miguel would follow him, but Miguel did not. He replaced the gun in the holster and ran to the car. It would be better to get out of there, better to spend the night in the car parked in some deserted place than with two corpses.

They had made a left turn into the driveway when he first arrived. Miguel's captors must have assumed he wouldn't be able to orient himself in a strange city, or perhaps they were worried about attracting attention, for they hadn't bothered to blindfold him. But Miguel had etched every detail along the route in his memory. He knew they had passed two houses built right at the edge of the road, a factory that made garden tools, and a suburban train station. He had to find his way back to Paris, where a non–French-speaking stranger would not arouse suspicion.

Turning right out of the driveway, he passed, one by one, each of the landmarks he had fixed in his memory on the way from the airport. Finally, he turned onto a street in a more populated area. It was a small village; the train station should be close by. He parked the car in front of a sports store and walked in the direction that looked most promising. After two very long blocks he realized he was in danger of getting lost and decided to try asking directions. Stopping in a café, he acted as if he were a deaf-mute at first and then, feeling ridiculous, decided to talk, using Portuguese words which he knew were close to the French ones.

"Um café!" he called out.

He was waited on and that made him feel good. The man at the counter accepted a hundred-franc note, mumbling furiously, and handed him lots of small coins in return. Miguel decided it was time to try his luck again.

"Estação de trem?" he asked.

The man behind the counter looked even more furious.

"Trem, viajar," said Miguel hopefully.

But the man didn't seem to understand.

Miguel grabbed a paper napkin and made as if to draw on it, but he didn't have a pen.

"Uma caneta?" he asked, mimicking the act of writing.

The man looked at him and stalked off toward the kitchen.

"Shit, he doesn't understand a word I'm saying," Miguel sighed out loud.

The man stopped and turned.

"Well, how about that! You're speaking Portuguese!" the man said, astonished.

Miguel laughed.

"Of course I am!"

"You're Brazilian," said the man. "I thought I was going nuts . . ."

"I'm lost," said Miguel. "I came to visit some friends and I don't know how to get back to Paris. Can you help me?"

"Of course, nothing to it," said the man in very Portuguese Portuguese. "You go down this street, all the way down until you get to a cross street at the end. Then you'll see a park, and the station is right there, you just get on a train to Paris. It'll stop at the Gare de l'Est."

"Thanks a lot, once I find the station I'll make out okay."

The Portuguese laughed. " 'I'll make out okay,' now that's a Brazilian talking."

"You take it easy," said Miguel.

A half hour later he was sitting in the tiny station. He didn't have to ask questions here, there were signs to follow. He bought a ticket and waited on the platform, just beginning to realize how tired he was. There were a lot of people—old women in raincoats with their carryalls, young rosy-cheeked kids with knapsacks, and men wearing baggy trousers and berets.

The train arrived fifteen minutes later, the loudspeaker announcing the route and all the stops along the way. Miguel settled into a plastic seat near the back. He felt like taking off his shoes but imagined this would shock the two old ladies dozing across from him.

He examined the train car, reading the ad posters and studying the map under plastic that hung beside the door. The doors linking the cars were locked. He confirmed this by checking the latches, to the surprised and reproving stares of the two old ladies.

It was a long ride, and the train passed small villages, highways, and crops in rows in various shades of green. Miguel counted the stations: there should be six before the Gare de l'Est, where he would get off. He didn't have a lot of money, but imagined it would be enough for a room in a cheap hotel overnight. As soon as he arrived in Paris, he would buy a map and try to locate the address indicated in Haidèe's instructions.

In the car behind him, pretending to be asleep, was the man who had escaped from Miguel. The blood on the back of his shirt had coagulated in dark rings and his filthy clothing made him look like a beggar. No one had taken the seat beside him, and he stretched his legs out conspicuously and crossed his arms, his dark, disheveled hair falling into his face. The French passengers gave him a wide berth; besides being dressed like a panhandler, he looked vaguely Arabic.

He had arrived at the station well after Miguel. He was amazed and impressed to find Miguel there, not expecting his charge to operate so successfully on unfamiliar ground. He'd lurked in the stairwell, waiting to board the car until the last minute, when the buzzers announced that the doors were about to close. In Paris he would settle accounts.

Without knowing he was being followed, Miguel struggled not to fall asleep. He had wrapped the .45 in a towel and cradled it carefully in his arms like a baby. The old ladies kept staring at him and whispering.

When the train pulled into the station, Miguel got off and moved confidently into the crowd. Following the press of passengers he soon found himself in the main waiting room and headed for the closest newsstand, where he bought a guide to Paris and a British newspaper; he knew enough English to at least peruse the day's news. Intermittently he looked up to scan the movement around him in the station. Purely a precaution. He was not expecting a welcoming committee.

The "panhandler" stood on the far side of the waiting room, shielded by a sign indicating arrivals and departures. He watched intently as Miguel leafed through the paper. When Miguel began walking, the man waited to see which exit he was heading for, wiping his nose with the back of his hand. Once Miguel started down a small staircase to the street, he left his hiding place and followed, tense as he passed two policemen who were looking at him suspiciously. That was all he needed. He'd already spent a night in jail and had been forced to alert certain contacts in Sûreté, who had acted promptly but charged dearly for the favor. He couldn't afford another screwup like that.

Out on the street, Miguel headed for a couple of hotels near the station that he'd seen advertised in the paper. The man watched Miguel go into the first hotel and come out almost immediately. Apparently the prices were not to his liking. He checked out a few more before finally choosing the most modest and disreputable-looking of them all. The man watched as Miguel carried on a difficult conversation, full of hand gestures, with the doorman. They were making him pay in advance because he had no baggage.

Miguel's pursuer turned and hurried back to the station. He knew where Miguel was staying and was certain he would not leave until the following day, to keep the appointment at La Coupole.

Miguel went up to his room, locked the door, and collapsed onto the narrow, creaky bed. He lay there, images of the two murders he had committed passing slowly before his eyes like a silent film, repetitive and sickening. He sat up and buried his face in his hands. In just a few days he had been transformed into a dangerous animal, exactly like his enemies. He simply couldn't fathom the underlying cause of this madness. And that was what hurt him most deeply, even more than the lives he had taken.

Suddenly an idea hit him like a thunderbolt and he leaped to his feet. Why hadn't he thought of this before? He was free. No one held him captive any longer, and for all intents and purposes he had disappeared forever in a foreign country where his enemies were as much at a disadvantage as he was. All he needed to do was make a phone call. He'd call Ruth. If she was out, which was likely, he'd call his father, who would surely be either at home or in his office, and who would be able to explain all this foolishness. His eyes darted to the bedside table. Of course. This was not the type of hotel to have phones in the rooms. And if he were to ask to make an international call at the desk, they would either throw him out or charge an exorbitant fee. But in the station he would surely find a phone booth, and he could place the call in English. The French operator would act insulted, no doubt, but at least he would be able to make himself understood.

He hurried downstairs and returned to the station, where the sight of a sign with a telephone outlined in blue and the letters PTT sent a thrill down his spine. Not just a booth but a telephone office, which would make an overseas call even easier. The blonde, heavily made-up woman behind the window looked at him and frowned. Miguel was beginning to think that everyone in Paris suffered from an excess of bile. It seemed that no one smiled; they were all ready to scowl and bluster at the least pretext.

"Do you speak English?"

The woman shot him a look, pursing her smeary, lipsticked mouth, and pointed to another window above which hung a large sign in English. Miguel moved down the counter and a young clerk, absorbed in reading a comic book, looked up, irritated.

First Miguel tried calling his apartment. It would be midday in Brazil, and Ruth was not likely to be home. Just as he expected, no answer. Next he tried Gouveia's office, with the same result. Which struck him as odd, because normally at least old dona Guiomar, his father's secretary for over a quarter century, would be there. But sometimes even the dona Guiomars of life fail you. The phone at his parents' apartment began ringing and his heart clenched.

No answer. He looked uncomprehendingly at the receiver, listening to the insistent ringing sound on the other end.

Miguel returned to the hotel crestfallen, trying to push away the sinister thoughts that were filling his brain.

As the streetcar rumbled through the arches heading for Santa Tereza, Rosa sat stroking her scraped knees and tried to come up with a plan. Her mind was fuzzy, but that was nothing new. She was used to living as if enshrouded in fog. Her life had always felt like that, indistinct, rarified—clear outlines visible only when things were in flux, then fading away in the mist. That was what had happened when she met Miguel at the Interior Illumination center. The fog had suddenly lifted, only to settle in again, thicker than ever, when the violence began. It had dissipated entirely at the moment she perceived the danger to Luciano, but now was falling down around her shoulders once more, clouding her thoughts, veiling her options. She tried to focus on the row of houses down below in Lapa and on the imposing facades that dominated the modern street, lavish among the old and worn-eaten buildings of this bohemian neighborhood.

The streetcar made its first stop in Santa Tereza. Rosa automatically got off. She climbed the steep, narrow sidewalk flanked by a decrepit retaining wall sprouting weeds.

She felt an intense need to meditate. She missed the tranquility she had found at the Illumination. But, when she thought about it, she realized even the Illumination had lost its charm. Everything was charmless, to tell the truth. She knew then that something important to her had ceased to exist, something she would never recover.

Rosa gazed up at her house, silent, planted solemnly above the city among the treetops. She opened the gate and climbed the steps. Maybe simply being at home would be good for her, maybe she'd be able to recover some of her self-assurance.

The front door was half-open. Rosa thought nothing of it. Sometimes she was like that, she'd walk out without locking up, as if she lived in another world entirely, where violence didn't exist.

Leaving the door open behind her, she headed upstairs to her bedroom. There was a noise in the kitchen. Mice? No, couldn't be. She turned and went back downstairs to investigate.

Walking into the kitchen, she found two men sitting at the table smoking.

She wheeled around, terrified, and stumbled into a third in the doorway. The fog was getting thicker, opaque, almost palpable. She felt a sharp pain in her stomach, then another, and another, pain upon pain. A succession of sharp bursts. The fog was no longer fog but smoke. She could smell it. Her body was leaving her. The fog suddenly turned radiant, almost blinding. And Rosa sank lifeless to the floor.

Luciano was leading dona Rita by the hand because she seemed to be in a state of shock. If not for the terror in her eyes, one might think they were just grandson and grandmother on a pleasant stroll through the Botanical Garden. As it was, it had been a painstaking walk from the National Museum and half-abandoned gardens of Quinta da Boa Vista on the other side of the park, where Luciano and dona Rita had been let out of the car. After their capture, the Veraneio had driven uninterrupted for half an hour. Then suddenly a radio patrol car attempted to pull them over somewhere in Manguinhos.

Refusing to stop, their kidnappers circled back toward Bonsucesso, Higienópolis, the police in hot pursuit. They managed to lose the patrol car in São Cristovão but still seemed unnerved, as if expecting another, similar confrontation.

They turned onto Quinta da Boa Vista, and one of the men got out and made a call from a phone booth. Luciano could see the look of apprehension still on the man's face when he returned to the car.

"Well, what did they say?" asked the one in command.

"Plans have changed. We're supposed to deep-six the contents."

"What? Are you sure you heard right? They really want us to knock them off?"

The other man nodded uneasily.

"No way we're getting sucked into this," said the leader.

And they simply let Luciano and his grandmother out of the car behind the National Museum.

Haidèe was having trouble falling asleep. The ambassador had gone, his trusty junior diplomat along with him, and she had taken some tranquilizers. But still she couldn't sleep; her mind crackled like a bonfire. As soon as the ambassador left she called Rogério, whom she'd met in 1963 when he was working in the Ministry of Education and Culture. A year later, with Haidèe's help, he had left Brazil for a prolonged exile, first in Uruguay (where she and her husband were living at the time), then Mexico, and finally Europe. Rogério was immensely likable and sharp-witted, and served as her contact with the Brazilian exile community.

By 1970, Uruguay, the proud Switzerland of Latin America, had begun to fall apart. The Tupamaros were acting as if they owned the country and revolution seemed imminent. No one was surprised anymore by the fact that bodies riddled with bullet holes were found on the streets every morning. No one cashing a check or making a deposit was unduly surprised to witness one of the guerrillas' speedy and brazen bank robberies.

One night, late in 1970, Haidèe and her husband were asleep in bed. The telephone rang and Haidèe answered; she was a light sleeper. Her husband snored beside her; in spite of being Brazil's diplomatic representative in Uruguay, his conscience seemed to rest easy enough, shielded somehow from the abominations performed in collusion with the military to maintain his job and climb the diplomatic ladder.

Haidèe picked up the phone and a woman's voice began talking. She identified herself as a spokesperson for the CIA and was calling to warn that security should be tightened because the ambassador was in danger. Hugo Jaffet didn't even use security men, confident that his nationality made him immune to threat, since Brazil was, after all, the neighbor and traditional friend of Uruguay. The strange voice on the telephone, meanwhile, said that the Tupamaros didn't consider the ambassador neutral and were planning to kidnap Jaffet and present certain demands to the Uruguayan government.

After delivering her message, the caller hung up. Haidèe stood with the phone in her hand, wondering if she were dreaming or if the whole thing were nothing more than a tasteless joke. But

Uruguayans were not prone to crank phone calls, and two weeks later the ambassador's car was in fact intercepted in the street by a commando unit.

The night of the phone call they had just returned from a reception at the Greek ambassador's residence, much frequented by the most right-wing of the Uruguayan military who admired the regime run by colonels in Greece. The high-spirited guests had sat on the veranda playing poker, drinking Chilean wine, and listening to the Greek diplomat's anticommunist harangues. As usual, Haidèe and her husband had not discussed the party after returning home. She didn't like the group's swaggering fascism, while her husband considered it the most highly evolved politics of the Western hemisphere. Hugo fell asleep and Haidèe lay there in the dark with her eyes open, the lingering taste of wine and the bitterness of a mediocre marriage in her mouth. She had just fallen asleep when the phone rang.

Instead of going back to bed afterwards, she sat and waited for dawn. The sun began to rise over the fog-enshrouded street, the blue morning air tinged with pale red. No movement outside. They lived in Pocitos, in a large, two-story house with five bedrooms, a house that harked back to the times of rich ranchers who squandered money constructing imitations of European mansions. Twice the Uruguayan chancellery had met with Ambassador Jaffet requesting him to organize a personal security staff, but he had done no more than hire a retiree as a watchman at the house. At the second meeting, deeply concerned that the diplomat was still walking the streets of the capital alone like any ordinary citizen, the Uruguayan authorities even offered him a three-man police squad to do discreet security work. Full of himself, Jaffet emphatically refused, maintaining that an armed bodyguard would give the impression that he represented the interests of a hostile nation.

Unlike the Uruguayan government, Haidèe didn't lose a lot of sleep worrying about her husband's safety. Hugo had turned into a gray, unimaginative bureaucrat. The marriage was dead, or at least crawling along on its last legs, and she felt suffocated. Since some point in the fifties, Hugo had been courting ultraconservative elements in Brazil. He participated in several conspiracies and quickly gravitated toward the extreme right. In 1952, as the recently named consul general in Lisbon, Hugo became so involved with the Portuguese fascists that she almost left him. Not that she was a leftist, or even possessed clear political views, but the fascists and conservatives were irritatingly obtuse and generally losers in the game of life, even when they might appear to be winners. Besides, they were moralistic, morose, and extremely paranoid, and they practiced avarice as a sort of preparatory antidote to the Communist deluge they believed to be imminent. Hugo himself had become so miserly that she suspected he refused to hire bodyguards because he didn't want to lay out the money. And so, half in spite and half out of an explicit desire to be free of her husband, Haidèe kept silent about the phone call. She decided to bide her time.

After watching the sunrise, Haidèe got dressed, drank a generous shot of whiskey, and went out. Hugo paid no attention to her except to complain when she spent too much money. She was obliged to live on what she considered a pittance, unable to buy a fashionable dress or spend an afternoon with her women friends gambling at the Clube Inglês.

It was not unusual for her to leave the house quite early, before the morning rush hour, and drive through the city. She liked the climate in Montevideo, it was so Spanish, so clear and ephemeral that her drives left her rested and less anxious.

But the morning after the phone call she didn't drive far. On impulse, she headed for Rogério's house. She maintained a matter-of-fact relationship with him, but she knew he harbored quite a passion for her. She had been able to overcome her husband's objections and hire Rogério for household work because he came cheap and worked hard. Though small and slender, Rogério was not the least bit fragile. Quite the contrary: he was extremely energetic, possessed a practical intelligence, and was utterly loyal to her. In recognition of his loyalty, Haidèe had rented a modest apartment downtown and offered it to him, so he could move out of the deplorable boardinghouse he'd been staying in where he never felt safe. But Haidèe had never permitted him to reveal his love or to get very close to her.

Rogério was still asleep when she arrived. The studio apartment was in reasonably good order for a bachelor's place: only the pile of dirty clothes rolled up in a corner bespoke a typically masculine condition. Haidèe had slipped in quietly with her own key, but Rogério woke up anyway.

"Sorry," she said, hesitating in the doorway.

He sat up in bed, alarmed.

"Is something wrong?"

Haidèe had a habit of showing up at his apartment when she had a job for him or simply needed someone to talk to. But this would generally be in the afternoon—never at 6:30 A.M.

"I got a phone call in the middle of the night," said Haidèe, hesitation in her voice.

"A phone call?"

"I think it was a prank," she said, to minimize the drama and at the same time make it more intriguing.

"What do you mean?" Rogério rubbed his eyes.

Haidèe's eyes widened when she saw that he slept with a gun under his pillow.

"I just have a thing about it," he explained, pushing the gun back out of sight.

"Are you afraid someone wants to kill you?"

"We're not all that far from Brazil, you know."

"Nobody's safe, are they."

Rogério pulled on an old bathrobe over his pajama bottoms. His naked torso, thin and childlike, seemed less insignificant without the pajama top.

"Tell me about the phone call."

"It was a woman, speaking Uruguayan Spanish, who said she worked for the CIA."

"The CIA!" he said with a chortle.

"Really! She said she was calling to warn us that someone was planning to kidnap Hugo."

Rogério got up and opened the curtains, filling the shadowy room with morning sun. Haidèe remained planted beside the door, keys still jingling in her hand.

"What do you think?" she asked.

"What do I think? Who knows! It's quite possible."

The jingling got louder.

"If you're worried, just tell Hugo to take the necessary precautions. It should be easy for him to arrange."

"He doesn't want to," said Haidèe dryly.

"Have you told him about the phone call?"

"No . . ."

Rogério went into the bathroom, splashed water on his face and hair, and toweled himself vigorously.

"I'm sorry . . ." said Haidèe.

"Sorry for what?"

"For coming here so early."

Rogério emerged from the bathroom with his hair wet and began choosing what clothes to wear.

"You don't have to apologize. I was about to get up anyway."

Even as he looked through his clothes he was studying her carefully.

"I wouldn't mind if it happened."

Rogério stopped what he was doing and his lips drew back into a funny grimace. He always acted comic when something shocked him, he had a special talent for reacting opposite to the occasion.

"What did you say?"

"You heard me."

He walked up to her and took the jingling keys out of her hand.

"Where do I fit in?" Rogério never put much stock in subtleties. "I don't have any connection with the heavies here. And that's the truth. I already got into trouble once . . ."

Haidèe took her keys back and walked to the window, where she stood staring into space.

"You've come to the wrong place, Haidèe. I'm against armed struggle, always have been. I can't see violence as a solution, it only provokes repression. Terrorism is a mistake . . ."

Rogério fell silent, because Haidèe had turned back to him and he saw irony in her eyes, and something else, something imperceptible but terrifying.

"What?" he asked, on the defensive.

She sat down on the bed, threw her keys on the sheets, and hitched up her skirt so that her thighs were visible almost to the crotch.

"Nothing, you idiot," she said harshly. "Did you think I was suggesting that *you* should kidnap Hugo?"

"Well, I didn't, uh, make myself clear . . ." Rogério stammered.

Haidèe smiled at his embarrassment.

"Do you think I'm too old, Rogério?"

Rogério cleared his throat and blinked several times.

"Well? Am I?"

"No, no . . . you're still very good-looking."

"Still!"

"I mean you *are*, you're very pretty, Haidèe."

"Maybe," she said. "Maybe I'm still pretty, just like a revolutionary who's hung up his cleats, is that the expression?"

Rogério cleared his throat again, as if he had a fish bone caught in there.

"What do you want from me?" he asked, looking like he didn't want to know.

"I want you to help things along. I want you to put the cleats on one more time and give the ball a good kick."

"Impossible!"

"I told you I'm no fool," she said gruffly.

"There's nothing I can do."

"That's a shame. Didn't you tell me you wanted to relocate in Mexico?"

He nodded.

"What do you need? A visa? Money?" Haidèe crossed her legs and looked Rogério in the eyes, arrogant.

"I want to go to Mexico, yes, but not that way. And pretty soon I'll be set to do it."

"When? When the Uruguayan military takes power and begins hunting down political exiles like rats? Where will you go then?"

"The Tupamaros won't let that happen, they have very deep links with the common people," he said and regretted it immediately.

"Ah! The Tupamaros . . . I thought you were against armed struggle."

"I am. But I still have eyes and ears."

"And a mouth, too. For what I want, those three things are all you need."

"Isn't it about time you show your hand, Haidèe?" he asked.

"All right," she said haughtily. "If the telephone warning proves to be prophetic, you win a prize. It's a kind of a bet. But I'll need you to give me some advance notice."

Rogério watched his hands pick up the clothes he had chosen to put on. He went into the bathroom and locked the door. Haidèe got up from the bed and walked out, her keys rattling in her hand.

Five days later, Rogério was at the ambassadorial residence doing some cleaning work. When he and Haidèe ran into each other after lunch he looked wild, positively comical.

"It's going to happen," he said between his teeth as she walked past.

"The day after it does you're going to be one happy exile," she replied.

A week later Hugo Jaffet was on his way to the embassy, nonchalantly trading opinions about the national soccer team with his chauffeur. He didn't notice anything was wrong until a van swung in front to block the street and ten guerrillas jumped out waving their guns. The chauffeur received a whack on the head worth eight stitches. He regained consciousness only to reveal temporary amnesia, which drove the security forces into a rage because he couldn't even recognize a picture of his own wife. At three o'clock that afternoon the radio announced that two North American technical advisors and the Brazilian ambassador were in the hands of the Tupamaros. The guerrillas were demanding that the United States government pay a million-dollar ransom for each American. They wanted only two hundred fifty thousand dollars for Hugo Jaffet's release, making it clear they would not accept the equivalent in cruzeiros.

Twenty-four hours after the kidnapping, Rogério was on an Aerolineas Argentinas flight to Mexico. In his pocket he had five thousand dollars and a letter of recommendation from the kidnapped ambassador, the last document Jaffet signed in his official capacity, not counting the three short letters the Tupamaros permitted him to write from captivity. The letter recommended Rogério to a Mexican company with whom the ambassador had close ties and which would prove to be as useful to him as the dollars.

Rogério and Haidèe lost touch after that, until a chance meeting on a Paris street in 1976. Haidèe brought him back to her hotel, treated him like a prince, and even let him sleep with her, to show how grateful she was for what he had done. Rogério never told her how he had encouraged the Tupamaros to go through with the kidnapping; perhaps he had done no more than to confirm that Hugo's name was on the list of targets. But Haidèe liked to think of Rogério as her liberator. For all intents and purposes, he represented the beginning of a new life for her.

Haidèe helped him in every way she could. It was through her that Rogério managed to insinuate himself at the embassy, becoming a kind of sentimental bridge linking government functionaries to the exiles, bypassing the organs of repression. He was always clever that way. Rogério was the person in Paris

Haidèe needed to see to find out things that not even the astute ambassador knew about.

She looked at her watch, it was eleven P.M. She couldn't just lie there in bed waiting. She dressed quickly, fixed her makeup, and left her room. The hotel was calm and quiet. She asked the doorman to call her a taxi and sat waiting in an armchair, watching the quiet street. This neighborhood was dead at night, everything closed early. But she knew some other sections of Paris, and she knew Rogério's habits well enough to stand a good chance of finding him there.

The cab driver was a woman, a grumbling neurotic with a playful and irreverent Dalmation beside her in the front seat. Haidèe ignored the woman's acrimony and ordered her to head for Boulevard Saint Michel. She got out near the bridge, paid the driver, and walked down rue Saint Andre des Arts, checking every bar, restaurant, and bistro along the way. It was a narrow, medieval street in the heart of the Latin Quarter, full of art cinemas and small bars frequented by bohemians and students. She had not gone far when she spotted Rogério sitting in a Vietnamese restaurant between two blondes dressed in black.

Haidèe strode into the restaurant and stood waiting for Rogério to notice her. He was absorbed in an animated conversation with his two tablemates. He raised his eyes to the door when a group of young people walked in, saw Haidèe standing there looking at him, stopped talking, and smiled. Without a word to the women, he got up from the table and went to greet her.

"I'm not even surprised," he said, "because you'll never again surprise me."

He kissed her on both cheeks and embraced her tenderly.

"Come, sit with us, there's room enough for one more beautiful woman."

Haidèe accepted.

"Who are they?" she asked.

"Two friends—they're French!"

Haidèe gave him a few complicitous pats on the back and smiled.

"You don't lose any time, do you, my friend."

At the table Rogério made the introductions.

"They don't speak Portuguese and they won't mind if you need to talk to me without their understanding."

"How appropriate!"

"I'm an exile," said Rogério, looking serious but wanting to express the precise opposite. "They understand that. Actually I think it turns them on."

They sat down and made small talk. The three had already ordered, but Haidèe wasn't hungry. She preferred to drink wine and asked Rogério to select for her. When they were done with their meal, Haidèe apologized for needing to speak with Rogério in Portuguese. The women nodded their understanding and sat looking grave, as if they were about to witness yet another decisive moment in the revolution that was consuming the Third World. Haidèe didn't condescend to look at them again; she knew that kind of person, hunter of the exotic.

"Have you been to the embassy lately, Rogério?"

"A little bit. Things seem to be hopping. It seems like they're beginning to distance themselves from the hard-liners. Is the same kind of liberalization going on at home?"

Haidèe shrugged.

"Maybe it's nothing to you, Haidèe, but for the people mired in shit over here . . ."

"Which is not your case, my friend."

He made a face and dabbed at his mouth with his napkin.

"You seem nervous, Haidèe. You have a problem?"

"Yes, yes, I do have a problem!"

"Can I help?"

"I hope so. I've been trying to get hold of you all day. You moved without leaving a forwarding address."

Rogério smiled shyly.

"My old paranoia. Sorry."

"You could have let me know . . ."

"What's the problem?"

Haidèe briefly summarized the situation, omitting certain details. The question of access to the money, for example. But she did mention Carlos.

"Carlos is dead," said Rogério.

Haidèe froze, though deep down she had suspected something like that.

"Of natural causes?"

"He fell down the stairs!"

"Poor man! When?"

"Two or three days ago; I'm not sure. He died last night, in the hospital."

Haidèe looked at her hands. With Carlos dead, there was no way to get to the money. The only beneficiary would be the Swiss government, into whose coffers it would be absorbed after a certain grace period.

"What does Carlos have to do with all you've told me?"

"Everything," said Haidèe, devastated.

Rogério leaned closer. "There are signs that his fall wasn't exactly a fall."

"What do you mean?"

"Like maybe he was pushed."

"Did he say something?"

"No. Carlos was in a coma afterward. Lots of broken bones; he was in bad shape. But he wasn't alone. A young woman friend of his took care of him till the end."

Haidèe brightened.

"Who? Do you know her?"

"She's Brazilian, an exile . . ."

"Where can I find her? Do you know her address?"

"Yes, but she left her apartment all of a sudden. A friend of mine was trying to get in touch with her, some school stuff or something, but she hadn't been back there in a while. The concierge said all her things were still there, but she'd just disappeared."

"Exiles. That's your lot, eh?"

"Or our luck," he quipped.

"What's her name?"

"Vivian, Vivian de Castro, or something like that. Her first name is Vivian, I'm sure of that."

"Are you positive that Carlos didn't confide in her?"

"I don't think so, but I'm not sure. I just couldn't visit him in the hospital. I'm terrified of hospitals, and I'm a real coward when it comes to people's suffering. I didn't want to see Carlos like that. But Vivian was at my place—well, I mean their place, I'm living with these two now—at a party we had. She didn't say anything about talking to Carlos once he was in the hospital. I don't think he ever regained consciousness."

"Do you know this girl well?"

"Not very. She's a little standoffish, keeps her distance from the Brazilian community. She hangs out with a couple of African guys. But she's real pretty. I only invited her because there was a guy who wanted to meet her."

"Really? Who?"

"Some crazy guy I was feeling sorry for because no one will have anything to do with him, you know how they are. He's a wild man, on drugs all the time, hardly the type the exile group goes for. I met him at the embassy. We talked a little, and I could see the kid was a lost soul. He kept insisting that I call Vivian, so I ended up sending her an invitation. But then something strange happened."

"Go on . . ."

"Well, he arrived early, really strung out, so we put him to bed in the spare room. We were scared to death he was overdosing and we'd have to call a doctor. Vivian showed up, with her two African friends in tow as usual, but the party was a fiasco. I didn't know about this until afterwards, but the guy took off with her. Somebody saw them go out the back way, and they didn't seem to be getting along any too well either—he was practically dragging her along with him. Then later we found out he was arrested. With no identity papers. Vivian herself called the cops on him."

"Quite the party guest! I'm not surprised the girl moved without giving you her new address."

"I know, but I didn't mean to get her into anything. I just felt sorry for the guy, he was so out of place here. And I know what that's like. But hell, he wasn't just looking for somebody to hang out with. He dragged her out by force. And disappeared. I never saw him again after he got out of jail, which is pretty odd. Without I.D.'s, you'd think he'd be deported, with the consulate footing the bill if he didn't have any money. But apparently he got out of jail, no problem, at least that's what a friend of mine told me. And the consulate wasn't even informed."

Haidèe was staring into the distance, as if meditating on Rogério's words. But then she dove back into the conversation.

"What's this guy's name?"

"He said it was Augusto, but since he didn't have any papers, who knows."

"What does he look like?"

"He's young, late twenties maybe, but he's a wreck, looks a lot older. Must be the drugs. He's got straight black hair, sort of long, and the kind of face that scares the hell out of the French: he looks like a lunatic Arab. Pretty well built, but a bit of a paunch. He's a real smooth talker, though, which isn't very typical of the druggie type, yet not at all interested in politics.

He said he was here in Paris because he didn't get along with his father."

"Oh, really?" This truly sparked her interest, though the combination of wine, fatigue, and tranquilizers was beginning to take its toll. "Did he tell you anything about his father?"

Rogério thought for a few seconds.

"No, not really. He was in a tight spot, with no passport and all. Got into a fight or something in Marais and lost his bag. These days the consulate's way of dealing with people who lose their documents is simply to give them a hard time, wear them down with red tape."

Haidèe was feeling pretty worn down herself.

"I'm falling asleep," she said. "I should go back to my hotel."

Rogério explained to his friends that Haidèe was leaving.

"We can drop you off," he suggested.

Haidèe consented, grateful.

She left the restaurant on Rogério's arm, the two Frenchwomen following silently behind. The street was still bursting with activity. Haidèe never had been able to understand those people's predilection for the foul-smelling holes-in-the-wall of the Latin Quarter.

The Volkswagen van hadn't been washed in two years, but the old Republican Spaniards were showered, discreetly perfumed, and neatly dressed. Each wore at his waist a German pistol, made before WWII but in perfect working order. They chatted animatedly in the front seat, Colonel Duran at the wheel and stocky Contreras beside him. They were happy to be doing something for their dead comrade and to be returning to active duty, just like the old days.

Vivian and her two African friends sat quietly in the backseat. Vivian hugged the leather briefcase from Austerlitz Station to her chest, her nerves on edge, but Kouma and Sanga couldn't stop smiling and Vivian knew they were making fun, in their peculiar English, of the two Spaniards. Leaving the apartment, Kouma had whispered: "Now I know why the revolution isn't going anywhere in Latin America—just look at the two revolutionaries you picked up!"

Vivian was too scared for repartee. She had to trust in all four of them to help her make contact. Contreras apologized for the condition of the van, which belonged to the bread delivery

business in which he was a partner. Painted across the side in
big letters was the name of the bakery: La Pasionaria. It was
nine-thirty A.M. when the delivery van of the Boulangerie La
Pasionaria headed out toward Boulevard Montparnasse.

Against all expectations, Miguel's sleep had been recuperative.
Poring over the city guide, trying to locate La Coupole and figure
out the best way to get there, he had fallen asleep fully dressed,
defeated by fatigue and the fears awakened by all his frustrated
phone calls.

Now, out on the street, he was alert, watching to see if he were
being followed, though the closer he got to the station the less
he worried. He went directly to the telephone office and placed
a call to his parents' apartment. It was the middle of the night in
Brazil, but he would rather get his father out of bed than go on
living with all his uncertainty.

A woman's voice answered.

"Mama?" Miguel shouted into the receiver.

The person at the other end seemed to have been struck dumb.

"Mama, is it you? This is Miguel. Talk to me, Mama!"

"My . . . God . . ." whispered dona Rita from the other side of
the ocean. "Son, where are you?"

"Mama, I have to talk to Dad, will you call him for me?"

"Where are you?" she asked again.

"I'm in Paris, Mama. I know it sounds unbelievable, but that's
not the half of it."

"Are you all right?"

"Yes, Mama, don't worry. I have to talk to Dad. Is he awake?"

A brief pause.

"Your father isn't home . . ."

"What do you mean he isn't home? It's the middle of the
night!"

"He's out of town. He and Ruth left early this morning, and . . .
they . . . they just haven't come back yet."

"I can tell you're hiding something from me, Mama."

"No, of course not, it's true," said dona Rita. "They're off
trying to straighten things out for you. We've all been very
worried, Miguel."

"Where did they go?"

Another silence. Miguel was getting very worried. Something
was wrong here.

"To, um . . . to Brasília," she said. "We were told you'd been arrested. I don't understand how you could be in Paris!"

"Me neither!"

"Are you in jail over there?"

"No, Mama. They brought me here, but I escaped. Everything will be cleared up soon. I don't want you to worry."

"You haven't even asked about Luciano! He's right here beside me."

Miguel swallowed hard. Of course Luciano was there, alert, curious as always, listening to the whole thing.

"Let me talk to him," said Miguel.

"Don't talk long, Miguel, it's very expensive and you must not have much money. Call collect next time, you hear me?"

"Okay, Mama. I love you." After a brief pause come Luciano's voice, childish, unreal.

"Luciano!"

"Miguel!"

Both were too choked up to talk.

"Miguel," said the boy again. "Are you okay?"

"Yes, I'm fine. What about you?"

"I'm okay, I'm here with Grandma." Pause. "Dad—what's going on?"

"I don't know, son. But maybe it doesn't even matter . . ."

"What do you mean?"

"Things just happened, Luciano, things just happened. And changed our lives."

"Did you do something bad, Miguel?"

"Me? No!"

"When are you coming home?"

"I don't know yet. This is new to all of us. I wish I could explain things better, son . . ."

"Dad . . ." Another silence full of electronic noise, and the boy spoke in a stifled voice. "Dad . . . I'm scared. Can you hear me?"

Miguel felt his legs go weak and his hands begin to sweat.

"None of that," said Miguel, though an enormous and shame-faced fear was sweeping over him.

"I love you, Dad," said Luciano.

"I love you, too," replied Miguel.

And they hung up.

Miguel left the booth radiant but trembling. He felt like dancing. But he knew there was something hidden behind his mother's words. Not the words themselves, but the hesitations. As he left the station, his hand closed around the automatic pistol he was carrying wrapped in a hotel towel. He hoped he wouldn't have to use it again.

He walked a few blocks and down into the *métro*. Suddenly it struck him. What was he doing? Why was he continuing to follow his old destiny, the route laid out for him by Haidèe? Curiosity? No, he didn't believe in curiosity. What, then? It was always like that with him. The last time he stopped to ask questions he didn't find any answers. He was still in the army in those days, up to his neck in fear and doubt. Suddenly he was drowning in questions. The barracks seemed strangely alien; something had changed. Military life had taken on dark coloration, full of secrets and suspicion. Camaraderie and friendship had deflated like balloons. Painfully, from discovery to discovery, he was learning not to go backwards. Never to go back.

In less than ten minutes he got off the *métro* at the Montparnasse station and found himself in an enormous subterranean labryinth. It was still early for the meeting, but he wanted to study the scene and calculate his chances. This might be another of Haidèe's incomprehensible traps. He wandered the underground corridors of the *métro* and let chance lead him to an exit. Taking the escalator up to the street, he found himself on a corner facing the tower of Montparnasse, just down the block and across a wide avenue from La Coupole, with its cream-colored wooden facade. A sign, not lit at this hour, advertised dancing upstairs. Even this early the place was bustling, tables packed with people talking over brunch. Miguel walked up Boulevard Montparnasse and stopped in front of a Multiplex cinema. He studied the posters for the various films being shown and at the same time kept his eye on the restaurant. He crossed the street, strolled slowly past La Coupole, and ducked into a small bookstore just a few doors down. As he browsed near the front window, he could watch the customers arriving and leaving the café.

Haidèe consulted her watch. It was nine o'clock. She had slept like a rock, but her head still felt heavy and achy. She finished the last few bites of the generous hotel breakfast and got dressed. Then she picked up a leather briefcase, hurried downstairs, and took a cab to the Champs-Elysées, the corner of rue Marbeuf, where there were several phone booths. After waiting for a smug businessman to finish using the only functional telephone, she made a brief call and walked the wide sidewalk to Rond-Point. She strode briskly, the briefcase clutched tightly in her right hand, and scanned the reflections in the reddish, polluted water of the Seine until she spotted a Brazilian flag rippling in the wind above #34 Cours Albert 1èr.

Haidèe strode into the Brazilian Embassy.

It was ten o'clock and the embassy was very quiet. A Brazilian colonel, in full uniform, recognized her on his way out of the building. He had the look of someone on his way to an official appointment. Middle-aged, dry skin, large mouth, and a pair of dark, inquiring eyes.

"Well, who have we here!" said the colonel.

Haidèe hung back a little, sweaty from the uncharacteristic exercise of walking.

"Colonel Sarmento! I didn't know you were in Paris!"

"By this time next month, I won't be," said the colonel, undisguised regret in his voice.

"Moving on to something more important, no doubt."

"I'm going back to the barracks."

"The Frenchwomen are going to miss you," bantered Haidèe, familiar with his courtly gifts.

The colonel smiled, but not very brightly.

"And how are you?" he asked. "Besides being more beautiful by the day. What is your secret, Haidèe?"

"You haven't changed a bit," she said, accepting the compliment with a faint smile. "I'm fine."

"Are you here to see the ambassador?"

"To vent my rage, as usual!"

The colonel made a face.

"He's upstairs. Bright and early, as usual."

"He's going to have a heart attack one of these days."

"God's wrath," said the colonel, flushing.

Haidèe extended her hand. The colonel bowed and kissed it.

"*Au revoir*, Haidèe. I'll be in touch—how about dinner some evening?"

"That would be a pleasure, dear Sarmento. If not here in Paris, I'll take you up on your invitation in Brazil."

"Not likely," said the colonel. "I've been transferred to the Amazon."

Haidèe watched the colonel get in his car and wave effusively as he drove away. Someone called her name and she turned to see the ambassador standing at the main entrance, his tie loosened, as was his style, wearing one of his badly cut expensive suits.

She shook the ambassador's hand, immune to the rebuke written all over his face. She had come to the embassy to investigate the identity of the Brazilian who had recently lost his passport. Why be coy anymore—everyone seemed to be coming out into the open, in Brasília and everywhere else. The pieces of the military regime were rising to the surface like debris from a shipwreck.

The ambassador escorted her to his office and invited her to take a seat beside his desk, which was piled high with papers.

"You have no idea how busy I am, Haidèe. Today's going to be a bitch of a day. The European Parliament's back in session and we have a full agenda."

Visibly annoyed by her presence, he walked around to the other side of the desk, but instead of sitting in the leather chair he stood nervously twisting his hands.

"Why are you here?"

"I need one more favor, darling."

The ambassador looked irritated and his voice rose a notch.

"I've already done all that I can for you, Haidèe. I simply cannot let myself become further involved."

Haidèe was about to respond, but the intercom buzzed. The ambassador picked up, listened, and replaced it without word.

"Wait here. I'll be right back," he said gruffly and stalked out of the office.

Haidèe couldn't resist leafing through the memos on his desk, opening folders, even peeking into one of the drawers.

"There's nothing here that would interest you, my dear," said the ambassador, sweeping back into the room. "But you did get a call from Brazil. My secretary took a message. What the hell does this mean?" He handed her the paper. She read it and crumpled it into a ball, visibly concerned.

"Haidèe, this is beyond the limit," said the ambassador, on the verge of panic. " 'The fruit was not delivered'? The SNI must be having a hell of a time trying to decode that."

Haidèe looked at him. She raised her eyebrows and ran her tongue over her lips. Then she unfolded the crinkled paper and reread the message.

He stared at her expectantly.

"I asked my brother-in-law to find out if Aldo really was in that sanatorium in Petrópolis. And just as I suspected, he's not. That's what the message means. I'm convinced that he's here in Paris."

"That's impossible," said the ambassador doubtfully. "I maintain absolute control over the comings and goings of our little 'community' here."

"Aldo is no longer part of any 'community.' "

The ambassador's face closed into a scowl. "What do you want from me?"

Haidèe's eyes flashed. "Do you get a lot of requests for replacement passports? I think our lunatic Aldo lost his papers. A guy fitting his description has been hanging around some exiles I know. Sounds like the spitting image of Aldo. Lost his passport in a fight or something in Marais."

"The consulate takes care of things like that," said the ambassador nervously. "But the whole idea's crazy. If Aldo lost his passport and showed up at the consulate to apply for another one, I'd have been informed immediately, because he could have entered the country illegally."

"Maybe he didn't go to the consulate. My exile friend has good connections there and says this guy was arrested but managed to get himself released from the French police, no strings. Under normal circumstances, they would have notified the consulate that deportation proceedings were underway, right? But that's not what happened."

"Very interesting," exclaimed the ambassador. "Whoever he is, this guy has good connections with the French police *and* the consulate. I'll check into it immediately."

"You do that," said Haidèe. "I'm positive this mysterious guy is Aldo. And we need to find him as soon as possible. But I can't hang around to hear what you find out, I have an important appointment, as you know."

"Yes, I sent a car to the hotel for you. It must have returned by now. My trusted assistant will accompany you."

"The little fag," said Haidèe.

The ambassador snorted and opened the door.

"Go!" he said, pointing to the exit.

Haidèe left the office and headed down a side hall to the parking lot. Time was getting short, she had to find the car and

get to La Coupole. She hoped the ambassador would manage to
locate Aldo, who had to be behind this whole business. They must
find him and neutralize him, hopefully once and for all.

Out in the parking lot, a uniformed employee approached her
with an inquisitive air.

"I'm supposed to have a car at my disposal," she told him.
"The ambassador arranged it."

The man consulted a clipboard and pointed to the same Citröen
that had picked her up at the airport.

"That one over there," he said.

She expected to see the young diplomat who had come to meet
her plane the night before, but he was nowhere to be found. Might
as well get in the car and wait. She opened the door and then
stopped, paralyzed. There inside, stretched out on the seat, lay a
dirty young man with long hair.

"Aldo!" Haidèe's voice cracked.

He fixed her with his bloodshot eyes.

"Aldo," she said, her voice a whisper. "What are you doing
here?"

Aldo's face twisted into a smile that was more like a scowl as
he motioned for her to get in the car.

"Hey, Aunt Haidèe," he said between his teeth. "Long time
no see!" His dark face was bruised. Years ago he'd looked like
an Indian, a trait inherited from his mother, but now he was
haggard and sickly. His slightly lopsided eyes were red-rimmed,
and although his athletic body was still muscular, it had become
a little puffy. He looked like an old man.

Haidèe didn't move. The floor of the car was littered with
cigarette butts and, off to one side, a disposable syringe.

"How are you, Aldo?"

"I'm just terrific, Auntie!"

Haidèe got into the car and picked up the syringe.

"What are you on?" she asked.

He scowled back at her. "Glucose."

Life had not been particularly good to Aldo. Haidèe had known
him since he was a child, and she had never gotten used to his
decadence. His choice to self-destruct had been obstinate and
irreversible.

They sat in silence. Haidèe was swamped with conflicting feelings. She didn't know whether to lament the boy's misfortune or
simply to accept the convenient explanation that he was just one

more of the regime's perverted creations.

She tried to stroke his hair, but her hand was roughly shoved away.

"Cut it out, Haidèe," he shouted.

"You're in a bad way, Aldo. You need help."

Aldo leaned his body across Haidèe's and pulled the car door shut. The smell of him hit her like a blow.

"What do you think you're doing?" Haidèe was beginning to panic.

"Look, *Auntie*, we have some business to attend to, isn't that right?"

"I'm leaving," she threatened.

"You don't want me to get out, do you, *Auntie?*"

Every time he said the word *Auntie* it was as if he had struck her.

"What is it you want?" asked Haidèe, intending condescension. She was hoping the young diplomat would appear and put a stop to the situation.

"You know what I want," he snarled.

"I have no idea!"

"You bitch!" yelled Aldo, pulling out a knife, and placing the sharp blade against Haidèe's face.

She didn't flinch, but she was deathly afraid. She knew he was just crazy enough to kill her right there, in the blink of an eye.

"I'm waiting, Aldo. What the hell do you want?"

Aldo slapped her twice.

"Never, never do that again," she said in a low, cold voice.

His response was to press the knife point hard against her neck.

"Bitch!"

"That much you've said already, no need to repeat it."

"I know you're on your way to meet the Communists to put the two halves of the account number together. I want that money. Those dollars are going to be mine."

"That depends," she replied defiantly.

"No, it doesn't. You have no choice."

"That's what you think, Aldo."

He laughed and slowly drew the blade along the crease in her neck. Her breaths were short and hollow.

"You think you've got me because of that lousy evidence? I can shit all over your stupid evidence. And once I get my hands on that money I'm going to disappear off the face of the earth."

"Oh, really," she said, her chin lifted in an awkward position, her neck irritated by the knife. "And what about your friends in the Falange Brasil Grande? What happens to them?"

"They're fucked, all of them! You sicked a mad dog on them. Major Portugal's probably settling accounts with the man upstairs right now. Your friend Captain Gouveia iced him yesterday afternoon . . ."

Haidèe's mouth fell open in surprise.

"At first I thought it would be worthwhile for us to get organized. Give a few headaches to the liberals in the Planalto. But forget it. Everything's falling apart and the boys are the only ones who don't know it."

"Let's talk like two civilized people," said Haidèe, gently pushing the knife away from her throat. He allowed this, but did not put it away.

"They came to see me one day at the sanatorium my old man packed me off to," said Aldo. "The place belongs to some doctor who worked for him. It was a cinch to set up. They needed some extra money, because they were planning to knock off a few big shots in the regime and let the Commies take the rap. Geisel really is going to revoke Institutional Act 5 and everybody's scared to death of ending up cannon fodder. Set fire to the past, you know how it is."

"You're mad, all of you!"

"No, it's not madness. It's the survival instinct. I see that now. Our only use to them now is to scare the shit out of the people who want the liberalization to go too far. The most troublesome will be eliminated—and that's not paranoia talking, the forgetting has already begun. Anyway, the boys came to me because they figured I'd want to get in on it. They didn't know anything about the dough you and old man Lyra tucked away in Switzerland. But hell, I broke into the safe a long time ago—I just didn't know how to get to the money. So here was my shot. I'd help them, they'd help me, and we'd all get a share. That was the plan . . ."

"And now you want it all!"

"Yeah, that's right, I want it all. The boys got fucked. I called Brazil last night and things look black. They've got the commander of the First Army and the people from CIEX on their backs now. That Gouveia's father is no joke. He wrote the whole thing up real pretty, and he came close to sending it to the press, to Brasília, you name it. Then the shit really would have hit the fan. Captain Maurício managed to intercept the guy, as well as the report, and Captain Gouveia's wife too, but even so. News of the situation was leaked within the military and everybody with three stars and up had to move their asses to keep the lid on. The group's country hideout outside Rio was sealed off and Political Intelligence raided the sanatorium that they were using as a last resort."

"Why are you telling me all this?" asked Haidèe gruffly. "You think I'm going to make it easy for you?"

"I don't think so, I *know* so. We can even split the money, half for me and half for you! Just put it in your pocket and wave good-bye!"

Haidèe shook her head.

"You belong in a straitjacket!"

"Don't get wise, Haidèe. I need that money. With Portugal and the sergeant dead, I had to fall back on my contacts with Sûreté. I owe them a bundle. And if I don't pay, they'll have my head. But I'll have yours first, you bitch . . ."

"What about Miguel? What happened to him?"

"He turned into quite an animal. We left him at our base camp and he killed the sergeant somehow; then when we got back he took out Major Portugal. I split or he would have gotten me too. I followed him to a hotel. He hasn't got much money, from the look of the place. I'm sure he'll show up at the meeting."

Haidèe's hand flew to her forehead. "My God, the meeting, I'll be late. If I don't show up . . ."

"I'll take you," he said quickly.

Haidèe looked around for the smooth-tongued escort assigned to her by the ambassador. But there was no one in the parking lot except the attendant sleeping in a chair.

Aldo smiled a hateful smile. "He's not coming . . ."

"What did you do to him?" asked Haidèe, trembling.

"Calm down," said Aldo, "the pretty boy's just having a little snooze over there in that warehouse. One knock over the head and that baby doll went all weak-kneed. But don't worry, I said I'd take you."

"You can't come to the meeting. The girl knows you. One look at you and she'll bolt . . ."

Aldo thought for a minute.

"You're out of the game, Aldo."

"No, no, I'm not!" he screamed desperately. "You're not going to get that money and throw me to the wolves. My old man has washed his hands of me. If I don't pay off the French cops I'm hamburger. And my father will celebrate—hell, everyone will celebrate. Except for yours truly, the one son of a bitch who didn't think twice about diving into the shit when he was needed."

"But think, Aldo. If you come with me, it'll screw everything up. Same thing if you try to stop me. No matter how you look at it, you're out of choices."

"No, I'm not!"

"Except for suicide, of course! You kill me and then jump off the Quai d'Orsay. That would make a nice epilogue."

Aldo shrugged and stared at his knife. His face was solemn, flushed with a certain nostalgia. Haidèe felt as if she were going to vomit.

"I won't throw you to the wolves, Aldo. Trust me. I just couldn't do something like that, though of course you deserve it."

A wild look crossed his face.

"You know something, Haidèe," he growled, clutching the knife so tightly that his knuckles whitened, "I should carve up that snotty face of yours real good, I ought to plant this knife all up and down your disgusting body, and finish off your sickening strain once and for all . . . You know what you are? You're a user, a profiteer, the kind that keeps everything for herself and lets everyone else wade through the shit. While we're out on the street doing your dirty work, you and your kind sit on the sidelines picking through the remains. Just like my father, the honorable General Lyra. And now I'm the poor soul and you're the charitable lady who only wants to help a maladjusted boy . . ."

"I'm not going to sit here for another minute listening to your lunatic raging."

"Go fuck yourself."

"Fine," she replied, purposefully grasping the door handle. "I've wasted too much time on you already, Aldo."

"Hold it just a minute, Auntie!"

"I'm *not* your aunt."

"What a shame! Considering your ethical gifts, you'd fit right in with the rest of the family."

Haidèe tried to open the door, but the knife flashed back into position against her neck.

"Are we going to start this again?" she asked impatiently.

"Just one more thing," said Aldo, pressing the blade to her skin. "How did you find out I was involved in this?"

Haidèe gently pushed the knife away again.

"Aldo, you're such a child. I don't know how you've managed to survive this long." Her tone was penetrating, as if she were trying to reach his innermost being. And she knew exactly how to do this. "It was simple, you idiot. You're the only person I know who likes to rape women and then burn them alive."

"But you thought my old man was in on it too."

"Of course. He was the only one with the necessary information. But you people miscalculated the amount of pressure to apply. Which is understandable, since you're used to dealing with the people at the bottom, people already backed into a corner."

Haidèe smoothed her dress and stepped out of the car. Aldo got out, too, and stood facing her.

"Anyway, I won't abandon you, Aldo," she promised. "You're sick, and extremely frustrated, of course . . ."

A thick, greenish glob of spit exploded from Aldo's mouth and struck Haidèe's face with a wet smack.

Haidèe's reaction was equally explosive. She pulled a small gold .22-caliber revolver out of her purse and shot him point-blank. A fine mist of blood spurted from a tiny hole in his chest.

The shot woke the parking attendant, who looked up, horrified, in time to see Aldo begin to topple, flailing wildly at the woman with a knife. With each impossible breath a spray of blood spurted into the air.

Haidèe returned the gun, which was still hot, to her purse and walked around the car, keeping her distance from the staggering young man. She saw the parking attendant stir from his paralysis and run toward the Citröen. The gate to the street was open and traffic coursed by indifferently. Without hesitating for another moment, she took a deep breath, ran to the sidewalk, and hailed a taxi.

After directing the driver to take her to Montparnasse, Haidèe settled into the backseat, wiping and rewiping the phlegm from her face.

General Lyra's office was as roomy as a large apartment and was decorated with huge blowups of the many business concerns

controlled by Life Chemicals, Inc., both in Brazil and abroad.
The office was on the top floor of a concrete-and-steel tower in
downtown Rio and overlooked the runways of the Santos Dumont
Airport, with its continuous shuttle flights and executive jets. It
also presented a dazzling view of Guanabara Bay.

Four men sat in leather-and-steel armchairs, silent and somber,
as if gauging the power of the multinational corporation by the
look of the place. A pretty secretary with a prominent bust and
big hair walked into the room carrying a notepad. With her
tight-fitting knit dress, high-heeled shoes, and perfect makeup,
she looked as if she had just stepped out of the pages of one of
the men's magazines flooding the newsstands.

"The general apologizes for the delay but will see you soon,
gentlemen."

The four examined the woman with the same interest they
had measured the ambience. Both were irrefutable evidence of
power.

"Would you like some coffee?" asked the secretary, all smiles.

The four men nodded and observed her proud, graceful motion
as she left. They sighed, almost in unison. The fattest one, in a
blue sport coat worn shiny around the collar, blinked and shook
his head as if to scatter improper thoughts.

The other three dropped their serious expressions and smiled.

"They've got it all, don't they," remarked the fat man. Lieutenant Fonseca had spent his life among very different sorts of
women.

"We didn't have anything like that in the barracks," said a
thin, elegant gentleman with white skin, thin lips, and an aqui-
line nose.

"You can say that again, Admiral Marcondes," said Fonseca.

A servant arrived to deliver the coffee and the men consulted
their watches: they had been waiting an hour already. And they
hadn't even requested the meeting; it had been General Lyra's
idea. Perhaps making them wait was just one more show of
power.

The general appeared before they had emptied their cups.

"Forgive me, please," he said. "There was an urgent problem at
one of our plants in Salvador, and I got stuck on the phone . . ."

The men stood and shook hands one by one with the general.
The mood was not exactly tense, but there was something in
the air.

"Please sit down, gentlemen," said the general, settling into a leather chair himself. "No need for preliminaries. We have serious business and we must act quickly."

The four took their seats.

"The distinguished lieutenant was kind enough to call and fill me in last night. And I can tell you that a number of appropriate measures have already been taken. The base of operations in Baixada Fluminense has been sealed and I believe that the operation at the sanatorium should be closed down by now, thanks to a number of phone calls and some butt-kicking."

"Butt-kicking!" exclaimed the admiral. "This requires more than just butt-kicking. This is a very grave situation, General."

The general waggled a hand and smiled.

"Oh, not all that grave, just the boys' high spirits."

"But they were planning a series of assassinations! The list of names even included figures from the armed forces!"

"Up to this moment, that is no more than conjecture," insisted the general. "The boys are hotheaded, I don't dispute that, but I just can't believe they'd go that far. They don't have the means. They can't do anything without assistance from certain channels—channels which have had their wings clipped. The man at the top was careful to trim all excesses."

The youngest of the men shifted nervously in his chair.

"Something bothering you, Brigadier?" asked Lyra.

"I'd like to know why we're here."

General Lyra smiled an understanding smile, but his affable mask could not altogether conceal his antipathy.

"It's very simple, Brigadier. The lieutenant here is responsible for your being brought in. He's trying to help his friend Dr. Gouveia, the eminent attorney much-cited in the press. If something were to happen to Dr. Gouveia, we would have a critical situation on our hands. Not so much for the negative repercussions of public opinion—I myself don't believe all the noise about that. There is no such thing as public opinion, there are merely opinions that are made public, if you see what I mean. But, as I was saying, we would have serious problems from the federal authorities, the guys in Brasília would come down on us like hungry dogs. They've made it clear on more than one occasion that they're not very fond of us. And here I find myself, not by any choice of my own, right in the middle of this problem." The general cleared his throat and crossed his legs. "Well. I've done what I can. I've slowed the boys' pace a bit at least. Now I'm counting on your cooperation."

"What kind of cooperation?" asked Fonseca.

"Dr. Gouveia prepared a document on the case, which he intended to disseminate widely. I've seen it myself, and I can assure you the thing is explosive. If the press gets hold of it, it will be the same as if the boys had managed to go ahead with their plans. The administration will be obliged to react, since the document unjustly incriminates some military chiefs, depicting them as conniving sponsors of terrorist activity and so forth. I'm hoping that you gentlemen will be able to convince Dr. Gouveia to give up the idea of making the document public."

Lieutenant Fonseca looked at the others and scratched his head.

"It won't be easy," he said. "I've known old Gouveia for over thirty years. I don't think he'll go for that kind of arrangement."

The general looked irritated. "We're not making any kind of arrangement!"

"Maybe I used the wrong word," said Fonseca, "but whatever term we apply, it's unlikely that Dr. Gouveia will accept the proposal."

"What the hell does he want?" roared the general, his face red and his hands pummeling the air. "I managed to arrange to get his son, some captain or other, out of this mess. And I can get him out clean, even though he killed two of our guys. Even more important, I stopped the boys from taking out Gouveia himself, which was no easy job, because in their minds there's nothing worse than a defender of Communists. So he gets his son back, no mileage on the odometer, and all we want is for him to keep his mouth shut. Who the hell does he think he is?"

Fonseca shook his head pessimistically.

"He's a man from a bygone era."

"I am, too," protested the general.

"But he's from the time when justice was justice. Of course he'd be pleased to get his son back. He loves the boy, his only child. But he wouldn't flinch to see Miguel brought before a court to answer for what he's done, if need be. He's not as interested in a low odometer reading as he is in seeing justice prevail, in seeing that those who break the law are punished."

"But that's impossible," snarled the general. He turned to the others. "You gentlemen will understand my position. You're in the reserves, for one reason or another, but still you're members of the armed forces. It's absurd, what this senile old attorney is asking for. We can't let the boys be cut down by some judge with a yearning to get into the history books. The minute we let something like that happen, we open the door to all kinds of accusations about the way we've struck at subversion. If just one of those boys were convicted, or even tried and found innocent, it would be tantamount to all of us being dragged into court. It would mean subjecting our actions to the evaluation and judgment of civilians, which is something we cannot possibly permit. The idea is unthinkable, and that is precisely what you will have to make Dr. Gouveia understand."

Cheeks flushed, the general stood up. His breath came out in an animal rush.

"I too have a son mixed up in this, gentlemen. Don't forget that! But the situation I've just outlined must be given a higher priority."

"We'll do what we can," said Fonseca doubtfully.

"No, you must do what has to be done. An unarmed man can suddenly fly in your face with a whole arsenal. The deal we're offering your champion of law and order doesn't go into effect until he agrees to abide by our demands. In the meantime, the old man stays there, in Petrópolis, in the sanatorium. He's being given excellent care by very trustworthy doctors. But there's always the risk of a lamentable mistake. Medicine is not perfect, gentlemen."

The men stood up, awkward and silent. They offered no handshakes this time, just vague nods of the head before leaving the room. The secretary, eyes lively and sly in a serious face, was waiting for them at the door. It wasn't just power that emanated from that enormous office, it was arrogance and contempt. On his way out the door, Fonseca noticed that one of the smiling secretary's teeth was angled across another. He was grateful, as he said good-bye, for the existence of that one defect that made her less poured from a mold.

The high Gothic window opened onto a mountain landscape. Dr. Gouveia opened his eyes. He was lying in a hospital bed surrounded by silence. It was daylight, morning perhaps, but he wasn't sure. He struggled to remember how he'd gotten here. Raising the sheet, he saw that he was wearing an unfamiliar

pair of faded blue pajamas, certainly hospital issue. A color-
less liquid flowed down a tube and into an intravenous needle
taped to his forearm. Plasma? He felt all right. Well-rested, a
clear head. But he couldn't remember anything about where
he was or why. It was a disquieting sensation. He let his head
fall back onto the pillow and his eyes retrace the vague, vio-
let profile of the mountains on the other side of the window
glass.

The door opened and a woman's face appeared in the morning
sunshine.

"Ruth!"

His daughter-in-law ran to embrace him.

"Thank God you're all right! I've been so worried about you!"

Gouveia hugged his daughter-in-law warmly and then hurriedly
disentangled himself from her arms.

"Where am I?"

"At a hospital in Petrópolis. They brought us here yesterday
morning. They threw us into separate cells, in the other wing."
Ruth wiped her nose with a handkerchief. "Then all of a sudden I saw them carrying you off on a stretcher. It was like
a nightmare. They wouldn't tell me anything. A little while
ago they let me out, gave me some breakfast, and said I could
visit you. I'm not sure what's going on, but something's very
different."

"Why here, in Petrópolis?"

"Who knows, just somewhere to keep us, but something must
have happened. The men who brought us here have vanished. A
doctor came to see me this morning in my cell and said there had
been a mistake. He's the one who's been taking care of you, they
say you collapsed from exhaustion. Fatigue, that's what he called
it. You overdid it, up all night working . . ."

Gouveia suddenly slammed his hand to his forehead and struggled to sit up in bed.

"You shouldn't—" protested Ruth.

"The documents! Ruth, where are the documents?"

"They have them, I'm sure. I haven't seen the folder you had
since we got here."

"My God . . ."

"Now, don't get upset. It's okay."

"How could it be okay? Everything's ruined, and here we are
in God knows whose clutches."

"The lieutenant is making some headway."

"Damn it, Ruth, stop hemming and hawing and tell me what you know."

Ruth took one of his hands in hers and patted it softly.

"I don't know much. But your friend called to say that he's on his way here. He must know what's going on."

Gouveia still looked impatient.

"I can't just lie here. We have to get out of this place."

"But you can't, Dr. Gouveia . . . you're not well."

Gouveia wasn't listening. He ripped the needle out of his arm and sat up in bed.

"My clothes—what did they do with my clothes?"

"I don't know," said Ruth, her voice faint and trembling.

"Then I'll walk out of this place in pajamas. Even rats struggle when they're caught in a trap. We're getting out of here, my dear."

"How?"

"On foot. We'll find a way."

"But they won't let us."

"They—who?"

"The doctor, the orderlies . . ."

"I was brought here against my will and there's nothing that says I have to stay here a minute longer."

Gouveia hauled himself to his feet and walked out of the room. Ruth followed. They were in a wing at the rear of the building, adjacent to the ward with less serious cases, patients in detox or merely getting away from it all.

"Which way to an outside door?"

"Over there, I think," said Ruth, pointing to a large double door. Through the glass they saw two orderlies get up and head in their direction.

"We can't go that way . . ." said Gouveia.

He spun around and lurched in the opposite direction, almost crashing into the lieutenant and the three gentlemen accompanying him.

"Okay, what the hell is going on?" yelled Gouveia.

"Simmer down, Gouveia," replied Fonseca, trying to smile and look relaxed himself. "Everything's under control. Why don't we go back to your room so we can talk?"

"No, I'm not going back in there. I'm getting out of this place. And my daughter-in-law too."

"Gouveia, please," insisted Fonseca. "We have urgent business to discuss, let's not waste time grandstanding."

Gouveia shot his friend a look and strode back into the room, studiously avoiding the bed.

"Sit down here," said Ruth, offering him the chair.

The old attorney accepted, his eyes riveted on the lieutenant and his three companions as they shuffled into the room. They weren't exactly from his circle of friends but their faces were familiar, from newspaper reports and a recent Amnesty meeting, if his memory served him. It was as if they'd stumbled out of some lost attic of history, those three men who represented a Brazil that rarely appeared on the street. Here was the austere General Silviano, clearing his throat behind a nicotine-stained mustache. Retired since 1964, General Silviano had been an active participant in various nationalist campaigns, especially the struggle for state monopoly of petroleum, and had become a living symbol of the fifties. The younger man beside him with the continual look of perplexity was Brigadier General Cardoso Moreira, celebrated for his dangerous rescue missions after an earthquake in Peru. Moreira had retired in 1968 after refusing to be party to the political assassinations planned by his superiors in the air force. Finally, behind Moreira, stood the unmistakably elegant figure of Rear Admiral Marcondes, who retired in 1964 in Porto Alegre after declaring himself in solidarity with President João Goulart during the events of 1961. Each of these men had paid a high price for clinging to the tradition of legality within the armed forces.

"Dr. Gouveia," began General Silviano, "last night we were informed of the regrettable events involving you and your family. While we are no longer on active duty, we could not just sit on our hands. We talked to the contacts we do have in positions of authority. Happily, the spirit of professionalism and discipline spoke louder than shoulder-to-shoulder loyalty, and our colleagues acted promptly. The fact that you and your family were being bulldozed and held against your will was clear proof that impunity has its limits. And the threat was lifted, thank God . . ."

Gouveia studied the general, solemn and intrigued.

"And what exactly does that mean?"

"That the danger is over. You've won, sir."

"I don't think so. How can we even talk about victory until those men have been brought to justice?"

The three military men shook their heads in sad agreement.

"We understand how you feel, Dr. Gouveia," said the general, a bit less sure of himself. "That's the outcome all of us hoped for."

"There will be no trial," said Fonseca, "because there's no one to try. Formally, nothing happened."

The rear admiral frowned.

"Any other alternative would have reactionary consequences," he said. "The military is still extremely sensitive. Judicial interference in the case would focus public attention on a painful issue."

"And the only beneficiaries of political reaction would be the terrorists," said Fonseca tentatively, trying to gauge Gouveia's response. "You have to understand! We did all we could at the present time."

Gouveia looked at Ruth and lowered his eyes, chagrined.

"What about Miguel?" asked Ruth anxiously.

The lieutenant put his arm around her shoulder.

"He'll be repatriated. He's in Paris now. Everything will be kept quiet. Miguel will come out of it clean if we accept the rules of the game."

"What game?" asked the attorney, anticipating the answer.

"None of this goes any farther than these four walls," said Fonseca.

Gouveia's expression changed from disapproval to disgust. Fonseca went on the defensive.

"Come on, Gouveia. You know what country we live in."

Gouveia sighed but the look of disgust remained.

"Yes, I do, my friend. And I feel the very weight and sadness of it. But I can't help thinking . . ."

Ruth knew her father-in-law well enough to understand his enormous dilemma. He felt impotent, entangled in this web of criminality. It was as if there wasn't enough oxygen. And then there was Miguel. Ruth had to agree, it was sickening the state the country was in, but she also had to recognize her own limitations. She could only hope that her father-in-law would be able to do the same, instead of taking an ill-timed stance that might put everything at risk. Brazil was no longer a sunny, communicative place but a sinister entity, a make-believe nation where waking horrors mixed with nightmares. Not exactly the best place for Luciano to grow up, but the only one she knew.

"Well, what do you say, Gouveia?" asked Fonseca.

Gouveia stood up walked to the bed. Then he lay down very deliberately and closed his eyes.

Fonseca exchanged looks with the military men and gave them the thumbs-up sign, along with a little shrug as if to say, *That's just what the man's like*. They filed out of the room, silently nodding good-bye to Ruth, who couldn't even summon the strength to nod back, her eyes brimming with tears and her head so confused that the rules of good manners flew out the window.

Ruth sank into the chair and surrendered to her tears. Gouveia was breathing audibly on the bed, eyes closed, lost in a place she was incapable of imagining. Suddenly he stirred, opened his eyes, and examined the room to make sure they were alone.

"Don't cry, my dear," he said affectionately. A tired, ironic smile played across his mouth. "We live in the land of the anything goes—'Where there's a will there's a way' is our national motto. People twist and twist reality until it becomes almost impossible to sort things out. Until everything begins to look the same, blotchy and undefined: justice and injustice, right and wrong, lies and truth. We have just witnessed one more episode of the evolution of general vagueness. We saw a couple of good men pushing the dung ball of our moral dissociation a little farther down the hill, gathering a little more horseshit. What can we do? Maybe nothing, except to adopt the posture of the Chinese bureaucrat of the Ming dynasty, olympianly computing the distortions in a kind of heavenly handwriting. My God," he sighed, "I don't want to live to see the day we discover that this paradise is actually hell."

Ruth went on crying, smaller and smaller in her chair.

"You're perfectly right to weep, my dear. Weep for the legacy we are leaving Luciano."

Part 4

The Vehicle of the Diamond

Miguel was still watching the restaurant through the bookstore window when Vivian arrived with her two African friends. Nothing about the trio caught his eye; they fit in well with the type of clientele streaming in and out of La Coupole. The two old men directly behind them looked suspicious enough, though, their glances darting here and there as if they expected some unpleasant surprise. Between glances, they seemed utterly fixed on the girl they had followed into the café. Miguel decided to keep an eye on those two older men, but forgot about them once they sat down a couple of tables away from the dark-haired girl and her smiling companions. The girl had chosen a table near the windows looking out on the sidewalk, in plain sight of passersby as well as patrons of the restaurant.

This was one of the most bohemian neighborhoods of the city, and the sidewalk was crowded with all kinds of people strolling the boulevard. La Coupole, he had read in some city guide, had been Jean-Paul Sartre and Simone de Beauvoir's favorite hangout. The famous existential duo had sat in that very restaurant, sharing meals and endless conversations with friends and university students.

Miguel was getting tired of feigning interest in the books and considered when the right moment would be to enter the restaurant. Five minutes remained before the appointed time; he would follow Haidèe's instructions to the letter. No reason to press things; he didn't need any more surprises.

He thought a thunderbolt had struck him when he saw Haidèe herself fly out of a taxi and hurry into the restaurant carrying a leather attaché case. That was one apparition he was not prepared for. Clutching the bundle with the gun to his chest, he left the bookstore and walked into La Coupole almost on Haidèe's heels. She turned, narrowly avoiding a collision, and broke into a smile.

"Miguel!" she said, throwing her arms around his neck. The bundle with the gun was pressed between them. "What a sight for sore eyes. You look marvelous!"

Miguel disentangled himself awkwardly. He wasn't exactly in the mood to respond in kind.

"Don't say a word," she warned. "You'll understand everything very soon. The nightmare is almost over."

Haidèe took Miguel by the hand and led him into the main dining room. Voices from dozens of tables of executives, tourists, and regulars blended together into a random tumult. Scanning the tables, Haidèe's gaze came to rest on a leather attaché case like hers, propped at the feet of the pretty, dark-haired girl seated between two black men. Without hesitation, Haidèe approached the table.

"Are you Vivian de Castro?" she asked.

The girl flushed and a wave of fear crossed her face.

"Don't be afraid," said Haidèe. "I was a friend of Carlos."

Vivian stood up hesitantly. There was only one free place at the table.

"Miguel, grab yourself a chair!" ordered Haidèe, taking a seat and making room beside her for Miguel, who just stood there wide-eyed. "He's a friend," she explained. "He's been a great help."

"Carlos told me about the locker only the very last time we met," said Vivian, still unsure of herself, looking for support from her Cameroonian friends and from the Spaniards two tables away.

"Who are they?" asked Haidèe, indicating the two older men.

"Friends."

"You're well-protected," remarked Haidèe. "That was smart. This game is deadly serious after all."

"Are you familiar with the instructions?" asked Vivian.

"My name is Haidèe, Haidèe Jaffet."

"May I see some identification?"

Haidèe removed her passport from her purse and handed it to Vivian, who examined it closely before returning it.

"I remember seeing your name on the papers Carlos left," she said, visibly more relaxed.

"Shall we invite your friends from the other table to join us?" suggested Haidèe.

Vivian beckoned to the Spaniards and Haidèe asked the

mâitre d' to find them a larger table. They were moved to an area separated from the rest of the dining room by a screen.

"This is much better," said Haidèe.

Vivian opened the attaché case and removed some papers.

"Let's follow the instructions," she said dryly.

"Of course," said Haidèe, smiling. "Where's the sequence of numbers?"

"Right here," said Vivian.

Haidèe examined the paper without touching it.

"Yes, that's it, all right," she said. "But I'd rather we didn't carry out the rest of the instructions right here. Could you accompany me to Geneva?"

"Impossible," answered Vivian. "My friends and I intend to proceed exactly as Carlos asked. We will personally deliver the paper in Geneva."

Haidèe seemed to acquiesce.

"Fair enough. But how can I be sure you'll do just that?"

The color rose in Vivian's face.

"How can I be sure that you won't simply withdraw the money? Once I've completed the sequence of numbers, this paper becomes a check to the bearer."

"We wouldn't do that," protested Vivian. "Carlos' instructions were very clear."

"Carlos is dead."

Vivian lowered her eyes.

"And we're all human," added Haidèe. "That account may still hold a considerable fortune. Besides, I don't intend for my participation to end here at La Coupole. I have things to take care of in Geneva."

"What sorts of things?" asked Miguel, joining the conversation for the first time. Vivian looked at him, curious, perhaps because he was Brazilian.

"I'm going to teach a lesson to a certain friend of mine!"

"I have nothing to do with any other business of yours," protested Vivian. "My only commitment is to the instructions Carlos left me."

"Carlos would approve of what I'm planning to do," said Haidèe.

Kouma and Sanga observed the conversation impassively, but the two old Spaniards were following everything with great interest.

"I'll try to explain briefly," said Haidèe, "because I can't go
into all the details. When I made this deposit at Carlos' request,
there were three million dollars in the account, but I'm sure it
has dwindled over the years. The expenses of armed resistance
were enormous, especially in response to the regime's repressive
methods. I know for a fact that a good deal of money was spent
greasing the palms of high-ranking military officials. The details
aren't important. But Carlos was afraid that the Swiss would end
up with the money, since access to the account was initially
assigned to Lamarca alone, whose life would naturally be at
great risk. Not surprisingly, that person died soon after, but not
before we had instituted this double control system to avoid the
eventual loss of the money."

"What are you saying?" asked Vivian, suspicious.

"It's simple," replied Haidèe in an undertone. "Now the money
belongs to whoever claims it."

Vivian almost leaped out of her chair.

"But I don't want the money!"

"Calm down and think for just a minute," said Haidèe, the
model of joviality. "Don't be too hasty. Great pains were taken
so that this money wouldn't fall into the hands of the extreme
right or revert to the Swiss treasury. And we don't even know
if there's anything left in the account."

"Carlos would not have asked me to get involved if there was
nothing left in the account," argued Vivian. "He might just as
well have tossed this attaché into the Seine."

"Now you're beginning to make sense," said Haidèe. "Carlos
was an extremely intelligent man. Think. What did he say that
might shed some light on all this?"

"Nothing, he never mentioned it at all. But he must have been
under incredible pressure when he asked me to hold onto the
key to the locker. And his instructions were that we should
turn the completed series of numbers over to Mr. Jean-Pierre
Grunt at the bank. He's supposed to know where to direct the
money."

"Monsieur Jean-Pierre will direct the funds where we instruct
him to," insisted Haidèe. "It's money without an owner."

"Maybe not," said Vivian. "Maybe the money should make its
own way in the world, independent of us."

"Let's talk about that some more," said Haidèe, languidly
regarding the girl.

*   *   *

Miguel was searching for the meaning of his experiences of the last exceptional days. Karma was an amazing thing, he thought. Just a light touch from the hand of fate had sent him spinning into other orbits, ever more distant from the path he had been previously seeking. In less than a week he had done things that would have been unthinkable before. He'd witnessed the violent deaths of several people and had himself killed several others. He, Miguel, had killed at least two men! Throughout this exceptional time, he had tried to untangle the thread of the story. What thread had he actually drawn out? The tantra, perhaps? Because everything was interconnected, this he firmly believed. His personal quest, his clashes with others, the political conspiracy, the whole circle of possibilities. The thread had been part of a tapestry which proved to him every second along the way that what was happening was an integral part of his own personal search. The path of experience was being illuminated by forces unknown to him, forces that were capable of annihilating the tenuous border of morality. Samsara: the state of walking in circles, the conscious sufferer in the cycle of death and rebirth. And there was no road back, he imagined. He'd taken the risks like a blind man; now he would have to open his eyes. Immersed in violence, he had felt like a warrior. Now he would have to allow the energy from this new part of his nature to flow freely. His military background had isolated him from other men, the arrogance of fraternity permanently conflicting with his need to understand others and his own human nature. But if, on the one hand, a military education had hardened his character, it had, on the other, given him discipline, the humility to accept hierarchy. He wasn't even interested in hearing Haidèe's explanations, the same explanations that he had sought so fervently when this all began. Explanations no longer mattered, they were part of the obstacles he had overcome. On the other side of the ocean was his family, anchored by the roots that he had just cut free of. Without recriminations.

"You're sure this is what you want?" asked Haidèe.

Miguel shone with an intense certainty.

The departure terminal of Charles de Gaulle airport was a confusion of exotic creatures loaded down with carry-on bags and boxes and packages. Women in saris mixed with young longhairs dwarfed by enormous backpacks. Noisy circles of North

American tourists hovered around the Air France ticket counter. A Hindu woman was having a heated argument with an airport employee who was insisting she couldn't hold her pet pig on her lap during the flight.

Haidèe opened the leather attaché case and handed Miguel a fat envelope.

"Here are your tickets, and the money."

"I don't want any money," said Miguel.

Haidèe shook her head disapprovingly.

"Take the money, Miguel, you may need it."

"The tickets are enough."

She stuck the envelope in Miguel's pack.

"Don't be an idiot. I'm not going to turn you loose in a place where cows roam the streets without a little money in your pocket. It's not much, but it'll be useful in a pinch."

Miguel smiled and set his pack on the floor. He placed his hands on his hips and raised his right leg, bent at the knee, ankle pointing up. He held this position for a few seconds and then repeated it with the other leg. He opened his arms horizontally, continuing the leg-raising maneuver, and twisting his back from one side to the other. Then he moved his right leg to the side and to the back, in a slow and concentrated choreography. He no longer heard the noise and bustle of the airport. He didn't even seem to be aware of Haidèe's presence.

His flight was announced, first in French, then in English and Hindu. Destination New Delhi. Miguel stopped his routine, picked up his pack, and vanished into a throng of passengers that looked too exotic for Haidèe's taste.

The odd dance Miguel had been doing, much to Haidèe's embarrassment and displeasure, was an exercise in balance called "the middle path," but that meant nothing to her. Watching him disappear, she had only one thought.

"The son of a bitch will come back to Brazil someday and get filthy rich founding a new sect," she mumbled to herself as she rushed out of the airport in search of a taxi.

There isn't a Brazilian who likes Switzerland. The entire country seems to be designed to drive Latinos crazy. The Caisse d'Epargne de Genéve was located in a small nineteenth-century building on a quiet, narrow street in the commercial section of downtown Geneva. The system was fast and efficient. Interviews with clients who had numbered accounts were held in a room off the mezzanine, which was richly decorated to soothe the consciences of suspect fortunes and protected by thick gray velvet drapes.

Jean-Pierre Grunt, wearing a suit that blended perfectly with the curtains, observed the two women on the other side of the lacquered table, a vase of yellow roses between them. He took no pains to conceal the maniacal order that reigned in his country.

The two Spaniards sat waiting impassively in the bakery truck parked outside. At Colonel Duran's insistence, the group had driven through the night on secondary roads until catching sight of the Jura Mountains at the first light of dawn. They crossed the border near St. Claude and rounded Lake Leman around noon. By the time Haidèe and Vivian walked into the austere and thickly carpeted foyer of the bank, they were utterly exhausted.

Vivian opened the attaché case and removed the paper on which Carlos had inscribed the sequence of numbers. Haidèe took the paper, examined it, and smiled. The clerk offered her a gold pen and she began carefully completing the sequence, without raising her eyes from the page. Finally she passed the paper to the clerk.

He opened a file, removed several documents, and meticulously compared the numbers on the paper to those on the documents, digit by digit. Finally he nodded.

"It's correct," he said dryly.

"Are there any written instructions?"

The clerk consulted the file and raised his eyes in an expression of surprise.

"Not that I can see, madame. Should there be?"

"No, that's fine," said Haidèe, throwing a significant look in Vivian's direction. "What is the balance, please?"

"There is eight hundred thousand dollars in the account," replied the clerk.

"Excellent!" exclaimed Haidèe, exultant. "Not such a bad out-come."

Vivian sighed. "No, not bad," she said, looking traumatized by the mere thought of so much money.

But she'll get used to it, thought Haidèe. She seems like a very realistic girl. Haidèe pulled another paper from her bag and handed it to the clerk.

"Check this account number, will you, Monsieur Jean-Pierre?"

"It will just take a moment," he said, and left the room.

"Well," said Haidèe, inexpressibly happy, "we can't just leave the money here to get moldy, Vivian. And the beauty of it is that no one will ever know. For all intents and purposes, the account was empty. Carlos would be happy with this solution."

"I don't know . . ." said Vivian.

"But you will, my dear. Just give it time. Fulfill some of your dreams. Before long you'll see it isn't really all that much money."

The clerk returned with another file. He sat down and ran his thin finger along the rows of numbers.

"Four million dollars," he said.

"It's our lucky day!" crowed Haidèe. "Lyra will be so much the poorer." Turning to Vivian, she said, "Have you ever heard of General Lyra?"

Vivian's dark face grew darker. Who in the left had not heard of the famous General Lyra?

Haidèe turned back to the clerk.

"These dollars are about to have a change of address."

"Very well, madame."

The transaction was quick and relatively simple. In under five minutes, General Lyra's money had been transferred to Haidèe's account and half of the eight hundred thousand dollars had been withdrawn and handed over to Vivian.

Haidèe stood up and swept out of the room. Following behind, Vivian felt a light touch on her shoulder and turned to see the clerk.

"Excuse me, miss," he said. He looked like a different man, his cheeks burning, not a trace of his earlier air of efficiency.

"You were Senhor Carlos' friend, weren't you."

Vivian nodded.

"He was an excellent friend," said the clerk.

Vivian shivered.

"We don't ask questions here, miss, but that didn't stop us from becoming friends. I wanted you to know that. I've lost a friend too." He adjusted his suit jacket and bowed solemnly. "Good-bye, miss."

"Good-bye," said Vivian, holding back her tears.

She slowly descended the mezzanine stairs and walked out onto the sidewalk with measured steps, lost in thought, remembering her friend, his tranquility and his sense of humor. Would he have approved of all this? Vivian had her doubts. The four hundred thousand dollars in the attaché case was heavy in her hand. What would she do with all that money? She didn't know. She nursed vaguely hopeful thoughts of speeding up her return to Brazil. Fulfill your dreams, Haidèe had said. Her greatest dream right now was to go home. Haidèe was waiting in the bakery truck and greeted her with suspicion.

"What took you so long?"

"Oh, nothing. The clerk was a friend of Carlos."

"A friend? How odd."

"I don't see anything odd about it."

Haidèe was beginning to get worked up. "You're hiding something. What is it?"

Vivian became irritated. "I'm not hiding anything. The man was Carlos' friend. He seemed genuinely upset about his death."

The two Spaniards exchanged looks. Haidèe seemed unsatisfied with Vivian's explanation.

"Carlos' friend!" she blustered, her voice full of irony. She looked to the men for support. "Well? Don't you find that a bit odd?"

"No, not really," said Colonel Duran. "Apparently, the young man merely expressed his regret about Carlos' death. It's a perfectly natural attitude, very human. Even the Swiss have feelings."

Haidèe shrugged and looked at the Spaniard scornfully.

Duran only became more indignant.

"The man expressed sadness and regret at the passing of a fellow creature," he continued, nailing Haidèe with his bright, sparkling eyes. "Where I come from we call that offering one's condolences, señora!"

"Let's go," said Haidèe, pulling Vivian by the arm. "If there's anything I can't stand, it's a show of senility."

As the two women made to leave the truck, Duran spoke up again, his voice choked with emotion.

"After all I've witnessed," he said, "I too would like to offer my condolences to this young woman. And not for Carlos' fate, since my compassion is not for him. I offer my condolences regarding your country."

Out on the sidewalk, the two women exchanged looks.

There was no trace of regret on either face. And there couldn't
be.

It was a clear summer afternoon, and these two Brazilian
women seemed to have forgotten that another's pain can have
the power to echo in one's own heart.

AVON BOOKS

TRADE PAPERBACKS

___	A Trail of Heart's Blood Wherever We Go by Robert Olmstead	$11.00 US/$13.00 Can	71548-1
___	Call and Response by T.R. Pearson	$10.95 US/$12.95 Can	71163-X
___	Gospel Hour by T.R. Pearson	$11.00 US/$13.00 Can	71036-6
___	The Jewel in the Crown by Paul Scott	$11.00 US	71808-1
___	The Day of the Scorpion by Paul Scott	$11.00 US	71809-X
___	The Towers of Silence by Paul Scott	$11.00 US	71810-3
___	A Division of the Spoils by Paul Scott	$11.00 US	71811-1
___	Lights Out in the Reptile House by Jim Shepard	$10.00 US/$12.00 Can	71413-2
___	The Bachelors by Muriel Spark	$9.00 US	71570-8
___	The Ballad of Peckham Rye by Muriel Spark	$7.95 US	70936-8
___	A Far Cry From Kensington by Muriel Spark	$7.95 US	70786-1
___	The Girls of Slender Means by Muriel Spark	$7.95 US	70937-6
___	Loitering With Intent by Muriel Spark	$7.95 US	70935-X
___	The Mandelbaum Gate by Muriel Spark	$9.00 US	71569-4
___	Memento Mori by Muriel Spark	$7.95 US	70938-4
___	The Lady at Liberty by Hudson Talbott	$9.95 US/$11.95 Can	76427-X
___	The Fugitive by Pramoedya Ananta Toer	$8.95 US/$10.95 Can	71496-5
___	Failure to Zigzag by Jane Vandenburgh	$8.95 US/$10.95 Can	71019-6
___	Girl With Curious Hair by David Wallace	$9.95 US/$11.95 Can	71230-X
___	In the Blue Light of African Dreams by Paul Watkins	$10.00 US/$12.00 Can	71640-2
___	Calm at Sunset, Calm at Dawn by Paul Watkins	$8.95 US/$10.95 Can	71222-9
___	Night Over Day Over Night by Paul Watkins	$7.95 US/$9.95 Can	70737-3
___	Winning the City by Theodore Weesner	$9.00 US/$11.00 Can	71554-6